How We Love Them

A HOPE IS HERE
NOVEL

MARY GRACE VAN DER KROEF

How We Love Them

A HOPE IS HERE
NOVEL

Cover Design: Mary Grace van der Kroef

Edited by: H.A. Pruitt

Proofread by: K. Ans

ISBN:978-1-0691537-1-5 (E-book)

ISBN:978-1-0691537-2-2 (Paperback)

ISBN:978-1-0691537-3-9 (Hardcover)

First Edition

Contents

Titles By Mary

Poetry:
The Branch That I Am
Words of Weight
Branches in Bloom
Calculated Hesitation
Fiction:
Our Road to Trust:
Interlocking Short Stories of Faith
How We Love Them:
A Hope is Here Novel
Visit www.marygracewriting.ca for more information.

The Vote

ARTHUR

FOREBODING FILLED ARTHUR AS he stood looking at the surrounding faces. Silence hung heavily around the boardroom table as each person hesitated. An invisible weight pressed down on Arthur's shoulders. If only he had a hat or a paper to clutch in his fists. He needed a distraction from the gnawing sensation in his gut, so he counted the people before him. One, Gary, two, Henry, three, Bennett, and so on until he nodded to Gail, the eighth, the church's secretary who sat perched uncomfortably on the edge of her chair.

Arthur cared about these people. Each was a partner in the running of Hope Is Here Church. But now? They sat against him. Some cast sad eyes his way, pity creasing age lines deeper. In the others, he sensed righteous indifference and even a level of disdain.

"Gentlemen." He coughed, emotion restricting his airway. "Gail."

"Arthur." Gary, the chairman, inclined his head towards him. He was an old friend, and his eyes softened at Arthur's unease. "I'm sorry we've got to hold a meeting like this."

"I understand. It's a necessary evil," Arthur replied. But he didn't, not really.

How can this be happening? Arthur had lost track of the times he'd prayed that question over the last week. Everything was crumbling so fast.

"Arthur, we all know the upheavals your family have faced these last few months. Amy's ongoing behavioural struggles, Rose being unwell."

He could only nod at the truth of it all.

God, this isn't fair. I've served these people so long. How can they entertain the idea of—

"It's all a weight on your home life, Arthur. We realize that ..." The pause Gary took to take a sip of coffee and clear his throat seemed to stretch a chasm between them. "But, since the developments with Rachel, people have raised questions."

"What questions?" Arthur couldn't help but jump in. "We haven't hidden anything from the congregation. I'll answer anything else you have to ask."

"Is it true Rachel is living with Pat Kenny's boy?" grey-haired Bennett from across the table asked as he adjusted his glasses.

"Yes. Yes, it is." The admission wasn't easy for Arthur as his heart shrank in shame. He'd raised his daughter better. But ...

"And she's been living with him for a while now, without your knowledge?"

Again, Arthur had to nod.

"I see."

A muffled muttering passed through the room. Arthur tightened his neck muscles and refused to look away from Gary toward the noise. The soft thumping sound of Gail's fingers on her laptop keyboard at the end of the table resembled a drumbeat riding the undercurrent of the room's tension.

"You being unaware of what was going on in your home, Arthur, is concerning," Bennett said. "As leaders in the church, we are all called to have our families in order." A pained look washed over the old man's face as he fiddled with a pen. "I have to admit, it doesn't seem like you've been able to do this with yours. As the lead pastor of this church, it's concerning."

Arthur was fast learning to hate the word "concerning". Why did the man insist on using it repeatedly?

"This is a difficult situation, Arthur." This time, Henry spoke. The man's black eyebrows, dusted with grey, almost touched as he frowned.

Nods rippled around the table. The wave almost stole Arthur's breath as his body tensed. He looked over at Gail, her fingers still tapping away. She refused to look back at him.

"I hope you realize this isn't something we want to have to do."

"Bennett, please, let's not make this seem like a decision has been made. It has not been." The look Gary gave Bennett was steel.

When his friend turned a strained smile back to him, a chime sounded from within Arthur's heart, only to be silenced by his friend's next words.

"We'll vote tonight. But the question is will we be voting to ask you to step down or for an extended sabbatical? Either way, we are asking you to step back from your role as Lead Pastor, for at least a time."

"Extended sabbatical?" This was news. Arthur stood straighter.

"Yes," Gary continued. "You need time to get your house in order, Arthur. But how much time?" Gary shook his head and held up a finger to stop Arthur from answering. "Only God may know that for sure."

Hope bloomed within Arthur again. Maybe this wasn't the end. Only a rest? A rest wouldn't be so bad. He could deal with that. How long had it been since he and Rose had taken a break from the ministry? He couldn't remember.

"What we would like to know, Arthur, is what you and Rose plan on doing for the next few months."

Arthur took his time with each word of his reply. "Rose is waiting to undergo tests. We haven't been told how long the wait might take, so we're resigned to being patient. She's dealing with pain, so our next few months will be finding a way to help her manage it."

"And?"

"And ... After that, it will depend on any diagnosis she receives."

"What about the girls, Arthur?" Gary asked.

"Amy's therapy continues, but I cannot see what that has to do with this situation."

"As a child still living under your roof, her conduct has a great effect on your reputation, Arthur. As our lead pastor, it affects us and this church," Bennett declared.

"I see."

"Do you?" The older man's gaze felt like a needle probing Arthur's chest.

"Is appearance all you care about, Bennett?" The man bristled, and Arthur knew he'd made a mistake in his choice of words, but he also refused to back down. "As for Rachel, her choices are her own, especially since she's left the protection of my house."

"Understood." Henry beat Gary to cut the conversation off before it turned uglier.

Gary quickly nodded and raised a hand of warning to everyone else in the room, silently letting them know to hold their peace. "I'm sorry, but we'll have to ask you to step out for the rest of the meeting, Arthur," Gary said, turning back to him. Strain forced his friend's voice to crack as he again reached for his coffee mug. "I'll text you when we're finished. I've no idea how long it might be."

Was there a point to even being present for this meeting? Arthur wondered as he left the room, closing the door behind himself. Immediately, muffled words flowed from under the door, rising and falling like a tide of judgment. The church hall was empty, the lights bright, and a headache was forming behind his eyes.

"You blew that," he told himself. "But, really, what did they want me to say?"

Gary was his only hope. Perhaps he could talk sense into the rest of them. Bennett and Henry had clearly already made up their minds. Had the others as well?

Arthur's vote was traditionally the tiebreaker for any tough decisions the church had faced. Depending on the issues at hand, the board often let other members of the church's ministry teams vote, but not tonight. None of them were here to watch their leader crumble under pressure. He'd thought that at least Jim, the youth pastor, would have come. Arthur had hoped the younger man would say something, or at least be present, to show support. But, no.

He and his wife were alone in this.

Rose sat waiting in an accent chair near the exit in the church office's foyer. Her face was pale and thin, wisps of dark blond hair had escaped the elastic at the nape of her neck to float around her face. The sight pinched Arthur's heart as he joined her by pulling over her chair's twin from the opposite side of a table filled with church leadership brochures. After sitting, he reached over to take her hand.

"How did it go?" she asked, bringing a tissue to her nose.

"Not well," Arthur admitted. "Seems some of them have already decided. Gary is pushing for an extended sabbatical over dismissal."

Rose slumped back against her chair. "That wouldn't be such a bad thing right now."

"No, it wouldn't."

Arthur squeezed her hand, and she squeezed back as the wall clocked ticked away what might be the last few minutes of Arthur's ministry at Hope Is Here. As they waited, his racing heart slowed. The feel of Rose's hand eased the ache in his gut, though he couldn't help but notice how thin her fingers had become as he cradled them. He couldn't bring himself to let them go.

The first hour dragged by. The second crawled. Still, neither one of them voiced concern about the wait. Arthur didn't want to upset Rose with the wandering of his mind as it slipped back and forth between defeat and hope.

Rose had closed her eyes and leaned her head against the chair's back. If it wasn't for her continued grip on his hand, he would have thought she'd fallen asleep. She only moved every once in a while to wiggle her fingers or wipe off moisture from prolonged contact. But she always reached for him again, and he made sure he was always ready to take back her hand. They were both in a silent daze as the door between the main church building and the offices opened.

"How long has it been?" The figure standing in the doorway asked while running fingers over smartly cropped hair.

"Jim?" Arthur had given up all hope of anyone coming to stand with him, and the sight of the youth pastor almost broke his emotional control.

"Coming up on two hours," Rose answered.

Jim shook his head. "Any idea what they're arguing about?"

"Extended sabbatical or dismissal."

"My vote doesn't count tonight, Arthur, or you know … I would have been here from the beginning."

"It's okay, Jim. You're here now."

"I got a text from Gary an hour ago. He said to come before nine."

Arthur pulled his own phone from his pocket and checked the notifications for the hundredth time that night. "I got nothing?"

So Gary had been sending texts during the meeting but not to him. That didn't bode well and left a sour taste in the back of Arthur's mouth.

A few more agonizing minutes passed as Rose asked Jim how his wife and kids were. Arthur couldn't help but stare at his phone, waiting. Gary had said he'd text. So why did his phone remain silent?

When the chime sound burst from Arthur's phone, he nearly dropped it before pulling up the notification screen again. "They're done."

"Finally," Jim said as Arthur stood. The younger man stretched as if he'd been the one sitting for hours.

Arthur noted the nervous drumming of Jim's fingers on his pant legs even while standing.

Rose remained seated but still held Arthur's hand. Her grip caused her fingers to blanch where their skin touched.

As the first board members walked down the hall, Arthur expected some kind of acknowledgement. Jim muttered in protest as the men ducked out into the main church building without a word. More people soon followed with only silent nods in his direction. Arthur's pulse quickened. Anger pooled at his feet as each board member refused to stop.

Were they all cowards? Too afraid to him the truth of what they had decided for his family?

Arthur couldn't help himself as a familiar grey head appeared. "Not even a goodbye, Bennett?"

Bennett stopped with his hand ready to push open the door. "I'm sorry, Arthur." He glanced at Jim as the younger man blanched and Rose let out a soft sob.

"Let him go, Arthur," Gary called, stopping him from following the infuriating man out the door. "I asked them to let me tell you."

"They didn't like the idea of an extended sabbatical, did they?" Jim whispered from beside Arthur's shoulders. The young man was standing so close, he could have wrapped his arm around his friend, but he didn't, and Arthur was glad of that. If he had, he wouldn't have been able to keep his composure. Gary grabbed his hand, and the firm shake captured Arthur's full attention, though his heart beat out a song of unbelief. Had they really just—

"Four votes for sabbatical, six for dismissal. I'm sorry, Arthur."

As Rose broke into tears, Arthur couldn't handle it anymore. He released Gary's hand, pushed past him and through the office entrance, before storming his way from the church building toward the darkness of the parking lot.

Gary walked Rose to the car as Arthur paced around it, kicking the tires in a show of testing them, ignoring every time another engine started and a once cherished friend drove away. Arthur ignored the envelope Rose held in her hand as he opened the car door for her. He didn't want to know what it was, didn't want to know what they'd written about this mess.

"Call me in the morning, Arthur," Gary told him. "If you don't, I'll be paying you a visit."

Arthur had no words for his friend and waved him off as he closed Rose into the cold vehicle. The late March air was damp and whispered promises of rain or snow, but which one, it would keep secret for now.

"I mean it, Arthur, call me."

Arthur didn't acknowledge his friend as he opened the driver's side door and climbed in. He didn't look to see if Gary watched them pull away. He forgot to look for Jim as well.

"I should have turned on the heat before you came out. I'm sorry, Rose," Arthur said. The windows fogged from their body heat.

"I'm fine," Rose assured him as he adjusted the vents. "It's going to be okay."

"Is it?" he snapped back and immediately regretted his tone.

"Yes." She sounded so sure, despite the tears. He wondered how she could be when they'd just lost everything.

Parsonage

ARTHUR

THEY BOTH KEPT THEIR silence as the light from street lamps streaked by. The engine purred, and the peaceful night banked Arthur's internal turmoil, leaving a weight of exhaustion as a layer of dirt over hot coals, smothering the flames but also protecting the embers, keeping them alive to flair again. What was done was done, and after all, hadn't he been expecting it?

Yes. He had. But still, the betrayal of so many friends burned deep.

The parsonage was lit only by the soft amber glow of a recessed light above the doorway. When they pulled into the drive and Arthur killed the engine, he sat there, looking at the classic white door and empty planters lining the three-step stoop.

"You know," he said into the darkness, despair riding the heels of his revelation. "We didn't just lose a job tonight, we've also lost our home and probably most of our friends."

It had always been a blessing to pastor a church that owned a parsonage. The cost of living had been upkeep and monthly expenses. No burden of rent. No questions about living affordability.

"Do they understand the punishment they've doled out on us? And for what? Because Amy is struggling? Because you're sick? Because Rachel's turned her back on us?"

"Arthur, let's not focus on that tonight."

The strain in his wife's voice should have clued him into the level of her exhaustion, but in his deepening despair, he missed it.

"With house prices so high, I don't know if we'll be able to buy. Will we even be able to afford rent? What other church will be willing to take on a disgraced pastor? What if we can't even find an apartment, Rose? What then?"

"Arthur, enough!" Rose's voice echoed within the small space of the car. "I can't do this tonight. I need time," she softly added, her voice catching on each word.

"Rose, I … I'm sorry. Let's get you inside."

Arthur got out and rounded the car, feet feeling like lead, and opened Rose's door. As she took his hand for support, he could feel her trembling and wrapped his arm around her waist.

"Tea?"

"Please."

He guided her slowly through the unlocked front door and switched on the hall lights. A rustling from the living room told him his youngest daughter, Amy, was awake and watching TV. He didn't ask what program she'd switched off as she peeked over the back of the couch. Her eyes were a deeper blue than her mothers and held a purity of the colour that her father's grey/blue lacked. Her hair was also a brighter blond than Rose's and the spiral curls that framed her face softened the sharpness of her gaze, where Rose's merely held wisp-like waves that demanded freedom from the combs that tried to hold them back from her face.

"You're late."

"Can you please turn the kettle on, Amy?" Arthur asked.

"Why the gloomy faces? Did they kick you out?"

When neither answered, Amy got to her feet and headed to the kitchen.

"Figures," she muttered. Soon the sound of a running faucet muffled her grumbling.

Arthur took his wife's coat and hung it in the hall closet before turning back and taking in her appearance. Her eyes were red, and her finger trembled as she lifted it in warning.

"Not tonight, Arthur."

He didn't argue but guided her frail frame to the kitchen, making sure she sat securely on a chair before searching for her favourite tea.

"No black tea tonight," she said as he produced a bag of Vanilla Spiced Chai. "Green is better. I need to sleep."

"Is the chamomile green?"

"No, herbal. But, actually, it's perfect."

It didn't take long for the electric kettle to heat and for him to pour hot water over the bag and hand her the steaming mug.

"So, what happened?" Amy asked as she slid into a chair beside her mom.

Rose looked to Arthur, silently asking him to say the words she couldn't. Her lips trembled, and Arthur swallowed hard as he watched her hold back grief.

"They voted to dismiss."

"Dismiss? Gosh, what a great word. So much gentler than 'fired'." Amy rolled her eyes at her dad's sharp glare. "I suppose it's my fault, right?"

"No, it's not your fault, Amy," Rose said, as she leaned over the steaming mug, fingers wrapped tightly around the porcelain.

"If you must know, it's more Rachel's fault than yours," Arthur admitted, unable to hold back a snort of derision.

"I knew it!" Amy straightened her shoulders, her face twisted into a devilish grin. "Miss Perfect falls at last."

"Amy! No more," Rose implored. "You as well, Arthur. We won't talk about it tonight. We sleep."

"Rose."

"NO, Arthur. Our hearts and minds need rest."

He couldn't argue with her. A weight grew on his shoulders and a deepening darkness in his mind. It threatened to swallow him as she looked over at Amy, her face still a twisted mess of glee.

"You have school in the morning. Go to bed." His instructions were firm but gentle, and with a final roll of her eyes, she left without arguing. They both listened to the sound of her slippered feet shuffle down the hall. "At least there won't be a fight with her tonight."

"She isn't a bad kid, Arthur," Rose reminded him. "Just confused and hurting."

"Just like the rest of us, then."

"Arthur ..."

"No, you're right, Rose, no talking tonight. Sleep. We both need sleep."

Rose didn't protest as he took the still half full mug from her hands and guided her down the hall to their room.

With the morning light, all the what ifs and what nows came rolling back into Arthur's mind. He'd never felt less of a desire to get up and start the day as he turned towards Rose's empty side of the bed. The alarm clock on the side table burned the number 8:30 on his retina, and it remained there after he closed his eyes again, searching for the numbness of sleep. He didn't stir until the mattress shifted with the weight of someone sitting down beside him.

He opened his eyes to the sound of paper being smoothed across the thick comforter. "What's that?" The words tried to stick to his dry tongue as Rose ran her fingers through his pillow-tousled hair, pushing the salt and pepper strands from his eyes.,

"You need a haircut," she commented.

"Hm. But what is that?"

"I guess you could call it an official eviction notice."

"What?" The emptiness of her tone worried him, and he sat up, taking the paper to read for himself.

Dear Grill Family,

This letter is the official request that you vacate the parsonage owned by Hope Is Here Church by the below date.

May 20th

The congregation will do its best to help you remove your belongings. Below is a list of known church property, including furniture and appliances still in the house. We have included it for your convenience and the sake of transparency. We wish you well in the new home God will provide.

The second sheet of paper held the list of appliances and furniture owned by the church. Arthur had to admit, it was a good thing to have on hand. After all, he was bound to forget a few of them after the last twelve years.

"So this is what took them so long last night. They weren't just voting ..."

A third sheet contained an official letter of dismissal for Arthur.

"They want me to preach for the next two Sundays."

Having already read it, Rose nodded and picked at the hem of her cream blouse. "Keep reading."

The last paper was a letter from the board.

Dear Arthur and Rose Grill,

We regret the circumstances that have led to your dismissal from ministry in our church, but we wish to clarify that you are still welcome as members of our congregation. We hope you will continue to worship with us until such a time as God opens another door of ministry for you or leads you to a new church.

"Well, how kind of them?"

Rose met Arthur's words and glare of distaste with smooth tones. "I'm sure they meant it that way."

All the board members had signed the last letter.

"Gary made sure his name was first here." Arthur pointed to the scrawl under the printing.

"He's letting us know he wants us to stay," Rose assured him.

The sheets rustled as Arthur dragged himself to the edge of the bed.

"I better call him before he thinks knocking on the front door is a good idea." As he rose from the bed, his limbs shook. "How ... how did they get all of this together in just a few hours, Rose? It's like someone knew already and was prepared." The thought made Arthur sick.

Arthur's conversation with Gary was a mix of apologies and questions, angry outbursts, and a flat out refusal to preach the following Sunday.

"I told them that was asking too much after last night," Gary admitted, when he failed to convince Arthur to change his mind. "Will you at least come to the service? The congregation deserves a goodbye."

"The congregation deserved their own vote, Gary. They deserve transparency. Half of them won't even know what happened last night!"

"I know. But too many board members decided it would bring unwanted attention to your family. They wanted to protect you."

"No, they didn't. They wanted us gone."

The next few moments of Gary's silence stung just as much as if Arthur had touched a hot stove element with a bare hand.

"Are you and Rose okay?" Gary's question broke the tension like shattered glass.

Arthur imagined the shards falling all around him, closing off his way of escape.

"No."

He hung up, and for a moment, Arthur stood there, staring at the ground and the imaginary fragments. "What now?"

"First thing. We need to remember not to sabotage friendships," Rose said from behind him.

Arthur took a step back, away from the invisible mess before him, and curled his fingers around Rose's.

"What's done is done, Arthur, and Gary is not our enemy."

"Really? The way he talks doesn't seem like a friend. He supported my stepping back. He wanted this—or a version of it—to happen."

"I know ... but maybe he's right." She pulled Arthur away from the imagined shards at his feet, unaware of the release he felt with her touch even as her words stung. As Rose steered him to the living room, the shards faded from his mind, leaving only the cool white of the tiles glittering beneath the hallway light.

"What now? Well, I think we go back to basics. What do we need to survive? Then, what do we need to thrive? Surviving this transition comes first. We need a new home and a way to put food on the table."

Arthur smiled as he watched Rose, her ever practical thoughts swirling behind her pale blue eyes. "How did I get such a wise wife?"

"God knew you needed me." Rose smiled back at him.

For too long, she had been so tired. The body aches and fights with Amy, zapping her joy along with her strength. The weight of what if was heavy on Arthur's shoulders, but those eyes. He could watch them forever when they danced with light as she smiled. He longed to reach for her and brush dark blond waves from the side of her face, to run a finger over her cheek. He held her with his eyes instead.

"We can't leave town. That would mean a change of doctor for you and Amy."

"Agreed. Not a good idea right now."

"So, places to rent and a way to pay that rent."

Rose nodded as she pulled a newspaper from a haphazard pile waiting in the centre of the coffee table. "Last week's listings come first until tomorrow's paper arrives."

She tossed the sheets towards Arthur, and he settled into the couch, pulling the paper open and letting it obstruct his view of everything else.

"I'll grab the laptop from your office," Rose said as she left the room.

Was it his imagination, or did her cheeks hold a bit more pink than they had for the last few weeks? Maybe ... just maybe this change wouldn't be as bad as he'd imagined.

A Bowl of Soup

ARTHUR WAS STILL POURING over apartment listings as Rose pulled her coat over aching shoulders. She'd sat too long, and pressure now crawled up her spine like slow-moving lava, sparking aches through her shoulders as a headache bloomed at the base of her skull. A painkiller had taken the edge off, but the discomfort lingered. A roll of the shoulders loosened tense muscles as she stilled her inner voice and its self rebuke. She had sat still for Arthur. It had been important.

Now? It was time for movement. Every Wednesday morning was Women's Bible Study and Coffee Hour at church. A year ago, she'd stepped back as a leader of one of the small groups, but she made it a point to attend as often as her health allowed. In the last few months, even that had grown more difficult. But that morning, she was determined.

It's important. When everyone hears what's happened, it's going to create fractures throughout the church. People need to know I'm okay.

"I'm off, Arthur. I'll be back before lunch."

"Where are you going?" he asked, looking up from the newspaper draped over his knees.

"Ladies Coffee at church."

"What?"

"It's important," she assured him.

"After what happened yesterday?"

The shock and hint of betrayal in Arthur's voice tugged at her heart. Rose looked away, smoothing down the front of her coat and inspecting the metal zipper for imagined broken teeth. She refused to look at him despite the sounds of rustling paper and shifting furniture as he stood.

"Rose ... is that a good idea?"

"I'll be fine."

He came to her, a hand gently wrapping around her arm. With the contact, she couldn't help but look up at his piercing grey-blue eyes. Their sharpness had lost the betrayal and now wavered with worry.

"I'll be fine," she repeated.

"Will you?" His hand slid down her arm before releasing its grip, taking with it his extra warmth. "Don't talk too much about this mess, Rose. Not yet. Maybe even not at all. Most of them won't even know what's happened."

"I won't hide it, Arthur."

He opened his mouth to speak, but she reached up and pulled his tall frame down, silencing him with a kiss.

"I promise I won't be the one to bring it up. I don't plan on causing a scene."

"Are you feeling okay?"

Was this a good idea? A slight tremble moved through her spine as her mind swam with questions and she felt a new pull within her chest. A tug of direction, a longing for connection.

"I need my friends, Arthur. I'm okay."

A second kiss sent her out the door, and the fresh air filled her lungs with hope. She wasn't sure how she could feel this way after last night, but she did. Guilt tainted the gentle light from the late winter morning sun, guilt at the loss of responsibility's weight, guilt that she could find hope in the middle of their family's heartache so fast when Arthur couldn't. She knew he wouldn't be able to let this go easily. His stubborn sense of justice would stoke the coals of anger and hurt. But could she blame him? The personal betrayal he was feeling would be deep. She felt it as well. Still, she saw the silver lining of freedom.

Rose parked her car in the usual spot close to the church's side entrance. Traces of last night's snowfall clung to the ground anywhere the shadows still held. She hadn't realized she was staring at the church building, lost in thought, until Sarah, Gary's wife, tapped on the car's passenger window before boldly opening it and sliding in to join her. The sound of the door slamming shut hurt Rose's ears, and she winced as Sarah turned in her seat and pinned her with a look of worry.

"You came."

"I did."

Sarah reached over and took her hand. "You are a brave woman, Rose. I'm so glad you did." Her friend sniffed and screwed up her face in defiance of tears. "I won't cry."

Rose chuckled and wiped at the dampness on her own lashes. "If we start that now, there's no way we'll stop before study starts."

"Shall we do lunch after?"

"Are you sure you want to be seen in public with your ex-pastor's wife?" Rose half joked, but as she said the words, emotion tightened the lining of her throat.

"Enough!" Sarah said in disgust. "We also won't talk about *that* before going in, or I might burn the place to the ground. Gary told me that's frowned on these days."

Rose couldn't help the tear that slipped down her face. "Lunch sounds great."

"Okay," Sarah said, taking a deep breath and looking out the windshield at the church building. "Then let's get this over with."

Rose loved Sarah's fiery spirit, and as she held Rose's arm they entered the church, her friend a guard against dark thoughts.

I'm so glad I came. This moment alone is worth it.

The buzz of women's voices engulfed them.

There had been a few wide eyes when Rose and Sarah entered the building, as well as a few tears, even a few disdainful glares as the morning sped by. It was exhausting wondering what each woman was thinking as she shook their hands in greeting or farewell. It was clear some of the women knew what had happened, some didn't, and some had only half the story.

"How am I going to tell them, Sarah?" Rose asked later as they sat at a local coffee shop, Bible Study over, porcelain bowls of soup and packets of saltines laid out in front of them.

"Let the church board do it." Sarah shook her head as she sprinkled crushed crackers into her minestrone. "I'm upset about how they've chosen to handle this."

Rose couldn't argue there, but she was also too tired to make sense of the mess.

"How is Rachel?" Sarah steered the conversation away from one painful topic to another.

"I'm not sure. We haven't heard anything from her in over a week." Pressure was creeping up the back of Rose's spine again, and she dug around in her purse for a painkiller. "There was a fight when she came to pick up the last of her things. It was right after her choice went public."

Sarah waited for Rose to continue as she spooned a steaming bite of creamy wild rice into her mouth then popped the pill in behind it. The hot liquid was like a balm to Rose's heart while the capsule was a reminder of how things were still not quite right.

"We've made so many mistakes, Sarah, so many." The spoon shook as Rose held it suspended before her, another bite ready. Focusing on it kept her emotions in check. "I had no idea how much our kids hated us."

"Hate? That is a really strong word, Rose."

"I know."

A tear welled in Sarah's eye, and Rose watched her friend dab it away with a corner of her sleeve.

"How bad was it?"

"I can't even remember most of the things that were said." Rose sighed. "It's all smashed together in my brain. But it was bad ... There is one thing I will never forget though. She looked right at Arthur, right at him, no blinking ... she said, 'I hate you. You and your stupid rules, you and your ignorant church, you and your make believe God.'" Rose choked on the words "make believe," and her heart shattered all over again as she relived the moment in her mind. Her baby, her firstborn, filled with such anger towards the most important thing in her parents' lives: their God. "So many mistakes, Sarah! I didn't see this coming. Not with Rachel."

Sarah got up and slid onto the booth bench beside her friend.

"Train up a child in the way he should go; even when he is old, he will not depart from it." Sarah's words were soft and slipped deep into Rose's heart as she recited the scripture from Proverbs 22:6.

Sarah knew the pain of watching a child walk away from the church. Their only daughter was now in her twenties, and though still a large part of their lives, she refused to have anything to do with organized religion. Her break from the church had been much more gradual and less public, happening while away at university. Still, it was a pain her mother carried every day and had shared with few besides Rose and Arthur.

"You need to talk to her, no matter how painful that conversation is bound to be, Rose," Sarah told her.

"I know."

Her friend ran a comforting hand up and down Rose's back as she finished crying. It felt so good just to sit there and be still and quiet for a moment, to be touched with a friend's love, to be accepted amid her imperfections.

"I know you have a lot to work out and work through," Sarah said as she moved back to the opposite side of the table. "But I don't want you to leave church. I can't imagine sitting in service every week knowing you're not there."

"Arthur won't be willing to go back."

"I know. I just ... needed to say it. So you know, either way. You're wanted, Rose."

"Thank you." Rose reached across the table and took her friend's hand. "Now, my soup is still a smidgen warm. Let's finish eating before any more talk."

They sat there for several minutes, fingers touching as they ate, uncaring what the world around them might think as people came and went. As the soup disappeared, Rose recognized something true as she watched her friend from across the table.

God, in the middle of this mess, I am still blessed.

It's All Mandatory

Arthur

IT WAS A DAY shy of a week later when Arthur pulled into the local grocer as rain pelted the pavement. He grabbed a cart from the carousel and groaned in disgust. The handlebar was dripping, and the cold from the wet metal bit into his bare hands, turning his fingers red. On reaching the store entrance, he wiped the water away with the sleeve of his sweater. Immediate regret swept in as the wet fabric brushed his wrists. It probably wouldn't dry until he reached home again.

Way to go, Arthur. Think next time, will you?

The store aisles were mostly empty of people, and Arthur was thankful no one was around to hear the choice words he mumbled while pushing into the produce section. The day before, he'd received his first rejection from a job interview. The hours he'd spent visiting places of business, handing out resumes and speaking with management had worn on him until he felt thin and used like an old worn out sock ready to tear.

What did you expect? It's only been a week. Where has your emotional stamina fled to?

Still, he'd never been without a job before, a purpose, a way to support his loved ones. The past week of failure had been pure torture.

A dark mood followed in his wake, threatening to pour invisible drops of self-loathing on his shoulders to join the dampness the rain had left behind. Starting the day engulfed in a gloom that expected situations to turn from bad to worse was new to Arthur. He'd never been an overly optimistic person, but neither had he been prone to pessimism. It felt oppressive. Try as he might to plaster a smile on his face, he couldn't help but let the edges of his lips droop.

"Apples, oranges, lettuce, potatoes," he recited the list Rose had given to him before leaving the house. Worry filled his mind as he reached for each item and read the prices printed on small yellow signs above or beside each. When had food gotten so expensive? It had been years since he had paid attention to details like that. He'd let Rose take the lead in running the house, especially the kitchen. But now that his situation had changed, he couldn't help but feel the strain on his shrinking bank account. The worry was almost palpable.

Do we need four sweet potatoes? He opened the clear plastic bag provided by the grocer. There were only three of them at home now. He set the fourth one back down in the display pile.

As he picked over the apple display, he heard raised voices emanating from the set of large doors at the back of the store.

"I quit!" a young man yelled and stormed by as he ripped off a green apron.

A middle-aged man followed, hot on his tail, relaying instructions in a hushed tone Arthur couldn't hear. The man's animated movements told Arthur to stay out of the way. The younger man threw his apron over a shoulder, and the latter picked it up with a curse. "If you can't be trusted at a grocery store, no one else will hire you!"

The disgusted exclamation of, "Kids these days!" drew a conciliatory chuckle from Arthur as he watched the younger man escape through the store's automatic sliding doors.

"Can I help you with something?" the man asked as he noticed Arthur.

The man's scowl should have deterred Arthur from pursuing a conversation, but it didn't. Their moods matched, and Arthur felt a kinship with the gentleman now wringing the discarded apron in frustration.

"Maybe. What was that about?" An idea sparked at the back of Arthur's mind.

"Someone's been stealing. I can't say for sure who, but storming off in the middle of questions doesn't look good, does it?" The man smoothed down the front of his white shirt and shook his head. "If they aren't sitting around playing on their phones in the middle of work hours, they're stealing. If they aren't stealing, they're smoking something behind the dumpster. Kids ..."

"Sounds like you need to hire someone other than a kid."

After crossing his arms and looking Arthur up and down, the man asked, "You looking for a job?"

"I might be. You looking for a new employee?"

"I am." Both men smiled, and Arthur knew he'd found his in.

"I've only got part-time positions available in the back." The man's smile flipped as he thought. "You look like someone who needs more than part time, my friend." Still, the man extended a hand.

Arthur accepted the greeting and returned it with a firm, yet brief shake. "Arthur Grill, ex-pastor, and right now I will take any hours I can get."

"Pastor? Really? I guess we'll all be minding our 'p's and 'q's around you, then. If you're interested, the job is yours. I'm Fred, the owner of this grand establishment."

Arthur felt a shade of gloom lift from his brain. It wasn't long before a second employee ran up and started asking Fred questions and urging him towards the dark double doors at the back of the store. Arthur would have walked out without another word, content to show up bright and early the next day, if Fred hadn't hushed his employee and turned back to him.

"Be here tomorrow morning at seven a.m. and I'll get Martha to start your training. I want you in the back, but we require every employee to know how to run cash as well. You know how to drive a forklift?"

"Not yet," Arthur replied, and Fred nodded before asking the boy still beside him if Lucas was working tomorrow.

"Lucas does the training in the back, Martha up front at cash. Penelope is our store manager and my right-hand man, or woman, if you would rather. She's here on weekends and afternoons. I usually open the store myself." Arthur could respect a man who took that much care of his own business.

As he loaded the groceries into the back of his car, Arthur allowed himself to feel excited. Things looked like they might turn in his favour just when he needed it most. As the trunk slammed closed, he stopped, his hands placed on the cold metal, his head bowed.

"Thank you, Lord, for your provision." He didn't even blink at the rain still spattering across the shell of his car.

Once safely seated with the door closed, he held his phone to his ear and waited for Rose to pick up. As rings sounded in one ear, a break in the clouds overhead poured light across the parking lot's blacktop. For a brief second, the puddles scattered across its surface turned gold. A moment's blessing? A sign his prayer was heard? Whatever it meant, Arthur would take it.

"Rose, you'll never guess what I picked up at the grocery store. No, not ice cream, I promised I'd remember that. No, I got a job!"

Hold on to that hope, Arthur. Hold on.

He looked back at the store as he spoke to his wife and made a mental note to ask Fred why it was called Ham's Grocer instead of Fred's.

"But will it be enough, Arthur?" Rose asked as she dragged her legs into the car. Her face was flushed, and her hands trembled. "I mean, part time? At a grocery store? It's not what I expected."

"No, but it's a start, isn't it?"

"Absolutely. It's just. You'll continue to look, right?" She leaned back against the headrest of the passenger's seat and glanced over at him. "When do you start?"

"Tomorrow morning."

"So soon?"

Arthur took his wife's hand in his and squeezed it. "Just think, this way we can start looking for an apartment and have a chance of being able to afford it."

Rose nodded, but Arthur couldn't help but notice how her eyes had dimmed. She was disappointed but trying to hide it.

"How did the appointment go?" he asked, hoping a change of subject would help.

"No definite answers yet."

"But the test results are back at least?"

"Oh, yes, she went over them with me."

"And?"

"She has theories, but again, nothing definite yet. Don't worry. When she knows what's going on, she'll tell us."

Rose's evasiveness troubled Arthur, but the excitement of finding a job and what it would mean for their dwindling resources excited him. "Alright, let's go home. What do you think Amy will say when she finds out?"

"Oh, no ... Do any of her friends have summer jobs there? If they do, you're going to get an earful."

"Are you kidding me?" Amy interjected, as the three of them sat around the dinner table that evening. "HOW EMBARRASSING!"

"It's not! It's a good start, Arthur." Rose said, as she put a finger up to stop Amy from continuing. Still, the smile she flashed him looked strained. "If anyone else in the house wants to look for a job so they can help pay bills, that would be great." Rose's pointed look shut Amy's mouth, and Arthur watched with a half smile on his face as his daughter held back words of scorn. "Just think, Amy, you could be your dad's coworker."

"Good Lord, NO! I would die."

"Then hush and eat your peas."

"I'm still looking for full-time work, Amy. If something comes up, I'll jump on it, but until then, I can't pass on this opportunity." Arthur pinned his daughter with his gaze. "I've also dropped off resumes at the hardware store, all the restaurants down Main Street, the newspaper had an opening at the printing press, oh, and the laundromat. I have a list ready for tomorrow evening after my training shift at the grocers as well. I think I need to spread out. Any more ideas?" Arthur asked as he handed Rose the list he'd laid beside his dinner plate.

He watched as Rose massaged her neck with thin fingers as she read.

"You okay?" he asked.

"Just tired, Arthur." The pink that had graced her cheeks after last week's drama, was gone. He missed it all the more after being reminded of how beautiful she was, kissed by her natural blush. Would her lost health ever return? He worried for her and wondered when answers would finally come.

"You haven't told me what Doctor Ingrid said, Rose." Arthur hoped he wouldn't have to plead for more information.

"My numbers are all over the place. That's why she's calling for more tests. Don't worry, Arthur, Ingrid is taking good care of me. Besides, your job is more important than me right now. We can't live without an income. We can't move without an income."

Arthur nodded in placating agreement. His wife's health was far more important, but she would only deflect his worry if he said anything more.

"How was church Sunday morning?" he asked, changing the subject.

"As good as expected with the pastor gone and an overconfident board elder in his place. They used one of your sermons from last year."

Arthur nodded. Gary had called him Friday night and asked for permission to use any sermons the church had on file.

"Who read it?"

"Bennett."

"I still can't believe you went."

"One of us needed to."

"Well, this has been fun, but I'm done," Amy interrupted and pushed away from the table. "Just don't get a job at MD's Dad. That would be the worst."

Arthur ignored the half snort of Amy's laughter as she walked out of the room. Once she was well down the hallway, he turned to Rose. "She isn't helping one bit."

"She—it's a defence mechanism, I think."

"That doesn't change the fact that she isn't helping."

"I'll talk to her."

"Mention it to her counsellor too. Maybe she can straighten her out. Lord knows she doesn't listen to us."

Wednesday dawned, and again Arthur found himself in the grocer's parking lot, thankful the morning was dry and the wind was blowing in from the south, pushing clouds across the path of the early morning sun. The small amount of snow, once left in the shadows of buildings as winter made a slow retreat, had disappeared in yesterday's rain, leaving the few patches of grass bare and brown, ready for spring to wake them.

Apprehension grew in Arthur's chest like a mushroom in damp soil, but he plucked it free with a cough and cast it aside as the glass doors slid open for him. Setting a smile firmly on his freshly shaven face, he found the customer service counter and announced himself.

"Ah! The new help." The woman behind the counter was round, and her smile stretched wide. Heavy makeup aged her in Arthur's eyes, but her handshake was firm and welcoming. "I'm Martha. I've got the computer ready upstairs with the orientation videos set to go. Then, when you're done with the first few videos, I'll be training you here at cash before Lucas gets his turn. Now, don't worry," she added as Arthur grimaced. "It's just formality stuff. Fred said he wants you in back. But, my, oh my."

Martha's hungry eyes roved over Arthur's tall frame, and he had to wonder if this woman was safe or if he should ask for a chaperone while she trained him.

"Come on!" She beckoned as she cast him a coy smile and headed down the nearest food aisle.

Arthur caught a few of his new coworkers watching them as Martha led the way to the back of the store and pushed open the large double doors marked with a sign that read "employees only". As they walked past boxes of foodstuff stacked on pallets and wrapped tight with plastic, Martha chatted away, trusting Arthur would be listening as he did his best to keep up.

"What did you say your name was, dear? Fred mentioned you were a pastor. What on earth brings you to Ham's Grocers?"

"I recently lost my job."

"Oh, what a shame. Or maybe?" The open question made Arthur uncomfortable as the woman before him swung her wide hips in a tantalizing rhythm.

"I was a ... I'm married." Arthur almost tripped on some power cords, despite them being taped securely to the floor with red duct tape.

"Watch your step!"

"Um ... yeah. It's a shame."

Martha paused and turned to look back at him, her eyes crawling up and down his frame. "Pity."

"Have you ever attended?"

"Attended?" The woman's eyebrows rose, and a laugh bubbled out across the space between them. "No, sorry to say I'm not the church type."

Red flushed Arthur's face at Martha's admission.

Turning, Martha led him up a flight of steps set against the very back wall of the last storeroom. It brought them into a hallway built on a second floor Arthur had never realized existed. Several doors stood open, all with windows built into red-painted surfaces.

"Here's the staff room. Computers in the corner."

She led him past a few square tables, waiting for tired employees on their lunch hour, to a dim corner. Three computers separated by wooden shields, creating small private cubes, lined the wall. "Welcome to Training" shone from the first monitor against a white and red background.

"Take a seat. Follow the prompts. It'll have you type in some of your personal information, but not too much. Fred will come to get your social security number soon. Got to get that paperwork filled out if you want a paycheck!"

"And I get paid for training?"

"Yes, you do!" As Martha patted the metal chair in front of the computer, she leaned over and clicked into a program using the computer mouse. "There, just go for it." She checked her watch. "I'll be back in two hours. Try to get through as much as you can. You won't need most of it, but it's mandatory for every new employee." She winked at him as he settled into the chair and turned again to wave as she left the room.

"Good Lord." Arthur wasn't sure if it was a prayer or not, but either way, he knew with that woman close, he would need the good Lord's patience. She swayed her hips as she left, and Arthur had to squeeze his eyes closed to keep from watching. How long had it been since he'd been able to come together with Rose as her husband? He'd lost track of the time. A deep sigh pushed its way up from his chest.

Rose.

He loved her too much to let a flirt distract him from doing what he needed to. She was worth the distance her health sometimes demanded. Still, the brazenness of Martha's attention was shocking.

Lord, what have I gotten myself into?

The orientation program was easy to follow, and Arthur watched video after video of employees dressed in green or red aprons talking about food and cleaning safety. One touched on what to do if the store was robbed. As the instructors droned on, Arthur reminded himself it was a necessary evil to get that much needed paycheck and shifted in his chair, determined to stay awake. At the end of each presentation, the program would throw up a short quiz. He'd have to watch the video a second time if he got over three questions wrong. Thankfully, that only happened once as he let his mind wander while the dull smiling face on the screen chattered away.

It was a sweet relief when Fred walked into the room, his white buttoned-down shirt neatly tucked into smart black pants. "Good morning. Finished with that video? I've got some paperwork for you to fill out." Arthur's new boss saluted him with a manila folder.

"Thank goodness ... These training videos are riveting," Arthur confessed, with a roll of his eyes.

Fred let out a laugh and shrugged, taking a seat at one of the square tables closest to Arthur. "It might seem boring, but it's all important information. Pay attention, you'll need all of it, eventually. Oh, and I'll be checking those scores at the end of each video."

"Of course you will." Arthur plunked through the last quiz as fast as he could then stood to stretch the kinks from his long legs. He smirked at the screen, grateful he hadn't had to do the video over again in front of Fred.

"Now, I need your SIN card, Arthur, and here, I need you to fill out this sheet for insurance purposes, and this one here for benefits."

Fred pushed several sheets of paper his way. When Arthur grasped their edges, they were warm, fresh from the printer.

"Please note, benefits are only offered for full-time employees who have worked over three months at the store."

"Only full-time?"

Fred nodded, the crinkles at the corners of his eyes moving as his gaze drifted away from Arthur to read over a few other papers. "Unfortunately, yes. We'll work you up in hours when we can. I like to hang on to my seasoned employees, Arthur. To me, your age is an asset as long as you settle in well."

"I'm still looking for full-time work elsewhere."

"I figured you would be. Still, let's see if I can persuade you to stay when the time comes. If this works out, that is."

The room fell silent but for the scratching of pen on paper.

"Stable work is a blessing, Arthur, even if it's not the work you first thought you'd be doing."

Arthur could only nod and keep his silence as cascading thoughts from the last few weeks crowded in, stalling his progress with the forms in front of him.

And if that stable work is enough to pay the bills.

The biggest question was rent. It loomed over him like an invisible presence looking over his shoulder. Part time wouldn't pay enough to cover food and rent for long. Would full time? Without an apartment secured, he had no way to know for sure how much he needed to make.

"Arthur," Fred asked after a few minutes, "If you don't mind me asking, what happened? Why is a pastor so desperate for a job at a grocery store?"

When Arthur failed to answer right away, Fred apologized for asking, but Arthur raised his hand and stopped him in mid sentence.

"It's okay, Fred. My family is going through some difficult things right now. The church felt it was better for us to sort it out with no added distractions of ministry. So I'm on break indefinitely."

"Sorry to hear that, Arthur. I'm not a religious man, but an eager worker is hard to find."

The door behind them squeaked as Martha walked in, her hips swaying as if she were listening to a private tune.

"Aw! Fred, dear!" Arthur couldn't help but notice the pause in her step and the change in her gait when she realized the new guy wasn't alone in the room. "Are you men all caught up on paperwork? It's time for some hands-on learning."

Boxes With No Place To Go

ROSE

THE SMELL OF CARDBOARD and dust threatened to make Rose sneeze. She filled the low table beside her with knickknacks and decor she'd pulled down from shelves and unhooked from walls. Methodically, she wiped each item clean with a damp cloth before placing it in a reconstructed cardboard box at her feet.

As she worked, she thought of Arthur and hoped his first day at work was going well. The house felt empty and quiet. Loneliness crept across the floor and held her ankles in place. The roller coaster of changes had come hard and fast. The question of what if was ever present in her mind while the silence gave it space.

She carefully arranged each item in the box where it fit best—a jigsaw puzzle with no sure lines to follow. A Bible verse plaque slipped into place between decorative cups wrapped in paper. She hoped the board would work as an extra guard against bumps, holding everything snug when moving day came.

Moving day.

They still had several weeks to find a new home, but right now, these boxes had no destination. What would happen if they couldn't find a suitable place? Her mind also wandered to her mounting health problems. Sometimes Rose felt like she was drowning in what ifs.

"God, part-time at a grocery store won't be enough of an income in the long term, and I can't work. These changes would be so much easier if you would just tell me what's coming next."

She closed her eyes to listen, just in case He gave her the answer she asked for right then. A buzzing from the table sounded, followed by the delayed chiming of an incoming call on her cell phone. The sounds pulled her from her dark speculations as she stretched down to reach the device. It vibrated against the smooth wooden surface, moving away from her.

"Hello, this is Rose Grill," she answered once she'd caught it.

"Hi, Mom. It's Rachel."

Rose almost tripped in place, her heart hammering as she heard her daughter's voice. A pause followed Rachel's excited greeting.

"I thought it was time I checked in on you. How have you been?"

The weeks that stretched between both of them had been painful.

"I've been okay." Rose swallowed the lump in her throat and moved towards the kitchen and a glass of water. "How have you been? We've never not talked like this before."

"I know. It's weird, but I wasn't sure ... I've got a job at the laundromat in the evenings. I'm still looking for something else, though."

"That sounds good. Does it get busy in the evenings?"

"Depends on the day. I've only been behind the desk for a week now. Jay got me the job. His buddy knows the owner."

"How's Jay?"

"He's fine. Say, are ... are you really okay? Jay said something happened at church, but I didn't quite believe it."

Rose told her daughter the whole story.

"You've got to be kidding me!"

"No, no kidding. I'm packing boxes right now. I wrapped Grandma's old tea cups in newspaper, but I'm still scared to pack them away."

"Oh, my God ..." Rachel's voice dipped to a whisper. "This is my fault, isn't it?"

"No, it's not. I think this has been coming for a while." Water glass in hand, Rose settled onto a dining room chair. "The last year was rough for the church board, and I've lost track of how many clashes of personality there have been between Bennett and your father. That and church politics? It's not always a fun thing to wade through."

"I'm sorry, Mom."

"I miss you, Rachel." Rose's fingers had gone cold, and she clutched the phone, afraid she might drop it if she loosened her grip.

"I miss you too, Mom," Rachel replied.

Rose heard a sniff from the other end of the call and asked, "Why don't you come over for dinner?"

"Can't. I've got work in the evenings."

"Oh, right ..."

"But maybe I can stop for lunch tomorrow? Do you need more boxes? I can ask around."

"That would be perfect. Bring all the boxes you can find."

The next day Rose felt like a kid getting ready for a long awaited play date with a best friend. She couldn't keep her nervous smiles hidden as she ushered Amy and Arthur out the door with kisses and waves. A bead of apprehension had settled in her gut when she'd started to tell Arthur about Rachel's planned visit. Did he need to know?

No. Better to wait until after, take things slow. She wasn't about to force a reconciliation before the time was right. Still, she inwardly beamed with the knowledge that soon she'd see her eldest child again.

"What are you on, Mom?" Amy asked before stepping off the front steps.

"On?"

"Yeah, like, did your doctor put you on some extra strength meds or something? You're acting like a strung-out teen ..."

"How would you know what strung out looks like?" Rose asked in shock at Amy's description.

"Everyone knows." Amy rolled her eyes and headed down the sidewalk, aiming for the bus stop at the end of the block.

"Well, that's terrible," Rose muttered as she watched Amy turn in the driveway.

"What's terrible?" Arthur put his arm around her waist and pulled her in for a kiss.

"Apparently, everyone knows what a strung out teen looks like except me, and I'm acting like one. Where does she get these ideas, Arthur?"

"Probably better not to ask." Her husband grimaced.

Rose didn't like his tone at all and returned his kiss with a peck on the cheek. "More training at work today?"

"Yep."

With the short answer, he was off down the steps and, in a minute, pulling the car out of the driveway.

"What a family," Rose muttered before heading back inside to clear the kitchen of breakfast dishes. She refused to let anyone dampen her excitement as she readied the space for lunch with Rachel.

By the time her eldest daughter knocked on the door, the kitchen was a wash of scents. They pushed past Rose as she greeted Rachel with a hug.

"Oh! Wow, Mom! I hope you didn't go to too much trouble. It's just lunch!"

"It was no trouble," she assured her, stepping out of the way and taking the armload of collapsed cardboard Rachel offered.

"Some of them might not be strong enough to put back together. But I can find more. These are just the ones I used ... when I left."

"Thank you. Come on in. Soup's on!"

Rose watched Rachel cast wary eyes around the hall and kitchen as they walked, her gaze stopping at each empty place on the wall that used to house a picture.

"It looks so empty," her daughter said as they sat down at the table.

"It does. Empty and dirty. Did you notice the spaces left on the wall after I took down the pictures? I'm going to have to scrub from the ceiling down, before we leave."

"I guess things build up over the years, don't they?"

"Yes, they do. Much more than we ever realize until something has to be moved. I thought I did pretty good at keeping this house clean." Rose's sentence was pregnant with more meaning than she'd meant it to hold.

"You did. You're a wonderful mom," Rachel assured her.

"Am I? My daughter left."

Rachel stared into her bowl for a moment before stirring its contents and lifting the spoon to lick it clean. It wasn't a full bite, but Rose watched her close her eyes in enjoyment of the warm liquid.

"This is so good, Mom. Did you make it?"

Rose shook her head. "Your father picked it up last night for me from Ham's Grocers. He got a part-time job there this week. Yesterday was his first day. They have a great soup counter and a salad bar. Your father brought home several discounted soups to stock the freezer with for these last few weeks in the house."

"Dad's working at *Ham's?*" Rachel's eyes grew wide, and she dropped her spoon.

It hit the tabletop with a clatter, and both women flinched.

"Yes. Today is his second day of training."

"Mom. *Jay* works at Ham's!"

"Oh!" Rose couldn't believe she'd forgotten. Or, maybe she had never realized. "Well ... that's going to make things interesting." Rose pushed aside the flutters in her heart as Rachel stared at her, mouth wide open.

"You think?"

"Don't worry, Rachel. This job is too important for your dad. Besides, he's an adult; he's had years of experience getting along with people he doesn't care for. And he knows Jay. Hopefully, steering clear of him won't be a problem."

"Yeah. Okay." But Rachel's eyes remained huge for a moment longer as the gears behind their grey-blue depths turned. "It's not Dad I'm worried about ..."

"Are you happy, Rachel?" The question was abrupt, and Rose immediately regretted it, but knew it was something the ache in her gut wouldn't let go of until she asked.

"Of course I am, Mom. I mean, there's always a space where you have to get used to each other in a relationship, right? Yeah, I'm happy."

The words, along with her daughter's shrug, did little to convince Rose it was true. But she left it there. She'd asked. Maybe just the question would get Rachel thinking. But she couldn't help but add in, "If that ever changes, you can always come home."

"I know, Mom. Thanks."

"Or at least we will make room for you wherever we find a place." Now it was Rose's turn to look around the walls of her kitchen, realizing afresh that it really wasn't her kitchen at all.

"I'll put a bug out for word on a new place, Mom. Jay's got connections. His friends are always looking for new apartments. I think he must know all the best rentals in town."

Rose changed the subject, not wanting to give in to the temptation to ask why Jay's friends were always moving. "How's school going? I love that you're here, but I have to admit, I completely forgot you should be in class."

"Can we leave that alone for right now, Mom?" Her daughter shifted in her chair and stirred her soup, the spoon sending out soft *clinks* as it brushed the sides of her bowl.

Rose nodded, but the wrinkles on her forehead deepened. She didn't like Rachel's hesitation. "The last few years of high school are so important."

"I know, but sometimes life just doesn't go the way you plan it. There are more important things to think about right now." Rachel abandoned her spoon and pushed back from the table. "I'll be right back."

Rose bit a dry ridge that had risen on the flesh of her lip. *Tread carefully, Rose, you can't afford to lose her again.* She prayed as she worked a small piece of dead skin free from its anchor. *God, give me wisdom and help me shut my mouth when needed.*

When Rachel returned, her face freshly washed, her sweater sleeves showed dampness at their edges. Was it from cleaning her hands or tears?

"I didn't mean to upset you," Rose said.

"It's okay, Mom. Let's finish eating before it gets cold. Then I'll help you fix the boxes up. I can help pull stuff out of the closets if you want."

Rose wiped away tears as Rachel walked down the front steps and zipped her jacket closed against the cool spring breeze.

"Think we might get snow again before it really warms up?" her daughter asked as she looked up at the sky to note the clouds rolling by.

"I don't doubt it. March and April can never make up their minds weather-wise."

"I'll call you, Mom. Try not to worry. It'll all work out, and I'm fine. Maybe we can find you an apartment next door. Would be second best to me moving back, right?"

"Right," was all Rose could answer as her throat closed with emotion. "Bye!"

Rose marvelled at her daughter's height and grace as she walked down the lane and turned at the sidewalk. Rachel's eighteen years looked like Rose's mid twenties. The realization warmed her heart while sticking hot pins into it. How could eighteen years of experience be ready for a life outside the four walls of her family home with such confidence? But Rose knew there was no use fighting the reality of her daughter's choice. She could drag her home, but it wouldn't actually bring her back. It would only push her further and further away emotionally until she was too far to return.

There had always been a struggle with rules, expectations, and reality within their family. Rose knew that. Being a pastor's wife wasn't easy and being a pastor's kid sometimes harder. Over the last year and a half, she'd been forced to acknowledge it and learn release, knowing she couldn't control the lives of her girls. Not even a little.

"God, please, whatever lessons I taught Rachel through my mess, help her remember them now."

Safe Place

RACHEL

A CHILL FOLLOWED RACHEL as she wandered the streets back to the apartment she shared with Jay. She slipped gloves on and pulled her hood up, but nothing stopped the draft from reaching down her back. Her mom had looked so pale, so thin and drawn. The familiar glint in her blue eyes was achingly absent. They hadn't talked about health problems, but they didn't have to for Rachel to know moving house wasn't the only struggle Rose was facing.

It had felt surreal being back home after weeks of no communication. As she walked past old neighbours' houses and familiar landmarks, she relived the day she'd packed her last suitcase.

Her parents had let the church's expectations run their lives for years, and when Rose had found condom wrappers in Rachel's garbage, she'd told Arthur. The confrontation with her father had been ugly and her mother's face lined with defeat as Rachel wheeled a final suitcase out the door.

"You're only eighteen, Rachel. You're not even finished with your final year of school."

"I'm not staying a moment longer in this house, Mom. I'm done with this bullshit."

Having already said his piece, her father had stood silently watching from a window, his arms crossed over his chest, his expression steeled disapproval. He'd made it clear there would be no more "living in sin" under his roof.

"You don't realize what you're doing!" Rose had said.

Rachel had turned and looked her up and down. "I do, Mom, I'm getting away from him, his ridiculous rules, his unfair expectations. I'm escaping Amy's constant drama. It hurts, Mom. Don't you realize that? You didn't even notice when I would sleep over at Jay's for the last year. Yes, year! I'm getting away from you and your empty promises. I'm going to a safe place."

"Living with a boy you're not married to is not a safe place, Rachel."

"It's safer than living here."

She hadn't listened to her mother's pleas that day. She'd shut her out. For Rachel, it was too little, too late.

"A safe place," she whispered to herself when she reached the apartment complex. The red brick building was old, and the three stories contained crowded one and two-bedroom suites. An electric key card let her in the front double doors, and immediately, she heard shouting from down the hall.

Rachel turned right instead of left as an elderly woman and middle-aged man yelled obscenities at each other, cutting off the direct line she usually took to the elevator. She winced while passing a young woman not much older than herself, a baby strapped to her chest and a toddler waddling behind her.

"Can you believe them?" the woman commented as Rachel turned sideways, giving the mother more space to make her way down the hall. "Screaming at each other in the middle of the afternoon?"

Rachel looked back over her shoulder as finger gestures emphasized the man's anger. "I can't believe he's talking to a grandma like that."

"Mrs. Call can be a real grump, but, yeah. Names like that are never called for." The woman pulled her toddler in front of her and covered the child's ears with her hands, letting the wrap she wore hold the infant to her chest as they walked on. Rachel felt bad for them as they ventured closer to the commotion, but she continued and turned the corner before pushing the stairwell door open—the perfect escape route.

The brightly lit stairwell still smelled of fresh paint. The apartment custodian worked hard to cover any graffiti that popped up now and then, but Rachel wondered if it wouldn't be more fun to let some of it stay or hire an artist to liven up the empty canvas the grey cement presented. A banging from above alerted her she wasn't alone, and she trotted up the steps as fast as she could, meeting several young men on the way to the third floor. They all parted for her, except one who was ignoring the rest. His ears were plugged with earbuds, his neck bent over a cell phone.

"Roger? What ya reading?" One asked as he stepped farther out of Rachel's way to make up Roger's deficit.

The man looked up and answered, "Texts and nothing," as Rachel slipped past and reached for the hallway door.

"Hey! You're Jay's girl, right?"

She stopped for a split second but didn't turn as she called, "Yeah," back to him. She didn't like the way his companions had eyed her as she passed. But the bright sunlight shining through the stairwell windows assured her it was too early in the day for them to try anything. Or she hoped it was.

"Tell him I'm waiting for his answer."

Answer? To what? Rachel wasn't sure if she wanted to know but didn't stop to ask for more information. The stairwell door swung closed behind her, and she breathed a prayer of thanks as it cut off the group's mutterings.

A safe place, she reminded herself as she unlocked and pushed open the door of apartment 302. The automatic lock *clicked* as she released a sigh into the room.

Echo Apartments wasn't necessarily a dangerous place to live, it was just different from what she was used to. She hadn't realized just how different until she'd carted in her final suitcase. Coming home to an empty apartment also didn't fill her with the same thrill that walking hand in hand with Jay had. Spending nights with him over the last year had been exciting, a forbidden refuge from the turmoil of her home life. The diversity of the people who shared the building had added to that excitement, giving her new experiences each time she visited. But now?

Her chest ached as if something important was missing. Had she made the right choice?

"It's a bit late for that question, Rachel." She rolled her eyes at the doubt she'd felt while visiting with her mother. She refused to allow it to plant roots as she pushed away from the locked door and kicked her boots off onto the entryway mat.

The door of the main hall accessed the apartment's open living space. She'd bought the mat herself the first week after moving in. Why hadn't she noticed how faded the carpet was before? Or the layers of grime embedded into it, solidified into a crust that resisted all her efforts to vacuum or scrub it clean? Had it been that way when Jay first moved in? Was it his sloppy carelessness that had caused the wear? Rachel wasn't sure, but it didn't matter. The mat was there as a guard and a screen. Now she didn't have to look at it.

The first week with Jay had been filled with scrubbing and sorting his mess. He wasn't really a sloppy guy. He just didn't think about wiping out the corners like her mother had taught her to do, and he never dusted. "Always dust first, then the vacuum will pick up the particles you scatter all over the carpets," Rose had told her repeatedly as a preteen. She never thought she'd be thankful for the knowledge.

The room felt too quiet, so she flipped on Jay's TV for background noise and wandered into the small galley kitchen while glancing at her phone's lock screen. She had time before her shift at Suds, the local laundromat, started. Jay would appreciate a hot dinner when he got home. But the question was what should she make?

Their stock of food was sad, but she pulled out rice and mixed frozen vegetables. Jay lived off what he could make in his rice cooker, and Rachel had found it had a slow cooker mode that she used when her mornings took her out early to school. She rinsed the rice and tossed in half the bag of vegetables. Was it too much? Maybe for Jay, but not for her.

After adding black beans to the concoction floating in carefully measured water and hitting the heat, Rachel flopped down on the living room couch and checked her phone. "Just one more hour." She told herself. "And think—you're doing the wife thing well today."

She'd already served herself and was sitting at the small dining table, complete with two mismatched chairs, when Jay pushed his way through the door.

"Hey," he greeted her, shaking his unruly black hair that threatened to obscure his vision.

"You'll never guess what I found out today," she challenged before he'd had time to pull off his shoes.

"Nope. But I bet you're going to tell me."

"You're going to have to work with my dad!"

"What?!"

"It's true. I had lunch with Mom today. She told me he got a part-time job at Ham's."

Jay shook his head in disbelief. "I didn't see him. Are you sure she said Ham's?"

"Yep. It's his second day."

"Terrific ... Did she say what position they're giving him? They always train new people up front first, even if they're working in back."

"No, she didn't. Be nice, okay."

"Nice? Aren't I always nice?"

"To me? Mostly." Rachel grinned as Jay rolled his stiff shoulders. "But never to my Dad."

"Yeah, well, can you blame me when the man disapproves of everything I do?"

"Not everything. He just doesn't like you sleeping with his daughter."

"He didn't like me before that either."

The conversation shifted as Jay walked into the kitchen to grab his dinner, eyeing the last few bites of rice and beans in Rachel's bowl as he passed.

"Black beans?"

"Yep."

"Eh, not my favourite." Jay wrinkled his nose as he opened the cooker's lid.

"Are you going to your mom's tonight?" Rachel was hoping he would say yes and she could count on leftovers appearing in the fridge when she got home from her shift at the laundromat.

"Nope. I have other stuff to do."

"What other stuff?"

"Just stuff."

"Some guy in the stairwell asked about you." She spooned the last bite of rice into her mouth and chewed slowly as Jay looked over at her, hand and spoon poised over the rice cooker.

"What guy?" he asked, an unreadable expression on his face that made Rachel swallow and clear her throat before answering.

"Just some guy. He said he was waiting for your answer to something."

"Must've been Roger ..." Jay muttered as he finished serving himself and took a seat opposite her.

"What's he want?" she asked.

"Nothing. Don't worry about it."

She didn't like his silence but didn't push the matter as he focused on his food, making it disappear in record time before getting up again for more.

"I work late," she told him as she stood with her own bowl in hand.

"Okay. You going now?" He looked up, the lift of his eyebrows lighting a spark in her gut. He knew that expression gave her butterflies.

"Yep. Wash the dishes for me?" She held out the bowl for him to take and place in the sink.

"Maybe."

"Yes. I would love to do the dishes for you, Rachel," she corrected while giving him a once over with her eyes designed to make his gut flip.

"Yes, Rachel. Maybe."

"Well, I'm gone." She turned, now rolling her own eyes at his refusal to promise to do the simple task.

Jay pulled his phone from a pocket as he walked back to the table, a bowl brimming full with a second helping, and proceeded to ignore her as she dressed for another walk in the early spring chill. She looked back at him as she reached for the doorknob.

"I love you, Jay."

"Huh? What was that?" He asked, still not lifting his eyes from the screen.

"Never mind," she muttered as her heart drifted into her toes.

A safe place. He's still my safe place, she reminded herself as she opened the door.

Forklifts

ARTHUR

FLOOR-TO-CEILING SHELVING LINED HAM'S GROCER'S stock rooms with a wide open space between both wings reserved for pallets stacked with goods and wrapped in thick plastic. It was all a labyrinth to a new employee, but Arthur was fast learning the layout. The path to the back of the room and the stairway leading to the second floor offices and break room were always a changing zigzag. But if he headed in the general direction he wanted to go, he'd usually get there. Eventually, all paths led to the exits. The back rooms were already buzzing when Arthur pushed his way in through the large grey double doors.

"Arthur!" Lucas, the stock manager, called across the floor. "Ready to learn how to drive this baby?"

Lucas stood with one foot on the running board of a forklift parked in the centre of the loading area, shirt sleeves pushed up to his elbows and a company cap placed backwards on his head. He was young but not so young that Arthur thought it was appropriate to wear a cap like a street kid.

Maybe you're just getting old. He checked his attitude. It wasn't always easy taking orders from someone younger than himself. But Arthur had gained respect for Lucas. The young man had demonstrated his knowledge and the ability to organize people in the few days Arthur had been on the team.

"Sure am," Arthur called back while fastening the last button on his company vest.

When they had him learning things in the storefront, he wore a green apron. But here in the back, the vest was all he needed. Lucas handed him a hard hat when he stepped up to the forklift.

"You finished the video on this machine yesterday, right?"

Arthur nodded.

"Good. Now, pay attention." Lucas tapped the top of a clipboard he'd pulled off the machine's driver's seat. "This is your official certification lesson. Yes, there'll be a test at the end."

He had his pupil settle in the seat and started explaining everything written out on the clipboard he held. Lucas liked to dive into new things fast and running hard.

"We're going to move some empty pallets around first. I got the rest of the guys working in stock room two this morning, so the open area is ours." Lucas pointed at the stack of empty pallets waiting for them. "You ready?"

Arthur nodded and pressed the ignition button beside the steering wheel.

"Then go for it and let me see what you understood from those videos."

In record time, Arthur had successfully moved two pallets from the pile and placed them on top of each other a few feet away.

"Good, keep it up!" Lucas yelled, and Arthur looked over his shoulder at the manager as he waved and beamed his approval of Arthur's progress.

A group of younger employees entered the loading area and called Lucas aside as Arthur focused his attention on the first pile of pallets. He manoeuvred the metal forks into just the right spot so they would slide cleanly in between the pallet boards, then with the pull of a lever, he hoisted it up above the pavement. Just before he hit reverse to manoeuvre the machine into a better alignment for dropping it on the second pile, he heard angry shouting and paused. He turned to glance at Lucas as one of the young men from the group raised his hands over his head. When the man spun around in a disgruntled exit, he looked right at Arthur.

The man's angry gaze nailed him to the forklift seat. Arthur's heart skipped a beat under the pressure, and he sighed in relief when the young man stomped off, flicking a company hat against the plastic-wrapped pallets around the edges of the room. It took Arthur's brain a minute to register the man's face, and by the time he realized who he was, he'd disappeared.

Lucas waved at Arthur, and he swallowed, killing the forklift's engine with the push of a button. Apprehension crawled into Arthur's chest and squeezed his heart like a pulsating fist. It was Jay, Rachel's boyfriend.

"What's wrong?" Arthur asked his manager as Lucas's mouth opened once before closing again without a word. His manager's brows knit together with displeasure added to Arthur's anxiety.

"You never told me you had history with Jay Kenny. I had you listed for his stock team this afternoon. He wasn't too happy about it."

"I wasn't aware he worked here," Arthur said while holding on to the steering wheel for support. "I have no problems with Jay as a person, but I can understand why he wouldn't want me on his team. Does this hurt my job?"

"Depends on if you two can be civil."

"I can," Arthur assured him while a sensation like ants on the hunt crawled up his legs. He leaned down to rub the fabric of his pants against his skin.

Lucas stared. "You sure?"

"As far as it depends on me, there won't be trouble."

"Alright, then. Let's see how this afternoon goes. Jay won't like it, but I don't have time to shuffle lists around. I'll revise teams for next week if need be, but ... I'd prefer not to."

Arthur nodded as Lucas stepped back from the forklift and motioned for him to continue.

Arthur could have kicked himself. How had he not known Jay worked here? With a sigh, he answered his own questions. *Because he hadn't spoken to Rachel in weeks. None of the discussions with her about her boyfriend ever touched on a job, or even if he had one. Because ... just because.*

As the forklift rumbled back to life, Arthur pushed his regrets from his mind. There wasn't time to dwell on it now.

Soon Lucas graduated Arthur to transferring a pallet loaded with large blue containers of water from one side of the room to the next.

"Try not to spill," he'd said as he patted the blue plastic bin before pulling off its lid.

Arthur's first attempt ended with a soaked cement floor as a lever slipped from his hand and the forklift dropped abruptly. But after a quick break to mop up the puddle, he'd gone back at it. Within the hour, Lucas called for him to quit and congratulated him on passing the test so far.

"Take your first break then knock on Fred's door and tell him you're ready for the written test. He'll ask you to hand in your phone so there is no cheating."

"Is that necessary?" Arthur asked.

"It's normal. You never know what people will try to cheat on these days." Lucas pointed to the crews walking around in groups of two and three. "I've already sent the boss a message about Jay. Expect him to have some questions."

Arthur wiped a bead of sweat from his temple.

"Just perfect," he muttered, none too keen on anyone grilling him about his personal life.

After finishing an early lunch, Arthur stood in front of the office door. His sandwich sat heavy in his gut, his hand refusing to knock.

This is stupid. Just get on with it.

But the internal pep talk didn't work, and he heard the ticking of his watch in the silence of the hallway.

"What on earth are you doing?" A voice from behind him asked.

Arthur jumped as he spun around, taking in the small black woman with arms crossed over her chest and a no-nonsense attitude radiating from her posture. She gave Arthur the impression she could ripple the surrounding air by will alone.

"Good morning, Penelope. It's still morning, right?"

"Yes," she said as she glanced at her own watch. "Not for long, though, and you didn't answer the question."

"I'm just here to tell Fred I've finished the first half of the forklift certification test. Lucas says I passed."

"Well, good for you," Penelope's direct gaze wavered. "It's strange to just be standing in front of his door for five minutes, then, isn't it?"

"Five minutes?"

"Could have been. I watched you as I walked the length of the hall. Now, come on." She flashed him a shockingly white smile from beneath her midnight toned skin.

This woman was the polar opposite of Martha and her overly friendly advances, but her firmness commanded respect, and Arthur had to admit from what he'd seen over the past few days, she was good at her job as Head Manager. Arthur shrank back as she reached past him for the doorknob and swung it wide.

"Fred, someone to see you!"

The office was much smaller than what Arthur expected, with three walls lined with desk space and above that shelves sagging with the weight of binders and books. It felt claustrophobic, even from the doorway. Fred sat in the middle of the chaos, bent over a paper scattered desk, bifocals perched precariously at the end of his nose.

"Hm? Hello, Penelope," he muttered.

"It's time to get your nose out of the books, Fred," Penelope told him as she pushed into the room. "And like I said, you've a visitor."

"Just a moment. I need to finish making sure this is all in order for the accountant—Penelope!"

The woman grabbed the back of Fred's office chair and spun him to face Arthur.

"Visitor, Fred." She pointed at Arthur. "He was sulking at the door for a good five minutes, just so you know."

"He was, was he?"

Heat rose into Arthur's face as Fred turned his attention towards him.

"Did something happen I'm not aware of?" Penelope asked as she looked back and forth between them both.

"No, or at least not yet," Fred said, then motioned for Arthur to enter the office as well. "Stop looking like it's the end of the world, Arthur. You're not getting fired. It's Jay's fault if he doesn't want to work with you. At least, until one of you tries taking any disagreements further than glaring at each other." As he spoke, Fred pulled the chair away from Penelope's grip and rolled backwards towards a stack of drawers stored under the desk. He counted the papers he pulled out before sighing. "Make a note we need to print off more of these, Penelope."

"*You* need to print off more of them, you mean?" Crossing her arms again, she leaned her backside against the nearest surface behind her, glaring at each of them.

"What?" Fred asked, smoothing down his shirt front.

"You going to tell me what's going on?"

"Arthur?" Fred looked over at him. "She won't be satisfied until she knows."

"As Head Manager, I need to know of any trouble brewing," Penelope told him.

The back of Arthur's neck tingled. He rubbed it before pulling his cap off and running his fingers through his salt and pepper hair. This woman had a way of making him feel like he was fifteen again and being reprimanded for breaking a plate in his mother's kitchen.

"Is it anyone's business?" he asked.

"Usually, no. But Jay has made it very clear he wants nothing to do with you, and their conversation has put Lucas on edge. He doesn't want trouble. What did you do? Excommunicate him from that church of yours, or something?" Fred's question clawed at the building pressure behind Arthur's eyes.

"It's nothing like that," Arthur said as he pulled the office door closed. Penelope and Fred exchanged looks as the handle's metal tongue clicked into place. "He's dating my eldest daughter. We don't approve of the match."

"Hm. Taking things a bit too far, is he?" Penelope asked.

"Yeah, she moved out a few weeks back."

"Are you going to be able to work around this? I won't tolerate fighting." Penelope's finger rose in the air and shook for a second with determination.

"We won't tolerate fighting," Fred added behind Penelope's statement.

"I'm not here to fight, Fred. I'm here to work. Just work. I promise, Penelope."

"Alright." Penelope's eyes softened as she pulled the papers out of Fred's hands. "I got this. You need to head up front. Martha needs you for something."

"Of course she does ..."

Penelope laughed as Fred stood, and Arthur opened the door for him. Cool air rushed into the room and chilled the sweat trickling down his spine.

"What's so funny?" he asked as Fred disappeared down the hall.

"He's scared of her." Penelope shook her head in mock disgust.

"Scared? I thought they were a *couple.*"

"Hm, it's hard to tell. He gets upset when she plays her games with any new blood she deems worthy of advances. But really, it's all highly inappropriate. Between you and me, I would have let her go years ago if Fred hadn't insisted on making her storefront supervisor. But—enough of this, Arthur. Let's get this test over and done with. To the lunch room please."

After all the Ts were crossed and Is dotted on the test papers, Penelope sent Arthur back down to the stockrooms. He wouldn't know if he'd passed until the next morning, but he felt confident in his abilities. The questions hadn't been difficult, and the information from the video lessons of the previous days was still fresh in his mind.

So much trouble just to drive a forklift.

He'd never thought that working at a grocery store would require studying. This behind the scene experience was eye opening. Had he been locked in a church office so long he'd forgotten what the lives of everyday people were like, even those who had sat through his carefully planned Sunday morning services every week? He thought he'd had a good look into the lives of those he'd served ... but this job and the hard doses of reality he'd experienced already because of it were stretching him in ways he hadn't expected. He sighed. Life was wandering down a different course than he thought it would. It wasn't all bad, but still ...

As he made his way through the zigzag of pallets and shelves that reached for the ceiling, Arthur missed the familiar faces of his ministry team. He'd give anything to be sitting at the board table facing down Bennett and his steely disapproval. The man had been a challenge to work with from day one, but his heart for Hope Is Here Church had always been apparent. Arthur missed Gary and the sureness of their friendship, a friendship he had been neglecting for the last few weeks. He couldn't help the sharp reminder of betrayal and the simmering heat of anger he'd buried over the past few days at the thought of his old friend. He wasn't ready to face that mess yet.

In the sea of boxes and strange faces, Arthur felt small and unimportant. He was no longer the one making decisions or guiding souls to God. He was drifting. It wasn't a sensation he liked at all. Where had his anchor gone? How had it disappeared so fast? Half the time, he felt the world moving past him at a muffled distance. And when things were clear, he felt present circumstances steered him away from what he'd always thought his life goals should be. Circumstances like this job. Arthur was grateful for the work, but could he be happy here? Really happy? Now that training was over, he needed to start making time to look for something different.

It's a good job, he reminded himself. *And we need it.*

Arthur was pulled from his internal musings as Lucas came into view. He held the always present clipboard and was tapping out a nervous beat while staring down an employee. All Arthur could see was dark hair peeking out from under a company hat, but the man's shoulders were rigid. As Arthur came closer, Lucas nodded in his direction, and the young man turned. The face that greeted him was Jay Kenny's.

"How'd the test go, Arthur?" Lucas asked.

"Well, I think," he answered, stopping well out of Jay's reach.

Jay screwed his face up into an ugly mask of disapproval, and Arthur felt heat rising to his face again. This time it wasn't embarrassment but anger. He narrowed his eyes, and crossed his arms over his chest, giving the young man a nod, but said nothing.

"You guys have got to keep your cool. Jay, I expect you to act like a junior supervisor, not a spoiled brat."

Jay's eyes flashed as he looked back at Lucas.

"I mean it. Get to work. We need the stock on the floor ready for shelving up front. If you finish before the second break, start shelving."

"Does the old man know what to do, or do I have to babysit him the whole time?" Jay asked.

"Disrespect will get you nowhere, Jay," Arthur said, his tone low but forceful.

"Martha had you stocking shelves already, right?" Lucas asked and turned towards Arthur.

Arthur nodded, uncrossing his arms to shove his hands deep in his pants pockets.

"Good." Lucas turned back to Jay as he unclipped a paper from his board. "He'll need basic instruction for the back shelves, but other than that, he should be good to go. Be civil. You got Ben sorting already, right?"

After Jay's affirming nod, Lucas waved them both down a long aisle, and Jay took the lead. "Grab a pallet jack and keep up."

Lord, help me, Arthur prayed as he turned to obey his wayward daughter's boyfriend.

Arthur pulled the heavy metal pallet jack behind himself like he would a wagon. Its two bright yellow forks rode on rollers that squeaked at an uncomfortable pitch. The third member of their team, Ben, had already located the first items on Jay's list and stood at the end of an aisle with shelving that reached near the high warehouse ceiling. He had a fast Indian accent that danced as he used jokes to lighten the heavy mood bubbling around Jay. Arthur quickly decided he liked the man but had to make sure he listened closely to catch every racing word.

"Slow down, Ben. The old man might miss something. When you're done loading that, go grab some oil for the wheel on that thing. The sound makes me want to rip my ears off," Jay called as Ben pointed out the first plastic wrapped pallet they needed to grab.

Jay's eyes shifted as he looked back at Arthur. "Ben will show you how to load the jack properly." With that, Jay thrust his checklist against Ben's chest and walked away.

Arthur's coworker frowned and fumbled before grabbing the paper, surprise bouncing out of him in a string of questions. "What was that for? Where are you going? What's wrong with him?" Ben directed his last question at Arthur as Jay had already turned down an adjoining aisle.

"He doesn't want to babysit the *old man,* I guess," Arthur replied as he let the pallet jack slide up in place beside them.

Ben just shook his head and instructed Arthur what goods they needed to grab and where they would need to take them.

"Do you think he's coming back?" Arthur asked after a good ten minutes of loading and shifting large boxes around to get what they needed.

"Your guess is as good as mine. But if he doesn't soon, Lucas will have something to say about it."

A New Home

An invisible weight threatened to pull Rose off her feet as she stood before a row of townhouses. The home she'd come to view was nestled between the others, their fronts painted a pale yellow, the flower pots sitting beside each door achingly empty. Her friend Sarah wrapped an arm around Rose's shoulders, unaware that the support was all that kept her on her feet.

"Come on. Maybe this is the one," Sarah said as her eyes roved over the yellow monstrosity. "And maybe you can convince the landlord to paint."

Rose laughed as Sarah's arm dropped from her shoulder to grasp her hand and lead her forward.

"Oh, I don't know, the yellow isn't so bad."

Sarah looked over at her, eyes round as saucers. "Really?"

"At least it's not pink."

"But see, I've seen cute pink houses."

Sarah's eyes shimmered as both women stood silent for a moment. Then laughter broke from both their throats, and Rose gasped for breath before shaking her head, a content smile spreading across her face as they reached the front steps.

A bit of the weight eased from Rose's shoulders, but she still held fast to her friend's hand.

After ringing the doorbell, the property manager greeted them. "Rose Grill?" The older gentleman asked as he shifted aside and motioned for them to please wipe their feet on the doormat.

"Yes, that's me." Rose raised an identifying finger. "Thank you so much for meeting with us today."

"My pleasure. I must mention that I've already shown the house to several others, and there are more interested parties on my list who'll be viewing it later. So if you're at all interested, communicating it right away will be important."

Rose nodded as she looked around the cramped space she'd just entered. A few mirrors on both walls helped give the feeling of more open space but couldn't hide the need to be shoulder to shoulder with Sarah. She could see several rooms branch off from the long narrow hall, and as soon as they'd finished wiping their feet, the women made their way to the first opening and the promise of more standing room.

"Here is the living room, and down the hall, you will find a three-piece bathroom, the kitchen, and a small bedroom and office. On the second floor, there are two more bedrooms and a closet washroom."

"The tub is on the main floor?" Sarah asked.

"No. This unit only has a shower."

Sarah looked over at Rose, eyebrow raised.

Rose let the property manager continue with his descriptions as she wandered the rooms. He enthusiastically answered all questions, and when the walk-through was done, they again stood in the living room space as she slowly spun in a full circle. Sarah watched her from the arched entryway.

"What do you think?" her friend asked.

"I'm not sure. I wish Arthur were here."

"Let me step out of the room as you two ladies discuss things," their guide offered.

"It's small," Rose noted as Sarah stepped forward.

"It is, but it's also cozy."

"Small for the price ... I'm not sure we can handle the cost long term." Rose couldn't hide the worry that crawled across her face.

"We could negotiate," Sarah countered.

"Yes, but with so many others interested? I'm not sure it would work. We have one more place to look at today, right?"

Sarah nodded. "The listing at Echo Apartment's Complex. I expect it to be even smaller than this, Rose. It's two bedrooms, not three."

"But more affordable."

Sarah again nodded, then stood in silence, letting Rose take one last look around the room and down the hall.

"Thank you for coming with me, Sarah," Rose said as she decided it was time to leave. The weight on her shoulders dragged her down again as she felt a fuzziness behind her eyes and a weakness spreading in her limbs. "We should move on."

Rose made her way out of the house as Sarah went to inform the manager they were finished. They would be in contact with him again after viewing one more property.

"I'm too old for this," Rose commented while her friend slipped into the driver's seat. Her legs had shaken as she walked down the steps. Now she held her knees tightly together, hoping Sarah didn't notice her weariness.

"You're not old, Rose."

She sighed. Was that true? At the moment she longed for the strength of even the last week.

I'll be fine. The drive to the next apartment means rest. I'll be fine.

"Are you alright, Rose?" Sarah frowned as she turned the key, sparking her car's engine to a healthy purr. "Make sure to tell me if you've had enough for the day."

"Yes. Let's keep moving." Rose couldn't help a deep sigh as Sarah moved the car out into the street.

On the way up the elevator at Echo Apartments, Rose wondered if she really would make it. Once the young woman showing them the apartment unlocked the door of suite 320, she looked around the empty space with a sinking heart.

Not even a single chair.

"Are you okay, Rose? You look very pale," Sarah asked as she slid a hand under her friend's elbow.

"I'll be fine. This is our last stop."

But would she? Her knees trembled as she took her first steps around the open living space.

Rose could see most of the apartment from the centre of the room. The open-concept living and dining area was partially sectioned off by a vinyl topped counter. Behind, cupboards with a full size pantry lined the wall next to a sink. Everything looked bright and open with no furniture but couldn't have been larger than the whole dine-in kitchen of the parsonage. The day had shown Rose that a drastic change in her expectations needed to happen. She felt grief as the knowledge warred with her heart's desire for familiar comfort in the surroundings she chose for her family.

"Well," Sarah said, "this isn't half as bad as what I thought it would be."

"I like to think I did a good job of cleaning the place up after the last tenants. They were a pretty good family, actually." The young woman had neglected to give them a name when they met her down at the building's main entrance. But she looked like a Jill or a Jenny to Rose with her bright smile, dark features, and long limbs.

"Is the flooring new? It looks new." Rose asked.

"Yeah. It was just installed last week," she confirmed. "We're trying to get away from carpets as they don't hold up well to heavy traffic most of the time. This is one of the first units with new hard floors. Easier to clean. The bathroom has been renovated as well."

Sarah took on a more active role in inspecting the apartment as she roamed about the rooms and asked questions while Rose moved slowly. Did Sarah notice her hesitation? If she did, she didn't say anything, and Rose silently thanked her while she placed a hand on the doorpost between the main living space and a short hall that gave access to bedrooms and bathroom.

"The rooms still look small," Sarah said. "And only two compared to the three in the last place."

"If room size is the biggest factor for you, we might have something bigger opening up downstairs in a few days. Still just a two bedroom, but the layout is more spacious, and the rooms aren't as restrictive."

Rose perked up at the news. "I would be interested in at least looking. My daughter lives in the building, and I would love to be close to her again."

"Well, let me see what I can do about setting up a viewing. It still has an occupant, but just a moment." The woman stepped out the door as she drew a cell phone from her pocket.

"That would be great, wouldn't it?" Sarah said. "How do you think Rachel would react to having you so close? And Jay?"

"I'm not sure. But we'll see if and when it happens."

Both women exchanged knowing grins, and Rose whispered a prayer of thanks as she walked the perimeter of the room, hand pressed to the wall for support.

No one could know how Jay would react if they moved in downstairs, but Rachel? Rose hoped her eldest would be happy with the idea as a bubble of excitement started to build within her own chest.

Rose gritted her teeth as pins and needles moved up her legs on the second elevator ride.

One more. Just one more!

Sarah slipped an arm around her as they exited the lift. "We're almost there," she whispered as Rose's feet dragged across the scuffed hallway floor.

When their guide stopped in front of a door and knocked, she looked back with a bright grin that Rose couldn't help but return. "I think you're going to love it."

It was perfect.

Not the perfect that Rose was expecting, but as she stepped into the apartment's entrance and felt the soft carpet beneath the large plastic entryway mat, it felt right. They were greeted by an elderly woman whose white curls framed her head in a soft halo.

"Hello, Susan. How is your mother?" said the woman Rose had decided to think of as Jill.

I really need to ask her name and soon.

"Oh, as old as ever! But please do come in and don't mind the stacks of boxes in the living room. We've been going through her things, deciding what to move with her and what to give away."

As Rose and Sarah stepped farther into the room, Rose squeezed her friend's arm as her legs wobbled with exhaustion.

Sarah took one look at her face and called to the elderly woman who had turned her back to lead them into the kitchen. "Is it alright if my friend rests on the couch for a moment? It's been a long day, and she's a bit winded."

"Oh! Of course, that's no problem. Make yourself comfortable and take your time."

Sarah led Rose to the couch and patted her knee. "Now, what's your first impression?"

"I don't know why, but it somehow feels right in here."

"You're only a few feet in the door."

"I know, but go and look for me. I'll follow in a moment."

"Alright," Sarah agreed and gave Rose's hand a gentle squeeze. She walked around the first room, her steps muffled by the well-kept carpet.

There was no open concept here but a grouping of well lit and laid out rooms. Both bedrooms were larger than the ones in the first apartment, and somehow the large arched doorways between the eat-in kitchen and living room held the spaces together like a hug, instead of feeling like a stark barrier. Maybe it was the curves instead of hard corners.

After Rose managed a walk through, she sat at the kitchen table while their gracious hostess bustled between the kitchen and a bedroom that housed her mother, Silvia. The ninety-year-old woman looked like she lived in the recliner that held her slight frame. Rose could just see the old fashioned handmade quilt thrown over her lap through an open doorway.

"What do you think?" the show woman asked as Rose looked around the room.

"We're interested. I would like to take home any paperwork and information on rent amounts for my husband to go over this evening."

"Perfect. I had a feeling this suite might work better. We'll miss Mrs. Silvia. She's been a perfect tenant for years, and I have to say"—the woman looked around the room herself—"has kept this place in perfect order. There won't be much to do before moving in the next family."

Rose agreed and felt a weight lift off her shoulders.

God? I think I've found a home.

Moving Day

ROSE

TIME FELT LIKE A rolling snowball to Rose as moving day approached. It sped faster and faster, gaining in significance until it hit the obstacle of moving day and broke to pieces.

"I really think you should sit down," Arthur called from across the living room.

She moved from one stack of boxes to another, checking labels. "I'm fine. The more of these we have organized before everyone arrives, the easier loading the trucks will go."

"But, Rose."

Her breath came in large puffs as she pulled one box from a pile and shuffled off in a new direction with arms wrapped around her load. "I'm almost finished."

In preparation for this day, packed boxes were stacked near to the ceiling.

When volunteers from Hope Is Here Church arrived, familiar faces and friends carried boxes back and forth as rooms slowly emptied of Rose and her family's belongings. Questions like "Is this one for storage?" and "For the bedroom or kitchen?" regularly flew by. She continued to shuffle from pile to pile, pointing out heavy boxes that were more suited for packing lower in the trucks.

Rose could soon tell that having so many of their former congregation together at once was hard for Arthur, especially when they still referred to him as Pastor. His eyes roved over the crowd in sweeping motions while his words grew fewer and fewer. The look he gave her when they passed in the hall was filled with suppressed panic. She reached for his arm. He smiled and gently patted her fingers before pulling away.

Their help is a blessing. There is no way we can sort and move it all ourselves.

As the boxes shifted from the halls to the lawn, ready for the moving truck, Rose wondered if Arthur was repeating a similar mantra to himself.

The new warmth of late April gave the crowd energy as boxes from the house moved to piles strewn across the lawn. Rose stood on the newly green grass and double-checked each box, directing them to the correct truck for loading. The first fourteen-footer was destined for storage, and the second, whose insides were quickly turning into an intricate 3D jigsaw puzzle, would leave for the apartment within the hour. Rose's heart thumped and squeezed when Gary, Sarah's husband, and Jeff Cooper, a church friend, flipped the couch and hoisted it up above the boxes stacked tightly underneath the kitchen table. They'd covered the tabletop with a quilt, but still, Rose refused to look as they slid the couch across its surface.

"We can fit a few of those under-the-bed bins up in here now, Mary," Jeff called to his wife as she eyed the pile before her, looking for just the right sized item to fit snugly into each crevice.

As Rose continued to inspect boxes, Amy approached her from behind. "My room's empty, and I'm hungry. Are we feeding all these people?"

"Sarah's on her way to pick up pizza," Rose assured her daughter as she refolded the cardboard flaps of a box she'd just inspected, making sure its contents matched the thick black marker scrawled across its side. After tucking the last flap under the first, Rose looked up and caught her daughter's scowl.

"Ironic, huh? So helpful now that we don't go to their church. It's almost like they can't wait to be rid of us completely."

"Amy, that's not true."

Her daughter only grunted, wrinkling her nose at people as they smiled while passing.

Rose's heart sank. She watched Amy turn, stomp up the entrance steps, and disappear into the house.

She'll head to her room. Her empty room.

Her daughter's mental health was fragile, and Rose couldn't help but be proud of her for holding up as well as she was under the mountain of change. But one never knew exactly how much Amy could take. Over the last year, her disruptive and angry outbursts had calmed from constantly bursting flames to smouldering embers that only flared now and then. But those flares scorched everyone around her when they jumped to life. She was difficult, her humour razor sharp, her mind absolutely brilliant but vindictive.

A stone of worry sat in the pit of Rose's stomach as well, worry that while more change flooded in, Amy would lose ground. Rose even felt herself slipping as she did her best to jump from one stone of God's promises to another. At first, their release from ministry had brought with it a feeling of freedom. It had been invigorating. But now? Rose was tired. The change was so draining.

God, be with Amy today. Please help her find a spark of hope in the middle of our mess. Help me show it to her.

A collective shout of joy rose as Sarah arrived, managing to slip her car past the first moving truck and up the driveway.

"I hope you're all hungry," Rose's friend called as she pulled an armload of pizza boxes from the passenger's seat. "Paper plates are in the trunk, Jeff. Is there still a table to put these on?"

Rose almost laughed as Jeff looked at the table stuffed in the centre of the moving truck.

Sarah did laugh. "Counter it is, then!"

Everyone crowded into the kitchen, and after listening to Arthur lead them in a collective prayer over the food, Rose searched with her eyes for Amy.

When Arthur appeared at her elbow with a plate of food, she turned to him and squinted. "Arthur, I don't see Amy. She was asking about food. I think she might be in her room."

"I'll find her," he reassured.

She squeezed his hand and took the plate from him.

After a moment the scent of pizza and people became oppressive, and the hum of voices tickled a pain behind Rose's eyes.

"Sarah." Rose gulped. "I need to move outside."

Her friend stepped up beside her, worry creasing her brow. "What's wrong, Rose?"

"I need air." Sparks filled Rose's vision, and she grasped the arm of the nearest person.

"I'll find a chair. Let's get her outside, Paul. Gary, can you help Paul?" Sarah called for her husband across the room, and the crowd hushed while the men helped Rose out the door.

"Do I need to find Arthur?" Gary asked.

"No, no, he's looking for Amy. It's okay. I'll be fine." The fresh air tamped down the sparks, and Rose released a rush of breath back into the world after filling her lungs to bursting. "Yes, this is much better. Thank you. I just need a moment."

One of the men relieved her of the plate of pizza while Sarah pressed her into an unfolded deck chair. Once she was settled amid the box strewn lawn, Sarah squatted down beside her as she nibbled on a slice of pizza.

"Look at you. There is no way you're in your forties," Rose teased as Sarah's eyes flashed with mischief.

"My birth certificate says differently. Now—"

A shout echoed from down the parsonage hall and out onto the yard where Rose sat, causing both women to turn back towards the door. The pit in Rose's stomach grew several sizes as people started leaving the house, glancing back over their shoulders.

"Rose—" Mary Cooper started as she joined the friends, her face plastered with worry.

"What is it?" Rose asked.

But Mary didn't get a chance to answer before Amy came hurtling out of the house. She turned, planting her feet firmly on the drive. Her curls almost stood on end as her face screwed up into an ugly mask. "I hate you. I hate ALL of you!"

"Amy, that's enough!" Arthur shouted as he followed her, stopping just short of the threshold.

"Make me! You're all a bunch of disgusting hypocrites." Amy flung the empty paper plate she'd been holding at her father.

The crowd of people stood stunned, watching as the flimsy piece of cardboard caught in the air and spun backwards then fluttered harmlessly to the ground.

"Amy!" Rose added her horrified voice to the conflict.

Amy's face turned beet red as she swivelled her gaze to her mother. "All of you," she repeated, her voice dripping with disgust. "What's wrong? Am I making you all uncomfortable?" She asked no one in particular. "Well, then, it's a good thing you're packing us up and seeing us off, isn't it?"

Rose began to stand as she reached for her daughter, but Amy stepped backwards.

"I'm gone," she said as she turned and waved her hand over her head in a dismissive farewell.

Rose's right leg buckled and refused to move as the distance between her and her daughter grew.

"Amy, if you're not at the apartment before three, I'm coming to find you!" Arthur shouted, his sharp tone bouncing against the tarmac and the sides of the moving truck.

"Arthur!" Rose called, her breath catching in her throat.

"I don't know what happened, Rose. All I did was ask her to come eat. I'll never understand that girl."

"Arthur! I can't move my leg."

"What?"

Rose felt the blood drain from her face and shook as her bottom hit the chair again, hard. Sarah was too late to ease Rose's fall as she reached out for her friend, but she held her on the chair as Rose felt her body slump against her friend's shoulder. Weakness wormed its way through her leg and up her side. Rose felt panic squeeze her heart. An unnerving tingle found its way into her right arm. She tried to lift it, but it refused to listen to her.

Mary Copper pushed her way forward. "Rose. Can you still talk?" The woman nearly squealed as she added, "Is she having a stroke?"

"I can still talk. I don't think ... but I can't move."

"Arthur, hospital, now," Sarah said as she helped hold Rose against him when he leaned down to take his wife into his arms.

"But the move!" Rose tried to struggle against her husband's chest. There was still so much to do. So many people watching, expecting.

"I've got it," her friend said. "Go."

"I'll find Amy," Gary assured them both as Arthur carried Rose to their car parked and ready on the street.

Her husband slid her half paralyzed body through the open passenger's door, his face looked as white as her own.

"Arthur," she whispered as he leaned over her to secure the strap over her chest, "I'm scared."

"Me too," he replied, hands shaking as he buckled her in.

Poutine Please

AMY

AMY KNEW HER FATHER'S words had seemed completely normal to him as he'd opened her bedroom door and found her sitting in the middle of the empty room, staring at a wall.

"There's still a lot to do, Amy. You shouldn't be hanging out in here while everyone else does the work."

"Everyone else." That phrase had stirred the banked embers in her heart.

"My room's empty. I did my part."

"Your part's not done until the whole job's done, kid. Come on. Sarah's brought the pizza. Let's eat with everyone and then finish this."

"It's always about other people with you, isn't it?"

"What do you mean? Look, we have a house full of people who've volunteered to help us. We can't make them do all our work."

It was then that the flames licked up through the stones she'd placed so carefully to guard the coals within. They were a shield she only moved around when necessary, examining each and every week with her counsellor, learning why she'd placed them within her heart years ago and how they both guarded and fed the red waves she had such a hard time controlling. She'd been getting better at it. But those two words had stuck a poker past them and stirred things to life.

"Look, it's difficult for me to have them here too, but we can't do this alone." He'd opened the door wide and expected her to follow him to the kitchen. She hadn't.

He'd come back a second later with an empty paper plate in hand to wave at her. "Come on, at least eat."

She'd gotten up and taken the plate, blinking away the red that threatened to flood her vision.

You can hold on.

You can make it.

Count to ten.

She'd thought it had worked until she'd entered the kitchen swarming with hungry bodies.

It was all too much, and she couldn't help the hate and resentment that swelled in her chest like a balloon filled to bursting. Her control popped. So she'd had her shouting match with her father and then done the only thing she thought she could to remove herself from the situation.

She clutched the cell phone in her pocket, a finger threaded through the stand loop on the back of its case, anchoring her to a digital world that often felt more real than the one she walked through right now. Thinking like that wasn't healthy; she'd been told that repeatedly. But who cared when the real world oozed toxicity?

A cool breeze pushed her bouncing blond curls out of her face but also slid in between the knit of her sweater, raising bumps across her skin. "At least you've left a lasting impression on them all, Amy. They'll never forget the pastor's daughter they survived."

She kicked at a loose cement fragment perched on the edge of the sidewalk. It skittered across the street to land in the gutter as she sighed. Now what? She hadn't gained anything from her outburst but the ability to walk away from the crowd of onlookers. It was a measure of freedom, but really, what good was freedom when she didn't know what to do with it? She decided against just walking to the new apartment. Rachel would be there, wiping out cupboards and closets in preparation for putting everything away.

"Rachel, the ever helpful. Rachel, the one who gets away with fornication, just to weasel her way back into the family."

It angered Amy. She didn't hate her older sister, but it all felt unfair. How were Rachel's mistakes forgotten so fast, when every small thing Amy did wrong people held against her for years? They'd all forgotten that it was Rachel's fault their family had lost the church ministry position. She kicked at a second loose cement fragment before deciding it was better to just walk somewhere. The weather was nice enough. Maybe the skate park would bring her distractions. If not, she could always walk downtown. The perks of living in a small community meant downtown was never far away.

As she walked, the embers in her heart cooled. She blinked away tears as they tried to gather. She'd have none of them, though. It was pointless. She wasn't sorry for what she had said, and she wasn't sorry for leaving the rest of the work to people who wanted nothing to do with her anymore. But she had to admit, it had hurt when all the adults showed up and not one of her old friends had come along.

Once she'd been popular. The girl everyone strove to please. Her good looks added height to the pedestal of being a pastor's kid. But now? Things were just different. She was glad her family was moving on. No one was left worth being friends with in that crowd—well, not many.

All those years of striving had built nothing but a castle of empty cardboard boxes.

As she approached the cement platforms of the skate park, voices rang out as rubber wheels and plywood slapped against the ground. Churches were not the only place a sixteen-year-old beauty could find friends. First, she saw caps bobbing as riders rolled up and then back down the sides of the small cement jumps. She'd never tried it herself, but watching was great. Her favourite was the bowl. If the skaters knew what they were doing, they could ride its walls forever.

When she stopped at the metal fence that ran the length of the park, a boy with curls to match her own peeking out from under his yellow cap, waved at her. She barely stopped from rolling her eyes at his lanky arms flailing in the air.

"AMY! Hello!"

His call made her turn red, and she almost continued her walk to nowhere. But he flipped his skateboard up with a deft stomp to land against his hand then walked towards her. "I thought it was moving day for you. Is it all finished?"

"The adults are taking care of it. My room's empty."

Glen Edwards could have passed for her brother. She'd known him for years, but with him being closer to Rachel's age, they hadn't been close. His mother Abigail had taken over much of Rose's roles in the women's ministries when her mother had slowed down over a year ago. He was bright and loud, and Amy always felt like she had to one-up him to stay in the youth group spotlight. He had always ceded the floor to her willingly, not caring to cause a scene or argue. That was infuriating. As if the attention wasn't worth it to him when it meant everything to her.

"Well, I hope you enjoy living in Echo Apartments. We're neighbours now!"

Amy hadn't remembered that the Edwards lived there too.

"We're the closest ground apartment to the parking lot. Perfect for Mom and her chair. I think you guys are just around the other side of the building."

Amy let him drone on about the apartments and the new people she would have to call her neighbours. "Yeah! You'll like it after you get used to it. Anyway, do you skate?" He held out the board to her, and she backed up a step, realizing he was offering to lend it.

"Ah, nah. I never learned. I prefer watching."

"You okay, Amy?" He asked, a frown pulling down one side of his mouth. "You're much quieter than usual."

"And how would you know my usual, Glen?" she asked while crossing her arms over her chest and cocking her head to the side. "It's not like we're best friends."

"No, I guess not." He said with a half laugh that ended in a sigh. "But you're usually the first one to talk. You know ... it's been weird since you all left—the church, that is—doesn't feel the same. I'm sorry about what happened."

A lump formed in Amy's throat. She didn't know what to say as Glen looked down at his board, giving it a nervous spin while balancing it on its rim.

"I kinda wish you'd all come back."

"Well, that won't happen." She sniffed. "But thanks for saying so."

"You want me to walk you home? I mean, to the new place?" He asked after wiping the frown off his face and replacing it with a toothy grin.

"Um, thanks, but no. I'm not going home, not yet." As she backed up, she waved, and he waved back before she spun around.

"Catch ya later, Amy!" He called after her, and the tears that had pooled in her eyes earlier got their chance to flow again. She chided herself for not staying longer and asking him to introduce her to the other teens around the skate park. He could have been the perfect person to find her a new in crowd. But man, was that boy weird. His open honesty made her uncomfortable when his lean face lit up with an eager smile.

Again, she was unsure where to go from here. Maybe heading for the apartment *was* best. But she wasn't ready to deal with Rachel and her cold calculations. Maybe a bit of window shopping was in order. Maybe even a bit of real shopping. She could use a new jacket. Goosebumps rippled up her arms as the breeze pushed through the knit of her sweater again.

Window shopping turned into eating out when Amy stepped onto Main Street. Her stomach rumbled, reminding her she hadn't eaten. Archie's Food Truck was always parked down by the local drugstore, its fryers only turned off in the worst of winter weather. Amy was sure it would be bubbling hot today as the sun was bright and people would be out enjoying it. The owner was a First Nations man who made the best poutine in town, maybe even in the whole district. Amy's mouth watered just thinking about the hot crisp fries, the sharp flavored cheese curds, and thick gravy. She often got chopped green onion and bacon bits sprinkled on top as well.

How long had it been since she'd enjoyed a large fry cup with friends? Months. As she walked up to the food truck, its canopy open, windows fogged with steam from the heat of the fryers, she looked around to see if anyone she knew was out and about. The crowd was a mix of colours and ages, but no one from school seemed to be there.

You don't need them.

But regret dipped its edge in loneliness, and she couldn't help but be chilled again by the emotional dampness that spread through her.

"What can I get ya?" the food truck owner asked after her short wait in the order line.

"One small poutine, please, with extra green onions and an iced tea."

"Can or bottle?"

"Bottle"

Amy produced her debit card and inserted it into the portable payment terminal handed to her.

"Where's the rest of your crowd?" asked the owner. He leaned out the window to look around.

"Eh, not sure. I'm hanging with myself today."

It felt good to be remembered, and she smiled up at him before stepping aside for the next person in line. It wasn't long before she was walking towards a picnic table painted in faded red, steaming cardboard bowl in hand. She sat on the edge of the seat, enjoying the heat seeping through the bowl's sides as well as the sun shining on her head. It was a beautiful spring mix of warmth and chill from the breeze.

People came and went as she sat there, jabbing each fry and melted cheese curd with a small three-pronged wooden fork. At first, she didn't notice a group of boys sitting down at the far side of the table, but one of them scooted up beside her, making his invasion of her personal space impossible to ignore.

"How's it going?" he asked, flashing her a bright white smile.

When she didn't answer him right away, he slid closer, his leg almost touching hers. "I'm Roger." He extended a hand as if he expected her to return the greeting.

"Um, good for you," she muttered as she realized he was older than she first thought and the group of boys behind him weren't really boys either, but men of varying ages. This Roger looked to be in his twenties and had some kind of tribal tattoo peeking out from underneath his shirt and crawling halfway up his neck. The pattern wasn't anything Amy recognized, and the man didn't look indigenous, but that didn't mean he wasn't. The community of Barton, Ontario was historically a healthy mix of those with European ancestry as well as Ojibway, Cree, and Metis Peoples.

Amy's heart thumped an unsteady beat as she pivoted her legs away from the visitor.

"What's a pretty girl like you doing sitting all alone?" The white smile never left Roger's face, despite her dismissive reply.

"Who said I was alone?" Her legs tensed, ready to jump up at any second as he leaned over and brushed shoulders with her.

"I was just observing. I'll leave you alone if that's what you really want."

She lifted an eyebrow at him as her heart hammered out a warning while somehow his presence weighed her down, gluing her rear to the bench even as the voice in her head screamed to get up and walk away.

"Hey! Sorry, I completely forgot your bacon bits." The sudden interruption surprised both of them, and Amy looked up to see a woman with long dark braids holding up a plastic spice shaker.

"I didn't or—"

"I'm really sorry. It's so busy!" The woman didn't wait but grabbed Amy's bowl right from her hand and started shaking small red bits out onto the fries remaining in the bottom. "Come on. I'll get you an extra scoop of fries to make up for it."

The woman nodded towards the truck.

Lost for words, Amy got up and followed her over to the side entrance, away from the crowd of hungry patrons and Roger. The man's eyes followed her, and Amy flushed with a wave of anger.

"You okay?" The woman whispered, her expression shifting to serious as soon as she opened the fry truck door and motioned Amy inside. She didn't wait for Amy to answer as she rushed her up the metal steps and into the heat.

Amy stepped inside a cramped space. Counters lined both walls, and cooking utensils hung within easy reach of busy hands. Above those top cupboards, boxes clung to the walls except where the service windows gave access to the outside. Above the fryer was also open with a vent letting heat escape overhead.

"Did you make the call?" the woman asked the truck owner as he jiggled a batch of fries in a vat of oil. He nodded at her as she handed Amy back her food.

"What just happened?" Amy asked, her skin rippling with goosebumps despite the heat.

"That guy's no good." The owner motioned with his head out the window but didn't look up from his work. "Don't worry. He won't come in here."

"Never seen him be so forward in broad daylight," the woman observed as she plunged a scoop into a metal basket and hauled up a large portion of perfectly cooked and drained potatoes. "Don't leave until they're gone. Okay?" she said when she saw Amy eyeing the closed door.

What had she just escaped from? The bumps that covered her arms somehow wiggled beneath her skin and settled in her stomach like a bubbling mass of sick. She looked down at the paper bowl in her hand as her rescuer dumped new fries on top of her leftovers.

"Want some more curds and gravy?"

Amy shook her head. There was no way she could eat it now.

"Who'd you call, Archie?" Amy asked the owner.

Amy noticed even her rescuer's hands shook as the woman grasped the countertop.

Warmth from the fresh fries spread into the cardboard bowl, and Amy willed herself not to drop it.

"Actually, it's not Archie. He was the guy I bought the truck from, and I never got around to changing things. Most people call me Mike." The man wiped his hands on the white apron he wore over a plain grey t-shirt and blue jeans. "And don't worry. I have some friends who know how to get rid of trouble. But you need to stay inside until they *all* leave."

He looked like he wanted to shake her hand and paused before holding it out to her. She was trembling all over, and confusion swam across her face in waves of shifting expression. Amy blinked as red crept into the corners of her vision.

Not now, not here, she prayed as anger tried to swamp her fear.

"I think our guest needs to sit down, Carmen."

The woman produced a small stool from in between the clutter of cupboards and, taking Amy's elbow, gently asked her to sit down.

"If you hadn't come to get me, what do you think would have happened?" Amy asked her.

The woman shrugged and tugged on a braid as her own confusing emotions flickered across her face. "Nothing good," she finally said before moving to the other side of the food truck to stir a vat of gravy sunk into the metal counter.

The world slowed as Amy sat waiting. The crowd outside the food truck had thinned, but Roger and his group stuck to the picnic area. Some of them stood around, hands deep in their pockets, acting like they were on the lookout for something. The rest lounged around the benches, and one even crawled on top of a table and sat. Mike shook his head in disgust as the man scraped a shoe against the inside of the bench, flaking mud and who knows what else onto where customers sat to eat.

Mike looked at his watch and stuck his head out the service window to look around. He was grinning when he pulled his head back inside and nodded at Carmen. "Here we go."

Amy strained to see as Mike pulled the service window closed then started wiping down the counter.

From the far right, a new group of people entered the stage that seemed to be spread out in front of her. They were a more diverse mix of skin tones, and a large man, in both height and build, stood at the back, his gut cinched with a belt that looked ready to burst its buckle at any moment. The new crew all seemed to look at him, and as he nodded, they moved in a line, walking in a sweep across the area allocated for Archie's Food Truck.

"What's going on?" Amy asked, her eyes wide.

"Don't worry, they won't take long," Carmen said as she slid over towards her.

Carmen was right. Within seconds of the line of newcomers moving in, Roger and his crew stepped away from the picnic bench. The man sitting on it scrambled off, a split second behind the rest. He turned, puffed out his cheeks and extended his arms to either side in a gesture that Amy couldn't interpret as surrender or defiance. Then he turned and followed his friends down the wide sidewalk. Amy stood in an attempt to watch what was happening as they disappeared to the left of the window, but Mike held up a hand of warning.

"Not yet."

She stopped, half standing, her back still in a crouched position, when a hand reached over from the side and tapped on the glass closest to Mike. Amy jumped at the rap.

Mike tapped back before opening the window to shake hands with someone just outside Amy's view. When he closed it again, Amy looked over at him with questioning eyes.

"Now we wait for the cops. They won't be far behind," he said. "And they're probably going to want to talk to you."

Amy's mouth went dry in one breath as she placed her uneaten fries down on the counter. She hugged herself and blinked away red bursts of colour that flashed in her vision.

"Why me? I didn't do anything wrong."

Trouble

RACHEL

THE COLLAR OF RACHEL'S shirt sat snug against the bridge of her nose as she strained into the fabric. She'd dumped too much bleach into her cleaning solution, and now all she could do was scrub as fast as she could with the vent fan on high and the bathroom door wide open. Her eyes watered as she held in her breath for as long as she could.

Almost done.

This was the last room to finish before everything was ready for the moving truck to arrive. She knew the many shoes and boots would track in fresh dirt, but as long as the deep cleaning was already done, all that would need to follow was a second sweep and wipe down. Her mom wouldn't have to worry about finding any surprises lurking in cupboards or corners, not if Rachel could help it.

She'd jumped at the chance to be a part of the move when Rose had called to tell her about the new apartment. Having her mom so close again while the rift between them healed would be great. But to have Dad and Amy here as well? Rachel's feelings were mixed. She reminded herself she still lived with Jay. He was her safe place. After all, they wouldn't be forcing their way into her boyfriend's apartment now, would they?

Her hands were slick with sweat when she finally pulled the cleaning gloves off and backed out of the small room. Her head swam.

"Done and done. Thank. God."

The rest of the apartment sparkled, and Rachel smiled in appreciation of her own work. She fished her cell phone from a pocket and sent her mom the all clear message before finding a seat on the floor to wait. Resting her head against the wall and closing her eyes, she let the world drift away as her body relaxed and her mind wandered. The fog of fumes lingered in the hall, reaching out to her, but she ignored it as she dozed off.

The ringing of her phone woke her, and the haze of sleep refused to leave her vision as she rubbed her eyes.

"Hello, this is Rachel," she answered.

"Rachel, your mom's on the way to the hospital."

"What? Sarah?"

"We aren't sure what's going on. All of a sudden, she just went limp on one side. Your dad's with her. I'm coming over with the first load from the house. We promised them we would be able to handle things from here."

"Of course. I've got the cleaning all finished and ready. Mom should have gotten a text from me a while ago."

"She didn't mention it. Amy might show up on her own before we get there. She had a fight with your dad ..."

Rachel tucked a strand of hair that had worked free of the elastic still tight against the nape of her neck behind an ear, then let out an exasperated sigh. "I'll keep the door open for whoever shows up first." Rachel wasn't sure how long she'd been asleep, but it couldn't have been more than ten minutes since she was still sitting upright against the wall. "Mom's going to be okay ... right?"

"I'm not going to lie, Rachel. It was weird, and I'm worried." Sarah paused, and Rachel heard someone calling in the background. "God knows what's going on, Rachel. Remember that."

"Yeah ... right," she muttered as Sarah said goodbye.

As soon as the call dropped, Rachel sent a text to her mom.

Sarah called, are you okay? Let me know what's up when you can. No rush.

No rush for her, but her pulse quickened as she stood and stretched. What could possibly have happened? A stroke? Something worse? Was there anything worse? Her poor mother.

Her heart skipped a beat when she heard a knock on the door. She opened it to find not Sarah, but her husband Gary.

"Any sign of Amy?" he asked in a rush. "She left the house angry, and I promised your dad I'd find her."

"No, she hasn't been around yet," Rachel replied as she stepped aside to let Gary in. "Are the others right behind you?"

"They were just closing the moving truck doors when I pulled out."

"I'll open the sliding door. I think it'll be easier to bring in some of the furniture through there than navigating the halls."

Concern lined Gary's face as he nodded his agreement. "I'm going back out to look for Amy. Tell Sarah for me?"

"You got it. But, Gary, what happened?"

"It was weird, Rachel. That's all I can say. I'm just glad we are all here to finish this up for them." With a sweeping wave of a hand that took in the whole of the living room, Gary nodded and left.

The glass sliding door gave easy access to the outdoor alcove, framed on both sides by freshly stained wooden privacy panels. It opened directly onto a walkway that led to the parking lot and didn't actually give much privacy, but at least they wouldn't have to look out over rows of their neighbours' heads down each side of the building. The glass door was on a spring, and Rachel had to find the wooden brace that fit into the slats across the bottom of the frame to hold it open. Alternatively, the screen was mounted on a metal frame and could be held aside with a small hook and loop screwed into the exterior wall.

As Rachel stuck her head out the door and looked down the path, she sucked in a breath of fresh air. Turning back into the room, the smell of bleach leaking from the hall and bathroom reached out to her again.

"If only I had a fan to place in front of the door."

It wasn't long before Sarah and a row of box carrying volunteers from Hope Is Here Church found their way down the walk and into the carpeted living space.

"I brought the entryway mat. I thought it would be prudent so we don't ruin the carpet," Sarah said as she set the first box just inside the door and unrolled the mat before letting the others in.

As the train of volunteers continued, Rachel nodded greetings to people she hadn't seen in weeks, some even months. As she checked each box's label and directed them to the appropriate room, she couldn't help but wonder what must they be thinking.

They'd still have a pastor if it wasn't for me.

Unloading didn't take long, and soon, most of the crowd was on their way back to the parsonage for a second load. Sarah went along to make sure everything that needed to find its way out of the old home did. "Mary Copper went with the second truck over to the storage unit. She and Jeff will make sure things are stacked away carefully," she told Rachel before leaving.

An elderly church member named Hillary stayed behind to help Rachel start with the job of putting things away.

"Perhaps we should begin with the kitchen?" the woman offered. "That way, when your mom's able to come home, there will be a place to eat."

"The beds did come in the first truck, right?"

"I think they left them for last. It'll be easier to put things away without the larger furniture for now." Hillary rubbed her hands in an absentminded way, grimacing when she touched enlarged knuckles and finger joints. "How about you get up on that stool in the corner, and I'll hand you things. My old legs don't care for heights these days."

"Sounds like the perfect place to start," Rachel replied.

They had most of the kitchen odds and ends put away when the second truckload arrived. But the everyday plates and utensils still sat nestled in their boxes, separated by hand towels and kitchen paper. Rachel's head swam as she stood on the stool and placed her mother's favourite kitchen decor pieces in the space between cupboard tops and the ceiling. Best to have them up and out of the way so nothing would break. She scared herself after moving the stool over and almost falling into poor Hillary's arms when she'd gone to step back up.

"Perhaps a break is in order, dear," the older woman said, her matter-of-fact tone telling Rachel it was an expectation and not a question.

"I'm sorry, Hillary. It's those bleach fumes. It's taking them forever to dissipate."

"They were pretty strong when I arrived. But they aren't as bad now. Come down." Hillary patted her hand and insisted that Rachel sit down in one of the dining room chairs. "I'm glad these came with that first truckload. I'll get us a drink."

Rachel watched as the old woman rummaged through boxes to find the glasses and nodded thanks as she handed her a drink. She held back a grimace as she took the first sip of room temperature liquid.

"So, will you be moving back in with your parents?" Hillary asked.

The look Hillary gave Rachel made her squirm. "No, I'm quite happy where I am."

"Pity. It would be the perfect way to straighten out your life."

Rachel's jaw dropped open. "What?"

"In my day, if a girl lived with a man she wasn't married to, she at least knew it was wrong. But it's never too late, you know. You can always ask for forgiveness. God knows none of us is perfect." Hillary waved her fingers dismissively.

Rachel's face flushed red. Was it with embarrassment? Anger? *How dare she.*

"I–I won't—excuse me." Rachel stood, not giving the old woman a chance to say anything else. The wind she left in her wake would have blown papers off a table.

God, that is why I won't go to church, she prayed at the ceiling as she slammed the apartment's entrance door behind her. *And to think, she looks like such a nice old lady.*

Her eyes burned and her heart beat an unsteady rhythm as she walked the halls and took the elevator back up to Jay's apartment. She stopped herself for a second as she realized she still thought of it as Jay's and not her own. Why was that? She was helping to pay for rent. Surely, it was her apartment too. She entered apartment 302 as a mass of defeated tears, nervously typing on her phone to tell Sarah she'd left the apartment for a breather. The air drifting through Echo Apartment's hallways smelled faintly of wet feet, but it was preferable to the lingering odour of bleach that clung to the back of her nostrils.

In Rachel's distracted haste, she almost bumped into a tall man standing in the living room as she blinked away tears.

"What's going on?" she asked Jay, who stood across the room, his arms folded over his chest, eyes never leaving the visitor's face.

"I thought you were helping your parents today," he said as she stepped around the man. Tension rippled through the room.

"I am, I was—I needed a breather."

Jay blinked and looked at her, his pupils dilating. "You should go to the bedroom."

For a second time in just minutes, Rachel's jaw dropped open.

"Babe, I'm busy here," was all her boyfriend said to her wounded expression.

Did she hear pleading in his voice? Fresh tears sprang to her eyes as she passed him, turning once she got to the bedroom to slam the door closed. Why was this all happening and *now?* Her brain replayed scenes and words from the last few moments. Hillary's wrinkled features haunted her as her comments shoved pins into Rachel's heart, and Jay's cold words ... What was going on out there?

She stood with her back to the door and leaned against it before sinking to the ground, her knees rising to form tired, shaking mountains before her.

You're just tired, and everything feels more dramatic when you're tired.

It was as if a dark cloud floated over her, throwing her world into shadow. She wanted to crawl across the floor and pull herself up onto the bed, but her limbs wouldn't move. She closed her eyes and waited, listening to Jay's muffled voice coming from the living room.

"Not ready ... time ..."

She didn't pay attention to what he was saying at first until the other man's voice came rumbling under the door. "You're out of time."

It was a clear statement, and the low, forceful tone held a threat. She heard the apartment door close, and then the space behind the door filled with silence.

Diagnosis

ARTHUR SHOUTED FROM HIS parking place in front of the emergency room door, and a nurse in blue scrubs came running. A second pushing a wheelchair soon followed and helped Arthur push Rose into the emergency room as numbness left her leaning against the metal armrest. Arthur's voice climbed the scale as he answered the nurse's triage questions. A gentle hand helped support Rose's head from the side.

The nurse asked if she wanted a blanket. *How kind,* Rose thought as she sat waiting with the blue striped fabric draped over her legs and pulled up over her hands. She was so cold, the pinpricks on her defiant limb amplifying the fact.

"It won't be much longer," she mumbled to Arthur as he sat beside her, leaning forward, head cradled in his hands. If she'd had the strength to reach out to him, she would have. His body vibrated with each breath. She smelled the musk of nervous sweat. To her, it was a pleasant smell, a grounding smell. It held her in place far better than the odour of cleaning solutions that filled the ER halls.

Rose could speak and reason, though her answers came slower than normal. The nurse didn't think it was a stroke, so what was happening to her? As she closed her eyes and tried to grip the warm blanket with resistant fingers, she thought back to the many conversations with her family doctor. The blood tests for various diseases and deficiencies had come back clear, except for slightly low vitamin D that they were treating with liquid drops. As they eliminated the more common culprits for her symptoms, a growing sense of the inevitable built up. She knew it was something serious, whatever it was. Had something in her body finally snapped? Would it allow them to find an answer? In a way, she was thankful to be sitting in a wheelchair in a hospital waiting room. It meant it might be time for answers.

"What's taking so long?" Arthur whispered, and Rose was unsure if he was asking her or praying. His knees shook as his ability to sit still decayed. "Are you okay?" he asked Rose as he looked up. The colour from his cheeks had travelled to ring his eyes with red.

"No." There was no point in lying. "But I haven't been for a long time. A few more minutes or hours won't change things."

Arthur's eyebrows pulled together, then relaxed as he ran a hand over his face. He shared in her struggle as only a spouse could. He knew she was tired. Knew she was holding back thoughts and emotions.

"We have good friends," she commented.

"Yeah ... friends." He looked away.

She wished he would say more. After nineteen years of marriage, she knew the signs of a cluttered mind, just as he knew her clamped lips meant withdrawal from her emotions.

"They are still friends, Arthur."

He said nothing as he reached out and took hold of her fingers. The blanket dampened the feel of his touch. Numbness had spread from her leg, up her back, and into her right arm. She didn't want to think about what the lack of sensation meant, so she pulled her left hand over and covered his in an attempt to feel him properly.

"Is God punishing us, Rose? Am I that much of a failure?"

"God isn't cruel, Arthur, you know that."

He nodded while staring at her hand atop his own. She wanted to tell him that right now, in this moment, it wasn't all about him, but she bit her tongue.

They whisked Rose away for X-rays even before an examination room opened up. The nurse said the on-call doctor wanted to check for hidden fractures or pinched nerves in her spinal column. After the procedure, they left her in an exam room on a stretcher while the nurse went to invite Arthur back to sit with her. She still numbly clutched the blanket they'd given her, now draped across her prone frame.

When Arthur stepped in, his face was white. He placed her handbag on the floor and held out her cell phone.

"Rachel's been texting, asking how you are." The screen was password locked, so he had no way to answer her texts directly.

"You didn't message her on your own phone?"

He shook his head, and Rose sighed at his stubbornness. Why couldn't he reach out to his own daughters? He was so good at giving space and time to struggling church members, yet there was a block that kept him from his own girls. Rose couldn't understand it. It was painful to see. Watching him hold out the phone to her with a distant look on his face, she felt as if a pin had been jammed into her heart. Rose struggled to sit higher, and Arthur pressed a hidden button to lift the head of the stretcher.

He supported the phone for her while she unlocked it, fingers shaking, and slowly scrolled through her messages.

"We need to answer her," Rose said.

"What do you want to say? I'll type it for you."

"Just ... let her know they are doing tests and besides being hungry, we're holding up."

Arthur pulled up a stool from the corner and settled beside her, letting the silence stretch out as he typed Rose's words.

"And Gary says he's still looking for Amy. What could that girl be doing?" Arthur tried to hold back a snort of disgust but failed. The noise tickled Rose's ears, and she couldn't help but laugh. The laugh pulled wind from her lungs, and with no strength left, she found her head slumping to the side. Arthur reached out to cup her cheek, checking the movement.

"You sound like a warthog," Rose said as Arthur eased her head back to a centred position.

"What?" He held her face in his hand as the waves of mirth pulled tears into her eyes. Rose drew in a deep breath as a bit of colour returned to her husband's face. It called to her, and she smiled. They were so close, yet he seemed so far away. All she wanted in that moment was to pull him into her heart.

"You sound like a warthog," she repeated, now calm. "Really, Arthur, she is just like you in so many ways."

"Well, this is not how I was expecting to find you Rose," a woman's voice interrupted, and both Rose and Arthur turned towards the door. "Do I need to give you two a minute?"

Rose's family doctor, Ingrid, flashed a smile as she tucked a stray hair behind an ear. She was a small woman, and the white coat she wore swallowed her in brightness that washed out her already fair features.

Arthur coughed as more colour flushed his cheeks. "No! Come in."

"Dr. Ivan will join us soon. But he called me right after he read your file, Rose. I'm glad he did. I'm also glad to find you in good spirits. Hold on to them. It will carry you a far way through this." As she spoke, her voice switched from its initial lightness to a deeper, serious tone that filled the room with stillness.

"What did you find?" Rose asked, pressing her cheek into Arthur's hand, unwilling to let him break their closeness.

Ingrid shook her head as she pulled a second stool from the far corner towards them. "Nothing good."

Dr. Ivan soon joined them. The deep worry lines that creased his face stole years from a man Rose knew was close to her own age.

"What do you know about MS?" he asked, hands clasped tightly behind his back.

"Not much," Rose answered. "Ingrid and I have spoken about it briefly as a possibility, but no more."

"Ingrid tells me she has suspected this as your diagnosis but wanted to be thorough. She has done well." He nodded at the young woman. "But

I think this episode is enough. She needs to be referred to a specialist immediately."

Rose felt Arthur's muscles tense as she held him with her one good hand.

"I agree." Ingrid pulled her white coat tightly around her chest and held it there with crossed arms. "I'm sorry we didn't get to this sooner, Rose, it may have stalled this progression."

"Don't be—"

"What's MS?" Arthur asked, stopping the conversation dead.

"Rose ..." Ingrid began carefully. "What have you told him?"

"Not enough," she admitted. Her heart sank into her stomach, and the acids that were already clamouring for food danced along with her anxiety. "I didn't want to worry him or anyone until we had answers. Some kind of plan."

Ingrid swivelled her chair towards Arthur, her eyebrows drawing together. "MS is short for Multiple Sclerosis, a disease that affects the brain and spinal cord. Its severity and symptoms can be drastically different from person to person, making it hard to diagnose. I'm only a general practitioner, so I can't officially say this is what we're dealing with, Mr. Grill. But, after eliminating most other possibilities ... You need to know that we have no cure for MS. It's a lifelong disease and can cause lifelong disabilities. I believe your wife has been masking small symptoms for years. And for some unknown reason, her flareups have escalated at a disturbing rate over the last few months. If I am right ..."

"It's concerning," Dr. Ivan added.

"If I am right," Ingrid concluded. "If I'm not?" The small woman sighed and shook her head.

Hearing it all at once took Rose's breath away. She looked over at Arthur, whose face showed blatant shock.

"You have a hard road ahead of you both," Ingrid continued. "But you're not alone, regardless of what the specialists think."

"So, what can we do? How bad will it get? Will she—" He couldn't finish, and for the first time in years, Rose watched heavy tears roll down her husband's face. "Is it fatal?"

Both doctors looked at each other. An expression Rose didn't understand passed between them, and she bit her lip as it started to tremble.

"Only in very rare cases is MS directly responsible for the death of a patient, Mr. Grill." Ingrid's voice was soft, her words slow and calculated. "But, depending on the disease's severity, it can cause complications that lead to disabilities and, yes, even death."

"Arthur." Rose attempted to tighten her grip on her husband as he let out a pained gasp.

"But as long as we can get things under control, there is no need to fear things progressing that far any time soon." Dr. Ivan pulled a second stool from the corner of the room and joined Ingrid. "Stress, worry, despair … in my experience, Arthur, these things can be even more deadly than any disease. We are a long way away from the worst case scenario. So let's discuss some options I think the specialist will bring up and go over some important questions you will need to ask."

Questions

RACHEL

RACHEL FELT THE TAPPING against the door on her back before she heard it. Jay's visitor had left, and for a while, complete silence reigned in the living room as tears dried on her face.

"Rachel?" The door muffled her boyfriend's voice. "Can I come in?"

"No," she answered but couldn't be sure he'd heard her.

She heaved a sigh of relief at the sound of fabric brushing wood and then the gentle creak of floorboards as Jay moved away. She let her legs relax and slide out in front of herself. It opened up the muscles in her chest, and she dragged in a deep breath, wiping itchy salt residue from her cheeks. What was going on with her and with Jay? She looked at her phone again. Still no messages from her mom or dad. She hadn't expected it from Arthur, but still, it would've been nice if he would update her.

Rachel wrinkled her nose at a sudden whiff of bleach. How was that possible so far removed from her parents' bathroom? She gave the front of her shirt a sniff for good measure. She caught the subtle scent of bleach. She groaned.

No wonder I've felt ill. I've been breathing the fumes since starting on that bathroom this morning.

"Rachel?" Jay was back again, and she'd missed his approach. "I'm coming in."

The door shifted behind her back, forcing her to shuffle sideways as it slowly inched open. Jay poked his head around the side, shoulders still trapped in the in-between.

"We need to talk."

She looked up at him. His six-foot frame forced him to crane his neck to see her sitting on the floor. She chuckled at his grimace, an itch in her throat making it sound strained as she shifted farther, letting him enter the room. The door clicked closed, and soon Jay sat beside her on the floor, his back resting where hers had been, his long legs stretched out past her shoes.

"I'm sorry if I scared you."

She nodded at his apology but looked away. Their bed was a rumpled mess of blankets. She was sure she'd made it up before leaving the apartment this morning. Jay must have been napping before his guest arrived.

"Who was that man?"

"Just some guy ... some guy I owe money." He coughed, lifting a fist to his mouth to stifle the noise.

"Money?"

"Well ... it's his boss I owe the money to."

"Jay, what did you do?"

"I needed a way to pay rent, okay? The price is going up again this month. The memo came in the mail three weeks ago, and we were already behind from last time." Rachel watched Jay run shaking hands through his mass of black hair, his head falling towards his chest as his voice broke while his tone rose. "I asked Mom for a loan first. She said no."

"But I'm working now and just gave you my first paycheck."

"It's not enough, Rachel, not with food and all the extras."

What extras?

"Are we going to lose the apartment?" Rachel asked, a string of fear and shock pressing her voice up an octave. It was Jay's turn to look away from her.

Her heart squeezed as he slid his arm around her back and pulled her close.

"Nah, they got a way for me to pay it off. That's why he was here, to tell me the plan."

"What plan?"

"Don't worry about it. Just keep doing what you're doing at the laundromat. I know you have a lot on your mind with your mom not feeling well."

Rachel sighed. "They took her to the hospital in the middle of the move." She lifted her cell phone to glance at the lock screen. "Dad hasn't told me what's going on."

Rachel looked back up in time to see Jay's adam's apple dance as he swallowed hard.

"He's a hard man," Jay said.

"He's not so bad ..."

Jay raised an eyebrow at her while wrinkling his nose. "He's a strait-laced brown noser, and everyone at Ham's loves him."

"And they don't love you anymore?"

"No, not so much. But I don't need them to love me, do I?" He gave her the impish grin that curled her toes before continuing. "Remember how we used to talk about moving to the city after you graduate? Well, you only have a few more months left. That's what I'm aiming for."

Rachel had almost forgotten. Life had changed so fast since she moved in. "Isn't it more expensive there?"

"Yeah, but once you can work full time and I take care of this trouble, it's just a matter of finding the right spot. Won't be fancy." His eyes held a question as they roved over her face.

"I don't need fancy, you know that."

"That's my woman." He pulled her against his shoulder, and her cheek found just the right spot to nestle in close. How long had it been since they'd taken the time to just sit together like this? Was this how it was for old married people? Losing track of each other until something bad happened and forced togetherness?

Rachel could have fallen asleep on Jay's shoulder, but he shifted after a moment of silence.

"Got to go make some plans. You okay now?"

"I think so. I just ran away from a mean old lady from church. I'm tired, and my shirt smells of bleach. You took a nap?" She nodded towards the bed.

"What mean old lady?"

"Hillary Shear."

"That cranky hag from nursery?"

"Well, I wouldn't call her a hag, Jay. But, yeah, her."

They both laughed as he got up, lifting his arms over his head and placing his fingertips on the ceiling as he stretched.

"People at that church never change, do they?"

Rachel shook her head.

"Maybe it was for the best that they kicked your family out, then. Maybe your dad will finally lighten up."

"Maybe ..." Rachel mumbled as Jay left the room. She couldn't picture a lighter version of her father right now. When would they message her? She checked her phone again.

Just waiting for the doctor.

Finally, at least things were moving. She leaned her head back against the wall and drew her knees up to her chest, wrapping her arms around them to keep them in place. It had been months since she'd purposely prayed. But a tug at her heart pulled words from her mind.

God, please be with my mom. She needs you, and she deserves some answers. Please. As an afterthought while she clambered her way up off the floor, she added, *And be with Jay and me. I don't want to lose him to whatever mess he's gotten himself into.*

AMY

The officer that questioned Amy was young with hair oiled to a shine and freckles that crowded his fair-skinned face, but his grin was sharp, and she couldn't quite bring herself to trust him. His partner was his opposite—a shorter, doughy man with greying hair, a warm smile, and a tender voice. She wished he'd been the one to scribble her account down in a notebook, but instead, he'd talked to Mike and Carmen before taking a walk around the area to see if anyone else was lurking about.

Now Amy sat cloistered in the squad car's back seat as both officers sorted notes. The kids at school were never going to believe she'd ridden in the back of a cop car. She almost didn't believe it herself as she crossed her arms over her chest, hooked her ankles together, and leaned back into the seat, heart still pumping with adrenaline. A wall of black metal lattice kept the officers safe from any violent passengers they might carry, but right now the plexiglass that attached to their side was open, and she could hear everything they were saying.

"He should have called us first," the younger of the two muttered with a sniff of indignation.

"Of course, but you can't expect someone like Mike to come running to the law first. I'm just glad they kept us in the loop and didn't hide things. But The Brothers marching in broad daylight? Things are heating up, and it's not good."

"Makes you wonder what's really going on ..." The young officer glanced back at Amy. "You okay back there? We're just about ready to head out. Echo Apartments, right?"

Amy nodded but kept silent. His eyes roved over her in a way that made her skin crawl, just like Roger's. Yet he wore the navy blue of law enforcement. That meant he was safe, right?

"I'm done," the older one said as he finished typing something into the laptop mounted between the two front seats. He swivelled its stand away from himself and buckled up before nodding back at her. "Let's get this kid home."

Amy thanked God when the younger officer opted to stay in the squad car when they arrived at Echo Apartments.

"My family's moving today, so I'm not sure who will be here yet. Dad's got the whole church helping."

"Church?"

"He used to be the pastor. Don't *even* get me started!"

The officer whistled at that. "Sounds like you come from a good family."

Good family? If only you knew.

A small crowd of Hope Is Here members greeted them at the glass door.

"Amy's here!" a woman yelled, and Sarah came running.

"Thank God you're back." Sarah pulled her into a crushing hug. "Jeff, call Gary and tell him Amy's home. Gary's been out looking for you all afternoon. Is everything okay, officer?"

"Yes, ma'am, and can I ask your name and how you know this young lady, please?"

"Of course. I'm Sarah Davids, a close family friend."

The officer nodded as he shook Sarah's extended hand in greeting. "And Amy's parents are?"

"Currently at the hospital, I'm—"

"Hospital?" Amy interrupted, pulling on Sarah's sleeve as a flash of red invaded her vision.

"Yes, your mother had some kind of episode right after you left this morning. The stress of the move and ... the argument. It was too much for her." Sarah turned her head to address the officer. "Arthur, Amy's father, took her mother to the hospital, and as far as we know, they won't be home any time soon. We've been setting up the new apartment for them.

"Amy's sister, Rachel, lives upstairs with her boyfriend but had to step out before I arrived. I can call and have her meet us here if needed."

"No, that won't be necessary as long as Amy is okay with me leaving her here with you. Do you feel safe with these people, Amy?" the officer asked, making eye contact.

"Yes." Amy dipped her chin in firm affirmation.

"Alright. I'll leave it up to you to fill your parents in on what happened today. And don't worry, ma'am, Amy is not in trouble. But don't go walking around downtown alone for the next few weeks, okay?"

Again, Amy nodded.

After a thank you and good day, the officer left, the sound of his cheerful whistling drifting on the wind.

Amy's shoulders dropped, and her heart plummeted to her toes as she took in the crowded living room. Boxes filled every corner, and people stared at her as if she was a curiosity at a sideshow. They had no right knowing her business, but there was no way around it now. They would all be whispering about how she came home in police custody. Monday morning at school was going to be horrible.

"Come on, Amy," Sarah said as she pulled her closer and closed the door. "Let's go sit in your room, and I'll help you unpack," she whispered as they passed wide-eyed faces. "Are you *really* okay? What happened?"

Alone

ARTHUR

THE MEDICAL TEAM DECIDED Rose would stay overnight at the hospital. Before Arthur left, he watched nurses insert an IV and hook her up to monitors. None of it seemed real. Even Rose, as she lay in the hospital bed, pale, frail, and terrifyingly accepting of the situation, seemed like she'd taken a step out of his reality and onto the next. When the doctor explained things, his mind had gone blank, only to be shocked back to reality when she said the words, "potential life long disability." The flash of realization had been a pain he'd never experienced before. It cut sharp and deep. He was going to lose her, slowly, inevitably. As he walked back to the car alone, he recognized he already was. Her health issues had been going on for years without explanations. Now?

Amy's mental health crisis had forced Rose to step back from church ministry, and even though it had been an adjustment for everyone involved, it also meant she had more time to take care of herself. His wife had finally asked her doctor about the strange numbness and tingling she experienced throughout her body. Her fatigue had grown with the stress of parenting teenagers, but it was only now they'd taken the time to register that something serious was going on. Arthur wondered just how long Rose had been ignoring her symptoms.

"Why didn't I pay attention? Why didn't I make her step back sooner and take care of herself?"

Because I'm selfish.

Rose was the perfect pastor's wife, always ready to jump in when needed and able to gather people around herself to get things done. No one was as good at organization as Rose. Without her?

Without her, I'm expendable.

Arthur's thoughts swarmed like hornets in his ears. He was so, so tired.

Each step from the hospital entrance was a strain. His feet were lead bricks that clomped across the pavement. The shadows were deep around him, and the tall lights scattered through the parking lot did little to illuminate the world. The weight on his ankles affected his driving as a heavy foot sped him down the highways. He first turned towards the parsonage's neighbourhood before remembering it was no longer home, then ran a red light. The curse he spat out lingered in the air, tainting it with the taste of bile. He thought of the fine he would receive in the mail the next week because of cameras over the traffic light. It meant money gone out the door that they couldn't afford to lose.

His palm hit the steering wheel in a flash of frustration. The impact sent an ache through his wrist as his bones vibrated.

He found a parking spot beside Gary's car at Echo Apartments but sat in the solitude, unwilling to face questions, unsure how he would answer them. Then his mind turned to work and the fact he had a shift tomorrow. A text to both Penelope and Fred about Rose being in the hospital and needing to be with her the next day cleared that immediate stress away.

Fred told him, "Don't worry about it and let us know if you need Monday off as well." Penelope sent a long message about how she expected him to take care of his wife and that she wanted regular updates. "I'm praying for you," she wrote.

That woman. She could be hard, but she was undoubtedly good.

At least one person's praying.

Arthur had been a pastor for over half his life, but the thought of talking to the God he professed to love stirred mixed emotions in his gut: doubt, anger, resignation, a strange hesitation he'd never felt before. He'd often told people in his congregation that God was close even when he felt far away. Yet he couldn't bring himself to open his mouth and heart, to say the words that burned the tip of his tongue.

He closed his eyes. *Why? Why her?* It was all his mind could manage at the moment. Was it enough?

His cell intoned an incoming call as the evening light dimmed around him. The caller ID read Amy.

"Hello?"

"Dad? Where are you?"

"In the parking lot."

"I'm hungry, hurry. Sarah says we won't start without you."

He kept the phone at his ear for a minute after the line dropped and the screen went black.

She didn't even ask about her mom.

He didn't bother entering the main building and instead followed the walkway that skirted it, passing small private alcoves hiding the sliding door entrances to the larger apartments on the main floor. He counted them as he walked. "101, 102, 103."

"104, 105, 106." Arthur stopped and turned towards the light spilling out of a glass door still free of curtains. The smooth surface glowed with warmth as beams hit it. He should have opened it immediately, but he stood on the footpath, looking into the living room filled with boxes. Some were open and half unpacked. Others lay stacked against the wall, waiting. He'd let the Hope Is Here congregation do too much work for them—his work, now that Rose wouldn't be able to help. He couldn't rely on them anymore. They were no longer *his* people. He felt the sucker punch of the thought as a physical blow and gasped, leaning forward, trying to absorb the force of it.

His cell phone rang. It was Amy, probably ready to yell at him for taking so long just to walk from the car to the table. If she really wanted him, she could have gotten up off her rear and found him. Why didn't she just come?

She's just a girl, Arthur. You're the parent.

Why didn't she ask about Rose? Why did the fact make him so angry?

He cancelled the call and instead straightened, took a deep breath, then pulled the screen and glass doors open.

They'd shifted the clutter of unpacking into the corners of every room, leaving the kitchen table and dining chairs ready for tired, hungry bodies.

"It's about time!" Amy said as Arthur breathed in delicious scents spreading out from the oven.

"Abigail brought us supper," Sarah told him as she pulled out a chair beside Gary, inviting him to sit.

"Where's Mom?" Amy asked.

"At the hospital."

Amy rolled her eyes at his obvious answer. "Ya think? But really, why didn't she come home with you?"

"The doctors want to monitor her overnight. She still can't walk."

"Oh …"

"Did they say anything? Do they know what happened?" Sarah asked.

Arthur felt his throat constrict as he opened his mouth to answer. It blocked his words and his wind, and he closed his eyes to calm himself. Gary placed a warm hand on his shoulder as Sarah found a glass and filled it with tap water.

"What's going on, Arthur?" Gary asked, his voice gentle but his eyes piercing when Arthur looked back.

"Nothing's confirmed yet."

"But they suspect something. Come on, Arthur, it's written all over your face," Sarah pressed.

"They think it's MS."

"What's MS?" Amy asked, staring at the empty plate in front of her.

"Multiple Scloooorosis?" The word felt like needles on Arthur's tongue.

"Multiple Sclerosis," Sarah softly corrected.

Arthur nodded. "It's not confirmed. They're referring her to a specialist."

"But what does that mean?" Amy lifted her eyes to her father's. Her look demanded answers, and Arthur grasped the edge of the table as shivers ran up his spine.

"I'm not sure Amy. We just have to wait and see."

"Is she going to die?"

"No!" Everyone jumped as Arthur's fist came down on the table hard, the dishes clattering against the wood as it shifted underneath them, knocking an empty glass over. Amy's sudden and silent tears stopped the words that wanted to spill from his heart. His hand ached where it had made contact with the table. It was the same hand he'd struck the steering wheel with, and he now felt a bruise forming under the skin.

For a moment Amy caught him in the headlights of her gaze.

He blinked.

She blinked back.

"I'm sorry, Amy."

Arthur pushed away from the table and made a hasty retreat to the hall, sliding past stacked boxes to find doorways. The master bedroom was dark, and he groped around the room for the light switch. Finding none, he searched for the bedside lamps that should have found their way from the parsonage to his room in the moving truck. Only one sat out on a bedside table. It was enough. He flicked it on as the anger drained from his mind, leaving behind slow, tired thoughts.

You're acting like a spoiled teenager running away from a difficult situation.

I lost control. It would have been worse if I stayed in the kitchen.

Rose would be ashamed if she knew how you acted in front of your friends.

He had often been so hard on Amy, and here he was, acting just like her. Rose's teasing words from the ER floated into his mind. He was like Amy. Or rather, she was like him. Was that why they butted heads so much? Her crass attitudes chafed. But had he been any different at sixteen?

Yes, he had been different. As different as a teenage boy could be from a teenage girl that shared the larger parts of an extroverted personality. But still, he failed to relate to her. Utterly failed.

Pitiful, and to think just a few short weeks ago, you were a senior pastor of the largest church in town. How the mighty have fallen.

The small lamp on his bedside table poked a hole into the darkness around him as he sat on the edge of the bed. Were the shadows closing in? They felt oppressive as he huddled within the small pool of light.

"God, where are you? I feel so lost."

Arthur didn't leave his room that night after receiving a message from Gary that he and Sarah would take Amy home and bring her back after church the next day.

"But we need to talk, Arthur," Gary's message insisted. *"Something happened to Amy after she left the parsonage, and you and Rose need to know about it. Don't worry for right now, though. She's okay."*

He hadn't been paying enough attention to her again, and shame mixed with confusion as Arthur listened to his friends leave the apartment, taking another of his responsibilities with him. Children were supposed to be a blessing from the Lord. He'd read that line to the Hope Is Here congregation dozens of times when welcoming a new baby into the church. They were treasures, they were important. Why did his daughters weigh on him?

He slept on a bed without sheets, finding only a quilt stowed away in a plastic bag. Strange and half-formed shapes and sounds romped through his dreams. A loud bumping on the opposite side of the wall woke him as someone thumped their way down the main hallway. He searched for his watch. Seven a.m. Who would be tramping down the halls so early on a Sunday?

"Apartment life is going to take getting used to."

Once he was awake, the noise of the building intensified and lying in bed became sensory torture. Irritability increased Arthur's sensitivity, and he made his way to the kitchen and the leftover dinner stored in the fridge. He struggled to remember who had brought it over and sighed when he failed.

The sight of cold congealed fat across the top of the sauce-covered meat turned Arthur's stomach, so instead, he headed for the door and a warm drink from the closest coffee shop. His stomach lurched as he paid for it alongside a breakfast sandwich he knew he couldn't afford, and he prayed that Rose would forgive him this indulgence. When he pulled into the hospital parking lot, it was still before eight a.m.—too early for visitors—so he sat watching the minutes flip by on his car stereo, his sandwich cooling beside him on the passenger's seat.

As soon as the clock flickered to eight, he was walking through the hospital's front doors, signing in at the front desk and riding the elevator up to Rose. Her room was dark, and he tiptoed past the first bed in the room occupied by a sleeping elderly woman. With coffee and sandwich in hand, he was ready to make an offering of it if Rose couldn't stomach the hospital food. When he passed the curtain that gave privacy to Rose's side of the room, he stopped, catching his breath at the view of his sleeping wife.

She was still pale, and dark circles ringed her eyes even as she slept. Her hair was frizzing against the white hospital pillows, but at the edge of her cheeks, he spied a touch of colour that hadn't been there yesterday. If he touched her right hand, would she be able to feel him now? He deposited his breakfast on the bedside table and quietly pulled the visitor's chair closer. The plastic bed rail was cold, but he slid his hand through it and gently intertwined his fingers with hers.

"Don't take her from me, God, not like this. She's too full of life and love. Don't let her waste away," he pleaded.

"I'm not going anywhere yet, Arthur," Rose whispered. She didn't open her eyes, not even when he raised her hand above the rail to kiss her knuckles.

She turned her nose up at the offered sandwich a few minutes later and gratefully waited for her hospital breakfast of oatmeal with milk and orange juice on the side. Soon Rose sat up slowly, spooning the grey goop into her mouth as her husband watched, nibbling on his now unwanted food.

Thank you, Jesus. She can feed herself this morning.

He told her about what had happened last night, and she nodded and grimaced when he confessed to losing his temper.

"It's okay, Arthur. I mean, it's not *okay*, but I think it's expected. All of our emotions have frayed. We need to thank Gary and Sarah for stepping in like that."

"What do you think happened to Amy?" He didn't expect her to have an answer.

She offered him a lopsided shrug, and pinched her lips as her eye brows dipped in a tired expresion. "You didn't speak to Rachel, did you?" Rose asked him.

"No, she wasn't there."

"How is the apartment?"

Arthur shrugged and turned to look out the window. "Lonely."

"Maybe you should have kept your shift today instead of coming here."

He turned back to Rose and gaped at her. "What? And not be with you? Has your brain gone numb too?"

"Well, MS means at least something is wrong between the connections there."

"That's not funny, Rose ... Don't joke like that."

"Arthur, I'm going to be fine. The feeling is coming back into my arm, and soon I'm sure the leg will heal as well."

"But there isn't anything they can do, is there, if it's MS."

"There are medications, therapies, ways to hold off future episodes once we know exactly what's going on. But this is my first identified flare-up, if it is MS. We'll get a handle on it. Stop thinking ahead." She pushed the over-the-bed table away with her good arm. "Have you ever thought that maybe this is why God had us leave ministry? He knew ..." Rose bowed her head for a moment and rubbed a hand over her face. "Arthur, He *knows.*"

Arthur didn't want to think about it.

"It's Sunday. You should go to church. You still have time."

"What?" Again he looked at her like she was going crazy.

"You don't have to go to Hope Is Here. Go somewhere else. Go sit in *His* sanctuary. It's been too long, Arthur. You've never not gone to church like this before."

She was right, but where on Earth would he go?

"I don't want to leave you."

"You can come back right after."

Was that a dismissal? It hurt. But he listened and slowly headed for the doorway.

"Arthur, I love you."

"I love you too."

"I'm not going anywhere."

"Not until you can walk, that is." He let a grin pull up the corners of his mouth in response to her muted laughter. But it didn't stay as he turned and left.

Where should he go? He could just sit in the hospital parking lot and wait it out, telling Rose he'd gone somewhere to keep her happy. But no, he couldn't lie like that. Not to Rose.

After driving around for a half hour, he pulled into a large parking lot that dwarfed the small white and blue building at its centre. The congregation here was elderly, and the pastor matched his people perfectly. Arthur remembered him to be a calm man with full head of grey hair and a surplus of wrinkles around his eyes. Only a few cars rested in the lot as he chose a space. The welcome sign told him there was still a half hour before services started.

He pushed through the front doors to a small, unassuming foyer. Only a few coats hung on the racks that stretched along both sides of the space, but Arthur took his spring jacket with him to the sanctuary. Old-fashioned pews lined the room and crowded the small raised pulpit. A few gaps in the rows looked like someone had cut a pew to form an open space, and after choosing a seat at the back and far into a corner, he found out why. An elderly woman pushed her husband into the room, his wheelchair fitting precisely within the first gap. Others soon followed, and the first few rows filled. It looked as if everyone had a home pew, and they fit together like snug puzzle pieces. A single toddler ran around the room, drawing a smile from every grey head he passed.

Another elderly woman took a seat at the antique organ beside the pulpit, and the service started as her hands and feet prompted the first few notes to life. Arthur was struck by the difference between this tiny congregation's service and what he was used to at Hope Is Here Church. His former congregation was the largest one in town, and the building vibrated with the laughter of children before and after services. Hope Is Here's music, though not as modern as some churches, was definitely several steps above an organ.

Arthur couldn't help but hear the fervency in every voice raised as they began to sing. Some old voices wobbled on the notes, some held strong and true like glue between those that wavered. The little one ran across the front and back again, and not a single person batted an eye in annoyance.

Arthur's shoulders relaxed into the weight of his body as the service continued. He slumped down in the pew as the pastor took his time with the message, not from inattention, but from emotional and physical fatigue. If he had let his eyes close, the rise and fall of the pastor's voice could have lulled him to sleep. But he held on, watching the little one up front pulling on his mother's purse strap.

When the service ended, Arthur remained in his seat at the edge of the room, waiting for the regulars to file out. It had been good to be here. He hadn't retained much of the sermon, but it had been a cup of peace to a parched throat just to be present. As he watched the last group of women leave the sanctuary, their voices a chorus of chatter, he turned to a tap on his shoulder.

Still seated in the pew, he swivelled to meet a pair of bright blue eyes shadowed by shaggy white eyebrows.

"I thought that was you. What a surprise, Arthur." Pastor Edwin extended a hand, and Arthur grasped it firmly.

"It's good to see you, Edwin. How are things?"

"As good as can be expected as time marches on, taking my body with it." Edwin chuckled and pointed at the pew seat beside Arthur. "I've heard the last few months have not been so kind to you and Rose. Can I assume that's why you're here and not worshipping at Hope Is Here this morning?"

Arthur nodded as he slid over, welcoming the older man into his space. "Unkind, yes, that's a gentle way to put it. But Rose told me she wanted me in a church this morning, so here I am. It's been a few weeks ..."

"And how is Rose?"

Arthur updated Edwin on the happenings of the last few days, his voice trailing off as he ended with the doctor's suspicions.

"That's a difficult cross for Rose to bear," Edwin said, his bushy brows knitting together as folded fingers supported the older man's chin in thought. "And an added burden on the shoulders of her husband. Perhaps that's the reason God's giving you a respite from open ministry?"

Edwin's words shocked Arthur as they echoed Rose's from earlier that morning. He clenched his fists in frustration. "I'm not on extended leave, Edwin. They fired me."

"I know, Arthur. But regardless of whether you have a church congregation to lead, your gifting is still the same. You're still a minister."

Arthur clamped his mouth shut. Was it true? He had not even considered looking for a new church to lead after finding a job at Ham's Grocers. Why was that?

"What good is a minister without a church, Edwin?"

"Plenty good. You think everyone who has the same gift as you uses it in the same way?" The old man crossed his arms over his chest. "My church is dying, Arthur. My people are aging, leaving, or moving on to eternity. I won't be standing up on that pulpit for much longer. The doors of this church will one day close, but my purpose doesn't change."

Edwin shrugged after unfolding his arms and leaning forward to look right into Arthur's eyes. "I have no idea what I'll do with my gifts after that, but I'm convinced God will have a new place for me to use them. Even if that is simply visiting with others housed in the same nursing home as me." Edwin's smile cut through the tension. "Now, are you coming over for lunch?"

Arthur smiled back, despite his brain swimming at Edwin's words. His perceptions had been flopped around like a rag doll. "I told Rose I'd head back to the hospital after church."

Edwin nodded. "How long will she be there? My wife and I should visit."

"We aren't sure. Perhaps another day? Maybe longer? I hope not too long."

"Alright," Edwin slowly rose from the pew and grimaced as his joints audibly crackled. "Then perhaps we will see you again today or tomorrow, and of course, you're welcome here next Sunday as well, and every Sunday after that, if you would like."

Plans

ROSE

ROSE'S HOSPITAL ROOM HAD become the town hot-spot, or that was how it seemed to her. She stole glances over at the curtain separating her bed from her neighbour's, hoping her family and friends weren't disturbing the poor woman. Arthur sat beside her in the only guest chair in the room. Sarah stood beside him, and Gary was leaning over the end of her bed, hands resting on the footboard for support. Amy sat on the floor near Arthur, her back to the wall as light from a window poured in over her head.

"They won't like so many people crowding into the room for long, so we'll be quick, but we had to come up and see how you were doing, Rose," Sarah said as she clasped Rose's hand. "How are you, *really?*"

"I'm doing okay," Rose reassured. "I'm regaining strength in my right side and will hopefully be coming home tomorrow."

Arthur cleared his throat and leaned back in the chair, the plastic fabric rustling with his movement. "I have work tomorrow, so ... we wanted to ask if you were available to drive Rose home, Sarah. If she's released during my shift."

"Of course! Just let me know as soon as you can when I should be here."

"They've already sent my paperwork to an out-of-town specialist, and we should be hearing about an appointment date soon. I'm hoping Rachel can help drive if it lands on a workday for Arthur." Rose squeezed her husband's hand, relishing in the sensation of touch that travelled unhindered across her skin. "Getting in as many hours as possible at work is important in case we have to spend overnight time in the city. He'll want to be with me then."

"Alright," Gary said as he straightened up and drummed a hand on the footrest. He looked tired and eager to leave.

"Thank you, Gary, for everything." Rose squeezed Arthur's hand again, tickling his palm with a finger. She tried to tell him to speak to his friend with her eyes, but Arthur just looked at her and shook his head.

"Let us know if you need us for anything. Really. Anything. I'll be expecting at least a text once a day from you, Rose," Sarah told her.

"I promise, and if you don't hear from me, you can always call."

"We'll be hearing from you, then," Gary said as he turned away.

Rose hated how awkward it felt as their friends left. The strain between their husbands was apparent and the distance painful. What must Gary be thinking of them? Should she be worrying about it so much? Maybe that was a question for Sarah's next phone call.

"What about me, Mom?" Amy asked as she leaned away from the wall for a better view of her mother. "I mean, am I coming with you to these appointments?"

"Do you want to? It would mean missed classes. I thought staying in school would be best, but—Arthur?" Rose poked her husband with a slender finger.

"We thought, I mean, your mom and I thought ..." Arthur shifted his chair backwards, opening up Rose's view to Amy. "We thought we should think about moving you from Hope is Here School to the public high school ... It's walking distance from the new apartment, so if Mom gets called away, you won't need help to get to classes."

Amy wedged her hands in between her legs, where they folded over each other. "Well, that's a thought, I guess."

"What do you think?" Rose pressed.

Amy shrugged without looking up. "Could be fun." Rose's youngest shifted in her position on the floor, pulling herself closer to the wall to sit up straighter before finally looking up at her parents. Her mother could see the wheels of her thoughts spinning as her daughter's eyes darted from one point between them to another.

"But?" Rose asked.

"But that would mean I have to get a new counsellor ... Right?"

"I'm not sure. We'll need to speak to the school about that," Rose replied.

Wrinkles formed along the bridge of Amy's nose as she looked down at her hands again. Rose shifted her position in bed, the pressure on her rear becoming a burden from sitting in one place for too long. She ignored the incessant itching at the site of her IV line.

"Amy—" Arthur started to speak but stopped as his daughter looked up with eyes shimmering with emotion. Rose squeezed his hand, and he pinched his lips together before sighing.

Rose couldn't help but wonder how many unsaid words floated around the space between them.

After a painfully drawn out minute, Amy nodded her head. "Sure, I mean, it's not like I have much left at Hope Is Here."

The defeat in Amy's voice broke Rose's heart. "If you want to stay there, we will do our best to make it work, Amy."

Arthur cleared his throat. "Rose." His eyes told her to stop.

She sighed.

They'd already talked about how much money taking Amy out of the Christian school and enrolling her in the public system would save, and right now they needed every extra penny they could find. But still, it all felt so unfair.

"It's okay, Mom, really. It'll be great, I'm sure." Amy pressed her lips flat and nodded, a determined look on her face.

Rose felt the bubble of tension surrounding her bed pop as Rachel appeared from around the room's dividing curtain. How long had it been since all four of them were in one place? She couldn't remember. A deep sigh escaped her as she slid down slightly in bed, pressing her tired back into the pillows, concentrating on where she could feel the contact her body made with the bed and where she couldn't.

"Hey, Mom. How are you feeling?" Rachel asked.

"Oh, I've been better." Rose didn't even try to hide the wobble in her voice as Arthur gave up his seat to his eldest daughter.

"Amy, you hungry?" Arthur asked as he beckoned his youngest to follow him out of the room.

"You don't have to leave because of me, Dad," Rachel said.

Rose watched the edges of Arthur's eyes crinkle as he narrowed his gaze. "I'm not, but I'm hungry and don't really have anything to say."

Rachel exhaled as Rose watched the pair disappear behind the partition curtain. "Really?"

Rose shook her head at the ghost of her husband's presence. "Give him time, Rachel."

"He can have all the time he needs."

"He still loves you."

"He has a funny way of showing it." Rachel's jaw worked back and forth as she shifted the guest chair closer to the bed before settling her elbows against its armrests.

Rose couldn't argue with her but also knew her Arthur better than any other human alive. She had read the rigidity present in his shoulders as he walked away, the canyons that had appeared as the skin around his eyes bunched, and she knew the far-off look he'd let fall on his daughter. "He regrets his shortcomings much more than anything wrong with his eldest daughter," she told Rachel.

"Sure ..." The disbelief dripped from Rachel's mouth as her lips parted, and Rose watched her swallow words for her mother's sake. "So, tell me, how are you, *really?*"

"Why does everyone keep emphasizing that word 'really' when they ask?"

"Because you don't always tell us the truth, Mom, and we *really* want to know."

Rose was tired of repeating herself, but for her daughter, she recounted every detail she could remember of the last twenty-four hours.

"As soon as you get some kind of schedule for trips, let me know. As long as Dad allows me to drive his car, I can ask for those days off. Most people don't want to work weekends, so it should be easy to shift hours around at the laundromat."

"What about your studies?" Rose asked.

"I'm taking night classes, Mom. Don't worry about school. I have it covered. I promise."

Rose hoped her daughter was also being truthful.

When Arthur and Amy wandered back into the room, Rachel rose to leave. Rose felt like the chair beside her bed was playing the supporting role in a sitcom, but she welcomed the warm cup of tea Arthur handed her as he sat back down, his clothes making loud swishing sounds against the plastic fabric.

"See you later, Mom! Let me know when you get released, okay?" With that and a look over her shoulder and a wave, Rachel left.

"You need to speak to her, Arthur. Our family has been divided long enough."

The snort he gave in response sounded like something from Amy, not her husband, and Rose couldn't hold down the bubbles of laughter that rose from her stomach.

"What?" Arthur asked, a scoop of ice cream on a small wooden spoon held just before his mouth. A drip fell from its flat edge to his pant leg.

Rose held a side with her good arm as it shook with mirth.

"Dad, you're dripping," Amy said, both eyebrows raised at her parents.

"Amy, grab your dad a napkin from the side table. It's just out of my reach."

Rose didn't know why she found the ice cream soaking into her husband's pant leg so funny, but the laughter bubbles didn't calm until Arthur sorted himself out and set the rest of his dessert aside.

"Really?" he asked his wife as she bit her lip and blinked before having to use a bed sheet to wipe a tear from her eye.

"I love you," was all she could manage to say between the bubbles as they popped inside her chest.

"Like *really*. How old are you two?" Amy muttered as she settled up against the wall under the window again. "And when are we going back to the apartment? I want to finish unpacking my room."

School

AMY

The parking lot at Hope Is Here School sat was mostly empty as Arthur and Amy pulled in the next morning. Amy's head filled with shadows as sleep clung to her brain, cushioning her thoughts like cotton balls. She pressed herself deeper into the passenger's seat, knowing her slow pace was irritating her father by the glances he kept throwing her way, but she couldn't help it. The new apartment might be home now, but it didn't feel like it. It always took her time to get used to new places, and sleeping soundly was going to be the last thing to happen once her mind settled in.

"Ready?" Arthur asked.

"I suppose so." Her shoulders sagged with reluctance.

Despite the warming spring sun, Amy had chosen to wear a black tuque with stars along the folded rim. It contrasted well with her loose blond curls that billowed out to the sides of her face and then hung down past her shoulders. It was a change from her regular pink tuque, meant to send a signal to the other students. She wasn't sure if she wanted them to ask what was going on or if she hoped they would take it as a warning sign and ignore her the whole day.

"Alright then, let's get this over with," she said as an impatient look from her father had her slithering out of the car and plodding into the school behind him.

"Chin up, Amy. This move will be good for all of us."

"Sure ..."

The school secretaries welcomed them both with chipper hellos before Arthur set to discussing Amy's transfer of schools with them.

Amy tuned them out and looked around the room. One wall was floor-to-ceiling glass windows, and she watched as teachers slowly trickled in from the front entrance, making their way down the halls to classrooms.

"Dad, I'm gone!" she called as she spied the clock inching closer to nine a.m. and made an exit before any of the kids could enter the building and see her standing in the offices. Many of them attended Hope Is Here Church, and everyone knew her father.

Would they see him standing in the office behind those exposing windows?

She didn't want the constant whispers she heard behind her back increasing. Not today. She wouldn't be able to handle it this time. She'd pick her own time to tell everyone about the change in school and the why.

Hope Is Here Christian School was small compared to the other local high school, and because of that, Amy's age group didn't move around the halls from class to class but stayed in set rooms just like the elementary grades. Amy was already at her desk and ignoring her teacher as best she could while the woman shuffled around the room when her classmates began to arrive. The noise in the hall that preceded them started as a low hum and grew to a wall of chatter and stomping feet as the crowds visited their lockers and then swarmed the classroom doors.

Amy kept her attention squarely on the notebook open before her and the blue lines on the page as the surrounding desks filled.

"Good morning!"

"Is it ever getting warm out there."

"Did you hear what Gregory said on the bus?"

"Yes! I don't believe him."

The urge to look up and ask what Gregory had said was strong as the conversation floated over her head, but she refused to give in to it. The black of her tuque seemed to work as no one greeted her directly, or maybe it was the way she scowled down at her desk's top.

The lack of attention was what she wanted, wasn't it? Still, it stung. Last year would have seen her leading the crowd in through the classroom doors, chatting about her weekend escapades and letting everyone know what was what. Her world had fallen apart as her mental health burst into flame in public view, forcing her parents to sign her up for therapy. The other kids didn't understand. A pastor's daughter wasn't supposed to have problems like that. Well, her father wasn't their pastor anymore. So really, who cared now?

That question—who cared now—spun around her head all morning as she listened to the teachers drone on about history and social studies.

Iris, a girl from the grade just below her, was the only student who dared to find a seat beside her at lunch. Amy had thought the outdoors and the cold cement picnic bench would give her a reprieve from the noise of the halls. It both did and didn't. As Iris sat down, Amy could feel the nervousness radiating from her friend.

"So," Iris asked, "you okay?" The girl pulled a plastic bento box from her bag.

"Why wouldn't I be okay?" Amy pulled a carrot stick from her own bag and munched on the end. She hated carrots without ranch dressing, but she hadn't found any in the fridge that morning. She grimaced but continued to chewed on it.

"I heard your mom was in the hospital."

"Oh? Yeah. She should be coming home today. She might even be back at the apartment now."

"And the move went well? What's your new room like?"

"I can hear the neighbours through the walls." Amy bit of her carrot, snapping the crisp orange body in half before working it into a pulp.

"Eh, that will take some getting used to."

"Yep." Amy let her short answer punctuate her irritation.

Iris coughed into the pause, drawing Amy's attention away from her food. The girl's hair was neatly braided. The weave came up to her forehead, holding all the ends in place before plunging back in a straight line to the nape of her neck. Amy thought it made Iris look like she was still elementary school age, but she bit her tongue before she could comment on it.

As if letting someone else do your hair for you is bad. Really, Amy.

She hated it when her mind went to nasty places. It was such an effort to drag them back to the moment and shut down the red that threatened to wash over her vision. But at least she had control of it for now. Her counsellor had once told her it was a self-preservation mechanism, something she could unlearn if she really wanted to, but it would take time. She needed to listen to that second voice inside that warned and reprimanded.

"It's your conscience, Amy," she'd been told. "Learning to count to five and letting it speak to you will help. Don't squash it, listen to it."

Amy tried. But on mornings like this ...

"Well ... like ... are you really okay? What's with the black hat? You look—"

"You noticed, and you still came to sit with me?"

"Oh, my God. I'm just asking if you're okay."

Iris shifted away from Amy, and while she watched, Amy bit her tongue again. The knowledge that the words she often chose to say were rude and inappropriate chaffed against her desire to change. But did she really want to change? Or did she just want people to stop judging her as if they knew what was really going on behind her blue eyes and blond curls?

"Sorry, Iris." Amy shoved her food back into her sack lunch and swivelled away from her friend. She would just have to remove herself from the situation if she really wanted to control how Iris was seeing her.

"One of the girls said she saw your dad in the office this morning."

Amy turned back after standing up. "So what?"

"Are you moving schools?"

Amy's mouth hung open for a second too long, and Iris nodded as if she'd guessed exactly what was what. A red haze rose like a cloud in Amy's peripheral vision.

"Why would you even think that?" Amy snapped. Her lips curled up from her teeth as Iris slid away again, almost falling off the other side of the picnic bench.

Amy knew she shouldn't feel satisfaction as she watched her friend's retreat, but she couldn't help it. She'd only come to sit with her to get information, not because she cared. Amy's chest felt swollen with emotions as she took a step forward, causing Iris to leave the bench and retreat around the table, as if putting something solid between them could protect her from Amy's ire.

"You want me to leave, don't you? This is what you've all been waiting for, isn't it?" As she spoke, her voice rose as if someone was sliding the sound up on a volume dial, slowly and methodically. "You can't wait until Amy Grill is gone and you don't have to put up with her anymore. As if all the time we spent together as friends doesn't matter at all! As if everyone who used to follow me around like devoted puppies is celebrating my fall from grace!"

A curse shot from Amy's lips with Iris's name attached to the end. It flew across the table, and Iris flinched as if slapped across the face.

Amy realized she'd gone too far when a shout broke through the red clouding her sight. The voice opened up a small hole that let in light and spread out, breaking the haze to pieces. Amy's anger boiled over, and more cursing filled the air. She spit the words like venom in every direction.

"Amy Grill, office, NOW!" Mr. Orville, one of the fifth grade teachers, charged up from behind at the same time a woman on yard duty laid a gentle hand on Iris's arm while asking if she was okay.

That's right, comfort the quiet one, even though it was her that pricked the beast and woke it up.

Amy blinked away red and water as she noticed tears in Iris's eyes.

"I'm sorry I asked, Amy," the girl said as the woman pulled her away.

Amy followed Mr. Orville back into the school building. His back towered above her like a brick wall. This wasn't the first time he'd escorted her to the office. His bulk was a protection that most other teachers didn't have. Amy didn't know if that meant he was the one they sent to deal with the troubled kids or if he took it upon himself to safeguard the other teachers.

It was too quiet in the hall. How loud had she been shouting at Iris? Did she scare the whole school away?

When they reached the familiar wall of windows, Mr. Orville turned back to her and shook his head. "You know better than to drop the f-bomb at school, Amy."

"That's what you're mad about?" She was ready to drop another one at his feet if he continued. But when she met his eyes, she clamped her mouth shut.

They shimmered as he looked down at her. "You're better than these outbursts, Amy."

Was that really true? It looked like he believed it for some reason, even wanted her to believe it. But, no, she didn't feel better than this behaviour. In fact, this behaviour felt exactly right to her racing heart. "Don't hold your breath for me, Mr. Orville. You might pass out while waiting."

Just Work

ARTHUR

As Arthur finished his first break of the day, the ringing from his pocket stopped him mid hallway. Ripples of apprehension moved through his arms and legs as he clutched the phone to his ear, forcing himself to listen to all the details of Amy's outburst.

"Do I need to come get her?" he asked. "I'm in the middle of work."

"No, Arthur," the voice on the other end of the call assured him. "It didn't get physical. Just be ready for a second call from the principal later. What time does your shift end?"

When he'd left Amy earlier that morning, he'd felt good, at peace even. The weight of school bills was soon to be lifted from his shoulders, and it felt like his family was truly moving on from the ties that wanted to drag his mind back to standing in that church board room, hearing and seeing the disapproval of men who showed no care for what they were going through as a family, except for Gary ... Arthur's mind wandered to the pointed looks his friend had given him as he stood at the foot of Rose's hospital bed. He needed to fix the block that now lay between them, but not yet. He wasn't ready.

He'd thought Amy would be excited for a change as well. Didn't she complain constantly about "those people" at church and school? The scheduling difficulties with her counsellor were an obstacle for sure, but she'd be able to carry on after the move. This change would get her away from judgmental eyes. Why had she chosen today of all days to lash out? They were all so close to moving on.

Arthur's shoulders slumped as the school secretary said goodbye.

After shoving the cell phone into his back pocket, it soon became a lead weight that pulled his thoughts and slowed his footsteps. But the noise of the stock room wouldn't let him wallow in private misery. Shouts of instructions and friendly banter between coworkers flowed over the top of stacked boxes. The rooms smelled of rubber and glue with faint traces of body odour as workers passed each other in sometimes cramped lanes. Arthur answered the call of his name from the far right of the room with a wave as the forklift rumbled past, forcing him to sidestep and pause.

His hard hat hung on the wall over his work vest. While still donning his gear, he stepped out onto the grey painted cement floor behind the forklift. He winced at the noise and the ringing it left in his ears.

The loading dock door was open to the outdoors, and a semi filled with foodstuff waited to be unloaded. If he had been faster with his break, it might have been him called to drive the forklift and unload the plastic wrapped pallets. He'd proved to be good at it, and even though the vibration of the machine sometimes rattled his middle-aged joints, he rather liked the job. Instead, Ben waved him over to the first pallet resting in the centre of the room. The man flashed Arthur a white smile made all the more bright by his dark features, as he leaned on the handle of a pallet jack.

"Ready?"

"Ready," Arthur answered.

"Lucas put me in charge today. He's got Jay and Arron unloading the delivery truck with Hammond supervising."

"Hammond supervising?" That surprised Arthur, and he squinted over at the men gathered around the now stalled forklift.

"I guess they're giving Hammond a promotion."

"And Jay?"

"There to observe how he handles things? Who knows?" Ben shrugged and pressed a button on the pallet jack's handle, lowering the heavy metal lever.

Arthur admired the man as he put his full weight behind it, moving the jack carefully into position and sliding it under the first unloaded pallet. "Since you're in charge, shouldn't I be doing that?"

"That'd be no fun!"

They both laughed as Arthur checked how secure the load was and Ben began to pull it all towards the side stock room. Ben was so different from him, but he felt fortunate to be paired with such a hard worker. They were a good team, and Lucas had noticed. It made it easier to keep Arthur separated from Jay, but still, they inevitably ran into each other.

Arthur felt he did a good job of holding his peace, letting the younger man be the one to run his mouth or disrupt the work routine. But often it felt like they were playing high school games of popularity. It sucked his energy and the little enthusiasm for work that he'd been able to gather over the last few weeks. Amid their work environment, Ben was an oasis, and with no other job prospects presenting themselves, it looked like Ham's Grocer would be Arthur's calling for the foreseeable future. With Ben taking more of a lead, it couldn't be that bad, could it?

The line of pallets shrank as Arthur and Ben found each a home then started the job of unpacking the ones with smaller goods that needed to be placed up front on store shelves. In the midst of all the sorting and back and forth conversation with Ben, Arthur began to forget his apprehension about the call with Hope Is Here School's principal.

Amy will be all right. She will be, and we'll have a good talk when I get home.

They walked back to the loading dock for one final haul before their second break, stopping to look at each other as shouting and shuffling erupted from just in front of the truck ramp.

Ben grabbed Arthur's arm as he stepped forward. "Wait! That's Jay on the bottom." His coworker's firm grip stopped Arthur short of pulling the tussling pair apart. "It won't be good if you get involved."

Ben was right.

You're not the boss here. Arthur blew out a loud breath, an attempt at tamping down the surge of adrenaline that rushed into his head at the sight of the twisting, thrashing bodies rolling over the floor. *Ben's right. It's not your job to break this up.*

Arthur stepped back and let Ben be the one to try and break up the tangle. It was no good.

A fist came up, and a meaty *thud* sounded as it made contact with a face. Arthur saw blood leaking from Hammond's nose as he backed off Jay and let him stand. Jay cradled his fist to his chest, eyes dark, curses spewing out into the air.

"I saw what you did," Hammond said, the words muffled as he held his nose, blood dripping down his chin. It must have stung something awful, but the man never lost his feet as he stepped forward in a refreshed challenge.

"What's this?" Lucas yelled over the rumble of the still running forklift engine.

"I saw him!" Hammond said again, this time turning his burning gaze on Lucas as the manager slipped between the two men. "He was passing off boxes to someone over the ramp ledge when I came back from break."

"I don't know what he's talking about!" Jay yelled. "I was unloading one of the crates when this toad jumped me from behind."

"I know what I saw. He's been helping someone lift goods. He's the thief Fred's been looking for!"

"Did anyone else see anything?" Lucas asked. He spun in a circle, making eye contact with everyone in the crowd, quickly forming around the scene.

"The oaf doesn't know what he's talking about. He's too stupid and blind to know what's happening right in front of him," Jay shot back.

"Enough!" Lucas roared, his face now beet red. "Ben, find Fred. Now!" As an afterthought, he shouted at Ben's retreating back, "Get Penelope to pull up the cameras and call the cops!"

At Lucas's words, Arthur watched as Jay tensed, his eyes darting around the room and his coworkers crowding around. The young man's mouth twisted in a scowl, pure panic flooding his eyes.

"Oh Jay," Arthur whispered. "What have you done?"

Jay heard him and turned, eyes filled with indignant fire. "Nothing!"

Work slowed to a crawl until the police arrived. After that, Lucas sent everyone back to their assignments. They'd all be interviewed later, one by one.

Ben threw Arthur a bottle of water.

"Penelope is handing them out," he said. "She's got juice and soda as well, but I wasn't sure what you would want."

"Water is great. Thanks, Ben."

"You talk to the officer yet?"

Arthur nodded. He'd been one of the first few interviewed, but he didn't think he'd been much help. All he and Ben had seen was the fight, but he'd done his best to remember any small details that he might have not realized was important.

"What I want to know is where Arron's got to. He's up and disappeared," Ben said as he unscrewed the lid of his own water bottle.

"Do you think he had something to do with it?"

"Why else would he leave in the middle of his shift? Looks wrong." Ben shook his head, the motion so deep, it moved his shoulders back and forth. "This is bad."

Arthur agreed. His mind kept jumping back to the scene they'd witnessed. Was it possible Jay had been telling the truth? With Arron missing—could it have been him that Hammond spotted handing out boxes? Or maybe it was him receiving them, and he'd run for it?

Arthur's breath caught as he watched an officer leading Jay down the steps from the second floor offices. His hands were cuffed, and his eyes smouldered with hate as he scanned the room. The boy's gaze settled on Arthur last. The look made his skin crawl.

He couldn't understand why his daughter's boyfriend seemed to hold so much hate for him. Then, as he watched the officer march Jay out of the back entry, both guiding and propelling him by a hand on his elbow, Jay mouthed something.

"What's he trying to say to you, Arthur?" Ben asked as he watched the scene as intently as Arthur.

"I'm not sure." It irked him how this boy had gotten his claws so deeply under his skin. "Unless ..." In a flash of realization, Arthur pulled out his cell phone and scrolled through his contacts, selecting Rachel's number.

If Jay was in trouble, did that mean Rachel was as well?

Close Call

RACHEL

Lunch was in full swing as Rachel walked through the halls of Barton Public High School. A constant wave of voices bounced off the cement walls, the press of bodies around her filled her nostrils with the scent of half eaten meals and hormone induced body odour. The crowd jostled for space in the bottle neck that was the lunch room hallway. Rachel barely made it through the press without losing the notebooks she clutched to her chest. She promised herself she'd organize her backpack that evening to make room for the overflow. The relief of another day of morning classes completed, propelled her though the labyrinth of hallways towards the front entrance and freedom.

Not much longer, and you will be done with high school forever.

As her fingers touched the glass entrance door's handle, her fingers shook with anticipation.

A handful of students crowded around the side steps outside. Some concentrated on sack lunches while others dithered their time away as they waited for third period.

As the fresh air hit her face, the emotions churning in Rachel's gut along with the growl of her stomach made her swallow bile. Still, it was freedom. She raced past them all. Lunch waited for her at Jay's apartment.

Jay's apartment.

Rachel's last year had been anything but settled. She sometimes missed the title of model student she'd once held at Hope Is Here Christian School. When she transferred to the public system, her focus had shifted from studies to Jay. She now followed an alternate schedule, attending morning classes two days out of the week, and slipped in night classes on the other three. Slowly, she'd pulled her grades back up to where they'd been a year before. It was an accomplishment that she never thought she'd have to reach for and one that she felt had been harder to achieve than it should have been.

Still, she took pride in the knowledge she had done it and done it on her own.

Night class was with adults who'd dropped out as teens or other people like her in difficult situations but with enough determination to get their diplomas. It was a judgment-free space. Above all, Rachel needed that: freedom, safety, and acceptance.

Her feet tapped out a steady rhythm as she left the noise of the school behind and headed out into the real world.

Rachel used to dream of living as an adult, making her own rules and telling her dad to stuff it. But now? She had work, bills, Jay's problems, and school to finish. As her mind flitted from one issue to another, her foot failed to lift high enough over a prominent crack in the sidewalk, and the toe of her shoe clipped the pavement. Thank goodness no one was paying her any attention. She caught herself before a fall, but the yelp and flailing arms were none too lady-like.

The few people walking the street with her were intent on making it back into the school before the bell rang.

The sun was hot, and for the first time that spring, it beat down with oppressive rays. April in Northwestern Ontario could be a fickle thing. It had been chilly earlier that morning, so Rachel dressed in layers, but now she peeled out of her light sweater and even pulled off the T-shirt she wore over her layering camisole. The lace around that last layer of hem had seen better days. She sighed. There was no room in her backpack for the garments, so she wadded them against her chest along with her notebooks. As she balanced the awkward stack and raised a foot to continue on, her cell phone rang. She pulled it from an inside pocket to read the caller ID.

Dad.

Her heart fluttered at the thought of talking to him as she pressed the cancel call button.

He'd be angry with her for that, but *s*he told herself she didn't care. She didn't live under his roof anymore and didn't need to cater to his rules.

It was true, but her heart did a flip-flop. She still held the phone when it buzzed again. This time it was a message, and she opened it immediately.

Jay's been arrested. They think he's been stealing from the store. Call me.

Rachel froze.

Bile gathered at the back of her throat as she read the text a second time.

Oh, God, Jay. What have you done?

All apprehension about talking to her father disappeared as she held the icon above his name down with a finger and waited for her cell to dial. She tapped her foot against the cement, willing it to speed up the ring.

"Hey," Arthur answered, his voice hesitant.

"What happened?"

"I don't have all the details, but there was a fight. One of the guys screamed accusations. Jay denied them. They just cuffed him and took him out."

"Oh, God."

"Rachel, he gave me a weird look as he left. It was like he wanted me to tell you something. What's going on?"

"I don't know, Dad."

"Where are you?"

"Just heading home from school." Rachel looked around. The street seemed quiet enough with only a few cars passing by. All the houses up one side of the street were quiet, their owners at work or school. The other side was open, and the school parking lot spread out behind her. A small group of shops started just past the blacktop. She could see the top of Echo Apartments rising into the cloudless sky as the buildings in that direction gained height.

"Rachel, don't go back to Jay's apartment."

She stopped herself from grunting a protest as the memory of Jay's last unexpected visitor flashed into her mind. What if the man came back looking for him? "Okay, Dad, but then what? We live in the same building now."

"I know, but your mom should be home from the hospital any minute. Go to her."

Rachel continued her paused steps, setting a brisk pace that would tell onlookers she was on a mission, hiding the murky fear that threatened to drown her already heavy heart. What was going on? Why was her life falling apart? What would she do with Jay?

Rachel crossed the street and stepped onto the curb a block before Echo apartments, heart thumping, the building just in view. She still held her cell phone and glanced down at the screen. There were no new messages. She hoped the silence from her mom meant she was doing okay.

Rose's tendency towards forced positivity sometimes worried Rachel. Was her mother withholding from them? That was the mystery and always had been. She had watched Rose break upon the rocks of other people's problems as her weaknesses stopped her from protecting herself. Rachel didn't want to be like that ever.

Traffic increased as Rachel neared the apartment building. She felt the wind of a car's passing as it sped by, ignoring the speed signs that read 50 kilometres an hour zone.

"What a jerk."

The sudden comment startled her, and Rachel jumped back as a man she recognized but couldn't quite place pushed off from the wall of a small convenience store. Where had he come from? She was sure he hadn't been there a moment ago. She'd only just turned to watch the car speed by before turning back.

"I guess they can't read signs," she offered, preparing to quicken her pace.

The man chuckled as he stepped closer. It was then she noticed another man, younger, taller, with a black bandana tied around his neck, walking across the street towards her.

"Excuse me," she said as she tried to step past, her eyes touching the apartment building with longing.

"What's the rush, Rachel?" The use of her name snapped her eyes back to the first man, and she looked him up and down while clutching the load of her belongings tighter to her chest.

"Whatever it is you're after, I'm not interested. I need to get home. My mother will be arriving soon."

"Have you heard from Jay today, Rachel?"

He used her name again.

Why was he using her name?

"Jay? No, I haven't."

"That's too bad. I hear he's been busy. How about I take you to see him? He would probably appreciate the support."

"What?" Rachel almost dropped her cell phone as her palms became wet. "Please, leave me alone."

The second man was closing in as she stepped backwards. What was his name? She knew she'd seen him before ... In the stairwell. That was it. He'd asked about Jay that day and told her to tell him he was running out of time.

Rachel was afraid to turn her back to the man as his lips curled up in an ugly smile, but she couldn't run backwards. Where had all the other pedestrians gone? Hadn't a couple been ahead of her a few moments ago? The cars still whizzed by. If he touched her, her only chance was to scream and hope someone stopped to help.

"Come on, Rachel, we're wasting time." A hard glint had come into the man's eyes.

She needed to turn, to run.

Before she could, someone wrapped an arm around her waist from behind. Whoever it was shifted the weight of her backpack to the side as she was pulled against a hard body.

She froze as she felt a large, strong hand holding her waist and a face popped up over her shoulder, almost brushing her cheek.

"Wow! Gentleman, what's going on here?"

Rachel stifled a shriek as she felt soft curls poking out from the owner's cap brush over her skin. He gently pulled her body tighter against his own.

"Sorry for startling you, babe. You okay?" At first, she didn't recognize who it was holding her, but he held out a hand that clutched the rim of a skateboard, his strong wrist keeping it flush against his arm, and she knew exactly who he was: Glen Edwards.

A wave of relief and dizziness washed over her, and she relaxed into his lanky body. He must have realized she recognized him as he felt her relax because he pulled her uncomfortably tight to himself and dared to lean in, kissing her cheek. "You wouldn't be muscling in on another man's territory, would you? Now, I don't blame you for trying. She is quite a catch. But I think I heard her say she needs to get home. Come on, Rachel."

She'd never realized how strong Glen was. He looked so skinny with his skater clothes hanging off his sharp angles. He almost picked her right off her feet with one arm as he took a step ahead.

"She's not yours. She's Jay's girl," the first man said while holding out a hand in warning to the second man, now only a few feet away, a foot resting on the curb. The second man stopped moving forward but planted his feet shoulder length apart, arms over chest.

"Used to be Jay's girl." Rachel caught Glen's cocky smile as he flashed it past her. "Now, I didn't catch your name?" As he waited for an answer, Glen whispered in her ear. "Call the police."

As Rachel fumbled with the power button on the side of her phone, the first man snarled and waved his friend off. He looked them both up and down before retreating past them.

Glen didn't let Rachel turn to see where they went but immediately started propelling her down the sidewalk towards Echo Apartments. He didn't let go of her until they reached the parking lot, and as they walked, she listened to his mumbled prayer of thanks.

She couldn't help but add her own amen.

"My house first." It wasn't a question, but a statement, and Rachel didn't mind one bit. "Are you okay?"

"No," she admitted, adrenaline racing through her arms and legs so fast, they felt like they were vibrating.

"Got your phone on? You should still make that call. Holy cripe, I can't believe they tried to pick you up in the middle of the day. What's going on, Rachel?"

Glen soon had her sitting on his parents' couch giving an officer a report of what had just happened by phone.

"Yes, I'm safe now. I'm at my friend's apartment," she assured the officer.

Glen handed her a cup of water as she nodded while listening to the reply. They would send someone by to patrol the area. The officer recorded her name and address as well as her parents' and Glen's, so she could be found when they arrived.

After she hung up, Glen asked, "How long do they think it will be before someone comes?"

"He couldn't say. I don't think the people who answer the phones are even in town. I think they run the calls from the city department."

"Eh ..." Glen's nose scrunched in frustration.

He sat in an overstuffed recliner, his elbows propped on his knees as he leaned forward towards her.

"I'm sorry. I lied, and I kissed you." His face contorted in several expressions that showed first his shock and then what might have been fear.

"I forgive you, and thank you."

Rachel smiled as the fun glint came back into Glen's eyes. He visibly relaxed and pushed up from his elbows to his hands. "Don't tell my mom the details. She is going to kill me if she knows I kissed you without permission."

They both laughed. It sounded nervous at first then lightened.

"So, what's going on with Jay?"

Rachel squirmed under Glen's direct look. "I don't know. But Dad called right after I walked out of school. Jay was arrested while at work."

"Well, that's ... not good."

Rachel had never seen Glen Edwards lost for words before. He was always a bubble of energy, a rush of words. But here he was, his mouth hanging open in shock, and the flow of intelligible speech stopped.

"He's going to be mad when he finds out I claimed his girl," he said after regaining a bit of composure.

"Well, he can stuff it if he is." Rachel felt bubbles popping in her stomach as she spoke. "He should be grateful you were there to step in." Her heart hadn't stopped racing since the strange man's first wicked grin, and now, even as she sat in safety with a friend, it hammered out a song of fear. Silence stretched across the couch for a moment as Rachel tried to fill her lungs with full breaths but managed only a few half gulps. "Excuse me—" She stood and let her eyes dart around the small room. "Glen, I need the washroom."

"Just down the hall, first door on the right."

Rachel bumped her way down the hall, a sudden desperation gripping her mind. She thanked God for the clean lemony fresh room as she threw open the bathroom door and let it swing behind her. She raced for the sink and leaned over its basin, her heart threatening to crawl up her throat and fall into its cupped embrace. She shook and beads of sweat broke out on her temples as tears burst their dams to flow freely down her face. She hiccupped then groaned at a sudden spasm in her side. Her throat burned.

The sudden release of emotion was terrifying and freeing at the same time.

She heard Glen moving in the hallway then the *clink* of glass as he set her unfinished cup of water a few feet into the washroom before shutting the door for her, giving her privacy.

Coming Home

ROSE

SARAH PUSHED ROSE AND her rented wheelchair into the carpeted living room. The wheels slowed to a crawl as they hit the freshly vacuumed fibres.

Rose let out a tired gasp. "I know I sound like a recording on repeat, Sarah, but what time is it?"

"Just after three."

The rest of the apartment was silent, and the revelation of the home Rose had that first viewing was achingly absent.

"Rachel didn't make it over first."

"Doesn't look like it. But don't worry, she should be along soon. She's usually pretty punctual, just like her mom."

"Except for today."

It had been a long, boring wait for paperwork and final discussions with doctors and nurses before Sarah had been allowed to load Rose into the car and drive her home. Rose felt exhausted from doing nothing, her brain jumping around like a bunny coated in molasses. Agitation and exhaustion mixed. She hated the feeling. Was it from the new medications?

Could be. I need to keep an eye on that and write it down somewhere.

"Sarah, could you hand me my purse?" She dug through the medium sized faux leather bag and pulled out a notepad and pen. Her right hand trembled, but as her fingers gripped the pen to write, she smiled. What a gift it was just to be able to hold one again and scribble a few notes. She'd been told to document how she was feeling and any new emotions as well as physical ticks, no matter how small, over the next few weeks. The notes would be important for her appointment with the specialist in three weeks. Nearly a month of waiting ... She sighed, and that was after they labelled her file urgent. She'd been told she was lucky to get in that fast. Some people waited months before being seen.

She was grateful, but honestly, she didn't feel lucky. Luck would have been to find out the attack was nothing more than a pinched nerve that would go away in a matter of days or weeks while taking relaxants. Luck would have been not being diagnosed with MS. But still, it was a diagnosis, and now they could make plans.

Don't give in to despair, Rose. It will kill you. Arthur still needs you. The girls need you too.

But would she really be any help in the day to day anymore? Or was she doomed to become a burden to her already taxed husband? Would her daughters drift away as they lived their lives, leaving her alone to shrivel until God finally knocked and told her it was time to come home?

I said don't give in.

She shook the dark thoughts out of her mind as she focused on writing her notes and hoped they would be legible enough to read when the time came. These dark thoughts were also something she needed to note. Feeling overwhelmed with the weight of health and family issues was nothing new, but she'd been told in straight language by Doctor Ingrid that declining mental health was also a very real danger to those experiencing tough diagnoses. Grief was real, and it wasn't to be ignored. Rose wasn't sure why Ingrid had been so forward with her about it, but it might have something to do with Amy. Did she see traces of Amy's struggles within her own patient? Or just the evidence of a tired mother trying to help her daughter navigate teen years as well as added mental stress?

"Thank you, God, for a perceptive doctor." She would hold on to gratitude. Placing her mental foot down, she drew a line through her mind that she promised herself she'd never cross.

"Help me keep this promise," she added to her prayer as Sarah moved boxes out of the way to make a clear path to the kitchen.

A pile of broken down boxes in the middle of the room served as a sure sign people had been busy putting this part of her world to rights in her stead. But moving usually took longer than expected. After all, they were shifting years' worth of collected possessions. Some of them would never find a home without Rose herself to place them in just the right spot. They also had far less room to arrange so many memories.

"You okay?" Sarah asked as she came to finish wheeling her friend onto the smooth flooring in the kitchen.

"Yes. Just thinking of where to start with this clutter. Oh! And we should ask Rachel if everything is alright. She really should have been here, Sarah. She said she was coming."

"I'll text her, but, Rose, you don't really mean to start unpacking already? You just got home."

"I'm fine. Besides, everyone has done enough for our family already. It's time I did my part."

"Rose—"

"It won't hurt me to sit here and go through a few boxes." Rose swivelled the wheel of her chair towards the wall where a lopsided stack of hopeful items rested. "And if Rachel doesn't answer the text after fifteen minutes, we'll call."

"Alright, but, Rose, you should wait to do that."

"Sarah, I've sat in a hospital bed doing nothing for days."

"You weren't doing nothing, you were recovering."

Rose's heart had started to pound during the exchange, and she sighed as she looked at her friend's strained expression. "Just this one box, if you could help lift it onto my lap. Then, when the tea has steeped, I will stop."

"Alright ..." After lifting the smallest box she could find from the pile, Sarah sent the text before heating water and pouring it over tea bags she liberated from the jumble shoved under the table.

"I can put more of this stuff away if you tell me where you think you'd like it to go. It might be best to find places you can reach from that chair. Just in case."

Rose sized each cupboard door up. "Why don't we open them all and let me have a good look at what the others have done so far? Then, if we need to move anything around, we can do that. Make it easier, hopefully."

"But after tea." Sarah pushed the steaming cup towards her friend.

Rose smiled back. "Thank you." The box on her lap had swiftly been emptied, and several precious items now lined the tabletop. She looked up at the gap between top cupboards and the ceiling as packing paper crinkled in her grip.

They should wait for the younger girls to climb up there. Or perhaps some display shelves were in order. They could go on the opposite wall or even in the hall.

A short singsong chorus rang from Sarah's phone, and she thumbed it awake. "And there is Rachel ... She says she's at Glen Edwards'. And she'll be right over."

Rose set the now empty box on the ground before taking the first sip of tea. Her hands shook while adding in a few splashes of creamer, but as the warm liquid ran down her throat, the kinks in her shoulders loosened. Her newly movable hand luxuriated in warmth as she clutched the cup tightly. First, it would be Rachel, then Amy, then Arthur coming home. They would all be together again. She ached for this. Rachel might live with Jay, but just having her in the same room for a few hours would fill a hole whose bleeding edges were threatening to scab over and heal empty.

I just want my family together, God. Then we can work on being happy again.

Rachel's state shocked Rose when she walked into the kitchen. Her daughter's camisole sported wet spots on the front, and her red eyes told everyone those spots were from tears. She was holding her sweater in shivering hands like she hadn't even considered putting it on.

"What happened?" Sarah asked as she stood up from the table.

Glen Edwards was behind Rachel and ducked around her shoulder, placing a backpack beside the table before nodding a greeting and then bowing out before anyone could ask him to stay.

Rachel sat down next to Rose, her fingers picking at a small pill in the fabric she held. At first, she didn't speak, focusing on breathing above anything else. Sarah and Rose exchanged glances while they waited, both women too afraid to pop the fragile bubble of control Rachel held.

Finally, her daughter looked up and said, "Jay's been arrested."

Rose's mouth fell open.

"What?" Sarah asked from across the table, her voice high and breathy.

"Arrested. Dad called me on the walk home from school. Said he watched the whole thing but doesn't know exactly why yet. Then ..." Rachel coughed and shoved her sweater sleeves into her eyes. "Some guys tried to grab me. They would have if Glen hadn't intervened."

"Grab you?" Rose couldn't believe it.

"Like, they said they wanted to take me to Jay because he was in trouble and needed my support. I knew they were lying. Dad had already called."

Rachel's face was a picture of devastation. It wrung Rose's heart like a used rag.

"Oh ... my ... God," Sarah stammered.

Rose had no words, but she reached out to her daughter, her right arm shaking in its weakness and determination. Rachel slid into her mother's arms as Rose's heart ached to take her grown body into her lap like a toddler. Wheelchair wheels swivelled, and soon Rachel was kneeling on the floor with her face in her mother's lap. Rose cradled her daughter's shoulders as best she could while Sarah dashed behind them to lock the chair's wheels. Sarah then leaned down beside Rachel, and the three women became a pile of love and tears.

"The police are going to come to take down my story," Rachel said once the emotions had drained them all to silence.

"Between this and what happened to Amy ... What on earth is going on?" Sarah asked.

"Wait. What happened to Amy?" Rachel looked up, eyes round saucers brimming with worry.

Rose grew light headed as her heart pounded, and her breaths came in soft grief filled gasps as Sarah told Rachel what happened to Amy at Archie's Food Truck. "She said the man who approached her used a name like Ray? Or was it Roger? Do you know who it was that tried to grab you, Rachel?"

The wheel of thoughts whirled behind her daughter's eyes, and Rose did the best she could to steady her as Sarah scooted her chair closer while she rose from the floor.

"I think I met him in the stairwell once, going from the first floor up to our apartment. He used his name then, but ... I can't remember it."

Rose felt her lungs straining for breath as tingles sparked from her lower back to travel up her spine. She closed her eyes and groaned.

"Rose?"

"I'm so sorry, but I think I need to lie down."

Frustration mingled with Rose's shock as Sarah fussed over her and Rachel assisted with the transfer from the wheelchair to her bed. As Sarah tucked a blanket around Rose's lap, Rachel crawled in beside her mother, her head resting on her father's pillow, a tissue crushed in her hand and held to her nose.

"I'm sorry, Rachel. I suddenly felt so weak."

"Don't be, Mom. It's nothing to be sorry about."

"I'm going to start supper," Sarah said, her face pinched with worry. "Amy will be home soon. Any idea about Arthur?"

"Just after five is when he should walk in the door. At least I think so."

Sarah nodded and then backed out of the room, leaving the door ajar.

"Sometimes I wonder if that woman is an angel," Rose said as she leaned towards her daughter, the crush of their bodies against the mattress pulling them closer together.

Rachel smiled through her tears.

"You can't go back to Jay's apartment right now, Rachel. It's not safe."

"I know."

"You will stay with me tonight, won't you?"

"Will Dad ...?"

"He will insist. You just wait and see."

Resting in her own bed after so many days in the hospital was a blessing. Rose thanked God for the soft mattress and familiar furnishing that eased a bit of the tension in her body as she watched her grown daughter nap beside her. They both needed sleep, but despite exhaustion, no matter how long she lay there squeezing eyelids together, that sleep refused to come. Did her mind subconsciously think of the walls around her as still strange? Maybe it was the smell of freshly cleaned carpets and scrubbed surfaces. Someone had really been going out of their way for her, Rose realized. What a blessing. What a burden to know she was now someone else's responsibility.

She flexed the muscles in her legs and arms to quicken the push of blood through her veins. The returned feeling unfurled petals of gratitude in her heart. She felt hope, hope she would be back on her feet soon, hope that this attack on her nervous system would retreat and any further deterioration would again be slow and almost unnoticeable.

She was starting to come to terms with the reality that if Ingrid was right, there was no cure. The small woman had reminded her that they still didn't have a confirmed diagnosis and wouldn't until the appointment with the specialist, but Rose could tell her doctor's certainty was growing. Another bittersweet blessing. Rose's thoughts wandered back and forth through the experience of her hospital stay then ran back to the memories of searching for answers, reaching for the moment her health had first started to turn against her. She just couldn't remember exactly when. The creeping pain and numbness triggering tingles could have been slipping under her radar for years. Years ...

It doesn't matter much now, Rose, it's time to look ahead, not behind.

A soft brush against the bedroom door pulled Rose from her internal battle. Amy poked her head into the room, and immediately, Rose noticed the wrinkles across the bridge of her nose.

"What happened, Amy?" she asked.

"The usual. I've made a mess of things ... But I'm glad you're home."

"So am I. Come on in and tell me about it."

Together

ROSE

AMY'S STORY CAME OUT in hushed, fragmented sentences as she sat on the end of the bed. Her shame was plain, but so was her resignation, and the sight of it pained her mother.

"Even after a year of progress, Amy, a relapse is normal. You're still learning how to control your emotions while under stress. Don't let this set you back. It's just a bump in the road. When life smooths out again, you will find you are stronger than you think."

Amy's head bobbed, throwing her curls into her eyes. "Still, four more days. I guess I had to burn the bridges behind me." Anger bubbled to the surface of Amy's cheeks as a flush of red. "It's just—why did she have to ask? Why? Why can't people just leave well enough alone? I didn't volunteer the information *for a reason*. People are so stupid. I hate them." It had been a long time since Rose had heard that level of vehemence in Amy's voice, and it worried her.

"Breathe, Amy," she reminded her.

"I am breathing, Mom!"

The mattress shifted as Rachel moved and stretched, almost knocking her mother on the shoulder with a fist.

"What's wrong with sleeping beauty?" Amy asked, the skin over the bridge of her nose wrinkling.

"She's had a rough day too." Rose wasn't ready to tell Amy the rest of the family woes. She had enough stress for herself with the move and the change in schools. Still, it would all come out soon. "Can you go help Sarah in the kitchen? I feel so bad that she's in there all alone, serving us like a maid."

"Alright." The roll of eyes that accompanied Amy's exasperated compliance relieved Rose some. That sass. It was a sign her Amy would be okay.

It was less than five minutes before Amy was back in the room letting them know that a police man was at the door asking for Rachel Grill.

Rachel blinked and stretched again.

"What did you do, Rachel?" Amy asked, a nasty smile turning up the corners of her mouth.

"Nothing."

"Oh, really? Well, at least it's not for me this time."

"Huh?"

Amy disappeared before Rachel could ask her properly what she meant, and Rose sighed as her eldest daughter looked back at her.

"She had a police escort home after her own incident."

"Oh …" Questions lingered in Rachel's eyes, but she didn't ask them while straightening her camisole and hair. Then she left.

Rose could hear the officer's voice from the living room entryway as a rumble and hum. She lay quietly, the door open. The bustle from the kitchen had quieted as Sarah and Amy listened in as well.

"God," Rose prayed. "The last few months have been torture. When will our respite come? I was hoping this forced time out meant peace and healing for all of us … Don't you want that for my family? Is there something else we're supposed to do? I'm not sure we have the strength to take any more. We are breaking."

A crash from the kitchen punctuated her whispers and was followed immediately by the sound of Amy cursing. "No, God, we're already broken. How long do I have to wait until you start sticking us back together?"

Rose closed her eyes and let the weight of her head sink deeper into the pillows. She couldn't remember ever experiencing a quick answer from God. Sometimes she waited months just to be told no as He closed doors in her life. But sometimes, He answered yes in the most precious ways, and those times were worth waiting for. She would wait. She would listen and hope He would choose to answer sooner rather than later.

It was difficult waiting while everyone else made themselves busy. Rose had to call for help to make it to the washroom after Amy had brought her a glass of water. She rejected the wheelchair for the process, as time was short and her strength was coming back. Her right foot still refused to lift all the way, but she felt triumph as she shuffled to the toilet with the support of Sarah's arm.

Moving into the living room exhausted her again, but Rose refused to return to bed.

"I'll wait for Arthur here," she insisted and sent Amy in search of a lap blanket.

The minutes crept past the five o'clock hour, and they still waited. The food was ready, and Sarah prepared to take her leave.

"You don't want me to help you move anywhere before I go?" her friend asked.

"No. I'll eat right here if I need to. Arthur will be home soon."

They all said their goodbyes, and Amy waved to Sarah from the kitchen.

"Keep things warm until your dad gets here," Sarah instructed as she waved back. "I'll call tomorrow, Rose."

Soon after, Rose caught sight of Arthur as he walked up to the apartment through the back. He stopped just outside the sliding glass doors, his cell phone pressed to his ear, his head nodding while he squeezed his eyes shut. He reached out a hand and placed it on the glass. She could see the lines in his skin, his fingerprints bearing his weight as he leaned in for support. Why was he waiting? Who was he talking to?

Impatience fluttered in Rose's chest. She missed him. All it would take for the reunion would be to slide the glass out of the way. She longed for the strength to get up and greet him, to be the one to open the way and welcome him with a kiss like the old days when the girls were small.

But here she sat, trapped in a body that ignored her longings. So she tamped down her impatience, watching the creases around Arthur's eyes deepen as he looked up and through the glass at her. He smiled as his gaze met hers. He put away the phone, and the door slid open for him.

"How is it being home?" He kicked off his shoes and crossed the carpet to squat down in front of her, placing his hand on her knee.

"Home. Yes, it feels good to be at home. Still strange, but also good. Sarah cooked dinner for us before leaving. You should eat while it's hot and before it burns. *Amy* is keeping it warm."

"Amy …" A deep sigh escaped her husband. "I was just talking to Hope Is Here's principal. They think it best Amy doesn't return to class this week and only comes in for her counselling sessions."

"Seriously?" The vehemence of Amy's disgust vibrated the word around the still mostly bare walls of the living room. "Like, good grief, I didn't hurt anyone."

Arthur opened his mouth to give a retort, and Rose tensed in anticipation of an argument, her gut gurgling with worry. "She already told me what happened. Let's leave it there for now, Arthur." The strain in Rose's voice turned her husband's attention from Amy back to herself. "I'm surprised. Suspension seems pretty harsh, and her last day is so close already."

"I guess they feel all the changes are causing disruptions in her whole grade level." Arthur shook his head at his own words. "Carla is going to call you tomorrow morning, Amy."

Amy slunk back from the kitchen entryway to be replaced by Rachel, who'd been hiding around the corner since she heard her father's voice.

"Hey," was all she said as she hugged herself.

"Hey, kid," Arthur replied.

Rose watched her husband's eyes soften for the first time in months as he took in the sight of his eldest daughter. She moved her hand to cover his as it gently squeezed her knee again.

"It's bad, Rachel," Arthur said, his voice catching on her name.

"How bad?"

"They found drugs in a few of the boxes of goods delivered to Ham's this morning. The truck driver is missing, as well as one of our employees. He was regularly scheduled to work on Jay's team …"

What little colour had been in Rachel's face drained away.

"They think it was those boxes Jay was handing off when caught. What was he thinking?"

A fresh tear slid down Rachel's face.

Transitions

AMY

The Barton Community High School building sprawled across its campus grounds, leaving an imprint that was almost three times as big as the Hope is Here School. When it came into view, Amy's heart fluttered. Rachel walked beside her, an unenthusiastic guide to this new chapter in her sister's life.

"Is it even worth coming this late in the year? Like, why can't I just stay home until fall?"

Rachel shrugged at the question. "They don't want you running the streets and lighting the town on fire with scandal."

Amy scowled at her sister's words.

"Chill. Today is just to get you acquainted with the layout of the building and learn your schedule. You jump from class to class here, remember? It's not a small private school where they make teachers come to you." Rachel gave her a sideways smirk. "You're not scared, are you?"

"Scared?" Amy wrinkled her nose at the word and let a groan slowly ease out of her mouth. "More like annoyed."

"Come on, I'll show you where the office is."

They trekked up the cement walkway that met the steps to the main building. Accessibility ramps enclosed the school's front steps, and handrails bordered each side with one running right down the middle, sectioning everything into pathways. It all looked tidy to Amy until she was halfway up the cement blocks and turned to look back. From the new vantage point, she could see gaps in the hedges that bordered the school grounds to the left where people had pushed their way through instead of walking around on the sidewalks. A large flower bed to the right had freshly turned earth, ready for planting, but deep footprints at the sides showed where feet had trampled the work and dragged mud up onto the pavement.

Early classes had already started, and she saw few people walking the grounds. Amy wondered where the culprits of the footprints were. Maybe she could spot students with muddy shoes later on.

"Come on, Amy," Rachel called back from the large glass doors. "I don't have all day."

Amy trotted past her sister into the school's foyer where everything was grey except for a large blue and yellow mural of the school's hockey team logo on the wall. That wall ended and funnelled into the first of many halls to the left. A reception desk stood to the right, separated from the foyer by large glass panels. They looked like they'd been a later edition to the design.

"Is that blast glass? What do they think is gonna happen? A shooting?"

"Maybe."

"You're not serious."

"Why wouldn't I be?"

Amy didn't like the sound of that. "But this is Canada!"

"No, really?"

Again, Amy scowled.

Rachel rolled her eyes. "It's still a high school. I guess everyone thinks it's better to be prepared."

Her sister led her up to a window with an opening above the counter only a few inches high. The woman on the other side of the glass seemed preoccupied, and her eyes kept shifting from them to a computer screen as Rachel introduced her to Amy and asked for the schedule that should be waiting for her. "Is there a guide set up for my sister?"

"Peggy Lays," the woman replied while checking her watch. "She should be along shortly. She's usually a very punctual girl."

"Peggy Lays?" Amy asked after Rachel had accepted a clipboard and a pass for Amy to hang around her neck.

"Yeah, I don't know her personally. I think she's part of the debate team."

"Oh ..."

Debate team? She sounded uptight and not someone Amy would have chosen to spend time with. But, if she was volunteering to help new students, she couldn't be all that bad ... could she?

Rachel left her on a bench against the left wall, the glaring bright blue and yellow logo beating down on her from above. Amy couldn't tell what it was supposed to be and decided she didn't care. She only watched hockey when it had meant access to the popular boys at Hope Is Here School. She pulled her pink tuque farther down over her ears, causing her thick curls to stick out around the rim in a golden cloud. Where was this Peggy Lays? She was taking her sweet time.

A fresh wave of students entered the school, most of them looking like they belonged to a higher grade, and Amy made a game of guessing who she thought would land in the tier above hers, especially the guys. Few noted her. She followed them with her eyes as they walked down the hall and scrutinized the cut and shade of a tall black-haired boy as he rolled his shoulders before turning a corner.

"Don't even think about it. He's taken, and if she saw you ogling her man, she'd rip you to pieces." The voice was high and girly, and when Amy turned her head towards it, she blinked in surprise.

The newcomer stood with her arms crossed over a slight chest and a hip slanted to the side as she cocked her head at Amy. Slanted eyes and pale skin proclaimed her Asian heritage. The girl shook her head at Amy's lifted eyebrow, throwing back her long hair highlighted with bright pink extensions that peeked out from underneath glossy black strands.

"Pieces? She could try."

"She would succeed. But really, forget about them. They're all bad news." The girl's tone held no malice, just sad resignation as she glanced down the hall where the group had disappeared. She extended a hand to Amy and flashed her a bright smile. "Anyway, I'm Peggy Lays, and I'll be showing you around today."

Amy stood and shook the girl's hand, though not without a large lump of apprehension lodged in her throat. "Nice to meet you, Peggy. I'm Amy."

"Well, let's not doddle. We've got a lot of ground to cover. Where's your schedule, and what's your first class this morning?"

They found Amy's locker and copied the combination code carefully into her binder. "You can never be too careful," the girl assured her.

As they continued down the hall, Amy learned they shared an age as well as several classes, but tomorrow she would have to find her way alone. Barton High School felt huge. It was good to have someone with her, paying such close attention to details she wouldn't have thought to ask, someone who didn't know her past and held no judgment in her eyes as she rattled on about shared classes and the other students they passed in the halls.

It felt good but was hard for Amy to bite her tongue as the desire to halt Peggy and take charge of the conversation plagued her. She was used to being the one giving advice and throwing shots at others behind their backs. Not that Peggy was the sort to throw verbal darts at people to rack up points. No, quite the opposite. Amy got the feeling she was the kind of person who stuck to the facts as well as one who didn't care what other people thought of her.

Must be nice to be so free.

Peggy's chatter slowed as they entered Mr. Shift's math class.

It was still early afternoon when the pair made their way back to the school's entrance. Peggy had several classes left, but Amy's day was done. Tomorrow would be her first full schedule, and as she sat down on the bench she'd started her morning at, she willed her head to stop spinning.

"You going to be okay from here?" Peggy asked.

"Of course. Why wouldn't I be?"

"You look like you might be in shock," Peggy answered. A few lines near the bridge of her nose underlined her worry.

Amy raised an eyebrow. "Why are you so concerned?"

"First days, or even weeks—no, actually, first years at a new school aren't usually easy. I know."

Amy felt the truth simmering under her new acquaintance's words, but didn't pry into the why behind them.

Peggy waved a hand and turned to leave. "I'll meet you here tomorrow morning. I'm looking forward to getting to know you better, Amy."

Amy slumped back against the grey wall as Peggy disappeared.

She's looking forward to getting to know me better? Really?

Amy wasn't sure how she felt about the revelation. Did *she* want to get to know Peggy? She sat motionless, thinking about her day—the unfamiliar faces, the classes, Peggy's incessant narration.

The girl was cute but also quirky and almost too kind. Amy didn't understand why the girl would be drawn to her, and that made her feel uncomfortable. She'd cultivated her friend group carefully while attending Hope is Here School, and Peggy would never have made the cut. But this public school was definitely different from a small Christian one.

She could reinvent herself here. What kind of person did she want to be?

As Amy rose to leave, she noticed the same group of teens she'd watched that morning making their way back up the hall. A blond girl hung off the black haired boy's arm. Both looked Amy up and down as they passed.

Amy couldn't help it. She flinched. The girl smirked.

Red crept into Amy's vision, and she sat up straighter, curving her lips in a wicked smile to rival the one she'd received. The girl pulled on her partner's arm, and they stopped.

What's she doing?

The group was a healthy mix of genders and skin tones. The tallest boy stood near the back sporting a spiked stalk of purple hair and a cross earring that flashed at her as it swayed below his lobe. He gave her a coy look and pressed his shoulder forward as he whispered down to a shorter boy whose darker skin complimented his salmon coloured polo shirt and light jacket. The shorter one smiled back at his friend, and Amy blinked at the affection she noted in his eyes.

None of the other girls in the group matched the blond's height, but all of them could have been sixteen or twenty-five with the way they dressed. Not a single one was afraid of low-cut tops, and one sported a skirt so short, it almost made Amy blush.

Her gut gurgled with apprehension, and she tried to blink away the red tendrils that floated into the picture before her, but without success.

The air sparked with electricity, and Amy knew this was going to be an important first meeting.

The tall blond stepped forward and lazily extended a hand toward her. "Hello, I'm Clara."

Amy hesitated before reaching out and accepting the girl's limp grip with a firm handshake. "Amy," was all she offered as she let her eyes wander from Clara's face right down to her toes.

The girl bristled, pulling her hand away as Amy smiled at her reaction. *She's not nearly as confident as she wants people to believe.* Amy noticed how the girl tugged on the hem of her shirt as it rested just above her jeans, letting the smallest flash of skin escape.

"You're new, right?" The tall black haired boy stood directly behind his woman.

"How perceptive of you," Amy answered, her eyes never leaving Clara's.

The girl took a step backwards as the tall boy reached out a hand and placed it on her shoulder. He extended a hand past his girl and offered it to Amy, a lopsided grin turning his features boyish by revealing a single dimpled cheek. "I'm Brad. Welcome to Barton High."

Amy accepted the handshake. As the boy's grip matched her own, she wondered if she'd misidentified the group leader.

Brad pulled Clara against his chest, his arm wrapping the girl from shoulder to shoulder. "What do you think, baby?" he asked against her ear.

"I don't know ..." She was again looking Amy up and down.

And there it is.

Clara was nothing but a pet—maybe one of the top popular kids in school, but still a pet. The sight of Brad nuzzling the girl's hair with his cheek turned her stomach, and she snapped her hand back from the boy's grip.

"Well, maybe not," Brad purred.

The strange noise coming from a nearly full grown man lifted the hairs across Amy's arms.

Amy swam in confusion as Brad released Clara and they both turned away. Clara looked back over her shoulder and offered a coy wave, her fingers fluttering as if she were flirting with a new toy.

Bad news? I think Peggy was right ...

Amy pulled her bag onto her shoulders as she watched the rest of the group turn to follow their leaders like an obedient pack. But the tall purple-haired one kept looking back at her. Disappointment flashed in his eyes. His hand was resting on his shorter friend's shoulder, and they whispered as they walked. Amy gave him a quizzical look, silently asking, "What?"

He paused his steps, and Amy gave him the same up and down she'd laid on Clara as he walked back towards her.

He fished a small card from a pocket as he let a sly grin light up his eyes again. The strands of his purple hair must have been glued in place, as they didn't shift at all when he cocked his head to the side while handing her the card. "We're having a get-together later this week. You should come."

Amy snorted as she looked down at the precisely cut rectangle of paper. The name "Josh Pluck" was printed in sweeping script above a phone number and email address.

"Aren't you with him?" Amy asked, motioning towards the shorter boy, who stood by the entrance waiting for his friend.

"I am." Josh flashed his teeth in an even wider grin. "But I'm also with whoever I want to be," he winked and spun on his heels, leaving her standing open-mouthed as he strolled back to drape an arm over his friend's shoulders.

Amy's mind spun as she worked backwards through the encounter in her memory. Definitely bad news, all of them. But still ... that grin Josh had given her was devilish, and for some reason, she felt a pull towards it. He'd come back after all the others had dismissed her. He could be her doorway to the in crowd.

Be careful, Amy, Barton High is not Hope Is Here. The people and rules they live by are clearly very different.

Still, the encounter had been intriguing. She needed to learn how to navigate this new world, and fast, and Josh looked like he might be a better teacher than Peggy Lays.

Break Up

RACHEL

RACHEL RESTED A HAND against the bathroom wall, ignoring the slightly sticky feel, willing the chill of the cement blocks to shock her senses and wake her up. Exhaustion had bogged her steps the last week as sleep had rebelled against her mind, sweeping in thoughts of what if and why. She shook her head to clear it. Her morning classes were over, and her attempt to freshen up before a shift at the laundromat was failing terribly.

Her heart quaked at the thought of walking to work, and the idea of calling a cab flashed into her mind. She shook that away as well, unable to stomach the cost.

"At least I don't have to worry about Amy for the rest of the day." She glanced up at the mirror above the long triple-sink washstand. Her skin had an unusual pallid sheen, and she winced at the circles under her eyes.

What's wrong with me?

She shifted over as a younger girl with long black hair sporting pink under-colour stepped up to the middle sink beside her.

"You okay?" the girl asked softly.

"Yeah. You're Peggy, right? How is showing my sister around this morning?"

"Your sister? Amy? She's your sister?" A bright smile stretched across the girl's face when Rachel nodded yes. "It's going well. I'm just heading back to her before we trek over to the gym."

"Is she treating you alright?" Rachel couldn't help the disbelief that crawled through her chest as the girl nodded, sending her bangs swishing across her forehead.

"Why wouldn't she be treating me right? She seems like a nice person, so far anyway. Maybe a little conceited, but it's normal to talk one's self up in a new place. I'd probably try to do the same thing if I had to change schools."

"She's been known for her sharp tongue. But hey, maybe this change has helped soften it. Just don't let her walk all over you."

Peggy giggled, and her slanted eyes squinted almost closed as she flashed another smile. "I'll be careful." She turned away and stepped for the door only to turn back and lower her voice. "You sure you're okay? You look a bit, well, wan."

"I'm sure. Please don't tell Amy I said those things. She isn't all that bad, really. Or at least she's gotten a lot better."

Peggy mimed zipping her lips as she walked from the room, leaving Rachel alone with her reflection.

Rachel turned back to the mirror.

Am I really okay?

A bead of sweat formed between Rachel's shoulder blades as the sun beat down on the nylon fabric of her jacket. She contemplated taking it off, but as larger buildings and shops with doors open directly to the sidewalk crowded up to her, their shadows did as well. Soon the light sheen of perspiration had her shivering, and she rolled her shoulders and blew into her cupped hands. Her breath did little to warm them.

How can it feel ten degrees colder in the shade?

She couldn't help but be uneasy walking in the shadows. Was someone watching her? Dread stalked her on each walk she'd taken since the day of the attempted abduction. She never felt completely safe anymore.

She quickened her pace when she saw the sidewalk shadows shrink back to let the sun reach in. Only a few other people were roaming around, looking into shop windows and crossing the streets. Monday had everyone moving as if half asleep.

A man tried to step around Rachel as she paused in the warm sunbeams before plunging back into the shadows under a taller building. The man bumped her shoulder as he blinked lazily across the street. For a second her breath caught, but he didn't offer the typical Canadian, "I'm sorry," as he walked past.

Rachel swallowed her own apology. Did he even see her? It didn't appear so as he stepped off the curb and the jolt of the unexpected step down woke him from whatever he'd been daydreaming about.

At least I'm not the only one who's tired today.

Being tired and jumpy at the same time was a horrible mix. She stepped up to the next line of shadows and took a deep breath as she plunged back under them, pushing herself until the space around the sidewalk abruptly opened for a small parking lot and the single-story clinic building.

Rachel had passed this building on the way to school dozens of times. She'd visited on and off while a child for routine checkups and the occasional ear infection or other heath issues, but it had been a year or so since she'd paid it any mind. Just before the entrance, an announcement board held posters of all kinds. She wandered closer to read the brightly coloured words.

Sign up for birthing classes today!

Is your child up to date on their vaccinations? Make an appointment now.

Ask about the grief support group inside.

Mental health is important too. Don't wait to seek help.

As Rachel paused before the large windows and board, she let her eyes wonder over the words, heart pounding. Was something here for her? Something that would cut the fear, the questions, the doubts?

A buzzing from her pocket made her jump.

Rachel looked up through the wide front windows at the reception desk and the busy woman behind the counter as she lifted her cell phone to her ear. She flashed an apologetic smile at the woman as their eyes met for a brief moment then stepped further away from the glass.

"Hello?"

She stood in the bright sunshine before the squat building, but her skin dimpled with an unshakable chill.

"Hey, Rachel. It's me."

Her gut flipped at the sound of Jay's voice.

The urge to hang up on him was strong, and her thumb hovered close to the small red cancel button. But it stopped as her heart crawled in to her throat.

"Hi," was all Rachel could get out as she turned her shoulders away from the clinic to face the buildings across the street. She shivered.

"Hi ... You okay?"

"I'm fine ... You?"

"Hanging in there."

Rachel wasn't even sure if Jay was out of jail. They hadn't had contact since that horrible day a week ago. She tried to ask, but the words stuck in her throat.

"Rachel? I got—they are kicking us out of the apartment. I got a letter. Called Mom about it yesterday. She's going to come clear out my stuff this week. Have ... have you talked to her?"

"No." Rachel hunched her shoulders against the chill flowing through her veins. Her fingers trembled, and her feet shuffled nervously against the pavement. She wanted to hang up. She wanted to forget everything that had happened in the last few weeks. She wanted ... She didn't know what she wanted, but it wasn't this.

"I'm sorry. They're holding me until my first hearing. The courts are backed up. It's supposed to happen tomorrow. The lawyer said there is a chance we'll be bumped to the next day since we are schedule for the late afternoon." Jay coughed, and Rachel heard him thumping on some kind of surface as he continued. "He told me I've got to sit in the holding room at the courthouse until they get to our case. I could be sitting there all day and not even get in. Disgusting."

"Yeah, disgusting. I can't believe they are treating a ..." She stopped herself as tears burned her eyes. Anger mixed with grief, and the weight of it crushed her shoulders. "Why are you there and not here with me, Jay? What were you thinking?"

"Where are you staying?" As he avoided her question, the drumming sound from his side of the call intensified.

"With my parents."

"Okay ... Okay, Mom will let you know what day she is cleaning the apartment out. You got your stuff?"

"No, I haven't been back up." For a moment, nothing but Jay's nervous drumming connected them. "They tried to grab me, Jay, last week, on that day. They tried to grab me."

"They what?" His voice wavered. "What do you mean? Who tried to do what?"

"That man. The one who asked about you a few weeks ago. He was in the stairwell with a group."

"Shit ..."

"What did you do, Jay?"

"Nothing."

"That's a lie."

"You've got to stay away from him, Rachel. You hear me?"

"No kidding ..." She was full on crying now. Her throat ached with disgust and hurt. "What did you do?"

"You can't go back to the apartment. Oh, God, why'd your parents have to move in downstairs? Okay ... Okay, Mom will have to clear it all out alone. Maybe send your mom or dad up to grab your stuff. You can't go back there."

"I still live in the same apartment building, Jay."

"I know. But maybe they'll forget about you if they don't see you around that door anymore. They'll know I lost the apartment. You just got to stay away from them, Rachel."

"I can't be with you anymore, Jay." She felt her chest constrict as she said the words, but say them she did. They came out firmly, her voice only breaking as she said his name.

The call dropped.

She hadn't known she was going to say it before she did, but once the words bubbled up, she couldn't stop them from spilling from her mouth. In that moment, it was the right thing to do. Still, the sound of the dropped call followed by silence, the flash of her phone screen showing a red call symbol, and the stalled timer broke her.

Every part of her shook as she held in sobs. She bent, pulling the hem of her shirt out from under her jacket and running it over her face.

Thank God the street was mostly empty.

She stood still, cradling herself as she shivered with emotion.

"Oh, Jay."

They were supposed to be together forever. Every plan she'd made for the future had put him front and centre, but ... She could still see the amused flash from that man's eyes as he'd reached for her on the street. The ache in her heart burned. It hadn't been Jay there to keep her safe. Then a wave of guilt slammed in, and all she could think of was how selfish she was being. Jay was in jail. It had been a week since she'd seen him. He hadn't had a chance to explain what had really happened, but ... he'd just lied to her. He was keeping secrets.

"Excuse me, miss, are you alright?" A gentle touch on her shoulder made Rachel turn to find the clinic receptionist standing behind her and holding out a brown paper bag, its top rolled down and crumpled beneath her fingers. "All appointments this morning are booked, but ... is there something you need?" Worry creased the woman's pale face as she looked around the quiet street. "I know this is very forward of me, it's just, you looked so ... lost."

"No. But ... yes. I guess ... I don't know." Rachel said, her voice strained as she pulled it past her sore vocal cords.

"Are you in trouble? Do you need me to call someone?"

"No! Oh, no ... I'm fine. I'm sorry. I–I was just distracted by the flyers on the bulletin board.

"Do you need to make an appointment?"

Rachel thought for a moment before shaking her head.

"Are you sure?" The receptionist looked concerned as Rachel took a step away, but she didn't make to stop her, only held out the bag. "Here, I thought ... Just in case you needed something."

"Thank you." As she received the gift Rachel couldn't imagine what was inside it, but the woman's kindness was touching. Still, she took another step down the sidewalk, a broken heart mixing with embarrassment as she felt her face flush.

"Are you sure you don't want an appointment?" the woman asked before Rachel could fully turn away.

"No, thank you," Rachel answered, her heart hammering.

What have I done?

Exactly what I needed to.

He's all alone in a jail cell, and you just broke his heart.

They tried to pick me up and who knows what else. Sell me? Use me themselves?

I did the right thing.

She had, and she knew it even though she wished it didn't have to be so. Her feet sped down the sidewalk as she crushed the brown paper bag to her chest. More paper crumpled within it, but she also felt several small boxes and other bits through the bag's thin sides.

It had been a long time since she'd prayed, really prayed. But as she turned down the street that would lead her to work, she let her spirit pour out in silent anger.

God, I still love him. But it's not safe to be with him right now. Are you punishing us? This isn't fair.

Coming Summer

ARTHUR

ARTHUR FELT THE LONGING for summer and its warmth in his bones as the chill of early mornings nipped at him each workday. His coworkers talked of planned outings and vacations with family. Shoppers commented on the warming weather and what they'd do when children were home from school for the summer in a few short weeks. The crews working in the back of the grocery store whispered of time off and denied vacation days. Arthur hadn't asked for any. With only a part-time position, every shift he picked up was a blessing to his wallet.

Still, the turmoil of the last two months had begun to settle, and it felt like a weight was lifting from his chest. He sat in the break room at Ham's Grocers, eating a cold-cut sandwich and thinking of his whole family under one roof again. They were all together. The knowledge felt good.

"How did you get a yes?" a young woman not much older than Rachel asked from across the room.

"I put my request in back in February," someone else replied.

"February? Seriously? How can you plan that far ahead?"

"You get used to it."

Arthur looked around the room as he wiped his mouth on a napkin. It was Wednesday, and he saw the mid-week strain on most faces.

"I made it a point to ask for later in the summer when I knew most people will be wanting to pick up some kind of schedule again as school gets closer."

"Perks of not having kids, right?"

The conversation bounced from person to person as Arthur finished his meal. Ben, his usual partner for stocking shelves and moving goods, wasn't working today, and he felt alone in the waves of questions. None were for him. He paused as he stowed his leftovers back into his lunch bag. What would his family do this summer?

Amy had settled into her new high school much better than Arthur had expected. He had even heard talk of friends. Rachel was again under his roof, and no one had heard from Jay in weeks. Arthur wasn't sure if he was still behind bars or released on bail while he waded through his legal mess.

Arthur sighed in relief at the knowledge that Rachel was safe from the boy's bad influence. At least for now. She hadn't even gone up to his apartment to collect her things but had let Arthur receive them from Jay's mother.

The woman had been sad and broken when they'd met on the third floor of Echo Apartments. Both had inquired about the other's health, but beyond a few words about Rose and well wishes for her continued recovery, there had been no further conversation. How long had it been since the woman attended Hope is Here Church? Arthur couldn't remember when he'd stopped seeing her sitting beside her son during services. He guessed Jay had only been coming for Rachel in the end. The thought irked him, but he shrugged it away as he headed out the break room door.

It had been about a month and a half since Arthur started his new position, and the faces of coworkers, though he hadn't learned all their names, were becoming familiar. He nodded as a pair passed him in the hall before descending to the stockrooms. He'd decided he didn't mind his job but also wondered if that meant his heart was healing. Was it time to look towards the future? Financially, his family would need something more, and soon. Could it be time to look for a new church? Was he ready? Would any want him after what had happened? Was that what *he* really wanted? He wasn't sure, and that fact alone sent fresh doubt through his mind.

It might be easier to stay the course I am on right now and just see what happens.

But he didn't know if that was something he truly wanted. Could he live with walking away from ministry forever?

He grabbed his work vest and hard hat from the hooks at the bottom of the staircase, ready for an afternoon of moving stock around, the questions in his heart forming a lump in his throat. What did he want to do? What should he do?

Lucas stood in the middle of the stockroom floor directing a new trainee through the same test with a forklift he'd given Arthur when he was first hired.

Good, we need more people.

They were always short staffed, yet Fred, the owner, was reluctant to give most of his workers a full forty-hour week. Arthur wondered if he'd choose to stay if offered a full-time position. Could he be content here, shifting goods from the back to the front, offloading delivery trucks, rubbing shoulders with people who were so different from him? So different ... He slipped one arm into his vest and went in search of the small crew they'd assigned him to that morning.

As he drew near, he heard shuffling feet and laughter. Skirting the end of the last aisle, lined with shelves stacked high with goods, revealed two younger men crouching low and circling each other. One swiped with a hand and knocked the other's hard hat. A booming laugh sounded, and Arthur glanced over to see Hammond, the man who had fought with Jay the day he was arrested. He held his sides while laughing and watched his two younger men charge each other.

"I guess we all took a break?" Arthur commented as he slid his hands into pants pockets.

"Just blowing off some steam after a disagreement," Hammond replied. "Okay, both of you take off for lunch. I expect you back in exactly thirty minutes."

Before the pair broke their circling, one took a final swat and landed a slap on the other's cheek. The sound of skin connecting with skin made Arthur flinch, and he raised an eyebrow as the victim swore at his friend.

"Sorry!" As the first man bolted up the aisle, he threw back a wicked grin before disappearing the way Arthur had just come.

"That hurt," the other man said, rubbing the side of his face as his eyes flashed. His steps were slower, but soon he turned the corner as well, and all Arthur could hear was shuffling feet and muttering as he moved down the line of goods.

Hammond shrugged at Arthur's raised brows. "He'll shake it off, and if he doesn't, I'll ask Lucas to split them up for a week."

"What was the argument about?"

"Eh ... Nothing important. Come on. Let's grab those paper goods and get them up front before Martha—or worse—Penelope comes back here looking for them."

Arthur grinned at the thought of Hammond being called out by either of the female managers.

Together they found the plastic-wrapped pallet piled high with toilet paper and paper towel packages. Arthur pulled it out from the back with a pallet jack onto the storefront floor, parking it at the end of the appropriate aisle before removing a section of the plastic holding the goods secure.

The sounds of a busy grocery store fluctuated all around, but the men worked in silence. Arthur stepped right up onto the bottom shelf, and Hammond handed him packages to line the back of the space. A single pallet filled half the large shelf, and soon they headed back for a second load.

"I can't believe the entire shelf cleared in a day," Hammond commented. He pulled the jack back through the stockroom doors while Arthur lent a hand to hold them open for him.

"I think it was only half filled yesterday," said Arthur as he let the door swing closed and watched it flap for a second on its double spring hinges.

Hammond shook his head. "Lucas is letting things slide, then. It should always be full after a restock."

"I was on the forklift yesterday, but the stock teams were short again."

Hammond didn't reply, and silence stretched between the two men. They'd lost too many employees over the last few weeks, and neither had anything to say about it.

"Jay out of jail yet?" Hammond's work shoes squeaked against the floor.

Arthur almost tripped at the question. His heart skipped a beat as he blinked for a second at Hammond, brain void of any reply.

"He's dating your daughter, right?" Hammond added as they pulled up to a second pallet of paper goods.

"*Was* dating my daughter," Arthur answered.

Hammond manoeuvred the pallet jack prongs into place, and the second load of goods was ready to go. But instead of pulling the load on, he leaned against the handle, giving Arthur a direct look. "You got that much control over her?"

"Control? No! She's pretty upset with him." Arthur hadn't broached the subject with Rachel. The memory of her trembling lips and clenched fists as she fought for self-control sent a chill up his spine. "Jay will never be welcome in my home again. Never."

"Why?" someone from behind them asked.

"Good," Hammond cut in before Arthur could answer his coworker's question. "He doesn't deserve her if he's going to pull shit like he did." Hammond rubbed a jaw with a trembling hand, and Arthur wondered if he was remembering a well placed punch.

"Jay wasn't so bad," the second coworker said as he joined the first. He glared at their supervisor even as he stood beside him.

"Come on, you plant it here with Arthur and finish this. I got a new job for you." Hammond's finger jabbed towards the first man, and then his thumb pointed farther down the line of shelves.

The first guy shrugged as he turned and walked away but threw back a wink at Arthur and the other man who sent dagger-like looks back at him.

"You know Jay?" the second man asked Arthur as they both turned back towards the pallet jack. If it wasn't balanced right, they'd lose the whole load across the store floor.

"Yes, unfortunately."

"Oh," the man let his gaze drift away as Arthur grabbed the jack's handle and started pulling the pallet out into the aisle. "I didn't think he was that bad of a guy. Sure, he made a stupid call, but don't we all sometimes?"

Arthur didn't answer the man as his load swivelled, and he double-checked the way to the storefront doors was clear.

"I thought pastors were supposed to forgive people. You know, Jesus Christ and all that stuff?" The man muttered the comment as he walked past Arthur's shoulders to lead the way towards the double doors, but they forced him to pause.

"Forgiveness doesn't mean you give someone permission to put the pastor's daughter's safety at risk," Arthur said back.

His coworker swore at the floor and looked back up. "Sorry."

Arthur pulled the car visor down to shield his vision from the sun's evening stab. It was getting late. He should have been home over an hour ago, but his shift never gave him enough time to get everything done. An extra hour on his timecard would mean a higher number on his paycheck. Why wouldn't Fred shift a few more of his men to full time? Arthur couldn't understand. He shook his head at himself and turned the key in the ignition.

I thought pastors were supposed to forgive people.

His coworker's comment had stuck in Arthur's mind like a pin. The pain wouldn't ease no matter how many times he lifted a hand to rub at his temple. Pastors were supposed to be forgiving, but they were only human, and he found he had no forgiveness left to give. Not to a boy who stole his daughter away and led her heart down a wicked path. Not for a boy who put her safety at risk and broke the law for a bit of extra cash. Not for a church that forced him out ... His blood heated just thinking about it.

I thought pastors were supposed to forgive people.

He turned on the radio to drown out his thoughts then immediately switched it off, irritated by the untimely voices of a Christian talk show. Why couldn't they just play music?

He drummed his fingers on the steering wheel at a red light and followed hot on the heels of the car in front of him when green replaced red. He heard a honk and backed off a bit.

"Calm down, Arthur. You don't want to upset Rose when you get home."

They'd been able to return the rented wheelchair, and Rose was now able to move around with a walker. In the house, she often left it by the door and used a cane on her weak side, placing the other hand on a wall or piece of furniture if she needed extra support. He was so proud of her. He recognized her strength as he watched her struggle. The sight often tore at his heart just as it warmed with pride. She'd always been so strong, so quietly capable. He'd let her down in so many ways over the last few months. He didn't want to bring this cloud of anger home, but so often it seemed to stick to him like tar once stirred up.

I remind myself of Amy.

The streets flew by, and as he turned into the shadows of a side street, he found his heart reaching out for something beyond himself, something it hadn't done in weeks.

God, things have finally started to settle in my family. Please help me tamp down this anger.

Prayers used to slip from his lips with no effort, but his mind now often resisted even this silent plea. It wasn't just other people he held anger for.

Don't let me be a source of stress that might stall Rose's progress. Help me find a measure of control and peace.

It felt like his thoughts fell to the car floor to roll around his feet as he pressed the brake pedal and pulled the car into the last turn before entering the Echo Apartment's lot. But once they were out, rolling around under him, he felt a release in the muscles of his shoulders and chest.

A flicker of his old confidence flared, then shrank, then flared again.

I'll just ask Fred directly about more hours, and if his answer is a flat no, I'll know it's time to move on.

He should have done it the first week after the church board's vote. Actually, someone from the conference's office should have reached out to *him*. He wouldn't find a new church if he didn't try. A flash of fear, like a hidden flame leaping out of a banked fireplace, flared in his heart, giving him pause.

Am I ready?

Arthur had never experienced such a blow to his confidence before. All questions of character, of method, of doctrine he'd been able to face head on. What was the difference this time? *Was it control?*

I've only ever been questioned about myself.

Maybe that was part of it. The balance of control within a leadership position was always something to juggle, but he had been doing that for years, and he had good people on his team. He thought of Rachel, of Amy, of Rose.

Everything has changed so fast.

We are no longer the picture perfect family we once were.

Or had that all been an illusion to begin with? Arthur realized that was a distinct possibility. He loved his girls, but with the demand of ministry, he hadn't been the most hands-on father around. Rose had been their guard against the world and judging eyes.

Yes. That was part of it. But still, the rationale didn't seem complete.

Is it really important to figure this out? Maybe I should just ...

No, Arthur knew he'd never be able to just let the matter drop. The questions would eat him from the inside out if he didn't try to understand what was going on in his own heart, and what had happened, what had led to this fall. He hadn't seen it coming, but there had been strain in his position as Lead Pastor at Hope Is Here for the last few years.

The answer teased his brain as he stepped from the car and double-checked it was locked before starting a slow plod down the sidewalk and around the building to the apartment's back door, then fled as he mentally reached for it.

What do I want?

What do we need?

What ... What does God want from me now?

A Long Drive

ROSE

ROSE SOAKED IN THE shades of green as the shapes of blurred trees rushed past. A warm travel mug rested in the cup holder between the car's front seats. Rachel had opted for a large reusable water bottle that didn't fit in the holders, so she'd slid it between her thighs for easy access as she drove. Rose's gut fluttered as they bounced over potholes in the weathered highway, but the pain in her limbs had eased over the past few weeks to resemble pinpricks that only troubled her when she overexerted herself. Her steps were still not as steady as they should be, so they'd folded and stowed away her walker in the car's trunk, laying her cane across the back seat.

She alternated between looking out the window at the passing scenery, searching for glimpses of wildlife, and glancing over at her daughter as the morning light lit her face. Rachel looked tired, and it worried Rose, but her daughter's hands gripped the steering wheel firmly as she turned it to follow a bend in the highway.

"Don't be nervous, Mom," Rachel said as she flashed a smile. "You've been recovering so well. I'm sure this means the specialist can help you get your symptoms under control."

Under control ... because MS had no cure.

"Thank you, Rachel. I'm sure you're right."

"But?"

Rachel had always been a perceptive girl, a powerful blend of quiet and confident intelligence that Rose knew would take her far in life if only she made the right decisions now.

Rachel's word hung in the air between them, and Rose sighed. *"But life has been so uncertain these last few months, it's hard to hold on to positivity."*

Rachel nodded, her eyes trained on the road ahead as they coasted down a hill and the tree line broke to reveal the shimmering green-blue of a small lake. The highway hugged its edge, and both women smiled as they stole glances at its wild beauty.

"I don't mind missing church on a Sunday morning for this one bit," Rose said as a house came into view, red vinyl siding highlighting it against the landscape. A long dock that jutted out into the lake was visible at the back of the house for just a second before it all whizzed by and the tree line veiled the water from view. "I wonder what it would be like to live all the way out here."

"Quiet, that's for sure," Rachel said.

Rose shifted in her seat, stretching out a leg when sharp pins and needles pricked her heel. It eased as she moved.

"You okay, Mom?"

"We might need to stop for a stretch soon," Rose admitted.

They'd set out early because Rose required many stops along the long, lonely highway.

"Sure thing. I'll keep an eye out for the next rest stop."

Rose nodded and looked back out the passenger side window. The four-and-a-half-hour drive down this road was a lonely one, but as she pulled in a breath, a bubble of gratitude lifted from her gut to envelop her heart. It might be lonely in places, but with her daughter beside her, she felt gentle peace. Spring was waking all around them. It was beautiful.

Gravel crunched under the car's wheels as Rachel pulled them over and then down a tree covered lane. The rest stop would have been perfectly concealed but for the small bright blue signs with a picnic bench depicted in white that first gave a heads up and then pointed out the turn to travellers. Rose wondered what it would be like to drive this road in winter when the highway was snow covered and these stops were closed to the public. She prayed they wouldn't have to make many trips after the winter landed.

The morning air still held a crisp chill when she opened the passenger door and slowly pulled her legs over to rest her feet on the gravel drive. Rachel raced to her side and helped support her mother as she stood, grabbing the cane for her mother but refusing to let a supportive hand drop from Rose's arm as she planted the tip on the ground.

"Did you need the bathroom?" Rachel asked.

"I will, but not yet. Let's walk first and brave the outhouses last."

Rachel nodded, and Rose led them in a slow stroll around and down as the pavement turned amid the trees.

They'd parked close to two tan buildings, their sides and floors cement blocks, their doors painted a forest green, one for men, one for women, and no one enjoyed using them. Still, the townships kept them well stocked, and they were usually clean. Rose didn't know who maintained the highway rest stops, but she was grateful for whomever they were. A few wooden picnic benches were dotted beneath the trees, whose full canopies sheltered the whole area. The surrounding ground was grass covered and the trees, a mix of evergreen and deciduous varieties Rose didn't know the names of. They were all beautiful, weather needled or sporting buds and baby leaves. They looked so fresh in the morning sun.

"I'm glad these stops are open again. It will not be an easy trip once they close for winter," Rachel said.

"We have months before then. Let's not think about it until we have to. And maybe we won't have to be travelling as often."

"This isn't the stop with the little lake, is it, Mom?" Rachel asked as she looked around the area.

"No, I think that one is farther down the highway."

Rachel looked disappointed.

"I really like that one too. Here, let me sit for a moment." Rose pointed to the closest picnic table, and they shuffled over the grass to reach its grey, weathered bench.

The wood creaked under their weight. Rose ran her hand along the grain of the bench board's end. The weathering left it a mosaic of grey and black shared with speckles of green. A clump of silver edged moss clung to a crack in the wood.

"I wonder if this thing is going to last the entire season," Rachel said as she leaned back against the tabletop and the bench groaned under her.

Rose didn't offer a guess as she watched a squirrel jump between branches in the canopy overhead. Soon a *chit–chit–chit* echoed off the tee trunks.

"He's cursing at us." Rachel grinned.

Rose snorted as she crossed her arms over her chest. "What makes you think it's cursing? Maybe he's welcoming us."

"You can't mistake that tone, Mom. Can't you just hear him saying 'What do you want, stupid human?'"

"Oh, come now, he wouldn't be calling us stupid."

"Are you sure? I wonder sometimes what creatures really think of us, rumbling into their spaces with loud metal contraptions, bulldozing their homes to make way for our roads and cities."

"Hm, yes. I guess they might call us worse things than stupid. But humans deserve a habitat as well." Rose pulled a tissue from her pocket and dabbed a drip from her nose that had formed in the chill air. "Just a minute longer, then a walk back to the bathrooms."

Rachel nodded and kicked at the turf before them with the heel of her shoe. "Mom ..." she started, but Rose heard her swallow as she paused. "Mom ... There's something I need to tell you. But it's hard." Her daughter coughed, and Rose shifted on the bench to face her better.

"Is it about Jay?" Rose asked softly. "You know, Rachel, I love you no matter what choice you make with him."

"Thanks, Mom. It is, and it also isn't."

Rose waited, watching the pensive look on her daughter's face.

"I ... I can't live with you, Dad, and Amy much longer."

The wind escaped Rose's lungs. She didn't mean for it to come out in a gasp, but it did, and she watched Rachel's brows draw together as she wrapped her arms around herself.

"I know you want me with you, but ..."

Rose had known this would happen. But she had hoped she would have had more time. "Why?" She couldn't help the desperation she felt from slipping into her voice.

Rachel shook her head. "It's hard to explain."

Rose waited. She slid her arms around Rachel's shoulders and pulled her close. The weight of another body pressing on her plus the tilt of her head as she laid a cheek on Rachel's hair sent tingles along her legs and arms, but she ignored them.

Rachel's shoulder shuddered, and Rose squeezed her as hard as she could.

"I need ... to find where I am safe." Her daughter's words were little more than a whisper.

Tears burned Rose's eyes. "But Rachel, you are safe with us! With me ..."

Rachel turned in her arms and tried to look her mother in the eyes. Rose's heart burned for her daughter as Rachel's eyes dropped to the ground. She felt her trembling. Rose trembled along with her.

"Mom. I don't feel safe. Not with you, not at the apartment, not in this town."

"But—" Rose paused as her daughter shook her head.

"No, Mom."

Could she blame her? As Rose bit her lip to hold her silence, she knew she couldn't. Not after everything that had happened. "Where will you go, and when?"

"I don't know." The smile Rachel gave her mom was sad. She looked so frail in the early morning light with the shadows of leaves drifting across her face.

How had Rose not noticed the strain of pulled skin at her daughter's temples as she squinted out into a world that had betrayed her? Her pale skin enunciated the dark moons under her eyes.

"Oh, Rachel."

"It will be okay, Mom."

But would it? How could it when her daughter was planning to leave again?

They stopped at several more scenic spots before the highway widened to two lanes. The first sign that they were coming into the city proper was a stoplight that funnelled vehicles of all kinds onto Main Street.

The noon hour had passed, so they stopped for lunch before pressing into the heart of the city, searching for the hotel they'd booked for the night. Rose's appointments were early the next morning.

"I can't believe how much traffic there is on a Sunday." Rachel leaned forward over the steering wheel, looking both ways before sitting back, straightening and then pulling a left onto a side street.

Rose clutched at the stationary section of the door handle as her rump slid across the seat. "I know. I never liked driving in the city on any day. Thank you for bringing me."

"Do you see the hotel sign? I was sure this was the street. I might have to pull over and check. Map's on my phone."

As both women shifted to look around, uncertainty hung in the air.

"It's okay Rachel, we have all afternoon to find the hotel."

"I tried to memorize the route so I didn't have to have you holding my phone the whole way." Her daughter was clearly upset. Her emotions had been all over the place since their chat at the rest stop. "I didn't think it would be this hard," Rachel muttered.

"There it is!" Rose pointed as a large blue sign with red letters came into view.

It took Rachel a few minutes to manoeuvre over into the turn lane and then wander through the maze of streets and parking lots that crisscrossed before finding the entrance to the hotel parking lot. "This layout is a mess ..."

Both women sighed deeply when they pulled under the entrance canopy.

"Just let me check us in," Rose said.

"Do you need help to get out?"

"No, no. I will bring my cane and take it easy on my way inside. Why don't you go ahead to park so we're not blocking the entrance? Grab the bags and come find me. I'm sure it'll take several minutes to check in."

It felt good to wobble her own way into the building. Weariness crawled up her legs, and her arms felt heavy, but it wasn't unbearable. It was almost welcome as it reminded Rose that she was strong enough to travel and walk on her own again, even if a cane was necessary. Tomorrow she would use the walker as it gave her a place to sit and rest wherever she was. The large city hospitals always meant a lot of walking.

It took only a matter of minutes for the black woman behind the counter to wave her over and begin the check-in process. The woman had a perfect smile that Rose admired and a warm accent that rolled vowels as she spoke.

Rachel joined her as the woman handed Rose the key cards to their room and gave general directions to the elevators.

When they reached the third floor room, Rachel pushed the heavy door open for her mother and held it wide.

"Not bad," she cooed as Rose stepped into the room ahead of her. "Were you expecting a sofa?"

"No, I wasn't. But now that I see how high those beds are, it's a pleasant surprise. I'll call your dad and let him know we made it safely. Why don't you see what kind of coffee there is and how much?" Rose waved at a coffee maker set out on a table that also sported a phone and binder. She assumed the book held advertisements and phone numbers any traveller might need as well as the hotel layout.

"You won't ... Please don't tell him," Rachel said as their bags dropped to the floor with a sudden *thunk*.

Rose looked back at Rachel, noted her flushed cheeks, and nodded. "Of course not."

"And when we get home?"

"Rachel."

"I know. He has to be told. But ..."

Was that fear Rose glimpsed as her daughter's eyebrows pulled together and her shoulders slumped?

"It can wait for now, but not forever."

Rachel nodded.

Rose paused, not knowing what to say next.

Rose paused, not knowing what to say next.

Who, Where, When

ARTHUR

ARTHUR INSISTED THAT AMY attend Barton Community Church with him on Sunday morning. She complained, but in the end, they'd arrived on time, and Arthur enjoyed the service. Amy filled the drive home with eye rolls and groans from the passenger's seat.

"Can't I just go out already?"

"Go out where?" Arthur had looked over at her, irked at the placement of her seat belt. He bit back a sharp comment about what might happen in a crash if she didn't wear it properly. She wouldn't listen anyway, and the sharp words wouldn't help their relationship.

"I don't know! We never know exactly. We like to walk around town."

"Just walk around town? We don't have money for you to waste on eating out on a whim. Lunch at home first."

"Come on, Dad!"

"Your friends can wait for you."

"Fine."

Arthur sighed as his daughter crossed her arms and glowered out the car's window.

As Arthur glanced every few minutes over at Amy's rigid posture, he missed his wife acutely. Her absence left a gaping hole in his parenting skills. She was so good at asking the right questions and was much better at keeping her cool.

"Who are you going to be with?" Arthur asked after a few minutes of letting Amy stew in her disappointment.

"Just some new friends from school. You don't know them."

"And their names are?" Arthur pressed before they pulled into their apartment's allocated parking spot.

"Oh, God," Amy groaned and rolled her eyes as she looked up at the car ceiling. "Josh, Rohan, Clara," she rattled off more names and opened the passenger side door on the last one. "Peggy, maybe. I have to ask her if she wants to come along. She doesn't always want to—Rachel knows Peggy. Why don't you ask her if you're so worried about who I'm with?"

Arthur flinched at Rachel's name. "And how am I supposed to do that when she's with your mom?"

"I wish *I* was with Mom."

Arthur and Rachel had avoided each other since she'd joined them in the new apartment. Arthur didn't want to rock the small, fragile boat their family seemed to finally be floating in, so he'd kept his mouth shut and let Rose do the reassuring and negotiating.

Amy had grudgingly shifted her belongings to half of her bedroom, making room for a secondhand bed for her sister. Arthur knew his youngest wasn't happy about having to share the small space, but so far the girls hadn't fought openly about it. Amy seemed resigned to the fact her sister needed to live with them again and had no other place for her to sleep except the couch, and that wasn't practical for the long term. Who wanted to have to tiptoe around a sleeping body every morning?

Long term ... Arthur felt the weight of that idea was both a comfort and a burden. One more mouth to feed. One more body to take up space in their two-bedroom apartment. Yet Rachel was his daughter, and she was home.

That was what he had wanted, right?

He rolled up the sleeves of his button-down shirt as he and Amy walked to the sliding door entrance of their apartment. The sun was warm, and the sound of kids playing on the sidewalks and in their own small backyard cubbies echoed off the brick building's sides.

"Okay," he relented. "But lunch first."

Amy snickered as he pulled on an apron and proceeded to make them each a grilled cheese sandwich. "What a lovely Sunday lunch, Dad. So gourmet," she scoffed.

He gave her a dark look but otherwise ignored her insults as he set the food on the table. It wasn't long before Amy had scarfed hers down and raced for the door again.

He called to her before the glass could slide closed, "Don't stay out late. School tomorrow!"

Arthur pinched the bridge of his nose and then shook his head at his daughter's empty chair. He couldn't stop her if he had wanted to, so better to just let it go. She really had been improving over the last year, and regardless of how difficult her attitudes often were, he was proud of her for that. A sigh of resignation released her from his thoughts.

He now faced a Sunday afternoon alone. It was a rare occurrence, and after eating and cleaning any remnants of his meal away, he looked around the small kitchen, lost. His fingers itched, and his heart pounded despite standing still. The quiet threatened to smother him, so he walked to the living room and turned on the TV.

The noise filled the lonely space, and he relaxed on the couch, face towards the screen but eyes unseeing. Sundays had always been one of the busiest days of the week, brimming with people, services, more people, prayers, visits, and special events like weddings or funerals thrown in on top of it all. Memories both sweet and bitter flooded in, and he blinked them away, his heart still racing.

"You're not made for sitting and doing nothing, Arthur." But what was there to do?

Several boxes still stood stacked in corners around the apartment, and he set to pulling one down and sorting through it.

"Office stuff." The sight of his desk lamp and stationery pulled something into his chest. He rubbed at the uncomfortable sensation. "I've no place for it now."

It should have been taken to the storage unit they'd rented for all the bits and pieces the apartment couldn't hold. He set the box aside and pulled another one open.

"More junk," he sighed and reached for a third.

As the stack of boxes shifted from the corner to the couch, each now open and their contents exposed to the daylight, resolve solidified where the ache had been a moment before. Maybe his desk things could fit in this corner if the rest of the mess wasn't there.

A message from Rose came in as he carried boxes from the apartment out to the car, and he smiled, knowing her trip was going well. Boxes soon filled the trunk as well as the back seat, and the satisfaction Arthur felt as he closed doors on the mess spread a grin across his face.

It took over an hour to drive to the storage unit, unload, extricate the pieces of his dismantled office desk, unbury his office chair, and load each of them into the car. He slid the desk top and legs across the back seat, praying the door would close, and winced when he heard a light *crunch* as the heavy door latched.

It would have to do.

As he pulled the furniture from the back of the car and hauled it into the apartment's living room, he told himself he could live with the crack and slightly crumpled edge. For the rest of the afternoon, he turned the living room corner into a cramped version of his former home office. As his gut grumbled with hunger again, he sat down, the wheels of his office chair protesting against the carpet.

Every man needed a home office. He had bills to pay and legal papers to keep track of. His fingers itched again as he remembered the sermons he'd penned at this desk, week after week, year after year.

While lost in thought, his cell phone chimed, a text from Amy telling him she wasn't coming home for dinner but not to worry. Friends had the food taken care of, so she wouldn't be spending his non-existent money.

Fine, he sent back to her, unable to think of an argument to get her home before dinner. *Just remember school.*

Amy sent no reply. He tamped down irritation and told himself it was fine.

His project finished, he rolled his unhappy office chair back against the wall and switched to the couch, flipping on the TV again but choosing a hockey game to play in the background as he scrolled the internet browser on his cell phone. He needed some kind of mat so his chair could roll despite the living room carpet. He forgot dinner as he searched for something in his price range, only to give up and wonder if Rose would allow him to swap the office chair for one from the dining room on a permanent basis. Maybe if he told her the wheels would help her roll around the kitchen and not worry about having to stand up and walk with the cane, she'd allow it.

He was kidding himself, and he knew it. Nevertheless, it was a thought.

Disgusted with the price of office supplies and decor, he left his phone on the couch and scrounged leftovers from the fridge.

No need to cook something fresh if no one else is home to enjoy it.

The evening dragged on, and he dozed on the couch, attempted to write a resume letter with his qualifications as a minister, then ended up back on the couch again, flipping through channels. His mind was numb but swirling with images he refused to take the time to puzzle out.

He glanced at his watch as nine p.m. approached and sent off a reminder text to Amy to make sure she was home before ten. The solitude was almost driving him insane, so he called it a night and went to bed.

"Amy!" Arthur called as he knocked on her bedroom door the next morning. "Amy, it's time to get up for school. I have to leave for work soon. If you don't get up now, you'll be walking, not to mention late!"

A second knock got him no answer, and he bristled at his daughter's irresponsibility. He hated invading her privacy, but ... He opened the door to gloom and two empty beds.

Arthur frowned at the crumpled bedclothes on Amy's side and the smoothed quilt of Rachel's. Walking into the room, he pressed a hand to his youngest daughter's bed. It was cold. Of course it was. It would only have been warm if she'd just been there. He told himself there was no need to be upset. Maybe she'd gotten up early to walk to school.

Arthur checked his phone, sending off a message to Rose to ask how her night had gone and another to ask Amy where on Earth she was.

A glance into the closet made him pause. Amy's school bag was still hanging in the back, just visible behind spring jackets.

Cold cubes of dread dropped onto his shoulders as he pressed the call button on his cell, no longer content with unanswered texts. Amy didn't pick up.

He called Rose instead. "Amy didn't come home last night."

"Wh–what? Arthur? What do you mean?" His wife sounded half asleep, and he forced himself to breathe, willing his heart to stop the incessant hammering. Amy wouldn't have forgotten her backpack.

"She's not in the apartment. When I found her room empty, I thought she'd headed out early, but her backpack is still in the closet."

"Where was she yesterday?" Rose now sounded fully awake, and Arthur heard her call to Rachel to get up as well.

"She went to church with me but headed out with friends after lunch. Rose, I don't know any of these new kids she's been spending time with. I don't know who to ask, who to call. She ... she hasn't mentioned a boy since moving schools, has she?"

"Rachel, do you know who Amy has been hanging out with at school?" Rose asked, and Rachel's response sounded over the call in low tones Arthur couldn't make out.

"She says Peggy Lays was the one showing her around her first week. And, no, she hasn't mentioned a boyfriend. Start there. Call the high school, Arthur, and leave your number for Peggy. They can't give out her contact information, but she should be allowed to call you. Look for Amy's school ID. It should be in her bag or in her room."

"Okay." Arthur pulled Amy's backpack from the closet as Rose continued.

"Did you have a fight about something? Was she angry with you for any reason?"

"No. We were fine. Maybe a bit annoyed about having to have lunch with me instead of her friends, but—I got the ID."

"She's never not come home before, Arthur."

"I know. I'll find her."

He would start at the school and wouldn't leave it up to some teenager to call him. He'd go there himself and find these kids she'd been hanging out with.

"Don't get upset, Arthur. You know how anger sets her on the defensive."

"I'll do my best. I promise."

"We'll come home as soon as my appointments are over. We won't stop."

"I'll find her, Rose, then I'll call you."

Arthur's heart fluttered as he said goodbye to his wife and headed for the door, his daughter's ID clutched tightly in hand. Why hadn't she come home?

Runaway

ARTHUR

THE WOMAN BEHIND THE glass jumped when Arthur rapped on the partition before him.

"I'm looking for my daughter." He held up Amy's school ID as the woman stood.

Her face flushed. "Sir! You can't just barge into the school like this. Who are you? Who buzzed you in? The bell for the first period won't ring for another fifteen minutes."

Arthur had followed a couple of early arrivals into the school, not thinking twice about how it might look to the staff, not caring what it might look like to the authorities later on. This was too important.

"She didn't come home last night, and I need to know if her friends have seen her." Arthur's words tumbled from his mouth in a rush as the woman nodded.

She then disappeared into a room beyond what the glass partition allowed him to see and reappeared a moment later, a strained smile on her face. "Just a moment. The school principal will be right with you."

Arthur paced before the glass as he ran his fingers through his hair. The strands on his forehead were damp. He wiped the moisture off onto his shirt and grimaced.

"How much longer?" he asked the receptionist, who'd followed him with her eyes ever since she sat down, trying to look busy behind a computer screen.

"Any minute, sir. Mornings are busy."

Amy might be a difficult child, but she wasn't stupid. She'd never stayed out all night before. The thought of what might have happened turned Arthur's stomach, and he longed to have Rose at his side.

You'll find her, Arthur. She probably went home with a friend and forgot to tell you. He hoped that the small rational part of his brain was correct and not the maddening thoughts of her taking off with some guy she'd met, or getting into an accident, or something worse. Was she scared of getting into trouble, and that was why she wasn't responding to his texts or calls? Yes, yes, that had to be what was going on. If it wasn't?

"Sir?" A second woman dressed in a smart tan pantsuit appeared at the receptionist's side of the glass. "I'm the school principal. How can I help you?" Her slender face was void of emotion, and her words beat a monotonous rhythm.

"My daughter," he held up her ID again. "Amy Grill didn't come home last night."

"I see." The woman nodded. But Arthur wondered if she really did.

"I need to speak to her friends. I need to know if they've seen her this morning. She isn't answering her phone."

"Maybe the battery died."

"I need to speak to her friends."

"Alright, sir." The woman held up her hands in what Arthur assumed she thought was a calming gesture, but the subtle lift in the woman's eyebrows stole away the intended sincerity.

"Amy Grill is a newer student, transferred from Hope Is Here," the receptionist sitting off to the side offered. She shifted so the principal could glance at the screen with her.

"I see your daughter is receiving regular counselling sessions from Hope Is Here's in-house counsellor while she waits for an opening elsewhere."

"Yes, that's correct."

"Has she run away before? Does she have a history of skipping school? Is she suicidal?" The questions pummelled Arthur like punches to the face. He stepped back from the partition and their brute force.

"Suicidal? What?" The words bubbled out of Arthur as panic rose in his chest. His thoughts flashed to the horrible day over a year ago when he'd raced to a church member's side after receiving an urgent phone call. Paul's wife, Debora, had taken her own life, and in the weeks after, her choice had left deep wounds in the whole congregation's hearts. "She would never."

"Are you sure, sir?" The principal leaned forward and placed a hand on the partition. Her face changed from blank to sombre, and Arthur had to swallow a scream of frustration.

"I need to speak to her friends. Now."

"Let's call the police in. We have them on speed dial," the receptionist offered, glancing from Arthur to her boss.

"I can't just let you talk to any kid, sir. It's against privacy and safety rules. But give me some names, and I'll ask if they're willing to come to you themselves. Do we need parental consent for this?" the woman asked her secretary as she grabbed a paper and pen then looked up at Arthur expectantly. The secretary shook her head and mouthed an "I'm not sure" while she held an office phone to her ear.

"No worries, we'll figure it out."

Arthur wracked his brain for the names he'd asked for before Amy had charged out of the house yesterday. What had they been?

"There was a Josh." He scratched his head as his brows knit together. "Peggy Lays? Yes, that was the last name she gave me. There were a handful of others, but … I can't remember."

"We know Peggy well. I'll call her teacher and ask if she's willing to speak to you when she arrives. Please. Take a seat while you wait." The principal pointed to a bench along the wall opposite the office. A garish mascot stuck out from the grey painted cement like a pimple on a teen's nose.

Sit and wait? How could he sit at a time like this? But he took a deep breath and forced himself back from the receptionist's glass cocoon. He needed to stay calm. If the police were coming, he would need to be rational, to give a statement.

The police? A bead of sweat rolled down Arthur's temple with the realization that the situation needed law enforcement involved. He perched on the edge of the bench, determined to calm himself but failing miserably as more beads of moisture joined the first on his forehead and his hands trembled as he clenched his fists.

Amy, where are you?

The bell rang, and the slow trickle of people entering the school turned into a wave of bodies pushing through the entrance and down the halls towards classrooms. Some students eyed him suspiciously while most ignored the strange man whose eyes couldn't help but dart over the crowd, searching for people he had no way of identifying.

The wave of kids brought a wave of sound and behind that, waves of smells. Perfumes, cologne, and blatant body odour slapped him in the face. It had been a long time since Arthur was in a high school. The bright mix of people shocked him. Barton had always been a small community with its population a mix of Caucasian and Indigenous peoples. Only in the last few years had new cultures and skin tones begun to call the small Canadian town home. Arthur hadn't realized how many new faces their community had welcomed.

The congregation at Hope Is Here hadn't changed in generations. When was the last time a fresh face not born into the church had greeted him from the pews as he preached? Arthur's heart sank as he looked around and realized how out of touch with his community he'd become. Why hadn't he realized before this? Even as he rubbed shoulders with different people at Ham's Grocer, he hadn't fully woken to his ignorance. But this place? It was a bucket of cold reality in his face.

Arthur fidgeted as the uncomfortable thoughts raced through his mind, mixing with images of his time spent comforting Paul last year as they all grieved for Debora, but he stood as he caught sight of a police officer through the school's glass doors.

As he did, he bumped into a short girl who had just stepped up to him.

"Excuse me, I'm sorry," he said, sparing her only a glance.

But she waited, and from the corner of his eye, he saw her fold her arms over her chest. Had she said something, and he'd missed it?

"I'm sorry. Did you ask me something?" Arthur glanced at the girl with pink hair strands peeking out from the dark, straight waterfall that fell over and past her shoulders.

"I said I'm Peggy Lays. The receptionist told me you're Amy's dad."

"Peggy?" The name pulled Arthur's full attention. "Have you seen Amy this morning? She didn't come home last night. Were you with her yesterday? She mentioned your name. Who are the other kids she was with? I need to speak to them."

As he spoke, Arthur watched Peggy's brows draw together, her lips pinch tight, but then her eyes slid off him and towards something over his shoulder.

She nodded and said, "Let's see what he wants first. Good morning, sir!"

The officer and Arthur both turned towards her.

"Good morning," the officer said, grasping his belt with both hands despite his generous gut that bubbled over the leather's edges, straining his uniform buttons

Peggy turned to Arthur, an unspoken question written all over her face.

"I'm Officer Thomas. The sweet ladies at reception told me you're the reason I'm here so bright and early on a Monday morning," the officer explained as he turned away from Peggy towards Arthur. "They said they had a distressed parent on their hands and a potential runaway situation."

"My daughter, Amy, didn't come home last night. I just need to talk to her friends and see if anyone knows where she is."

The officer's eyes lost the twinkle they'd held a moment before, turning serious as he pulled a notepad and pen from his left chest pocket. "And you are, sir? And the full name of the missing girl, please."

Arthur relayed the information and then fell silent as Peggy piped up with her own name and the fact that she'd seen Amy yesterday but had refused to go along with her and a group of others after they'd lunched at Archie's Food Truck.

"I know Mike the owner well," the officer said, nodding and scribbling notes as Peggy talked. "And who are these other kids?"

"Josh, Rohan, Brad, and Clara. There were a few others." She rattled off more names before the officer held up a finger for her to pause.

"These first few have last names?"

"Oh, sorry! I'm not sure how to spell Rohan's last name. It starts with a 'p'. We can ask the office, though. But other than that, it's Josh Martins, Brad Black, and Clara Fauster. Josh is tall and has purple hair. Amy's been hanging out with him a lot. Him and Rohan, that is."

"Is he her boyfriend?"

"No, Josh and Rohan are a couple. Or at least they are supposed to be. Sometimes it's hard to tell with Josh."

"Oh?" the officer asked, raising both eyebrows.

When Peggy didn't continue, Arthur swallowed the burning that crawled from his gut up his esophagus. "And–and she hangs out with these two guys a lot?" he asked.

Peggy looked Arthur up and down, her arms tightening over her chest. "Yes. I warned her the whole group was no good on day one. But Amy likes to do her own thing."

"Can you elaborate on that?" the officer asked.

Peggy let her arms drop and swing behind her back to clasp them there as she looked at the floor. Arthur noticed the colour rise in her cheeks.

"I've got no proof, but everyone talks about the stuff they're into."

"Like?" the officer gently prodded, taking a step closer but not invading her personal space. His voice dropped as he reassured her. "It's really important you tell me everything, Peggy, just in case something is really wrong."

The girl shifted her gaze to Arthur, her eyes shimmering with emotion. "Parties and drugs and ... some people call Clara 'loose'. But Brad is pretty controlling. They're a couple too. I honestly couldn't believe it when Brad let Amy into their circle. When I asked her why she wanted to spend time with them, she said that Josh wasn't all that bad, and he wanted her there." The girl's hair bounced as Peggy shook her head at her own words. "She just wouldn't listen to me. But ... but she didn't seem like that bad of a person herself. I mean, you are a pastor, aren't you?" she said, looking at Arthur again.

"Yes ..." Arthur replied as the officer looked from Peggy to Arthur and back again.

A second man in uniform, sporting a full jacket zipped closed despite the warming spring weather, appeared at the first officer's elbow.

"We've got a missing girl on our hands," the first officer said, pulling at his belt and handing his notes over to his colleague.

"Amy Grill? Didn't we have to escort her home a few weeks ago?" the second officer asked. He was younger, his hair as black as Peggy's, but his pale skin was peppered with freckles.

Arthur pulled at the collar of his shirt. It felt like the air had thinned and every breath fed his lungs less and less.

"Yes, we did," Officer Thomas replied.

Arthur remembered he'd been at the hospital with Rose the evening Amy was escorted home. Now he wished he'd asked her more about what had happened. He wished he'd drilled Gary about what she had told him. His assuming things were fine when no one spoke to him needed to stop. He sighed. Gary had tried to tell him, but he'd been too distracted to find time to listen.

"If I remember correctly, her parents weren't at home." The first officer looked to Arthur for an explanation.

"Yes. That was the day we moved. Rose, my wife, experienced a health crisis, and we were in the hospital with her when Amy came home. I'm ... I'm afraid I didn't push my daughter for a full account of what happened." It felt right and good to admit this failing, but the ease of it and the weight the words held as they dropped out of his mouth shocked Arthur. He took a step back and reached for the bench's edge, drawing in a deep breath. "I'm sorry. I should have pressed her. I ... I'm feeling a bit winded."

The trickle of sweat had moved from his temple to his back, and the sensation of drops down his spine chilled him.

"No worries, sir. Take a deep breath," Officer Thomas said, a worried look creasing his brow.

The next few minutes were a wave of more questions. What time had Amy left the house yesterday? When was her last text message, and what did she say? Did he remember her mentioning anything in particular before she left, and did she say where she planned on going? What had she been wearing? Did he have a recent picture of her?

Arthur began to feel numb as his heart rate settled.

It's going to be okay, he told himself when the officer switched from him to Peggy, pressing her for information in the same way.

Around them, the halls had emptied and the wave of sounds dropped away as the first classes began.

"Thank you for your time, miss," the officer said. He scratched his head as he scanned his notepad then scribbled something on a new page, ripped it out, and handed it to her. "You call me if you see, hear, or remember anything that might help."

Peggy stuffed the paper into a pocket on her jeans and turned to leave. But before she took her first step, she looked back at Arthur. "Mr. Grill?"

"Yes?"

"I'll be praying for Amy and for you." With that, she walked away.

Her words stunned him. When was the last time he'd prayed for Amy himself? He couldn't remember.

Officer Thomas instructed Arthur to come down to the police station to file an official missing persons report. That would require him to take the day off work.

"Isn't that a bit overkill?" the second officer asked before they left. "I mean, she's probably just at a friend's house sleeping something off."

"She's a minor! You can never be too careful," the first officer snapped back, his eyes sharp. "Besides, I remember now why we had to bring her home those few weeks ago. I've got a bad feeling ..." He turned away from Arthur and fell silent for a moment before turning back to continue. "Mr. Grill. Call every person you can think of. Every person who knows her and get them on the lookout. Maybe she's walking the street, and as soon as someone sees her, we can put this to rest."

As the noon hour approached, Arthur sat back at home at the kitchen table looking at the paper he'd hurriedly scrawled names on in an attempt to brainstorm people he should call. His eyes burned from holding back tears. His hand shook as he held a pen poised above the paper, at a loss of who else to add. The ring of his cell phone was a welcome break from the oppressive silence the apartment had settled into as he sat, thinking, worrying. He cleared his throat before answering.

"Has she come home? Have you found her? Is she at least answering her phone?" Rose's strained voice almost broke Arthur's control, but he jammed a fist into his eye before any tears could fall. He didn't trust his hands to hold the phone steady, so he switched to speaker mode, setting the phone down with a *thunk* on the tabletop, fingers trembling. A cough cleared his airway before he could speak.

"No, nothing yet."

He'd sent Rose texts as he filled out paperwork at the police station. She'd replied with names for his call list.

"How ... how are you doing?" he asked, wishing he had a glass of water to soothe his aching throat but feeling too drained to walk to the cupboard and grab one.

"I'm doing. The appointment with the specialist was difficult but informative. We'll grab lunch in the car soon and start for home."

"I'm sorry, Rose."

"You didn't do anything wrong. This isn't your fault."

He hadn't realized how much he needed to hear those words from her. His shoulders shook as they released the tension he'd been holding in for hours. He recognized the inability to get up and sate his thirst as shame. For some reason, he felt he deserved to sit in discomfort.

"She's never done this before," he murmured, and Rose's soft reply of "I know" fell gently on his ears.

"We'll be home as soon as we can," she continued.

"Okay. I'm ... I'm going to drive around the neighbourhood and see if I can spot her. Maybe she's walking the back alleys or something, afraid to come home because of skipping school."

"Let me know if you find anything."

Arthur nodded to the phone screen before remembering to say, "Yes, of course I will."

After Rose said goodbye, Arthur stared at the darkened cell phone and the list of names beside it. He'd managed to call a few people before his mind had stalled in an attempt to extend the list. Now there were a few still left to cross off, and the next one in line was Gary Davids. It had been weeks since he'd spoken to his friend.

Instead of calling, Arthur typed out a text and sent it on its way. He crossed out Gary's name with a thick black line of pen and moved down to the next name on the list.

Never Give Up

ARTHUR

THE STARK CONTRAST BETWEEN Arthur's reality and the way the world continued along at its normal pace sent flickers of irritation, jealousy, and anger through Arthur's heart as he grasped the car's steering wheel. His hands felt like he was touching pins and needles. He gritted his teeth against the sensation and sped down the street, taking care to slow down at the sight of the skate park's open lot. He searched for Amy's head of light, bouncy curls.

How could anything be normal, anyone happy, when his existence continued to spiral out of control? It didn't matter how hard he held on to things, they all slipped away.

He circled through the neighbourhood before parking downtown and walking Main Street. He paused at every alleyway and gap between buildings and entered each store, making a beeline for the cash registers and flashing a picture of Amy from his phone at everyone who looked his way. They all shook their heads.

The sun dipped towards the buildings and cast shadows across the sidewalks, slowly creeping towards the streets. He looked everywhere, ignoring people's stares as he stopped in awkward places. He was so intent on checking every crevice of Main Street that he almost missed the buzzing from his pocket.

When he fished his cell phone out and thumped the screen, a text notification blinked at him.

Where are you? I'm coming to help look.

Main Street, he sent back, hesitating with his thumb over the send button before adding, *Thanks, Gary.*

He didn't have to wait long before his old friend pulled up, parking mere feet away from where Arthur stood.

"Have you gone into stores to ask if anyone's seen her yet?" Gary asked as he rolled down his window.

"Just this side so far. Checking the back alleys and walkways too … just in case she doesn't want to be found." Arthur's shoulders sagged as he looked at his friend in defeat.

The urgency in Gary's tone and expression were a far cry from the numb response the high school principal and secretary had given. "Send me her picture and the description you gave the police. I'll take the businesses from here on. Most of them know me." Even the younger police officer hadn't seemed concerned. But Gary? Gary was on Arthur's side.

Arthur nodded and sent the photo through a text.

"Arthur, we'll find her."

Those words stirred more emotion for Arthur than he was comfortable with. The fact that they came from Gary, a friend he had been avoiding for weeks, stung even as they tried to reassure him.

He retreated into numbness, giving his mind over to something that pulled him along like the strings of a marionette doll. Any adrenaline he'd been riding fizzled out. Gary's gentle pat on his arm before disappearing into the closest store felt like hot irons on his soul, and he couldn't help but retreat further. He was so tired.

Gary didn't show any sign of having noticed, and Arthur shuffled down a tight walkway between two buildings. The way looked clear, but the shadows were deep. The soles of his shoes crunched on crumbling pavement and trampled dandelion plants just starting to throw hearty leaves over the cracks and crevices they'd helped broaden. The foul odour of decomposing trash hit him. Arthur wrinkled his nose as his brain began to surface from the cotton clouds of numbness. One question floated up as his shoulders brushed concrete and brick walls.

Why did Gary care so much?

He'd been a part of his family losing their normal, so why did he still care at all? Was it just his guilt? Arthur shook the questions off, unwilling to inspect any possible answers as he searched for his daughter. It wasn't important right now.

Focus on finding Amy.

The school secretary and principal hadn't seemed overly worried or shocked about a missing teen, but at least that first officer had seemed genuinely concerned and was taking this seriously. He could still trust a few people.

His cell phone buzzed again, and he checked the messages as he emerged from the small passage into the back alley, his feet hitting packed dirt where the broken pavement stopped.

Moving on to the next store. I'll meet you at the end of the street when I finish. Be careful back there.

Gary's focused words propelled Arthur forward. He scanned the alley before turning and heading to the right. He checked behind a dumpster and wooden pallet pile where he found a collapsed tent, a side ripped wide. Had someone been living back here? Arthur's heart pounded. He didn't see anyone.

When he reached the end of the alley, he turned down the sidewalk and headed for the crosswalk and waited there, watching the streetlights turn from green to red and back again.

The number of people walking down Main Street had increased. As he waited, Arthur rallied his courage and flashed Amy's picture via his phone screen at the people who passed. "Have you seen my daughter? Excuse me, have you seen this girl today? She's my daughter, and we can't find her."

A few people stopped to inspect it, but most simply glanced at the screen before moving on while shaking their heads. Every "no" was like a nail hammered into Arthur's heart. He stopped flashing the picture when Gary joined him.

His friend shook his head when Arthur asked if anyone had seen her. "Let's cross the street here, and you take the outdoors again while I go into the stores. Archie's Food Truck is up ahead, and there's always a small crowd hanging around this time of day. I would start there before visiting the alleys again."

Arthur agreed, and both men took off towards their targets as the light flashed green and the small green walking man appeared on the pedestrian light. Arthur passed the first handful of shops before space opened up and the drugstore parking lot spread out beside him. It gave Archie's the perfect amount of space for the two red stained picnic tables providing outdoor seating for customers. The scent of fried foods filled the air, and Arthur's stomach growled.

He sent a message to Rose as he approached the food truck, asking how close to town they were, and then started flashing Amy's picture to the people standing in line for food.

"This is Amy. Have you seen her? She didn't come home last night."

"No, sorry."

"No, I haven't. Cute girl, though. We'll keep an eye out for her."

"Nope. Have you checked the skate park?"

Arthur felt as if a large weight pressed him into the ground as the line made way for him to flash the picture to the food truck owner. "What will you have?" the man inside the window asked.

"Sorry, I'm just here looking for my daughter. Have you seen her?" Arthur lifted his phone high, and the man blinked as he looked at Amy's picture.

"Carmen, come here," the man said while motioning with his fingers to someone standing out of view. "Is that the girl we brought into the truck a while back?"

A young woman stepped up to the window and squinted as she leaned past the owner.

"Yes," she said, glancing at Arthur, then back at her boss. "She was here yesterday too, with a group of kids."

"She didn't come home last night. Did you see what way they left, or did she say anything else to you?"

Carmen didn't answer as she stepped back from the window, but the food truck owner motioned around the vehicle. "Come on back."

Finally, a lead. Arthur sprinted behind the truck as a silver door swung open, and the young woman took a seat on the set of pull-out steps bolted under the door.

"I don't know how much I can tell you," she said right away. "They ordered together, and I remember her hanging on the arm of a tall kid with purple hair. It was funny because there was a shorter kid hanging off his other arm like they were a threesome." Carmen laughed quietly to herself.

Arthur sucked in a breath but held back any verbal judgment. "Do you remember what time they were here?"

"Around noon."

"Anything else at all? Please … She's never stayed out all night before."

Carmen shook her head and looked up at him with sad eyes. "I'm sorry. That's all I know from yesterday."

"And you didn't catch any of the other kids' names?"

"No." Again she shook her head then paused. "But you know, the first time I met her—apart from serving—we brought her back into the truck because some creeps were paying too much attention to her. I was worried about her then, so we called the cops."

Arthur nodded as she told him the story, and the food truck owner stuck his head out the back door to listen for a moment before interrupting. "The line's getting long, Carmen."

She nodded and stood, balancing on a single step and again apologizing.

"It's okay, thank you. It helps to know the time she was here."

Carmen's boss let her slip back into the truck before he stepped out onto the fold-out stairs himself. He wiped his hands on a dish towel looped over his belt. "Here, let me give you my email and phone number," the man offered. "I'll put her picture up on the side of the truck if you send it to me."

"Thank you." Arthur gratefully received the man's contact information. As he worked on sending the photo, the man took a second step down, moving closer to Arthur, and lowered his voice.

"Father to father, those creeps paying your daughter too much attention are dangerous. The gang activity in town has increased over the winter and spring."

Arthur looked up from the email, and the man met his gaze with dark, solemn eyes.

"I've got connections up north, connections from my past that I am not proud of." He shuffled his feet on the metal step and let his eyes drop. "I used to be part of—no, never mind that. Still ..." He looked back up at Arthur, reaching out to lay a hand on his shoulder.

Arthur was too stunned by the action to move as the man leaned in closer and said, "If it was my kid ... If you find out anyone, anyone at *all* has taken her out of town, get in your car and drive west. Stop and ask after her at every tourist stop, every gas station along Highway 11. Don't stop until you get to Winnipeg, and then, if you still haven't heard of her, turn around and do the same thing coming home." The man's fingers squeezed Arthur's shoulder. "Don't stop until you find her. They never expect the doubling back ... It could be your chance."

Arthur's throat had gone dry as he listened, but he forced a question out with a cracking voice. "What are you trying to tell me?"

"Just ..." The man released Arthur's shoulders and stepped back. "If they have her, if they get her as far as Winnipeg, I don't know if you'll find her. But don't give up. Never give up."

Arthur felt as if his stomach had fallen out of his body and was lying on the payment.

If they have her?

The man nodded at Arthur's silence and closed the food truck door.

God, you wouldn't let that happen to her, would you?

After a moment of frozen bewilderment, Arthur hit send on the email with Amy's picture. The phone still in his hand buzzed as he moved back around the truck and passed the line of eager diners waiting to make an order. He thumbed the phone, expecting a text from Gary, and stumbled a step as he realized it was a call.

"Hello," he stammered as he pressed the phone to his ear, drawing his feet back under himself.

"Hello? Pastor Grill? It's me, Glen Edwards. Mom just told me Amy's missing. I saw her with Josh Martins yesterday at the skate park."

"Do you know how to contact Josh? The high school refused to give me contact information."

"I can do better than that. I know where he lives and can take you over to talk with him."

"Glen! Thank God! Thank you." A rush of relief made Arthur lightheaded, and he squeezed his eyes closed against gathering moisture.

"Amen, Pastor. I hope we can find her. I'm just getting off work, so I'll meet you at the skate park. We can go together from there."

"Thank you, Jesus," Arthur breathed as he raced down the street towards his parked car. He sent a text to Gary with the meeting location before climbing in and igniting the engine. *God, please don't let what that man said be true. Please keep Amy safe.*

Stones and Trashcans

ARTHUR

ARTHUR WATCHED GLEN AS he rolled down the last few feet of sidewalk on his skateboard. As the teen flipped his board up into a hand with a deft foot, Gary pulled into the lot as well and parked beside Arthur.

Rose had texted a few moments before, saying they were just coming into town and would grab something for dinner from the grocers. Knowing that the other two most important people in his life were safe helped Arthur breathe, but as Glen flashed him a smile, he found himself unable to return the warm greeting.

"It's okay, Pastor, we'll find her." The young man seemed so confident as he tossed his backpack and board onto the rear passenger seat of Arthur's car. "You won't make a scene, though, right?" It looked as if the possibility had just popped into Glen's head, and he glanced over at Arthur, his eyes wide. "Maybe we should call the cops and bring them along."

"I won't be making any scenes, Glen. I just want to find Amy."

"Good," was all the young man said as he took the passenger's seat, pulling the belt over his shoulder.

Gary rolled down his window before Glen closed the passenger door. "Where to?" he asked.

"Just follow us, Mr. Davids. It's a bit of weaving in and out of streets, but I know exactly how to get there," assured Glen.

Arthur wondered at the boy's confidence again and looked over at Gary just in time to see his eyebrows go up before the car door closed. Glen motioned for him to turn right when they left the skate park behind them.

"What can you tell me about this Josh?" Arthur asked as the car's wheels hit the street.

Glen hesitated before he admitted, "I don't know him well, but he doesn't have the best reputation. Under it all, he seems to be a pretty okay guy, but he likes to party. And ... he lives an alternative lifestyle." Glen pulled at a curl peeking out from under his cap before sliding fingers behind the fabric and pushing the strand up and out of view. "I was a bit surprised when I saw Amy hanging out with him, but, yeah. I guess she has to make her own way in a new school."

"Alternative lifestyle?" Arthur wondered aloud. "What exactly do you mean by that?"

"He's gay." Glen shrugged, and as Arthur huffed in protest, he added, "You can't expect everyone to live like a Christian, especially when they are *not* Christian, Pastor. He really isn't a bad guy, just making some bad decisions. Could be way worse."

Arthur didn't think he could take any more revelations about his daughter, and the people she had befriended before meeting this Josh person. His gut clenched as thoughts of Rachel and Jay swarmed in. *Jay could be described as not such a bad guy, he just makes some bad decisions as well.* He raised a hand and stopped Glen before he could continue. "Just show we were to go."

"You said no scenes, remember?"

Arthur gritted his teeth before glancing over at Glen. The young man's eyes held a measure of worry that pulled at Arthur's heartstrings. "No scenes. I promise."

Glen nodded, the bright smile back on his face. "Turn right up here and then go two blocks before turning left."

Arthur hoped he'd be able to keep that promise. It wasn't a question of how this kid chose to live, it was one of if he knew where Amy was.

Glen pointed to a house with faded blue siding and a garage whose door was bent and sagging in on one side. The driveway was empty, so Arthur pulled in right up to the crumpled door. The bend gave a warped window into the garage's dimness, revealing the clutter inside. A stack of boxes jutted out past the metal, and signs of water damage speckled their brown exterior. Arthur winced as Glen exited the car and yelled. "Josh! Hey, Josh! You home?"

The dilapidated state of the house gave Arthur pause, and he was questioning the wisdom of this visit as Gary pulled up behind them, the back end of the second vehicle hanging out onto the street.

Arthur swallowed hard. "We can't park like this for long," he said as both older men joined Glen in a visual search for signs of life.

Glen boldly approached the house and tapped on the front door, daring to peek into a slender floor-to-ceiling window that was meant to pull light into the home's entrance. Arthur couldn't see past the dingy white lace curtain that was drawn over the window. He wasn't sure he wanted to.

"I don't think anyone's home," Glen offered and ran fingers through his hair as his shoulders slumped. "I'm sorry if I bought you out here for nothing."

"It's not a problem, Glen," Gary told him. "For information on Amy, it's worth it."

Arthur watched the teen set his jaw at a determined angle and pull on an earlobe.

They all jumped as a *clang* rang out, the sound bouncing off rooftops. Gary and Arthur frowned, but Glen grinned, turned and slapped Arthur's shoulder, and barrelled past him to dive down a small walkway between the house and garage.

"Wait, Glen, are you sure this is a good idea?" Gary asked.

Why were they letting a teen lead? Apprehension sizzled over Arthur's skin as he did his best to keep up with the young man, leaving Gary a few steps behind to shake his head and retrieve his cell phone from a pocket. "Just in case we need to call for help," his friend muttered.

As they stepped past the garage's corner, Arthur's heart dropped to his knees.

Before them stood—no, tottered—a tall boy with a pale, strained face. The shocking purple of his hair lifted away from his scalp in haphazard spikes. The colour did nothing for his haggard complexion. Arthur's brain jumped to images of fresh zombies from TV as the boy lifted a rock with a long, gangly arm and sent it clanging into a row of battered garbage cans.

Glen shouted Josh's name, but the boy either ignored them or didn't hear as he half tripped over his own feet once the rock left his hand. His shoulders rose and fell in fast succession. As Arthur stepped closer, the scent of alcohol reached out to them. It stopped him in his tracks even as Glen doggedly continued.

"Josh, hey, Josh! Have you seen Amy?" Glen reached up to grasp the taller boy by his shoulder and was almost pushed over as flailing arms and legs turned towards him. Those arms contacted Glen's chest and the legs with his knees. Still, he stood against the assault. "Calm down, Josh. It's just me. Wow, who's liquor cabinet have you gotten into?"

"What?" The purple-haired boy shook all over as he blinked up at Glen, who held him on his feet. They both swayed, Josh's tall frame a significant weight.

"Pastor Arthur, we need to call the cops."

Josh's eyes rolled around in his head as he tried to focus on Glen's face. As the boy strained to look past Glen, Arthur spotted what looked like dried blood smeared across the side of his face.

"Son, what happened to you?" Gary said, his hesitation forgotten as he stepped past Arthur towards the boy now sinking to the ground as he clutched Glen's arms for support.

"Who are you?" Josh's words slurred as his intoxicated brain tried to work his mouth.

"Josh, what happened?" A tear rolled freely from Glen's eye when he turned Josh's head with a hand. The dry blood cracked, and a line of fresh red oozed from a gash up the side of the boy's head.

Josh struggled at the touch, trying to pull his face away, but Glen held him still.

"If he's got a gash like that ... It might not be just the alcohol making him loopy," Glen said.

Arthur, thankful he had added the officer's phone number from that morning to his contacts already, scrolled through a list of names as fast as he could.

"Hello, yes, this is Arthur Grill. Yes. I came to check on one of my daughter's friends, and ... looks like someone might have kicked him around. He doesn't look well." Arthur pulled the phone away from his ear as he asked Glen, "Do we need an ambulance?"

"I don't know. I can't tell how badly he's hurt." Josh thrashed in Glen's arms, forcing Gary to help hold him still. "Josh. Calm down. We aren't going to hurt you, but you might hurt yourself. Come on. Stop!" Glen's last plea was nearly a sob.

Arthur relayed the scene to the officer, who then instructed him to stay on the line.

"Hold his arms so he can't hit me, Mr. Davids. Yeah, like that." Glen gently patted Josh's face as the boy's eyes threatened to close and not open again. "Stay awake until they get here, man. I can't tell if you have a concussion or something. What happened? What happened to Amy?"

"Amy?" Josh blinked as Glen's pat roused him. "Amy ..."

Arthur's heart flipped as Josh convulsed. The boy's breath came with gurgling. What would they do if he died in Glen's arms? Then he realized the boy was weeping, unable to hold himself still as waves of grief surged.

"Amy," the boy whispered her name in between breaths as his body trembled. "Amy, I'm so sorry."

The pain in Josh's voice as he said her name ... Arthur joined Josh in his trembling as ice crystals formed in his veins. He didn't hear the officer's voice calling from his cell phone as he stood watching the rawest picture of grief, too afraid to register what it might mean.

"What happened to Amy?" Gary asked, his words a whisper they could barely hear over Josh's tears. "Why are you sorry, Josh?"

"You can tell us," Glen said as he again patted the boy's cheek. "We're here to find her. We can help you."

The boy tried to grab for more rocks that littered the ground where the grass was worn away and gravel mixed in with bare brown dirt. Gary retrieved the stones from the clawing fingers again and again as the battle of wills drew on.

Arthur took a breath at the sound of a siren from down the street. Help was almost there.

The first officer that appeared behind Arthur was a large black man with deep brown eyes and closely cropped hair. He was followed by a white companion who was much smaller but whose square stature screamed strength. Relief shuddered through Arthur as he came back to himself, giving over his phone to the first officer, who clasped his shoulder and asked him by name what had happened.

Arthur blinked at the name embroidered on his uniform. Gregory. Yes, he remembered now, this was the same officer he met last year when his friend Paul found his wife had passed away from suicide in their home garage. Officer Gregory took the phone from Arthur's hand and, after speaking with his colleague still on the other end, hung up.

Arthur licked dry lips as he finally answered the officer's question. "We found him throwing rocks, but as soon as Glen called his name, he started having some kind of fit. We don't know how he got hurt."

The second officer was on the ground helping Glen lay Josh flat.

"Hold on, young man, the ambulance is a minute away."

Arthur's brain felt like it was on fire. He couldn't take any more. Where was Amy? Why hadn't the boy told them where she was? The paramedics had taken one look at Arthur and tried to bring him along when they bundled Josh into the ambulance. Instead, Glen rode with the other boy as the second officer searched the outside of the house, looking for clues and information about Josh's parents. He'd been home alone.

Gary refused to let Arthur drive and forced him to leave the Grill's car stranded in a stranger's driveway.

"I'll get Sarah and Rachel to grab it, Arthur. Don't worry," Gary had said.

Now they both sat in the emergency waiting room, Arthur with his head bent low over his knees, his elbows resting on his legs, while Gary patted his back and told him to breathe. Embarrassment kept him from looking up at his long-time friend, but at that moment, Arthur had no idea how he would have made it without him. His mind and body had never behaved like this before, rebelling against his commands. Even now his lungs refused to pull in full breaths, leaving him panting.

Where is Amy?

"Why didn't he tell us where she is?" he stammered, unsure if his voice would bounce off the floor and reach Gary.

"He'll tell us, Arthur. As soon as they get him lucid, he'll tell us."

Glen was still with the boy and had sent Gary a text telling them that drugs had been found in Josh's system, but the amount didn't account for how out of it he was. The doctors had realized he was suffering from a concussion, and that mixed with alcohol was dangerous. The boy had supposedly tried to self-medicate with it. No parent had shown up yet, so they were letting Glen stay with him.

"He's a kind kid that Glen," Gary said as his hand on Arthur's back stilled.

"He just takes you as you are. No questions asked," Arthur added.

A wave of shame flooded Arthur at the thought. He hadn't been able to look past the boys' shabby living conditions, until he'd started convulsing. When had he become so judgmental? Or had he always been this way? Shouldn't he know himself better at forty-six years of age?

They waited a full thirty minutes before Arthur could lift his head and shudder into an upright sitting position. People around them came and went, nurses called names, and voices made announcements over hidden speakers. Arthur ignored most of it as his heart rate finally slowed.

"I'm sorry, Gary."

"Don't be. It's been a horrible day."

It took another hour and a half before Officer Gregory found them sitting in silence. A nurse dimmed the light slightly in the waiting room as night arrived, and Arthur was grateful for the eased brightness when he opened his eyes and tried to focus on the officer squatting in front of him.

"How are you holding up, Pastor Grill?" he asked. Gregory's voice was deep and melodic. It would have made for the perfect radio voice, but Arthur was glad that at this moment, it was meant just for him.

"I'm coming out of whatever's wrong with me." It was true, but his hands were still slicked with sweat.

"First time you've had a panic attack? They can be rough. Be kind to yourself, Pastor."

Panic attack? Was that what this was?

"I know that look, Pastor Grill. Don't be shaming yourself for your body's reaction. It is what it is, and it sure has been a shitty day for you. Now, are you up for some news?"

"Is it about Amy? Did you find her? Did Josh tell you where she is?" Arthur felt his words running away from him, the beat of his heart accelerating.

"Now, hold on," Officer Gregory held up a large hand and tamped down the air between them. "Hold on. I wouldn't usually consider offering it to a man in your condition, but we are already in hospital, so …"

"You're making it worse, Gregory," Gary said. "Please just tell us what's going on."

"Alright. From what we can gather, Amy and Josh attended a party on Sunday night along with a few other kids from school. Interviews with a few of these kids have already taken place, but most of them didn't give up much information." The officer sighed as he looked from Arthur to Gary and back again. "We think some of them, including Amy, took what was supposed to be some kind of recreational drug."

"My kid's doing drugs?"

"Details are pretty hazy there, Arthur. Josh isn't giving very coherent answers. It's a matter of piecing everyone's words together like a jigsaw puzzle to get the clear picture. All we know for sure is that drugs and alcohol were involved at some point during the night."

When Arthur filled his lungs with air, he felt them expand. The pressure assaulted his heart, and it ached as if being squeezed with a fist. Yet his lungs were hungry, and he sucked in again before coughing. Gary's hand moved on his back again, as if Arthur were a child and Gary was soothing his fears away.

"Josh is adamant that someone took Amy away. He said she was tripping and wasn't sure she fully understood what was happening."

"What do you mean 'took her away'?" Gary asked as Arthur stared at the officer's dark face.

It felt as if Gregory's dark eyes were sucking him into a bottomless hole.

"Josh believes she was abducted. He doesn't know by whom or why, beyond the fact that the substance he took was more expensive than what he was told. He couldn't cover the full cost. It's possible they took Amy to pay for the debt."

"What?" Arthur couldn't tell if he was yelling or whispering. All he knew was he felt like he would either faint or tear Officer Gregory apart with his bare hands.

I Don't Know

ROSE

ROSE BARELY RECOGNIZED THE man who walked through the apartment's front door. Arthur's eyes looked sunken as his pallid skin highlighted the dark bags under them. Gary ushered him into the room and found him a seat on the couch before bowing out to head home to Sarah.

Rose and Rachel had waited hours to hear any news after being told Arthur was on the way to the hospital. Then the call came. Officer Thomas had informed her that her daughter may have been abducted on Sunday night. She hadn't believed him.

"What do you mean?" The question had come out in a breathy voice, and the officer had asked her to repeat the question.

Rachel had burst into tears beside her as Rose placed the call on speaker. She'd reached over and squeezed her daughter's hand, not only to comfort Rachel but to ground herself.

"What do you mean exactly?" she asked again.

"I'm sorry, Mrs. Grill. I know this is a hard thing to understand. Alerts about your daughter are being sent out as we speak. We will do everything in our power to find her and bring her home to you."

It hadn't been enough. Those words hadn't been even close to enough. But the call had ended, and they had again waited for Arthur to come home.

Now that he sat before them, Rose didn't know how much information would be forthcoming, didn't know if she should even try to get him to tell her. He looked ... fragile. He blinked at her, but it didn't look like he even registered she was there. In his hand was a collection of white slender, rectangular boxes bound together with medical tape. Black and blue print scrawled across their sides in too small a size for her to read from where she sat snug on her walker's seat.

After several uncomfortable minutes of silence, Arthur's eyes finally focused. "I didn't find her. I'm sorry."

Rose stood and moved closer to her husband, pulling her walker along with her and planting its back legs into the carpet as close to him as she could. As she sat back down on the folded-out seat, their knees touched. With the contact, awareness washed back into Arthur's face, and Rose held back tears with a shuddering breath. "The search has just begun, Arthur. We won't give up. We will find her."

"They think someone's taken her."

"I know," Rose whispered and laid a hand on his knee.

Arthur laid his over hers, fingers trembling even while squeezing her fingers in a firm grip.

"The ER Doctor thinks I'm cracking," Arthur said. He looked down at the boxes he held and tossed them to the couch cushions. "Samples. To help me get through the next few days."

As the boxes rolled over, a paper slipped away from where it had been tucked in between two of them. "A prescription for helping with my *anxiety.*" He told her, though he refused to meet her gaze as he said it and instead lifted a hand to his mouth and wiped moisture from his trembling lips.

"There is no shame in needing them, Arthur."

Rose could have sworn she heard threads snapping within her husband as he let out a sigh. He released her hand to sink back against the couch cushions and pressed both hands to his face as if he could rub away the weariness that was etched there.

"I know. I just … I thought I was stronger than this." Was his resignation release or enslavement? Rose couldn't tell as she studied the curve of his jaw, the wrinkles around his eyes, the strands of hair that fell across his forehead, the desperation in his expression.

Her hand still rested on his knee, and she tightened her grip while willing the uncomfortable pangs in her gut to ease with a deep breath.

"You are strong, Arthur. But even strong people get tired."

Rachel appeared at Rose's side, two steaming mugs in her hand. "Herbal tea," she said. "For sleep."

"Thank you." Rose had to release Arthur's knee to take the offered mug, but once her fingers wrapped around its warmth, she realized how cold the rest of her body was. She shivered as chills danced up and down her spine, threatening to cascade down her legs. She moved her feet to ward them off.

I can't afford an episode right now, God. Please, fortify my body.

Arthur had turned his head towards Rachel but hadn't accepted the mug she offered. Rose watched with an ache in her heart as he looked at his eldest daughter, his expression raw and pained.

"I'm so glad you came home," he said to her.

The red that lingered around Rachel's eyes deepened as fresh tears welled up.

Rachel handed him the second mug. A few drops of warm liquid sloshed over the rim to drip down the side.

"I'm so...so glad you came home." Arthur's words were muffled as he pressed his sleeve to his eyes and nose then used it to wipe the side of his mug dry. "I'm so sorry I drove you away."

Rose wept the tears she knew her husband was struggling to hold back.

Rose hoped Arthur had found sleep. As she sat in the gloom of the dimly lit living room, staring at the empty couch and the gentle impression his backside had left, she'd told Rachel she needed some time alone and insisted she could make it to bed without assistance.

If she didn't take care of the stirring in her heart, rest would run from her forever.

Arthur hadn't asked about her appointment with the specialist. Of course, he hadn't. Their daughter was missing. Amy's situation was far more important. She was more important. Guilt married with the churning of disappointment in Rose's gut as she sat cradled by her walker and tried to hold back invisible waves of worry that crashed against first her knees, then her thighs, and steadily lapped at her waist before threatening her chest. She knew these waves well and hated them. They chilled and confined, pummelled and supported.

"God, I can't take it all. It's too much—too much all at once. Why are you letting this happen?"

Honesty slipped out of her and tumbled within the rising waves, floating on their surface like search beacons looking for land. She cupped her forehead with a hand and anchored her elbow on the walker's handlebar.

"We've served you for so long. We still do. So why are you letting this happen? Where is my daughter? What will happen to us? What will happen to me, to Rachel, to Arthur?"

Anger and grief dripped down her face.

"Arthur is breaking, but does he see that the rest of us broke long before this?"

Memories of her husband as he spoke from the Hope Is Here Church's pulpit flooded her mind. Confident, purposeful, and earnest, he had always exuded all those qualities in public. His care for their congregation has been deep and his empathy for those in difficult situations real. But ... that level of empathy and care had sometimes failed to transfer to his home life, to their children. Arthur, and as an extension all of them, had always felt the pressure to appear as the good and, yes, perfect pastoral family.

Behind closed doors the lack of that perfection wasn't only present in Arthur. It also resided within herself and in their daughters. After all, they were only human. So much energy spent on giving and appearing well put together outside the home left a deep lack once the doors to the world were closed. It was exhausting. Once the world was shut out, that facade crumbled.

"God, you are so good, and I am so ... not. But all these bricks at once are too much for me to bear. They're crushing us."

What could be done? Rose asked that question to her Creator, the One who had mapped out each of their existences before their births.

"Why? What now?"

She felt a question stir within her spirit as the seconds on the wall clock ticked away.

What is it you really want, Rose? She couldn't tell if the question originated in her own mind or somewhere beyond her. But it bubbled up to float under her nose across the surface of her worries. As it bobbed, it smelled of selfishness, and she turned away, shifting her sitting position and switching from the support of one walker handle to the other. But she couldn't help but shift back towards it, pulled by her need to understand something in this mess of all their lives.

"Is this what you use prayer for, God? To dredge up things I would rather not deal with while we sit in the middle of desperation? Why am I thinking of these things *now?*"

Guilt coated the question as it refused to disappear, and Rose almost gagged on the imaginary fumes that smelled and even tasted so real.

"God," she gasped, realizing she'd been holding her breath. "What can I do? What can I do when I am like–like this?"

She motioned to herself in the darkness like God was sitting in Arthur's place on the couch, able to take the sight of her in. "You have stripped my abilities away while handing me more trouble. We are already broken. How can we overcome this with less than what we had before?"

You are less, but I am more.

The thought splashed her in the face like God had dropped a stone in the waters before her.

Am I not enough for you, Rose?

Was he? Was God enough when nothing felt right anymore?

"God, right now, I don't know if you are."

Go!

ARTHUR

Darkness invaded Arthur's dreams. As the bed sheets twisted around his body, he wished the prescription he'd been given was for sleeping pills instead of anxiety. The bedside clock blinked five a.m. mocking him every time his eyes opened. He pressed his face into his sweat dampened pillow as if burying his eyes could shut off the terrible images his mind tortured him with.

Amy, all alone. Amy, afraid. Amy, at the mercy of men twice her age. Amy ... He groaned into the pillow.

If it was my kid ... Get in your car and drive west. Never give up. The food truck owner's words reverberated through his mind. *Get in your car and drive west.* It was strangely direct advice coming from a stranger. As sleep tried to wrap him in its arms and pull him back into dreams, he reached for Rose's side of the bed.

His hand met cool sheets.

Arthur bolted upright, his heart racing, his palms sweating, his legs shaking with effort as his feet hit the cold floor.

"Rose!" he called as soon as the bedroom door opened for him. "Rose, where are you?"

His heart stumbled in his chest at her soft reply.

"I'm here, Arthur."

The apartment had chilled overnight, and the cold kitchen floor spurred his feet onward even as the relief of hearing her voice had drained adrenaline from his body.

"Why didn't you come to bed?" he asked as he entered the living room, his toes digging into the carpet fibres in an attempt to forget the cold of the linoleum.

She sat in the seat of her walker. Had she not moved all night?

"I'm sorry." She turned to him, her tired eyes puffy but the light in them clear.

She was okay. She was here. She wasn't missing. She was safe.

Arthur swallowed at the sight of her trembling fingers clutching the handles of the walker as she made to stand. He didn't let her and slipped onto the couch in front of her, squinting as the light of early morning invaded the living room. The wall clock told him an hour had passed as he'd thrashed, half awake in bed. It was now six a.m. and just past sunrise.

Rose looked so frail, and Arthur watched her face crumple in grief.

"I was talking to God," she said, her voice raspy and weak.

Arthur shifted his feet on the carpet and scratched at his bare shoulder. He focused on her knees instead of her face as he asked, "What did you tell Him?"

"Everything." Rose's hands shuddered as she released him and let them fall to her lap. "I'm useless, Arthur, I can't help you find Amy."

Arthur blinked at his wife.

"I can't help you find her, but you have to find her. You have to go. Today. Before it's too late."

Get in your car and drive west.

"I ..."

"You have to, Arthur. Go find my baby."

"But the police—"

"I've been selfish, Arthur."

"You're never selfish, Rose—"

"Oh, yes, I am. I don't want you to go. I'm tired, in pain, and I want your attention more than anything. But right now, I don't matter. Amy does."

"Rose—my God, Rose. You matter to me. You're not useless. I can't believe that He would tell you that."

"He didn't, but ... I know. And I know needing you isn't wrong, but I know you, Arthur. If you sit on this couch and do nothing, it will kill you. It's already breaking you."

Arthur couldn't deny that.

"Amy needs you. Maybe you won't find her and the police will. But something inside me tells me she needs you to try. Arthur, you need to go."

The sound of Rachel moving around the kitchen interrupted them. Arthur opened his mouth to say something and then closed it again. Everything around him seemed to slow to a crawl as his brain tried to make sense of what his wife had just said.

Get in your car and drive west.

The food truck owner's face flashed into his mind again. Arthur remembered the conviction behind his words.

"Alright," he said.

"This morning," Rose urged.

"Okay." Arthur nodded. "I ... ah ... I'll get dressed."

Before he could stand, a knock rapped on the sliding glass door. His legs, still weak from restless sleep, threatened to let him down as he stood and reached for the lock. He wrapped arms over his bare chest, still dressed only in pyjama pants, but the faces on the other side of the glass beamed at him.

"What is this?" he asked as the door opened, letting in the bite of a cold early morning.

"Breakfast!" a chorus of three voices answered.

Glen flashed a smile as he pushed into the living room carrying a basket covered with a tea towel. His father, Ben, was right behind him, a steaming casserole dish held at arm's length. Behind them both was Glen's stepmother, Abigail. Arthur noticed the dark circles under her eyes as she manoeuvred her motorized wheelchair up to the doorway.

"You'll need to give me a boost over the lip here, Arthur," she said. "Ben? We need to make Rose some wooden wedges for this doorway so she doesn't have this problem if she needs her wheelchair."

"Right-o!" Ben called back from the kitchen.

Arthur blinked at Abigail for a moment.

"I don't plan to sit in this doorway all morning, Arthur," she said.

Arthur bowed before Abigail and, grasping the seat of her chair, he carefully lifted and pulled it over the sliding door's threshold.

"Thank you," she said as she patted his arm and manoeuvred past him to Rose's side.

"What's going on, Abigail?" Rose asked, her eyes filled with as many questions as Arthur's.

"We've come to help make a plan, and feed you, and—Ben?"

"Yes?" came the call from the kitchen amidst a squeal from Rachel and the clatter of dishes as people set the table. "Direct Arthur to the shower, will you?"

"Abigail. I think the man can bathe himself."

"I didn't say to jump in with him!"

Rose's laugh filled the living room as Arthur coughed and Ben came back into the room, his arms crossed.

"Come on, Arthur. She was up all night praying, and now she's got this fiery determination," Ben told him as he waved Arthur into the kitchen. "You know how she gets when that happens."

Lost for words Arthur let Ben usher him into the bathroom and watched as his friend shrugged apologetically before closing the door firmly behind him.

"Ben! Wait! I'm going to need clothes first unless you all want to get to know me really well after this shower."

Ben opened the door again with a sheepish look on his face. "Oh, yeah. I guess that's kinda important."

The clatter of dishes and the chatter of Glen and Rachel followed Arthur into his room then back over to the bathroom. It felt good to hear the sounds of something so normal. But as he closed the door again and the bathroom walls cut off the noise, his mind whispered to him, *Get in your car and drive west.*

Arthur noted the gentle grip Abigail held on Rose's hand when he joined the small crowd in the kitchen. Rose had fresh tears in her eyes, but she also smiled at her friend. Glen and Rachel occupied another side of the table, and Ben pulled out the chair closest to him for Arthur.

"I have to leave for work soon, so let's eat. Then I can get out of the way, and Abigail can do her thing."

"Her thing?" Rachel asked. She looked from her mother to her father.

Arthur shrugged. His tired body pulled him down to the wooden dining chair as if his lap were loaded with bricks. When he sat back and let Ben and Glen serve up the food, he wondered at his own passivity. His mind felt numb, and after a shared prayer, the warm breakfast casserole tasted like chalk in his mouth.

He felt Rose watching him and forced mouthfuls down, drowning them with hot coffee. The coffee helped. He was grateful for its warmth as his fingers tingled with cold despite the food, the friends, and the warming morning light.

He jumped when Ben clapped him on the shoulder.

"I'm off," the man said, nodding to everyone in the room before exiting the kitchen and then the apartment.

"Now what?" Rachel asked. Her chatter with Glen had slowed, and Rose and Abigail also slipped into silence.

Arthur felt everyone's attention as added bricks to his lap. He looked up at his eldest daughter to find his anxiety mirrored in her pale face, dark lines under her eyes, and a half full plate before her.

"I'm going to find Amy. I'm leaving as soon as I call work and get a few things together."

The sound that escaped Rachel as she listened to her father was a cross between a sigh and a whimper.

"Where are you going to look?" Abigail asked.

"West first. Into Manitoba and as far as Winnipeg."

Arthur wished Rose would speak. But she remained silent, eyes fixed on the crumbs from a biscuit Abigail had cut and buttered for her. She hadn't taken a bite, but crumbs littered the table as if she'd been playing with the food, crumbling bits to make it look like she'd eaten.

"And Glen and I will stay here while you're gone, Arthur," Abigail assured him.

Rachel dropped her fork, and the ring of metal on glass stung. "How long, Dad? How long will you be gone?"

"As long as it takes. On a normal day, the drive takes five and a half-ish hours. But I'll be stopping a lot."

Rose cut the heaviness in the air when she pushed her chair away from the table.

"I'll pack a bag for you," she stood and pulled her walker in close. "And one for Amy, for when you find her."

The next hour was a flurry of movement. Rose packed while Arthur endured a strained phone call with Fred, finally secured time off and the assurance that his job would still be waiting for him when he returned. Afterwards, Arthur pulled small things out of drawers and cupboards that he thought he might need. His phone charger and cord lay in a pile on the kitchen table, beside it a notepad and pen that Rachel set to writing every phone number she could think he might need but wouldn't have on his phone.

"Just in case you forget them," she said.

Their sleeping bags for camping were in storage, but Abigail made sure a heavy blanket was placed beside his bag.

"It might be nearing summer, but it's always best to have one in the car when travelling."

Rose agreed with her as she added the first aid kit from the bathroom to the pile.

Arthur added the last few items to a bulging duffle bag when the doorbell rang. He looked up as the sound of crying burst into the living room. When he turned, the duffle slung over a shoulder, Sarah was standing on the apartment's threshold, holding Rose in an embrace.

As Gary stepped into the room and reached for the bag Rose had packed for Amy, placing it on the couch, he asked, "Your car or mine?"

"What?"

"I'm going with you."

"I'm leaving town, Gary. Heading west towards the city."

Gary lifted his own bag so Arthur could see it over Sarah's shoulder. "Of course we are."

For the second time that morning, Arthur stared at friends, utterly bewildered.

Sarah peeled her face off Rose's shoulder and pinned him with a fierce look that left no room for arguing. "There is no way you're going alone, Arthur Grill. I expect you both to take care of each other."

"How did you even know?" Rose asked.

Rachel coughed from behind Arthur. "I told him," she admitted. "Don't forget these, Dad," she added, her voice lowered for only Arthur to hear. She held out the bundle of white prescription samples he'd brought home the night before.

Friends

ARTHUR

ARTHUR STASHED THE SMALL white boxes in the top of his duffle, closing the zipper on his weakness as if not being able to see them could dissolve the weariness in his spirit. He didn't have time to wait for the pharmacy to open, so the samples would have to sustain him through whatever came next.

Gary held his silence as they pulled up to a gas bar and Arthur filled the thirsty tank. The numbers on the counter soared as the machine took in its fill. Arthur ran a hand over his face groaning at the dent it would put in his bank account.

How high are these prices going to get? He grimaced with shame.

How could he let money bother him when Amy was out there somewhere, alone? Or not alone, and that could be much worse. Why had he let her go out at all? Why hadn't he insisted she spend a quiet weekend in the apartment with him? Why?

"Arthur?" Gary leaned across the driver's seat from the passenger's side and waved a long arm out the open door. "The automatic shut off."

Arthur blinked at him before realizing the gas tank was full and the pump had sensed it.

"Do you want me to drive?" His friend asked after Arthur had paid and settled back behind the driver's seat.

"No."

"Is there a plan?"

They hadn't talked before they'd both jumped into Arthur's car and waved goodbye to Rachel and Glen, who'd followed them to the apartment's parking lot. Now Arthur paused before pressing the tongue of the seat belt into the fastener. "We drive west and stop at every public place we can find on the way to the city."

"Okay ... We should stop at Ham's and get supplies before leaving. There's no telling how long that many stops will take."

The idea of going into the grocery store after calling in that morning turned Arthur's stomach.

"I'll go in," Gary offered. "We don't want anyone stopping you with questions."

"Good idea." Arthur breathed a sigh of relief. "We should get some ginger ale and ketchup chips. They're ... Amy's favourites."

"Done."

Gary emerged from the grocers with two bulging paper bags. A tear down the side of one threatened to let their supplies spill across the pavement, but by some miracle, he managed to get them in the back seat before losing anything.

As their small town disappeared in the rearview mirror, a lump grew in Arthur's throat. What would they do if they found her?

"We should let Officer Thomas know where we're going." He kept his eyes on the road as he handed his phone to Gary. "Number eight on speed dial, but I would ... just send a text."

Gary nodded and typed out a message to the officer. "Will he be upset that we are looking on our own?"

"Don't know. Don't care."

It wasn't long before the houses that clustered together at intervals along the roadside dropped off completely and the scenery turned from small farms and homesteads to wild tree cover broken up by sprawling fields. They stopped at a small convenience store set at an intersection where the great Canadian highway turned north. The First Nations owner shook his head, sadness creasing his forehead, when they showed him Amy's picture.

"How long has she been missing?" the man asked.

"Since Sunday night, Monday morning."

Again, he shook his head and blinked concerned eyes at Arthur. "They're still looking for the last girl that went missing ... last year."

The man motioned towards a bulletin board, drawing Arthur's gaze to a white poster with the face of a young girl printed in fading black ink. The paper's edges were curling, and a rip that someone had taped back together marred its side.

"You got a poster? You should have a poster."

Arthur shook his head no.

"You get me a poster, and I'll hang it up. It's off season, and we don't get much business before the tourists show up in June, but you get me a stack, and I'll even hand them out."

"Why didn't we think of that?" Gary asked as they walked out and down the weathered and greying wooden exterior steps. "I'll ask Glen to make some up. He can hand them out around town as well."

The smile of the other girl in the poster haunted Arthur as they turned north and drove on. She looked younger than Amy. She'd disappeared a year ago? Why hadn't they found her yet? Arthur didn't even remember hearing about her. Had he forgotten or never been told? Was his ignorance the failure to simply pay attention to what was going on in the surrounding communities?

Arthur coughed around the lump in his throat. What would it be like to have Amy's picture hanging beside that girl as the paper aged and people forgot? He shook his head to clear his thoughts.

"You want me to drive?" Gary asked.

"No."

Why does he keep asking?

Arthur glanced over at his friend as they strapped back into their seat belts. "I hope you're not going to ask me that every time we stop. I'm fine. If I need a break, I'll let you know."

Loose gravel ground beneath the car's wheels as Arthur manoeuvred out of the small convenience store parking lot.

"How's the gas tank? Stops get pretty sparse for the next bit, and there won't be a place to fill up."

"We have plenty." Arthur tried to keep his tone calm, but his irritation with Gary's questions bubbled out. "Maybe we should have brought two cars."

"Hey! If you don't want me here, Arthur, just drop me off. I'll call Sarah to come pick me up. It's her that insisted I come along." Gary reached for his seat belt even though the car had moved out onto the road. "You'll break her heart, not to mention Rose and how she'll feel knowing you're out here all alone. I mean, come on! We just *won't* think about what will happen if you find Amy. I'm sure whoever has her is friendly and won't mind her dad showing up and bringing her home."

"Gary!"

"No, Arthur. Do you really think you can do this alone? Really?"

Arthur slammed on the brakes, throwing both of them forward against the straps of their seat belts. The sound of shifting angry gravel under the car and his own heavy breathing sounded too loud in his ears. "Really, Gary? You want to fight right now?"

Gary paused before he could unlatch his seat belt. "If you'd waited a few seconds longer to stop the car like that—"

"What? You'd have broken your nose on the dash? Maybe it would have taught you not to play with the belt while in a moving car."

"Arthur, what's wrong with you?"

"What's wrong with me?" Arthur's hands shook as he gripped the steering wheel.

Gary's eyes were wide in shock when his friend turned his way.

"My kid's missing, that's what's wrong with me. She's been taken, kidnapped. Who else knows what—and here I am sitting in a car with one of the men who kicked me out of our church and fired me from my job. One of the men whose fault it is my family is even in this mess!" Arthur found himself shouting into his friend's face, all facades of control crumpled. He leaned over, and Gary instinctively pulled back until his head touched the passenger's side window. "Did any of you think even once about how your decision would affect my family? Amy wouldn't have had to change schools. We'd still be living in the parsonage, in a safe neighbourhood. Rachel would have been able to come home after what happened with Jay, not stay in the same building where she's been living in sin. Did you even think of that?"

"This is not my fault, Arthur."

"No? Then whose is it?"

Gary shut his mouth at the question, his eyes filling with sadness, his shoulders drooping. "It's no one's fault, Arthur. I'm your friend. I'm just here to help."

"Friends don't betray friends. Get out."

Arthur pulled the car over to the side of the road, and it rested with one wheel touching the grass starting to grow back now that spring was in the air.

The sound of the slammed car door rang in his ears as he watched Gary's retreating back. The man's hands were jammed into his pockets. He hadn't even grabbed his bag from the trunk.

Arthur knew the walk back to the small convenience store would only take his friend a matter of minutes, but sitting in the quiet at the side of the road alone cooled his anger. Shame crawled into his chest as he saw Gary glance back. Arthur couldn't remember ever losing his temper like that before. It was childish and selfish. He closed his eyes as he admitted the truth to himself and let his forehead drop to the cool smoothness of the steering wheel. He didn't move from that pose until he heard the driver's side door opening. The chill kiss of a spring breeze sent a shiver up his spine.

"Arthur?" Gary's tone was soft. He'd squatted down with the driver's door wide open to the road.

The touch of Gary's hand on his shoulder made Arthur flinch, and for a second, his friend pulled away but then changed his mind and tightened his grip instead. "We'll find her. Or someone will find her."

Arthur wanted to scream, but he swallowed the urge. The effort irritated his throat, and he coughed, averted his eyes from Gary's direction, and grabbed a bottle of water from the cup holder at his side.

"Maybe we need to go home. Maybe this is too much for us both," Gary said.

"No." Arthur's eyes snapped back to his friend, the hand on his shoulder tightening. "I'm supposed to try." Arthur hated the pity he saw flood Gary's face.. He hated himself for hating it. "I'm sorry," he said after a few swallows of water.

Gary nodded and released his shoulder. As he stood, Gary let a smile curve his lips. "I didn't realize it was from you that Amy got her temper."

"That's not funny."

"It is, a little. But … How long have I known you, Arthur?"

Arthur shook his head. Dates weren't something he was good at remembering. "Long enough," he finally answered.

"Did we ever fully know you, Arthur?"

What was that supposed to mean? Arthur opened his mouth in protest, but words caught on the lump in his throat, and he coughed again. Maybe Gary and his other friends from Hope Is Here Church didn't know him as well as he thought they did. Did Arthur even know himself anymore? These last few months had been surreal. He wasn't sure if he knew the answer to that question anymore. His reaction to the changes and the damage they'd left in his life had been so different from what he expected, that now he found himself second guessing every possible turn his family's lives were taking.

He closed the driver's side door at the same time Gary climbed back in on the passenger's side.

"I'm sorry, Arthur."

"For what?"

"For how it went down that night. It's just … you and Rose and the girls have been struggling for so long, and you never took a break. You never stepped back to take stock of yourselves. We were all watching you breaking. I just …" Gary looked down at his hands and spread his fingers wide before pulling them back into relaxed fists. "You needed a respite. I only wanted it to be for a time."

"No one ever said anything—"

"We tried. You didn't listen."

Had they? Gary was right, and Arthur knew it, but hearing it said out loud for the first time stung.

Silence reigned as the car pulled back out onto the road.

What now, God? Arthur prayed as he set his eyes straight ahead.

"You can still trust me, Arthur," Gary told him.

Arthur nodded, unable to form any more words as his shoulders slumped in exhaustion. He would have to ask Gary to take the wheel at the next stop.

Amy

AMY

Amy grimaced at the cream coloured pill in her hand. The lights above the bathroom mirror cast her in a too pale light. She shoved the anti-depressant medication into her mouth and leaned over, head tilted to the side, and drank directly from the running faucet. When she straightened, she swallowed before sticking her tongue out at the mirror and wrinkling her forehead.

"Good morning, sweetheart. Ready to do your thing?" she asked herself.

She was tired, and attending church alone with her father was the last thing she wanted to do. But she would, knowing that giving in to his request would make him more likely to let her do what she wanted with the rest of her day.

During the church service, she slouched down in the pew and watched the only toddler in the whole church run the length of his parents' seat as the couple sat at either end to corral him in the small space. The mother groaned a bit too loudly when he found an escape by diving under the pew. Amy silently cheered him on as the small congregation ignored his antics. He was much better entertainment than the elderly pastor and how he droned on about a story she'd heard a hundred times before.

When they arrived home after services, she wolfed down her lunch and raced for the door, hardly registering her father's questions about where she was going and flying through her haphazard answers.

"Rachel knows Peggy. Why don't you ask her if you're so worried about who I'm with?" She shouldn't have been so pleased when her father flinched. But she couldn't help it. He needed to get over hearing Rachel's name. He'd let her move in with them, after all.

Leaving him silent when she slammed the sliding door closed felt too satisfying.

The sky was a light blue with not a single cloud to cast shadows on her outing. She wore a light jacket and rolled the sleeves up as she walked in the noon sunshine. It was a good day to be out and about. A warm bubble grew in her chest as she walked towards downtown. As it expanded, she couldn't help the smile that spread across her face.

Freedom. The word floated in her brain, and she giggled as she pinched her smile closed, holding in laughter. It felt so good.

When Archie's food truck came into view, Josh waved to her from the picnic benches, purple hair waving in the breeze. Amy spied darker roots peaking through the dyed strands and smirked. "Josh! Your true colours are starting to show."

Rohan rolled his eyes as he held Josh's hand.

Josh grinned back, his sharp features highlighting dimples as his eyes flashed with mischief. "And wouldn't you like to get to know those true colours better, Amy?"

"Hell, no!" she'd assured him as she took a seat beside the pair.

Clara and Brad both groaned from where they were seated across the table, tangled in each other's arms. Emptied paper bowls and wooden utensils littered the table between the group. Clearly, everyone had enjoyed the meal despite Amy's absence.

Rohan smirked as Josh jostled Amy's shoulder. He was a quiet boy and the polar opposite of his boyfriend. He had a calm assurance about him that oozed intelligence. Though Josh flirted with just about everyone who would let him get away with it, it seemed that Rohan didn't mind and felt secure in his position beside him.

Their relationship had shocked Amy at first. But as she got to know both of them better, she realized she had never felt so accepted in her life. They held no expectations of who she should be, Josh especially.

Why had it taken her so long to find people like this? They were so different from the friends she'd had at Hope Is Here School. "Sinners" is what her old crowd would have called them. Amy herself would have turned her nose up at Josh's brash flirtations and personality if they'd met before she fell from popularity. But not now, not when he invited her lonely heart in with flashed smiles and outstretched hands.

One thing she couldn't understand was why they hung out with Brad and Clara.

As the thought entered her head, she heard a snort from across the table. Brad stood and pulled Clara along with him. "We're off!"

"Already?" Amy asked.

"Yeah. Got stuff to do before this evening. See you then, Rohan." Brad threw the smaller boy a thumb and finger salute before ignoring the others as they left.

Amy sat silent for a moment as she watched Clara's backside sway with every step as she followed her boyfriend.

Josh shook his head at the pair.

"I thought we were all spending the afternoon together?" Amy couldn't help her whining tone. "I texted ahead."

"Probably getting last-minute stuff ready for the party tonight," Josh said, his elbows bent as he leaned back against the picnic table top.

Amy looked from Rohan to Josh and back again. "Did I miss something? What party? On a Sunday night? We aren't planning on going, are we? There's such a thing as school on Monday, you know."

"Of course we're going. *All* of us are. My treat," Rohan said, eyes gleaming with an anticipation Amy had never seen there before.

"What do you mean?"

"They have a DJ from the city coming, and Sunday is the only night he was available. Brad said he's just passing through."

"He's a big thing, I hear," Josh added. He made googly eyes at Rohan before shoving one last wooden forkful of poutine into his mouth. "Thanks, baby. I was famished."

Rohan leaned backward until he could look past his boyfriend. "I heard he's the best DJ in the city. You have to come with us."

That settled it. Only one thing besides Josh could light Rohan up, and that was music. "We promise we won't stay too late," Josh said. "You're not the only one who cares about exams. Rohan needs to keep his grades up if he's going to be a big bad lawyer and get us out of this cesspool of a town."

"Right." Rohan smiled as Josh hooked an arm around him.

"Maybe we should take her with us when we leave, Rohan. What do you think?"

Both boys grinned at Amy's exasperated snort.

"I'm not playing second fiddle to anyone." She meant it, and any more jokes about threesomes stopped.

Amy could never tell if Josh actually meant the joking as an invitation. But though she was taken with his openness and his acceptance, she had her limits. She was happy for them both, but the thought of taking anything that far turned her stomach.

"It's just the good little Christian girl in you, Amy," Josh teased. "You'll grow out of it."

"Or she won't," Rohan added. "Nothing wrong with not growing out of it, Amy."

Josh grimaced at Rohan and turned the conversation away from religion.

Amy kicked at the pavement under her feet. "You guys finished? The smell of grease is getting to me."

"Oh, I'm done." Josh jumped up and threw his plate as if it were a freebie into the nearest trashcan. The fork fluttered to the ground, and he dashed for it and flashed another roguish smile as he planted the fork beside the plate with a flourish. "Now, Rohan, are we ready to go shopping?"

Rohan groaned and patted his wallet through his back pocket. "Of course."

The experience of shopping with Rohan and Josh ended in the three spilling out of the local sportswear store laughing. Josh had tried on nearly every pair of shoes in the place, even the women's sandals.

As evening fell, the purple-haired boy swung his bag of finds, and Rohan counted the few bills left in his wallet. The amount of money he'd just spent on his boyfriend made Amy wince but also intrigued her. More than once she'd wondered if she should leave them to their fun and find something else to do. But Josh's insistence that she stay stoked the warmth in her chest. So she had.

A bag of chips and beef jerky was dinner as the three walked into the residential district. She hadn't been to Brad Black's house yet, and the sight of the tall white building lit up with a lawn spotlight that cast a rainbow of stars across its siding made her halt.

"Brad lives *there?*" she asked, her eyes widening at the spectacle.

"Yep. His Dad is loaded. It's the only reason he gets away with half the shit he does," Josh said.

Rohan nodded as Amy looked over at him, questions in her eyes.

"Then ... then why do we hang out with him and Clara at all?" she pressed.

Josh raised an eyebrow. "Um, because he's loaded!"

Rohan shrugged at Amy's exasperated sigh. "Josh enjoys being where the action is. Nothing wrong with that, is there?"

"I guess not ..."

"Come on, it's time for fun!" Josh raced up the walkway to the house's entrance and rang the doorbell. "Come on, you two."

As the door cracked open, Amy caught sight of Clara and her straight blond locks. The girl's eyes flashed when she glanced down the walkway, and Amy ignored the muttered, "You had to bring her?" as she joined Josh.

Amy gave Clara her biggest, brightest smile and let her voice rise into a mocking, girlish tone. "Hey, girlfriend. Are you going to let us in? I've heard it's going to be a wild night."

Clara cleared her throat as she let the door swing wide. "You sure a church girl like you knows how to handle wild?"

Amy took in the sparkling white tiles and matte grey walls of the entryway. It was as big as the new apartment's kitchen. Amy had to swallow before answering, "Oh, you know it, Clara."

"Twenty per person." The disdain in Clara's eyes changed to mirth as she held out her hand in expectation.

"Twenty? That's a bit steep for friends, isn't it?" Josh asked.

"Brad insists. This DJ is not cheap."

"Makes sense," Rohan said as he produced his wallet and leafed through bills.

Clara made a show of stuffing the shiny green and yellow bills he gave her into the front of her low-cut blouse.

The plastic content of those bills won't do anything to plump up that chest, dear.

Amy let her eyes linger on the tightly pressed v of Clara's chest for much longer than a straight girl should have. She made sure Clara saw, and Amy laughed as the girl wrinkled her nose at them.

"Don't make her mad tonight," Josh warned. "We're in her boyfriend's territory."

"She needs to tuck it in."

"You need to let it out." Josh let his shoulder drift into hers with a gentle nudge. "Come on! This is going to be a blast."

And it was, literally, for soon the music was pumping from speakers in the living room and those dragged out onto a connected patio area, filling the backyard with electronic rhythms as the DJ practised at his turntable. Then the people started arriving, and despite the cool spring air, the living room grew uncomfortably warm. The house lights dimmed, and the DJ grabbed the microphone to begin his show.

It was a party unlike anything Amy had experienced before and had her questioning if she was really still in the little Northwestern Ontario town of Barton and not on main street Toronto City.

Bodies jostled against each other as people began to dance. Coloured lights flashed against the ceiling and broke the night as they swivelled past the large patio doors to the outside that also teemed with people. Food on folding tables lined the entryway, and drinks were being served at a small bar in the living room. Red plastic cups passed from person to person over heads. The noise, the people, the smell of bodies and alcohol, it was overwhelming, and Amy revelled in it.

"You ever party like this before?" Josh asked as he pressed in close, his lips almost grazing Amy's ear.

"Party? Yes. Like this?" Amy let her shaking head answer for her as she took a cup Rohan extended towards her.

Amy was popular back at Hope Is Here Christian School. There had been parties before, but nothing like this. How much had the food alone cost? Any alcohol her former friends had gathered only consisted of what lined their parents' liqueur cabinets. But here? Someone had definitely gone shopping to supply this event. She no longer questioned the twenty dollar entry fee.

Amy remembered one night she downed three cans of beer and kissed her first boy. If her parents had found out, she'd be dead. But back then, her dad had left her actions and whereabouts as something for her mother to keep track of. He'd never asked questions like he asked this morning.

Amy licked bitter foam from her lips as she remembered that boy. He'd fumbled when trying to find places to put his hands as their lips locked. She remembered laughing about it with her friends later on, careful to leave out the fact she was just as inexperienced as he was. He'd become a walking joke and never spoke to her again. She hadn't cared. Back then, she'd been the queen. Now?

Rohan smiled at her as he wrapped an arm around Josh's waist. Their height difference made Amy smirk, but the kiss Josh planted on his boyfriend's mouth made her look away.

No, she'd never been to a party like this.

Together, they found a spot on a curved couch at the back of the living room. Squished as they were, it felt good to sit back and take in the sounds of the writhing life around her.

When Josh got up for refills, Rohan slid closer to her and slipped an arm around Amy's shoulder, a bright smile stretching wide

"What do you think of him?" he whispered, his alcohol laced breath warming her cheek.

Who did he mean? She watched Josh struggle through the crowd to the bar then looked back to the DJ. "It's great!" She shouted back, not sure if she could sustain a conversation over the surrounding noise. She smiled and pointed to the man behind the turntable. Amy didn't think he looked like much, but the crowd clearly loved him.

"Josh told me you'd love it." Rohan's smile faltered. "Amy?"

She leaned closer, his voice so lost in the thumping beat around them, she had to watch his lips to understand. The look on his face pulled at her heartstrings.

"Amy. Don't take Josh from me." It was almost a plea.

"Rohan. I would never ..."

But her friend didn't look reassured as Josh returned, oblivious to his boyfriend's shift in mood.

"Come on! Let's DANCE!" Josh shouted, throwing his head back and laughing as beer sloshed out of the cup he'd just handed Rohan and dribbled down the shorter boy's shirt.

Amy grimaced as Rohan was pulled off the couch. The boy handed her the cup he'd just tried to drink from before being pressed into the crowd. His head disappeared behind the mass of bodies closest to the DJ's table, but Josh stood out like a brightly coloured beacon.

What had gotten into the purple-haired boy?

Amy laughed as she watched his arms flail above the crowd. He was a horrible dancer, but he knew how to put his heart into it.

He's so free.

Feeling a tightness in her chest, she mourned her own inability to follow his example.

Poor Rohan. She hadn't realized he felt so insecure. But she had to smile to herself. Rohan felt threatened by her. Warmth spread over her cheeks.

Amy was so focused on watching Josh and looking for the occasional bob of Rohan's head that she didn't notice a stranger slip up beside her on the couch. "Hey, cutie. Want something that'll make you happy?" The weight of the man's body pressed into the cushions and her leg slid to touch his.

She tensed, but the warmth from the beer in her belly had spread through her limbs, making her slow to shift away.

"No, thank you." She tried to stand, but with two beers in hand, she struggled to balance and only managed to slide forward. The stranger placed a hand on her leg, and she froze, thankful she wasn't wearing a skirt as his fingers and thumb gripped her jeans.

How old was he? She got a good look at his dark eyes and blanched.

"Come on. Tonight's a night to be happy."

"Let go of me," she stammered as she pulled away.

The man's face looked familiar, but she couldn't place him. He leaned in close, sliding an arm in front of her to rest on the couch. She was trapped.

"Just finish your drink, dear."

Dear? The word felt wrong as his eyes crinkled, and lines formed around his mouth. He smirked. His breath smelled of alcohol and smoke. Her stomach turned over.

"Come on," he coxed, releasing the couch arm to tip one of the beer cups she held up between them. Only the cup separated their bodies.

Fear ignited from the well of beer, heating her gut. Her core clenched.

"Be happy, baby. You're with me."

She tried to look around, to catch someone's eye, but the crowd was intent on the music and the DJ prancing behind his table.

The lip of the cup touched her mouth as the man directed it. It turned up and beer poured onto her face. At first, it flowed over her closed mouth and down her chin, but a hard hand grabbed her face and forced her mouth open. The shock of it was too much. She swallowed.

Why?

Why was he doing this?

The front of her shirt was drenched, and she shivered despite the warmth of the bodies filling the room.

Why did no one see her? The man was nearly sprawled on top of her.. She squirmed and tried to shout but coughed instead as the last of the beer found its way into her belly. The last swallow tasted wrong as a lump of grit passed between her teeth and over her tongue.

"What was in that?" she gasped.

"That's a good girl. Now up."

She dropped the last cup she held, spilling Rohan's beer all over the hardwood floor.

"Brad is going to kill me!" A strange, uncontrollable panic built in her chest.

"Up!" The man jerked her to her feet. Someone beside them cursed and shoved back, pushing the stranger into her chest.

"Watch it!"

Amy watched in sluggish horror as her seat was filled with strangers' bodies, and the man pushed her forward in front of him, a hard hand on her arm.

"Where are we going?" She asked as she was moved through the crowd.

She didn't struggle. She told herself she should, but a weight had settled into her arms and legs, and if she did, she knew she'd fall under the feet of the surrounding people. She slipped in spilled beer. Her fingers clutched the sleeve of the man holding her as he hoisted her up and almost carried her away from the couch.

"Come on, sweetheart," a whisper in her ear urged.

"How much did you give her?" someone laughed. But Amy's brain ignored the conversation drifting over her head.

"Not much, but she feels like a dead weight. Here, take her."

She was thrust against a new chest, and the jolt rattled her brain enough to clear some of the fog creeping into her vision.

"Where are we going?" she asked again.

"Nowhere—"

"Amy? AMY?" someone called for her. She could hear it as people pushed past.

The man pulled her in the opposite direction.

"What did you give her? She shouldn't be this out of it."

"The normal mix. Maybe she was on something else already."

"Come on—"

"AMY?" The call sounded like Josh. She could hear his voice move over the head of the crowd.

"Hurry. The party is getting too big, and it won't be long before someone calls the cops to break it up. *Move her out.*"

"You sure you got the right girl?" someone asked as Amy was pushed up against a doorjamb.

"Let me go. I want to go back—"

"Don't worry, kitten," a voice purred to her. It sent shivers up her spine. Hands shifted, and she was held on both sides. Then a face came close, and she blinked into eyes she knew.

"Brad, what's going on?" she asked.

Brad Black patted her cheek as he pulled Clara along beside her. "You tell me, church girl. These men seem to think you owe them some money. So, like a good friend, I said I'd help you pay them back." His grin was wicked as someone pushed her out the front door and down the steps.

"AMY?"

It was definitely Josh calling for her. His voice rang out from behind. Amy tried to pull away, tried to turn and look for him. The hands on her arms tightened, and someone shoved her off the last step but held her up and kept her moving forward as her feet slipped.

"Someone get rid of that kid, and do it fast."

Amy heard Clara beg Brad not to hurt anyone, but she couldn't see past the line of male bodies that surrounded her.

"Shut your girl up, Brad, or we'll take her too."

A dark car loomed at the end of the walkway. Strong arms lifted Amy off her feet. The sound of someone's hand striking against skin rung out. Then Clara was crying and screaming, and Josh's voice shouted above it all. "Let her go! AMY! AMY! Brad, you dick, make them let her go!"

"No can do—"

The voices cut off as Amy was shoved into a car and the door slammed behind her.

The interior was dark, and the way Amy had been shoved inside left her half kneeling on the seat. Her arms were stretched out across someone's lap, and strong hands pulled her in so whoever had dragged her out of the house could close the door cleanly.

"Hello, Amy," the man said as he pulled her up by her forearms, his nose mere centimetres from brushing against her own.

"Who are you?" She trembled under his vice grip. It hurt. She whimpered.

"You don't remember? I tried to get to know you better a few weeks ago." He paused as the car door opened and closed again. Someone slid in beside them.

The new passenger was large and pushed Amy right onto her captor's lap. A scream bubbled up from the well of beer still in her belly. The new passenger laughed and fumbled with a zipper.

"Let me go," Amy sobbed.

"No, but don't worry, we're taking you to meet a friend." The man who held her sniffed her hair as it curled around them in a cloud. "Now, hold still, and this will all go a lot smoother."

Horror threatened to stop Amy's heart as red waves filled her vision and hands grabbed her leg. Something sharp was plunged into the soft tissue of her upper thigh. It burned as she jerked.

The man holding her struck her face. "Inject it now!"

Amy screamed as something was pushed into her body, then the needle was removed. Her gut churned, and she gagged.

"Oh, God, if she pukes on me, I'm going to kill her!"

Amy's face was shoved down in between a pair of bony knees. It was all she could do to breathe as the red was washed from her vision and her whole body felt like it was floating.

Jay

AMY

AMY DIDN'T KNOW WHAT they'd injected her with, but as they drove away from Brad's house, she barely heard or felt anything. She was braced with her head between a pair of knees, looking down at the blackness of a car floor and the dirt from many pairs of shoes. But she didn't care. She laughed. She could have been bent over like that for hours or for only minutes. It didn't matter. She felt none of it.

She relaxed. Even when pulled from the car, she felt removed from reality, like her soul floated apart from her body. She didn't know where she was. She didn't care where she was. The laugh that bubbled out of her lips sounded far away.

She looked around, but all the houses were dark. Nothing sparked recognition. Then again, she didn't care to recognize anything. She was in molasses, resigned as it held her in place. Voices spoke, but she didn't care to listen to them. She didn't register any particular person until someone snapped a finger under her nose before grabbing her chin and forcing her to look up.

She had seen those eyes before. She recognized that grin. It made her skin crawl despite the floating sensation. What was his name?

"Feeling happy, are we?" he asked.

She laughed in his face.

"Go get him," he ordered.

She felt a hard chair beneath her. When had she sat down? Where was she? For a moment she cared and looked around to see walls painted a faded mint green. Stains streaked them, as if the roof leaked regularly, and other dark marks that crept up from the floor. Her addled brain couldn't tell what they were from.

Then she smelled a stench like a broken backed up toilet spilling its contents across a floor. She heard moans, groans, yells, and whispers. They came from the only door to the room. Still, they were muffled, only distant disturbances trying to reach her but failing. Understanding what they meant was beyond her drugged brain.

The man still held her chin as he stood in front of her. His legs pressed up against her knees, but he let her look around. Amy couldn't help the bubbles of laughter that spilled out of her throat as she looked at his face. It contorted as if it was clay and someone was crushing then reshaping it.

"Get him in here. We don't have all night!" the man yelled as he let Amy's chin drop.

Her head lolled on her neck for a moment as he removed the support of his hand. She blinked as her vision bobbed with the movement. There was shuffling. A stupid grin spread across her face as someone she recognized entered the room.

Jay.

Several other people flanked him. But she didn't care about them. Amy tried to reach out as she called his name. "Jay! How's it going, Jay?"

Why didn't he reach out for her in return?

His face blanched as his eyes fixed on her.

"There you are. See. I told you I would find you some incentive." The man she recognized but couldn't name laughed with her as Amy reached out for Jay again. He grabbed her wrist as someone pushed Jay farther into the room.

"That's not my girl," Jay said, his voice low and hard.

"No. But I figured her sister was the next best thing. Besides ..." The man hauled Amy to her feet, and she flopped against his body. "I think I'll be having more fun with this one. She's got more spunk. Can you believe she ignored me when I tried to get to know her better a month ago? I didn't know she was Rachel's sister then. But it just makes it all the sweeter now."

A hand squeezed Amy's backside, crushing her against a hard chest.

"Let her go, Roger. She's just a kid."

"NO!" His shout startled Amy. Her ears rang. She whimpered, her senses finally telling her that something wasn't right. The man lifted the wrist he still held in a vice grip, and Amy felt the revolting sensation of his tongue on her finger. "Make the run, Jay. Or I eat her alive. You owe me too much money after your mistake."

"Let her go, Roger." Jay's face was hard.

Amy tried to pull away from the stranger. He held parts of her he shouldn't be touching.

"Pay me back, or I'll take it out of her ass."

More people pulled Jay from the room, and Roger let Amy fall back onto the chair. She gasped at the abrupt hardness and the realization she had no strength in her legs to hold herself up.

"Where am I?" she asked, her voice shaking. Her earlier mirth had dropped away.

"Watch him and make her disappear. Tonight."

Roger stepped away.

Who had he been talking to? The shapes of people Amy hadn't realized were in the room with them drifted into her peripheral vision. How many of them were there? She couldn't count them all.

A new man with a shaved head and dark circles under his eyes appeared in the doorway. "The cop's here. He wants to know if you have the girl."

Roger growled as he pushed past the man, their paths crossing right in the doorway. "If he's here already, we have no more time. Get her out of here."

"He wants his cut. Says he'll take it from her." The bald one nodded Amy's way.

One of her hands clutched the wooden seat, the other the back of the chair. Her body wanted to slide forward, but she held as tightly as she could.

"We don't have time for this," Roger said, his voice now muffled as he stepped down the hall.

The bald one protested, and the last thing Amy heard as Roger disappeared deeper into the building was a grunt.

Amy could do nothing but hold on to the chair. Its smooth dowels resisted her weakened hands' hold. Tears slid down her cheeks as her body slumped. She'd never felt so grateful for falling into a chair instead of nose first to the ground. Fear thundered through her chest as the tall, broad shape of a man entered the room. Shuffling whispered of more people exiting the room.

"Ten minutes, then we're leaving," someone said. The newcomer nodded.

Amy whimpered at the flash in his eyes as he unzipped his uniform's jacket. She knew this man, too. He'd ogled her as she rode in the back of his squad car. Where was his partner, the older man with the kind eyes? Why was a police officer in a place like this? What did he want?

"Please take me home," Amy said as the man's jacket hit the floor.

Every Prayer

ROSE

ROSE WAS CONVINCED ABIGAIL was an angel in disguise as she watched her friend manoeuvre around the fellowship hall at Hope Is Here. The woman had called Pastor Edwin from Barton Community Church then the board members from Hope Is Here the night before. They all felt the bigger fellowship hall was the best place for Abigail's plans. Now, as the noon hour approached, she directed people, and they filed into the room.

Coffee bubbled in the large forty-cup silver percolator in the corner. Someone had laid out plates of cookies. Several women in the kitchen worked on finger sandwiches. The room was a bustle of industry that formed in waves and moved with purpose.

Rose trembled as she sat on the cold metal chair watching. Everyone tiptoed around her, and she couldn't shake the feeling that this was how it would feel at a loved one's funeral. The air felt filled with cotton. The people she'd known and loved for years moved through the puffs, every set muffled. Even their gentle hellos felt distant. Then Rachel sat beside her and reached for her mother's hand. Her fingers were cold. Rose entwined hers around them, squeezing gently. She wondered if her own felt as icy as her daughters.

Rachel hadn't wanted to come back to this place, this church.

Rose didn't hold the same animosity the rest of her family did for the congregation of Hope Is Here. But fear had still crawled up her esophagus in waves of heartburn when Abigail had told her about the prayer meeting she was planning. Not just a meeting, a prayer day. Abigail had said she would not close the church doors until Amy was home safe. Her eyes had flashed with light to match her cropped curly red hair, and Rose had loved the woman all the more. Still, as the cold metal of the chair bit into Rose's backside, she wondered if her own presence was a mistake. People didn't need her or Rachel to pray ...

"Are you okay, Mom?" Rachel asked, leaning in close to Rose's shoulder.

"No."

"Do you want to go home?"

Rose had to think for a good long moment before she answered. "No." Leaving now would bring more unwanted attention and add to the cotton that surrounded her, cutting her off from feeling truly present. An invisible weight held her firmly to the chair.

"There are more people here than I thought there would be. How many of them had to take off work to come," Rachel wondered.

"And more will come over the lunch hour. After that, the crowd will thin out, I think."

"I hate this, Mom." Rose heard withheld tears in Rachel's voice. Her daughter fidgeted with the hem of her shirt, took a deep breath, then blurted out, "What if it's my fault?"

"What do you mean?" Rose stopped scanning the other people in the room to concentrate on her daughter. "How on earth could something like this be your fault?"

Rachel swallowed. Her fingers, still joined with Rose's, trembled. She picked at a string that had come loose at her shirt's hem. "They tried to take me first. What if ... they took her because they didn't get me?"

Rose didn't know what to say. The possibility had never occurred to her. Finally, she drew in a breath and said, "It wouldn't matter either way. This is not your fault. They are evil people. You don't dictate their plans."

Rachel's eyes swam with moisture as she looked up into her mother's face.

"I love you, Rachel."

"I love you too, Mom."

What else could Rose say? She untangled her fingers from her daughter's and slipped her arm around her back. Neither had any more words.

Rachel's cell phone buzzed, and she shifted out of Rose's embrace to pull it from a pocket and look at the screen. Her expression steeled as she slid it away again, the notification cancelled. Rose held back her curiosity. It wasn't any of her business. Better to focus on Amy and what they could do to help find her.

Glen came bumbling into the room. His presence broke the tension as he bumped into a chair, jostling an older man, who yelped at the impact. "Sorry!" he said as he clutched a large stack of papers to his chest. "Are you okay, Mr. Stratfurd?"

The man nodded and assured Glen he was before asking why on earth the boy was in such a hurry.

"Just wanted to get these laid out as soon as they were done."

Rose assumed he meant the papers in his arms. But she didn't know what was on them until Glen held one up for the man to see. Amy's face, printed in black and white, smiled out at the room. The sight of the picture ripped open the cotton cloud around Rose. She pushed away from the cold chair and stood on tired legs.

"Mom?" Rachel asked, her tone worried.

"I'm okay." Rose walked over to Glen, hands shaking as she took a paper. The simple poster asked if the viewer had seen Amy Grill and listed several numbers, including Crime Stoppers, as places to report any sightings.

Rose couldn't hold back her tears as Glen explained that he'd gotten a text from Gary asking him to make them up. "He sent me a list of places to bring them to. I'm going to be asking for volunteers to drive them up the highways."

Rose nodded as Rachel came up behind her to place her hands on her shoulders. She trembled. She should have brought her walker, but it stood half-folded beside the metal chair she'd vacated. As she gave the paper back to Glen, she didn't know whether to thank him or scream in his face.

It wasn't okay.

How could he put her daughter's face on a missing persons poster? How could such a thing be needed? She held in her grief at the worry in Glen's eyes. He was helping. This was helping. Her reaction was not logical.

Breathe, Rose.

"We'll find her, Mrs. Grill. We will. I just know it," Glen whispered as she turned back to her cold chair.

She perched on the edge of the seat again, this time with Rachel holding her, and let the cotton reform, pushing the noise of the room back and away from her tired mind.

At twelve o'clock, everyone quieted when Abigail rolled to the centre of the room. "Hello friends," she said.

Rose tried to listen. Her chair had finally warmed beneath her after Rachel had found a lap blanket and bundled her up as best she could with it. Now her daughter pressed a warm mug into Rose's hands. Muscles, tense from the chill, loosened.

Abigail's voice was calm but sad as she continued. "You all know by now that Amy is missing. We don't know the full story of how or why yet. The police are knee deep in investigations. But ... they believe someone took her."

A collective gasp rippled through the crowd.

"Glen has a few ideas about how we can help find her. We'll need volunteers to drive posters around town and up the highways to the east and west. If you can help with that today and tomorrow, please let Glen know." Abigail nodded at her son, a wan smile on her face as he nodded back and tentatively waved a paper bearing Amy's face. "The rest of us are going to pray. There will be a church staff member here twenty-four hours a day until they bring her home. The doors will remain open for anyone who wants to be here."

The warm cup in Rose's hands grounded her as Abigail's words flew by. The reality of the blanket across her lap, the chair under her, and the daughter who sat as close as she could, a leg pressed against her mother's, were all arms bearing her up from the waves of worry and fear that sloshed at her neck.

Abigail's words drifted over Rose's head like distant balloons whose strings dangled down, asking to be grabbed and held, only to dart away when Rose strove to understand. Her sleepless night had caught up. With the relaxing of her muscles, her body sagged, and she almost dropped her coffee.

"Mom?" Rachel saved the cup from Rose's unsteady hands.

"I'm fine. We need to listen."

"I should take you home—"

"Not yet." Rose's voice was again soft but firm. They couldn't miss this.

Abigail glanced over at them as she continued laying out a timeline for the first few days. "We are praying every and any minute for a phone call that they've found Amy and she's coming home. So the schedule will change as soon as we get the word."

Every head nodded.

"I would also like volunteers to be with Rose when she needs to go home. People who can bring her back to the church whenever she wants it or be ready to drive her anywhere she might need to go if we get a call about Amy."

Rose wasn't sure how she felt about people going home with her, and Rachel opened her mouth to protest, but Abigail cut her off.

"I know you can care for your mother, Rachel, but it's not right to leave you both alone when Arthur is part of the search." The look Abigail gave them told Rose if they refused, she would place Glen or herself outside their door.

Abigail joined Rose and Rachel as people filed by on their way to the sanctuary, where quiet music already played over the house speakers. "If you need to be alone, Rose, don't worry. We will give you space, and hopefully, we will get word soon that this is all over. But until then? I won't let you be without someone lined up to help."

"Of course, Abigail. You're right. Rachel has a job to go to, and I won't refuse help. Not this time. I can't believe you've done so much already. There's so many people here giving up their lunch hour."

"Did you think we'd forget about you?" Sarah asked as she walked up to the small group. She waved her phone. "Just got a text from Gary. The going is slow with all the stops, but they're several hours down the road now. No luck ... No one has recognized Amy's picture."

Rose felt her heart constrict. "At least they're together."

Sarah nodded as she squatted down in front of Rose's. "I insist on the night shift, Abigail."

"Done," the woman said as she smacked the armrest of her wheelchair.

"For tomorrow as well, please. I work, but I want to be with you in the evenings." Sarah placed her hand over Rose's lying limply in her lap. "Rose! You're so cold."

"Mom, I should take you home," Rachel interjected.

"When all these people are here? No. We need to join them." Rose watched her daughter exchange looks with Abigail and Sarah. "Do not treat me like a child." Her words snapped, making her friends flinch, but Abigail held Rose with her eyes.

"I do not view you as a child," she said. She reached to add her hand to Sarah's in the grip of friendship. "I am sorry if I made you feel like one, Rose."

Rose's ire melted as the love and compassion in Abigail's face coated her quivering heart. Maybe her friends had been treating her like a child for a reason. Maybe she was incapable of sound judgment while wallowing in self-pity and selfishness. Maybe—

"I can tell you're thinking self-depreciating thoughts. Stop it." Abigail's whip-like tone matched Rose's from moments ago.

Rose waited for Abigail to continue, to say her thoughts were wrong, to stroke her bruised heart. But she didn't. The compassion never left Abigail's face, but her eyes also never lost their glint. She marvelled at how much her friend had grown over the twelve plus months since Rose and Arthur had asked her to join Hope Is Here's staff as the head of the Compassionate and Women's Ministries. Abigail had always oozed kindness and compassion for others. Now her confidence had filled out to match her other attributes. She was steady, a calm assurance. Someone Rose knew she could trust.

"I want to stay. I need to pray," Rose told her then glanced at her daughter with pleading eyes. "We need to pray."

All three women nodded. Rose grasped the arm of her walker, unfolded it, and stood.

Ignored Calls

RACHEL

IT HAD BEEN MONTHS since Rachel sat in the Hope Is Here Sanctuary. Her eyes took in the familiar burgundy upholstered seats on the polished wooden pews, and her heart trembled. She'd slowly grown to hate this place over the last two years. Coming into the building and enduring sympathetic inquiries of people who'd shunned her since moving in with Jay was a whole new kind of hard. Her gut had rolled with every hello and handshake. But she'd stuck it out for her mother. Rose still needed her. But as she slid onto a pew beside her, Rachel didn't know how much more she could take.

Instrumental worship music played softly in the background. The crowd from the fellowship hall sat around them, heads bowed. Some people whispered prayers while others sat silent. One gentleman talked aloud, though quietly, admonishing God to lead the police forward as they looked for Amy and to protect Pastor Arthur as he did the same. Some faces were screwed up in emotional agony while others were expressionless during their private internal conversations. So why did Rachel feel like all eyes were on her?

No one is looking at you, no one cares that you're here. They're thinking of Amy. Get a grip.

She tried to sit still, but as the seconds ticked by, her legs itched, forcing her to rub at them through the fabric of her jeans. She squirmed, she shifted, she closed her eyes, but couldn't bring herself to speak to a deity she wasn't sure was there. If He was, did He even care?

In the end, she abandoned the self-imposed mission of staying at her mother's side, mouthing that she needed to use the bathroom as Rose looked at her in question.

You're weak, her brain taunted. *You're useless and don't belong in this building.*

It must be the stress that made her brain swim and her thoughts race. A cold splash of water from the ladies' bathroom sink did little to ground her, but as she walked back out to the foyer and looked to the sanctuary where her mother sat, head bowed, at least she could breathe a little easier. The sanctuary felt like it was filled with heavy air her body refused to suck in. She dreaded going back to sit in it, so she lingered in the doorway.

A vibration from her pocket made her jump.

Her heart raced as she fished out her phone. Would it be her dad? Had they found something? She was sure the police would call her mother's cell, not hers, if they had news. Her heart sank as "Pat", Jay's mother's name, flashed across her notifications.

No, not right now.

She'd ignored several calls from the woman over the last week. Rachel felt bad for doing it, but Jay would probably try to reach her through his mom, as she had blocked his number from her phone and removed him from her friends' lists on social media. Not that she used social media much, but still. She wasn't ready to speak to him again. She didn't know if she would ever be ready. Not after what he'd let happen to her, not after what he'd done and what he was probably doing right now ... Her phone silently vibrated again as she held it, staring at the screen. A text came through that started with the name Jay.

Rachel shoved the device back into her pocket, ignoring a third round of vibrations. She almost stepped forward into the sanctuary, but as she raised her foot, she felt the thickened air resist her momentum, slowing her down. She planted the raised foot back beside the other, crossing her arms over her chest. She couldn't go back in there. She resigned herself to watching her silent, unmoving mother.

The phone in her pocket continued to vibrate, and Rachel closed her eyes, resisting the urge to grab it again. If she did, she didn't know if she would answer or power it off. She couldn't do either; her dad could call at any time. She sighed with relief as the phone stilled, looking around at the empty foyer, thankful no one had heard her, but as a ringing sounded through the sanctuary and Rose lifted her cell to her ear, Rachel's breath caught.

Rose turned to look for her. Her eyes searched and stopped on her daughter standing in the shadows. Rachel's heart sank to her feet.

Rose pulled her walker from where it rested at the end of the pew and dragged her body to the seat's edge with shaking arms. Rachel hurried back into the room. The sight of her mother's weakness pricked.

"I'm sorry, Mom, I should have come right back to you," Rachel whispered as all eyes watched them.

Rose didn't seem to hear her daughter as she struggled to keep the phone pressed to her ear and stand at the same time. "Are you sure?" she asked the soul on the other end of the call. "And you're positive?"

Rachel grasped her mother's arm and placed a supporting hand on her back as Rose shuffled forward, placing her hips between the walker's metal sides.

"You need to call this in yourself, Pat—no, I know it's hard … Alright, I'll do it. But be ready to get a call or visit from the police." Rose switched what hand pressed the cell to her ear. "Yes, Pat, I know. Thank you."

As Rose ended the call, the whole room seemed to press in around them. People slid closer, a mix of hope and dread in their eyes.

"Rose?" Abigail asked from across the room.

Rose ignored everyone. The steel in her eyes almost made Rachel release her grip on her mother's arm. "Jay called Pat a half hour ago. He told her who has Amy."

Jay knew? Knows?

Rachel raised a hand to her mouth as she gagged on guilt, frozen in place until someone pulled her along beside her mother out into the foyer. Someone else, she thought it was Abigail, shooed people away and directed them back to the sanctuary, asking for space for Rose while she called the police.

How long had Jay been trying to contact her? For how long had he known about Amy? Could ... could they have stopped her abduction, if only Rachel hadn't blocked him out of her life? Was this even more of her own fault than she'd thought?

No. No!

She didn't hear her mother on the phone with the police giving out the sparse details from Pat. No, she only heard her inner voice droning in her ears.

You don't know what they had planned for you.
What if they took her and brutalized her because you ran away?
What if they kill her because of you ...

Rachel hadn't realized she was moaning as the voices filled her mind. But someone gently shaking her shoulders brought her back to herself as bile rose in the back of her throat again.

"Rachel, are you okay? Rachel, calm down. Someone grab her a chair! We should have left her in the sanctuary."

Was it Glen? If he didn't step away from her, she was going to puke all over his shoes. She pushed him away with one hand while holding the other firmly over her mouth. Her eyes darted around, looking for the hall that led to the bathrooms.

"Rachel?"

She pulled away from the single hand left on her shoulder and dashed for the women's bathroom. The heavy door gave way as she pushed in. Cool, moist air engulfed her as the door swung shut behind her. Every toilet stall door was ajar, and her heart leapt with gratitude. No one else was there to witness her weakness.

A minute later, she grasped the edge of the toilet seat, her gut writhing in agony, her chest constricting with dry heaves, her mind and heart in tatters. She wanted to close the stall door and forget about the world outside. She reached behind herself to pull it shut when she heard the bathroom door squeak open.

"Rachel?"

If only they would leave her alone. If only she could sink into the floor, into nothingness, where the stress of the last few months meant nothing and her mind would finally have peace. But, no, the voice wouldn't leave her alone. Her hands on the toilet's rim shook.

"Rachel," someone called through the stall door.

"Please just leave me alone."

Rachel's heart pounded as her breathing became uncontrolled. She laid her head back against the stall wall and closed her eyes, willing whoever was on the other side of the door to go away. But they pressed on again.

"Rachel, the police are asking for you and Rose to come to the station."

Oh, God, no, anything but that.

What would they think of her? Her sister was in real trouble, and here she was paying homage to a toilet, unable to hold herself together, unwilling to do her part. She clenched her fists as she realized she had no choice. She had to go.

For the last two years, it has seemed like the whole world revolved around Amy. Her destructive behaviour had escalated. She had trouble with friends, trouble at school. Shouting and hate-filled words burst through their home every day. Rachel had fled into what she'd believed was the safety of Jay's arms and the apartment. Now she was being sucked back into the turmoil. Except this time, it wasn't Amy's fault. It was hers.

How was she going to tell her mother?

"Rachel?"

She let the stall door open, and Sarah came into view. Her friend crouched down in the doorway to lay a hand on her knee.

"It will be okay," she said, her eyes shimmering with moisture. "They'll find her. They'll bring her home."

Rachel's heart stuttered as she wondered if she really wanted that to happen.

Interview

RACHEL

THE POLICE STATION WAS a single-story brick building with a line of windows that looked out onto the street. Rachel shivered despite the sun shining through those windows, wrinkling her nose at the scent of window cleaner that lingered in the closed space. The five feet wide hall was enclosed by a white wall that blocked the natural light from the inner offices. Set into the wall was another window with a counter behind it. A metal circle with rows of holes punched through it glared at her from its centre. She let her mother shuffle forward and press a button beside the metal circle, sending a chime through the rooms behind the wall.

"Hello?" Rose said to the woman in a blue pantsuit and chunky black glasses that appeared at the sound of the buzzer. "We are here to see Officer Thomas. He's expecting us."

"Names and IDs please," the woman asked.

Rachel helped her mother look through her purse, drawing out her driver's licence before adding her own ID to a small drawer the woman pushed out from the wall for them. As the cards were received, the woman smiled reassuringly at them. Apprehension still crawled up Rachel's legs in shivers, and her mother looked pale and tired as she clutched her walker's handles with blanched fingers.

"He should be expecting us," Rose repeated as the woman turned, the light from a computer screen reflected in her glasses.

"I'll just let him know you're here, and someone will come meet you at the door to your left in a moment."

"Thank you," Rachel and Rose both said at once.

"I didn't realize visiting the station was such a process," Rose muttered as they stepped to the left towards a door painted white to match the walls surrounding it.

Rachel also found it unnerving, but she smiled for her mother's sake. The warm tea Abigail had forced her to drink before leaving Hope Is Here Church sloshed in her gut, and she hoped she wouldn't be reliving the scene from the church's bathroom here at the police station. She focused on breathing to calm her irritated nerves.

The white door cracked open, and a young officer with twinkling black eyes and a tribal tattoo scrawling over the left side of his neck greeted them. "Welcome, ladies. Come on back."

Rachel blinked at him for a moment. The young man took her attention in stride and smiled again, beckoning them both to follow. Blushing at her own rudeness, she obliged.

The young officer was patient as Rose made her way slowly into the second hall with Rachel right behind. As soon as the white door was closed on the stark entryway, Rachel felt her shoulders relaxing. Old-fashioned brown speckled flooring and blue walls warmed the space, and soon the second hall gave way to an open-style office area where their guide exchanged nods with one of his colleagues seated at a desk. Rachel didn't know how many officers the district employed, but it looked like most of them were out on patrol.

The young officer showed them to a carpeted room decorated with landscape art on each wall and furnished with a simple wooden table and four chairs.

"I'll get you ladies some water for while you wait. Officer Thomas shouldn't be long." He bowed out of the room as Rachel offered a chair to her mother.

"Well, this isn't so bad," Rose said. "I was afraid we would be sitting in an interrogation chamber complete with a metal table and chairs bolted to the floor."

"Oh, Mom." Rachel shook her head as she took the seat beside her. But she, too, was relieved at the warmth of the room. Still, she wiped moist palms on her jeans as they waited, dreading the questions soon to come.

"Mrs. Grill?" an older officer with a gut that pressed against his uniform shirt asked as he entered the room. His face was solemn as he set two water bottles down on the table in front of them, pushing one farther down the table for Rachel.

"Yes, that's me," Rose answered.

"I'm sorry to call you in, but I always communicate better face-to-face than over the phone. I'm Officer Thomas. Lead on the investigation into your daughter's disappearance. These are from Officer Benjamin." He motioned to the water bottles.

Rose let out a small gasp, and Rachel pressed a hand to her mother's shoulder in support. Her own throat threatened to close with emotion as the officer sat across from Rose, a large notepad and pen in hand.

"Now, I need you to do your best to talk slowly as you tell me exactly what Pat Kenny told you."

Officer Thomas leaned over the paper and took notes while her mother recounted the call from Jay's mother. With the man's head bowed, Rachel found herself focusing her attention on the balding patch exposed on the crown of his head.

"The call came in while we were in a prayer meeting. I'm not sure of the exact time, but I called in right after," Rose said. "Pam guessed that Jay was on the road somewhere when he called her. He wasn't using his usual number. He said he'd been trying to call Rachel for days ..." Rose looked over at her, and Rachel had to remind herself to breathe. "Jay told her he'd seen Amy on Sunday night, that the men who had her were dangerous. He—"

Rose stopped, and her shoulder trembled under Rachel's hand.

"Did Mrs. Kenny say if Jay told her where he was?"

Rose shook her head. "Only that she could tell he was in a car."

"Please try to continue, Mrs. Grill." The officer's voice was gentle, but he didn't look up from the paper as he scratched out a few more words.

"He said he was sorry, that he owed these people money. He told her this was all … all his fault, but he didn't know why they'd taken Amy. Pat said he was very upset and difficult to understand."

"Very good, Mrs. Grill." Officer Thomas turned to Rachel. "You're Rachel, yes? Jay's girlfriend?"

"Ex-girlfriend," Rachel corrected him.

"Alright, and when did you break up?"

Rachel pressed her lips together, and Officer Thomas arched an eyebrow as he waited for her answer.

"I know it's uncomfortable to talk about your personal life, but I need all the information I can get to paint a picture of what is going on. We need motive for actions to try to figure out what exactly went wrong. This is important so we can try to guess what the abductors might do with your sister."

"Guess?" Rose asked, her voice rising in surprise and objection.

"Until we have concrete information about where she is and who has her, I'm afraid it's all guesswork, Mrs. Grill. We're trying to get ahead of these people, but it's not easy."

Rose didn't look happy, but she stayed silent. Rachel worried that this interview would impact her mother's health. She looked so pale.

"May 1st, I got a call from Jay. He lost the apartment we'd been sharing, and … I ended it then," Rachel said.

Officer Thomas nodded as she spoke. "He would still have been in jail at that time, I think. How did he take the news?"

"He hung up on me."

Irritation tickled the back of Rachel's neck as the officer nodded at her again.

He's going to give himself whiplash doing that.

"And how was your relationship before the breakup? I reread the report logged on April 24th. You didn't mention if you and Jay were having problems before then."

Rachel didn't answer. Worry lines creased Rose's forehead as she listened, and then she coughed, drawing Officer Thomas' attention away from Rachel.

"Miss Grill … would you rather your mother step out of the room while we talk?" he asked.

Rachel rubbed an itch on the back of her neck and crossed one leg over the other, trapping her second hand in between them for warmth.

"I think right now is the perfect time for me to visit the bathroom." Rose stood from her chair with shaking legs and pushed her walker towards the door.

"Mom, no, it's okay," Rachel protested, but Rose shook her head.

"Perhaps the officer who showed us the way in could help me find my way?" Rose asked.

"Yes, of course." Officer Thomas rose as well and opened the door for Rachel's mother. He called out, and Rachel heard the young man reply before Rose disappeared out the door.

When he turned back, he asked, "Door open or closed?"

Surprise at the question made her stutter, "Um, is that ... is that normal?"

"As you are still a young woman, what's normal is what you're comfortable with. You're not being interrogated, Miss Grill. But all the information you can give me is relevant."

"Then closed."

Rachel could sense true concern from the man as he again sat down across from her and grabbed his pen. She'd never had much contact with the police before. She'd never been afraid of them or mistrusting. But over the last few weeks, their attention had been intimidating, no matter how needed it was. It helped that Officer Thomas was taking the investigation seriously. She also had nothing to hide. Sure, it was embarrassing, but she'd done nothing wrong. She didn't need to be afraid of honesty. Gratitude for her mother's willingness to give her privacy during this conversation intertwined with shame at having let her leave.

Rachel took a deep breath. "I guess ... things hadn't been going as well as I had hoped since moving in with Jay," she admitted. She told Officer Thomas about her doubts, about their money issues, about the man who had come to the apartment, about how distant the relationship had seemed for the last few weeks before that terrible day. She recounted a few moments of fear from her own experience of attempted abduction and shivered as a bead of cold sweat ran down her spine.

When she finished, Officer Thomas leaned forward and pushed one of the unopened water bottles closer to her. His eyebrows knit together as he leaned back again.

"Thank you for your honesty, Miss Grill." When he got up and opened the door again, Rachel felt lighter. When Rose reentered the room, she gave Rachel a once over before sitting down and patting her daughter's knee.

"Now, Mrs. Grill, I'd like to go over what you know about the incident Amy had at Archie's Food truck on April twenty-second. I was one of the officers to bring her home, so I have her statement and have reviewed it several times. But I wanted to know what Amy told you. As her mother, you might have been privy to more information."

Rose did her best to recall anything Amy had told her about the ordeal, but she didn't seem to have any new insights to offer.

Officer Thomas went on to ask about Amy's new school, her friends, old and new, and any past or present boyfriends. The list of questions dragged on.

"I feel like we've already given you most of this information, Officer Thomas," Rose commented. "Arthur was thorough with what he told you at the school and afterwards."

"I know. I'm just hoping we missed something. Even a small thing like a forgotten name or missed outing could help make a connection. I understand your husband is out of town looking for her."

Rose nodded, and Officer Thomas clicked the back of his pen nervously. "I think it's time he comes home, Mrs. Grill."

Rachel wondered why. Wasn't it best to have as many people out looking for her sister as possible?

Rose said as much as the officer stood to leave. "He is determined to find her," she said.

"That's what worries me. You have no idea what things people like this are capable of. The closer we get to finding them, the more desperate they may become."

"What are you thinking, Officer?"

He didn't answer before opening the conference room door. "Nothing I can tell you yet, Mrs. Grill. I'm sorry. Go home. Rest. Do some more of that praying you mentioned earlier. We need all the help we can get."

Truck Stop

ARTHUR

The driving, stopping, asking, and flashing of Amy's picture into any and every stranger's face seemed endless. Arthur's hands rested firmly on the steering wheel, but his shoulders sagged with a mix of relief and apprehension as a large paved parking lot appeared in the distance.

When they'd turned north earlier in the day, the clusters of humanity and places to stop had thinned, but on crossing the Ontario border and entering Manitoba, they'd increased in frequency. The landscape had also changed from hills, rock formations, and swaths of mixed evergreen and deciduous trees to sprawling fields that stretched past the horizon.

As the parking lot neared, a sign announced Crossroads Truck Stop.

Gary groaned as he stretched his legs in anticipation. "After this stop, if we press on, we should be able to reach the city sometime tonight. But with Officer Thomas wanting us to turn for home, what are you thinking?"

Arthur wasn't sure. The police weren't telling them much, and the messages from Rose had been desperate and brief. He understood Officer Thomas withholding information until he had hard facts and a plan for moving forward, but he didn't appreciate the fear he'd instilled in his wife's heart. Rose had almost begged him to come home. He'd reminded her about the pull to go they'd both felt early that morning, but it seemed like the tug had stopped for Rose as her day of waiting, wondering, and worrying had dragged on. Was she right? What chance did he have of finding Amy himself?

"I'm not ready to turn around yet," he told Gary despite the doubts.

"I'm not either," his friend answered.

A long, single-story building appeared as the parking lot grew in their vision. Little else surrounded the lot but roads, fields, ditches, and fence posts. The blacktop of the lot stuck out like a stain on the landscape. Arthur couldn't help but feel relieved when only a few big rigs and smaller vehicles peppered the space as they pulled in. When he turned their compact car towards the sign designating slots for smaller vehicles, a loud honk sounded as a rig with a bright red cab barrelled in behind them.

"What the!" Gary gasped.

Arthur pulled hard to the right to let the huge truck by. "At that speed, he couldn't have even slowed for the turn!" His heart skittered as the big rig passed and pulled to the left towards the extra large parking area. "He almost flattened us!"

Curses gathered at the back of Arthur's throat, but he bit them back and took a deep breath. Still, the word "idiot" rang through his mind like a gong as they pulled up to a long building and parked between generously spaced yellow lines. Maybe it was time to let Gary drive again. A shiver ran down his spine as he looked over at the semi parked in between extra long lines. The rig with the red cab had swung wide before pulling into a spot in the centre of the lot. Arthur didn't think he could handle seeing the driver get out and hurried to the raised sidewalk belting the building and pushed through its double glass doors.

A chime announced their entrance, and Arthur nodded to Gary as they split ways. Gary made a beeline for the bathrooms, and Arthur scanned the tops of shelves packed with snacks and other goods a driver might need on a long-haul trip. A few people roamed around the food aisles and coffee bar set against the back left wall, but Arthur headed straight for the checkout. He readied the picture of Amy on his phone before stepping up to the counter crowded with trinkets and small snack packs.

"Got a pump number?" the elderly man behind the counter asked.

Arthur shook his head and held up his phone screen. "I'm looking for my daughter. She's been missing from Barton Township since Sunday night."

The man squinted at the picture, and Arthur let him take his phone for a closer look.

"What's her name?" the man asked as his bush-like eyebrows knit together.

"Amy Grill. She's sixteen."

The elderly gentleman muttered a curse as he passed Arthur back his phone. "I'm sorry. I don't think I've seen her before. Have you got a poster or something I can hang up in the window? We get a lot of traffic through here, especially in the evenings."

The last drops of enthusiasm for the search dribbled out of Arthur. "No, I wish I did. We left this morning in a hurry."

"I can email you a PDF to print one yourself if you've got the supplies in your office." Gary stepped up behind Arthur, holding his phone in one hand and a dark brown to-go cup with steam rising from the vent in the lid in the other.

"We got a printer in back. I don't use it much, though. What's a PDF?" the man asked as he ran a hand through his grey and white beard.

"I can help you if you have the time," Gary offered as he set the to-go cup down on the counter.

The elderly gentleman typed a price into the cash register while they talked and nodded to the tiny three inch screen on the back of his monitor when finished. "For something like this, I can make time."

After Gary paid for his drink, the old man introduced himself as Austin Moore and called an employee's name into a microphone hidden behind the cash register's monitor.

Three other people wandered through the convenience store section of the truck stop, and it didn't take long for Arthur to approach them to ask about his daughter as he waited for Gary and Austin to finish in the office. After asking the last man, who'd looked at him sideways and merely shrugged at the phone screen, Arthur looked around the rest of the building. Where the gas station and convenience store ended, an open area held signs pointing toward paid shower facilities. A rack of brochures about local tourist attractions and local businesses, like auto repair shops, was placed in the centre of the large room. A few benches lined the walls, magazine racks and fake plants separating the seats.

At the end of the open space was a wall of windows that looked out over the parking lot and a small blue building made from a repurposed shipping container. It was raised on grey cinder blocks and fitted with windows and a slanted roof. The windows were dark, and a sign on the door that read "closed" in a dark red caught Arthur's eye. He walked over to the farthest window and read more words painted on the glass of the door: Truckers' Chapel. The red letters of the closed sign glared brightly back at him. It was sad to see a house of God, no matter how small, closed.

Empty and unwanted. Like me. Arthur mused as he turned his back to the sad sight, hoping Gary would be finished. *Will it ever be what it once was again? Will I?*

The three men all converged at the check-out counter together. Gary smiled brightly as he pointed to Austin and the stack of papers in his hand.

"I'll leave a few of these on the counter here for the guys to take with them. You never know where they'll end up. Some drivers long haul all the way down to Florida and back in a week."

"That's perfect, Austin, thank you," Gary said as he clapped the man on the shoulder.

Arthur felt tongue tied, and all he could manage was a nod for the elderly man, whose eyes crinkled in a kind smile.

"I hope you find her, and soon."

Before Arthur could reach the door, a man, head down and hands hidden in deep pockets, shouldered his way in.

"Sorry," the newcomer offered as he almost clipped Arthur while passing.

"No harm done," Arthur replied and reached for the door, but the man lifted red-rimmed eyes at him.

"Was that you I almost hit coming into the lot?"

Arthur paused to look him up and down before slowly nodding.

Gary, who stood behind them, verbalized his affirmation with a "yes."

"I'm sorry about that. Must have given you a scare." The man's tone was heavy.

For a moment Arthur wondered if the stranger was mocking him but decided that, no, the puffy eyes looked more like grief than anything else. Arthur held back an aggravated "yes".

"I got a call right before the turn and should have passed to double back instead. I'm sorry."

Arthur didn't know what to say. The newcomer wiped a hand over his face before rubbing his nose against his dark long-sleeved shirt. His distress was palpable, and Arthur felt a tug in his heart he hadn't felt for months.

Ask him what's wrong.

The question tried to bubble out of Arthur's mouth, but he swallowed it down, heart constricting with doubt and anger.

I'm busy. I don't have time to counsel a stranger. Amy comes first.

"Kevin!" Austin greeted the newcomer as he stepped out from behind the counter. "How are you, boy?" The old man's exuberance dimmed when he looked at Kevin's face. "What's wrong?"

Arthur turned again to leave, his heart, mind, and body all reaching for the doorway in a spark of desperation to be away from someone else's drama, but Kevin's answer stopped him in his tracks. The tug on his heart became painful.

"Mom's gone. I got the call just before pulling in. The hospital said it was sudden at the end."

His mother? Arthur felt the muscles in his chest loosen. He couldn't help but turn back again, even as the voices in his mind argued.

One told him to stay, to pray, to help, that it was his job. The other said to move on. He had enough trouble as it was. What was done was done, and he couldn't help this man. Amy was more important.

"I'm sorry to hear that, Kevin," Austin said. He took the man by the arm and pulled him away from the counter.

"Thanks. I'll be fine. Was just the worst time to get the news." Kevin looked back at Arthur.

Was he never going to be able to leave this building? It felt like his feet were stuck in quicksand as the man threw a thumb towards them. "I almost drove over those two in their car. I'm just so sorry, guys."

Gary lifted an eyebrow in question at Arthur, as if to ask, *Why aren't you saying anything?*

Arthur wondered the same thing himself. All it would take to get out of this place was a single sentence of farewell. Why couldn't he just tell the man he was sorry for his loss and leave? His throat felt sore. That must be it.

"I think I should grab a coffee too. Give me two minutes, Gary." Arthur's voice came out as a croak.

A gust of fresh air teased as the door closed behind his friend.

Coffee. I just need coffee.

When his feet finally obeyed the command to walk back towards the coffee bar, Kevin and Austin's voices were a steady hum behind him. He chose the dark roast blend and was soon back at the checkout, ready to pay and make his escape. As he set the to-go cup on the counter, Kevin came up behind him, arms full of snacks for the rest of his haul. Arthur glanced back but said nothing as he handed over the money and waited for his change.

"Do I know you from somewhere?" Kevin asked.

"I'm not sure," Arthur replied, finding his voice after a sip from the steaming cup. "I'm not from the area."

"Wait. Are you from Barton?"

"Yes, but ..." Arthur blinked at the man, surprised to hear his small town's name on a stranger's lips. He took a moment to look him over carefully. Mussed brown hair almost fell into his eyes, and the beginnings of a beard covered his cheeks. His eyes had lost some of the redness they'd held when he first walked into the building. Kevin looked like an average trucker, a bit young, but still average.

"Wait!" Kevin's eyes lit up. "Aren't you the pastor at that church? Hope or something? My stepmom goes to that church."

"Your stepmom?"

"Yes, Tina. Tina Hearth."

"Tina's your stepmom? Really? And, yes. Or ... I was. I've been looking for other work for the past few months."

"Well, isn't that something." Kevin's face broke into a full smile. "How is Tina doing?"

"Not sure. Like I said, I haven't served there for a few months."

"Sorry. I guess I don't know much about how a church works."

"What's this about church?" Austin interrupted as he came to take over at the checkout again.

"This here is the pastor from my stepmom's church in Barton, Ontario. I just recognized him."

"Former pastor." It irritated Arthur that he had to repeat it to the man. It also irritated him that he got so irritated about something so stupid. Why couldn't he brush such a small thing off?

"A pastor, huh? Without a church, huh?" Austin gave Arthur an assessing look. "Did you show Kevin the picture of your daughter?"

The elderly man handed over a copy of the poster Gary had helped him print.

"She's been missing since Sunday night," Arthur said as Kevin took the poster. Asking this young man about Amy should have been the first thought in his head.

"I'm sorry, I haven't seen her. But I'll take this with me. I'm on my way home to Alberta. Funeral arrangements to make ..." A redness returned to Kevin's face.

"Thank you, and I'm sorry for your loss." Again, Arthur's heart squeezed.

Pray for him.

I'm not doing that in front of strangers.

You would have a few months ago.

Would he have? Austin and Kevin were looking at him with a question.

"I'm sorry for your loss," Arthur repeated but added, "I'll be praying for you."

Then, coffee in hand, he left the building, feeling the eyes of strangers on his back like hot brands of shame.

When Arthur made it back to the car, he found Gary had settled in on the driver's side.

"You doing okay, Arthur?" he asked.

"I think we should stop for the night." Arthur looked at the car's stereo and the clock that shone the time in bright blue numbers.

"Sure. There are a number of motels along this route."

Feeling defeated and ashamed after his interaction with Kevin, Arthur sipped his coffee in silence for the rest of the drive.

God? Where is Amy? Are you with her? Please. Protect her.

The Camper

AMY

THE COARSE BLUE BLANKET Amy held to her chin made it itch, but she didn't let go of it. Every pore of her skin felt sour. She'd never felt so dirty. The haze of substance induced amnesia drifted in and then out of her brain. It was strange being able to remember what was going on one minute, and then completely forgetting the next, only to have the realization slam back in and steal her breath.

The worst part? She was utterly helpless. She hated being vulnerable. It always welcomed the red waves of anger into her heart and vision. But in this place? The red was strangely absent. All control over her life and body had been erased. Cold fear coated the red waves of anger, reducing them to near nothingness. Only coals smouldered under a blanket of fear. Would they be given a chance to flare in this place?

She lay on a bed that lined the side of an old camper. The cushions under her were a puzzle, and a foot or leg often slipped down in between them to the cold plywood of the deconstructed couch. A second bed sat across the front of the camper. She wondered if that was where the table folded out. Old campers usually had a fold-out dining area, right? Another rumpled blue blanket lay wadded on the floor just before the bed. Someone had thrown a grey stained sheet over the cushions, and a ripped corner revealed ugly pea green covers.

What a terrible colour.

The thought drifted away almost as soon as she'd thought it, and the fog rolled back in. The camper jostled. The movement sent her heart into her throat, and she couldn't help but squawk with alarm. But it didn't matter. No one was in the camper to hear. No, the men who had pushed her in through the slender doorway and dragged her to the bed had left almost immediately. She remembered the sound of the lock. Had they forced her to swallow something before they left? She barely remembered the hands holding her chin and a bottle of water someone shoved into her mouth to wash it down.

How long have I been here?

As a wave of memory fog receded and she understood she was in danger, she thought about looking out the window to see if she could gauge what time it was. It was cold. It couldn't be morning yet.

But her hands wouldn't move from the blanket she'd managed to pull over herself in her first few minutes of solitude. Her body wouldn't listen to her. She shivered.

God, I just want to die. Please. Just let me go to sleep and never wake up again.

The camper stopped moving. Amy heard voices outside the door. Her whole body was stiff, and she shivered as the door opened, letting in a significant draft. She smelled moist, fresh air.

A head of oily black strands poked into the camper, but the owner didn't enter farther than the doorway.

"She's awake," he said before closing the door again. The *click* of a lock stabbed into her returned solitude.

Voices from outside the door moved off, and Amy flexed her fingers. The muscles screamed at her. Why did absolutely everything hurt? Her body and mind had started to recover from the drugs. But as their effects dissipated, her senses came back in full force, bringing with them heightened pain, cold, and hunger. The water bottle they'd used to almost drown her before the long drive lay by her feet. She'd been so out of it that she hadn't noticed it was still there. She grasped for it, every move reminding her of how wrong this situation was. What had they done to her? Places on her body she didn't want to think about screamed at her for attention. She felt an overwhelming urge to get up and see if the small camper had a working shower or at least a toilet. But fear kept her on the bed. She felt like a cat that couldn't find a secure foothold and kept massaging the cushions with her movement. At least the motion eased some of the stiffness in her joints.

She hadn't realized how dry her mouth was until the first drop of water coated it. She swished it around her mouth to remove a film-like texture from her tongue then gulped, her hands shaking, drips escaping the corners of her mouth to wet her chin. Where were they? Where were they taking her? How long until this all stopped? Would she ever feel warm again, safe again? The effort of thinking was exhausting.

Once her belly filled with liquid, it ached, and she groaned, praying none would work its way back up. She was hungry. The water did nothing to curb the gurgling of her stomach. If only she knew what time it was.

When the camper door opened a second time, she scrambled as far back on the bed as she could, pulling the blanket up until only her eyes could be seen. The man with oily hair stepped up, and the camper rocked with his weight. He looked over at her and grunted. But he only rolled his eyes as she drew back, pressing her shoulder into the cold panelling on the wall and the glass of the window over the bed.

The man opened a cupboard and fiddled with a metal panel. When he finished, stale air blew from somewhere above her. She coughed. Dust filled the air, and the man wrinkled his nose as he pulled off his coat and sat down on the second bed.

"Don't try anything," he said to her before scooting back and pulling the blanket from the floor up onto his lap.

The blowing air slowly warmed, and Amy sighed as she let the tension in her back relax. But the door opened again, and the rigidity returned as a second man entered the camper. As the small room rocked again, Amy felt her gut churn.

"Good morning, sweetheart," the newcomer drawled at her. "Do you think she'll be willing to show me some gratitude after I give her breakfast?"

He didn't look away from her as the first man mumbled, "I wouldn't count on it."

"Well, she wouldn't really have a choice, now, would she?"

The thought of his hands on her sent shivers up Amy's spine. She gagged on air as he stepped closer and dropped a plastic bag at her feet.

"You only have two hours to sleep. Leave her alone." The first man closed his eyes and tucked his hands behind his head. He was too tall to stretch out, so he lay with his knees up, the blanket tucked around his legs and chest. "And don't you dare do anything with me in here. That's just sick."

"Two hours?"

Amy thanked God. The first man didn't look interested in her at all. Her heart pounded as the second one sat on the edge of her bed and rummaged in the bag he'd dropped beside her. He cursed under his breath as he tossed a small sealed cup of fruit at her as well as a bottle of orange juice. Her hands scrambled for the food but didn't open it. The orange juice rolled and found its way under her blanket.

"Bathroom's there. If you need to use it, do it now, because once I lay down, you're not moving again." The second man's grin pulled Amy from the bed. Her legs wobbled, and she prayed she wouldn't collapse to the floor in front of him, but she made it to the small door, fumbling with the strange latch in a rush of desperation. She slipped inside, shaking.

The same fake wood panelling that lined the main room of the camper lined the walls of the bathroom. The smallest toilet Amy had ever seen stared at her, and the sink was nothing but a wedge on the wall, its basin barely big enough for a single hand to fit inside. The second man laughed as she relieved herself, and the first tears she'd shed all night leaked from her eyes.

God, how did this happen to me?

Why?

A deep ache in her chest hitched her breathing for a moment, and she struggled to stay seated on the small toilet. She didn't want to look down at herself and flushed away the toilet paper as fast as she could. She couldn't tell if she was still whole in body. She wasn't sure if she wanted to know. It was clear to her that she'd lost pieces of her heart during whatever had happened since being taken from the party. How long had it been? Hours? Days?

"Girl. You're done!"

The loud voice jolted her off the toilet, and she scrambled to rinse her hands in the cold water from the tiny plastic faucet.

The second man ripped the door open a moment later and leered in at her. "Get back in bed."

She obeyed without a word, mourning the loss of the bright ire that would have risen from her chest under any other circumstances. She imagined for a moment that nothing felt as good as crawling back onto that bed and pulling the rough blue blanket up to her chin. She found the fruit cup and juice bottle where she'd dropped them and hugged them to her chest as the second man eyed her while stretching out across the edge of the bed. His head rested on the opposite side, and his feet invaded her space.

"See you in two hours," he said and closed his eyes, pulling the zipper of his coat up higher under his chin.

As she sat there in the quiet, huddled in her corner, the sun rose, and shafts of light highlighted the dust that drifted in the air. When the breathing of both men settled into steady rhythms, she dared a peek out at the world behind the plastic blinds covering the window by her head.

All she could see was pavement and the large bodies of semi trucks. Most pulled huge white trailers. A few had flat beds with goods covered with tarps held tight by industrial bungee cords. She watched men come and go, heard the slam of semi doors, watched as engines rumbled past until the towering white walls of the trailers opened up and she was looking out across open fields. She didn't recognize any of it.

Help

AMY

WHEN ALONE AGAIN AS the camper trundled down the highway, Amy found the courage to peer out the plastic blinds and watch the world whiz by. They made few stops along the road, and her captors didn't enter the camper again until lunch when they rummaged around for food and completely ignored her.

They'd turned the heater off after their early morning nap, but the chill had been driven from the small space enough that the worst of Amy's shivering had stopped. She didn't dare grab the second blanket that the first man had left on his bed, but she stared over at it longingly. Instead, she pulled the itchy fabric of her own blanket higher, tucking it behind her shoulders, and dreamt of the thick quilt on her bed in the new apartment. Would she ever curl up with it again?

The scenery soon changed from open fields, to city suburbs, and then finally the city proper. They stopped once to gas up but then pushed through the busy highways. Amy felt her heart shrivel as the scenery again shifted to open fields.

She tried to sleep, but the ache in her body was too deep, the unrest in her heart too full.

Where are they taking me? What will happen?
Why?

Why?

Why?

She remembered glimpsing Jay in the dark hours before the camper but couldn't remember if she'd spoken to him, what he had said, or why he was there. Only his face above the shoulders of many faceless figures haunted her. Had it been real? Why had he been there? She wondered if Rachel was all right. Then she wondered if her family even cared she was gone. Were they looking for her?

Her absence might be a sweet relief for all of them ...

She remembered moments that had been lost in the fog of drugs, and tears burned her eyes. Someone had pulled her from the house party. Josh's voice called her name. Hands touched her body in places no one had ever dared touch before. She pushed the memories away before they became too much. She still clutched the bottle of orange juice to her chest. It had warmed with her body heat, and the acidic flavour burned a spot in her mouth that she'd bit down on too hard. She wouldn't let go of it, though. It was a small thing, and as each sip drained the bright liquid from the bottle, she wondered if she would soon be consumed in the same way.

Not knowing the time was torture, but at least she was sure by now she hadn't lost more than a night. It was still Monday. But they'd travelled so far already. She trembled again and pulled her fingers away from the plastic blinds, letting them close. She could do nothing but sit and wait, dreading the future, reliving the past.

It wasn't yet dark when they stopped for the night. She didn't know her captors' names, but the man with dark greasy hair sported patchy circles under his eyes. He stumbled when he entered the camper. He didn't speak as he climbed into the second bed and instantly fell asleep.

She looked towards the door. Had he locked it? Where was the second man? Should she get up? Should she try to leave? What would happen if she did? Her heart raced as the questions stampeded through her mind. She slowly, quietly slid to the edge of her bed, the puzzle of cushions shifting under her, trying to follow in a tumble to the floor. She stopped to push them back into place and stood.

What would happen if the second man came in and found her up? Would he hurt her while the other man slept? She stood by the camper's bathroom door. If she stayed there, she could always say she'd just been using it and crawl right back into bed. Light from outside called to her. She visualized reaching for the door and pushing it open.

The man with the greasy hair rolled over, and her heart skipped a beat. His eyes were still closed. She couldn't do it. She couldn't reach for that freedom that beckoned to her. Fear turned her blood to ice, and she shivered before climbing back onto the bed and pulling the blanket over her head.

She used to be so full of fire. Where had the warm flames gone? Her legs cramped from being in the same curled position for so long, but she dared not move. The second man slept beside her again. The first man's soft snoring filled the small space with a constant noise that irritated like an itch she couldn't scratch.

The heater blew warm air, and condensation formed on windows as the night chilled them. She wondered how far they'd travelled. Waves of emotional and physical pain radiating from deep inside washed over her. In the ebbs, numbness held her in its grip. She tried to hold its nothingness. It was a place to hide when she had no more tears and no more hope. Even if they were looking for her, she was too far away. They would never find her.

When they got to wherever they were taking her, what would she do?

"I'm not driving another minute. I'm too tired," the second man growled.

She'd learned it was Tuesday, and they'd stopped after only a few hours' drive that day. She couldn't tell if the parking lot they sat in belonged to a gas station or if it was a larger truck stop like the first one.

"No one's following us. I say we plant it for a day or two."

"We need to make the drop. The sooner we get there, the sooner we get home," the first one said around a mouth filled with sandwich.

"I say we get a hotel room. The girl stinks. I'm not sleeping beside that another night."

Amy winced at his words. Did she really?

"Roger wants her gone, the drop made, and us home," the first man said.

"Roger didn't have to miss sleep to get her out of town."

The first man shrugged, clearly too tired for a fight. "Fine, but when we get back, you're taking the rap, and you pay for the room yourself."

"Fine!" The second man slammed the camper door as he left, and the whole room rocked with his frustration.

"Idiot," his partner said as he looked over at Amy. "If it was up to me, we'd dump you at the side of the road. There's no way one girl is worth this trouble."

Nearly scalding water rolled off her body, but she still shivered. The second man had gotten his own motel room, and they'd allowed her to leave the camper for the first time. He'd held on to her arm the whole walk across the parking lot and into a room that smelled of old cigarettes and spilled perfume. He'd kept a sharp lookout for the whole walk and hadn't let go of her even once the door had closed. No, he'd marched her right up to the bathroom and shoved her in then tossed her a plastic bag.

Once the door had slammed behind him, she'd found a small pair of men's sweatpants and an old t-shirt with a logo so faded, there was no way to tell what it had been. She needed new underwear badly. But there wasn't even a fresh pair of socks.

She'd stood there in the quiet for a moment looking around the white-tiled room before resigning herself to her fate and peeling out of her old soiled clothing.

Once clean, she'd run shaking fingers through her blond hair, working thick strands into curls just like she'd do at home. The face that stared back at her from the mirror over the sink looked gaunt. She shook despite the warm steam that still filled the room and the warm sweatpants tied tightly around her waist.

"Trash your old clothes," the man had called through the door and then given her a five minute warning.

She'd obeyed and crammed the last remnants of her life into the small trash can under the sink before opening the door to the main room. She shuffled out but stayed close to the bathroom, too afraid to let her eyes wander around the room. The carpet was a disgusting brown. The man had been smoking, and she coughed at the smell of cigarettes and him.

She closed her eyes and prayed when he pulled at one of her curls and gave it a sniff, standing so close, the smell of beer puffed from his breath into her face. She'd almost fainted with relief when his cell phone rang, and after a string of curses, he'd marched her back out to the camper.

God, will this never end?

She's spent the last few hours of daylight sitting on that same bed, curled under that same blanket.

The first man had told her he'd snap her neck if she tried anything during the night before pulling his own blankets over himself and falling asleep, only to fill the camper with the sound of his snoring again. At least she didn't have to share the bed. She stretched out and stared at the brown panelling of the ceiling for a long time.

You're such a coward, Amy. The old you would strangle him in his sleep.

The thought nearly stopped her heart. There was no way ...

It was full dark. The familiar ache from not moving nagged at her, but she didn't dare shift too much and wake the man across the camper. She didn't dare get up to use the bathroom even though its door stood ajar and the forgotten low light within shone. It cast long shadows across the walls and floor. She didn't dare sip from the bottle of water she'd been given earlier in the day, its contents nearly spent. Instead, she rested her head against the camper panelling and stared at the fogged window.

Help! her mind screamed at the darkness outside. She let her mind wander and with it her fingers. She reached towards the window and wrote the word her mind screamed, unthinking. Then she let the blind fall back into place and closed her eyes.

Help.

Kevin

KEVIN

KEVIN WAS USED TO driving unforgiving hours, and today was no different. His hands gripped the wheel of his semi, the lump in his throat stubborn and grating. It didn't matter how many times he tried to swallow, it stuck.

He'd only reunited with his mother a few years ago, and now she was gone. He swiped moisture from his eyes and took in a deep breath as the air cushion on his chair lifted and settled after a tire found a pothole in the road.

His mother hadn't been well for years, maybe decades. She'd never blamed his father or the trauma of divorce and losing her son for her health problems, but Kevin often wondered if it had played a pivotal role in her decline. He didn't remember her being so frail when he was small. Did his childhood memories paint her in a different light than reality? Had he missed it? He cursed his father and the time lost because of him.

It had been good to talk with Austin Moore at Crossroads Truck Stop. The man was a whole different level of kind than the average human being. He remembered most people who frequented his business by name. Kevin remembered his second time stopping and how it had felt when Austin, rubbing his chin, told him he remembered his face, but he needed help with the name that went with it. After that, it had been, "Hello, Kevin, son," at every visit.

Kevin had been sorry to see the Truck Stop Chapel still closed. He'd never gone in for religion, not even when his dad had remarried and his stepmother Tina had insisted his father attend church every week. But on a day like today, he ached for a place to spill out his questions. He didn't know what went on in churches, really. But for some reason, he assumed he would find a quiet place to think in the chapel, maybe someone to talk to. He needed to talk. He'd wanted to talk more to Austin, but the man had touched his shoulder with crinkled, sad eyes and told him he was out of time after ten minutes of listening to Kevin's story. He'd told Kevin to make sure to stop on his next trip and he'd do his best to carve out more space. Maybe they could sit down and have a coffee together. He'd do it too. That was Austin's special kind of kind.

Kevin rolled his shoulders, still holding the wheel tightly. There was no use getting choked up. The man had done what he could, and Kevin was grateful. He looked forward to his next stop at Crossroads.

Push for home, Kevin. You have a lot of work to do.

But how was he going to handle it all? How did someone go about arranging a funeral? Just walk into a funeral home? Did he have to call first? Would there be someone at the hospital to tell him what to do? What if they asked him to view his mother's body? Would he be able to handle it? He shivered at the thought of her frail frame hidden under a white sheet shelved in the hospital morgue.

After that, he couldn't stop the tears.

Kevin kept a close look at his watch. The hours he could legally stay on the move wound down with each glance at the digital screen. He'd passed the city long ago, skirting around its edge on the fast moving highways. Exhaustion crept into his shoulders. The coffee he picked up at the last fuel station wasn't working. He'd have to stop. Pushing for much longer would be dangerous.

The setting sun threatened to blind him as a sign announced the next town and its population. It was small, but sometimes the small places were better. Less crowded meant less trouble. He needed a shower, so he'd get a motel room instead of overnighting in the bunk behind his seat.

As groupings of buildings started to close in around the highway, he spotted a fuel station and motel with fused parking lots. It gave ample room for larger vehicles.

Perfect.

Making spur-of-the-moment choices was an art form for a long haul driver. Sometimes he had no way to plan his stops. He pulled wide before steering into the lot and circling the buildings, finding a centre slot with the nose of his rig pointed towards the street, perfect for pulling out early the next morning.

As he looked over the hood of the truck, the road still called to him. But he reconciled himself to an agonizingly slow evening and marked down the time in his logbook, taking note of when he could get up and leave the next day.

Mom, I'm sorry. You're going to have to wait for me to get to the hospital and start things. I promise I'm coming as fast as I can. And ... I'll do my best.

Was it a prayer? Could people who had died hear their loved ones? Was anything left of her drifting through the earth's atmosphere, or was she now nothing more than a mass of wasting flesh? He shuddered at the thought, wishing he believed in something, anything, to give him hope. But he didn't. He couldn't bring himself to pray to the God his father had flirted with. No good deity would welcome a man like Herald Hearth. No good God would.

The air smelled damp as Kevin jumped down from the truck's cab. Would it rain? He reached back in and grabbed his coat from the back of the driver's seat. First, get a room, second, shower, third, ask around for the best place to eat within walking distance of the truck. He took a quick stroll around the loaded trailer before heading into the motel's office. He would find time for a more thorough once-over later.

The motel office was small and cluttered with file cabinets, but the man behind the counter was chipper and efficient. Kevin groaned when he learned only fast-food places were within walking distance of the motel. But the gas station next door had a good supply of convenience food, and every room had a list of the best restaurants that offered delivery.

"If there's anything else you need, just ask." The man winked as Kevin left the office, key in hand.

Kevin ignored the offer, not interested in the extras an emphasis like that usually meant. But he made a point of looking around the parking lot a bit slower, just in case there was a marker he could find that could tell him where to stay away from. His was the only rig. A small car and a pickup truck sat close together at the end of the building. Lights from the rooms in front of them were on, but all was quiet. Behind his rig and parked at the back of the lot was another pickup truck with a camper hitched to the back. The camper door was wide open, and a square man with greasy black hair sat on its small step, puffing on a cigarette. The man screwed his face up when he noticed Kevin looking his way.

"Oh, great," Kevin muttered and turned his back to the man. "Room first, then I'll do the walk around the rig."

He wondered if he should find a fresh parking space. He didn't like the man's look, and that camper was too close. Oh, gods, what would a camper be doing in a motel's parking lot? Kevin didn't want to think about what it meant. He groaned as he found his room's door and threw it open. If he moved the rig, it would draw too much attention. He'd just have to keep his head down when out and about. But first, he needed food and a shower.

It was dark, and the wind pulled at his coat. Kevin hadn't bothered to zip it closed and now struggled to marry the ends as shivers rolled through his shoulders. He stumbled but caught himself before a fall as he walked on, all the while struggling with the zipper.

Why had he stayed so late at that bar? He'd known he needed to walk back to the motel. What kind of idiot was he? He was going the right way, wasn't he? He had a good buzz going and suppressed a giddy feeling in his gut as the two ends of the zipper finally connected. The local crowd at the bar had been sparse. It was midweek after all. While downing his first drink, he'd felt more like crying than laughing, so he decided to keep to himself instead of seeking a hand to hold, no matter how badly he needed one. One lady with an especially short skirt had captured his attention from across the room.

Oh, that skirt.

She'd noticed him and had eyed the stranger for the rest of the night. But she'd looked almost old enough to be his mother, and since the phone call earlier that day, he just couldn't, not tonight.

The sidewalk slabs felt uneven as he dragged his feet across them. He spun to reorient himself. Yes, this was going the right way.

"One foot in front of the other one will get you back, Kevin." Yes, he was definitely buzzed. Talking aloud to himself? Really? He shook his head. Maybe he'd call his dad tonight. With the liquid courage running through his veins, he thought he just might be able to. Then he remembered the tears he'd spilled on the bar table.

"Liquid courage, my ass." Besides, yelling at the man wouldn't bring his mother back.

No, no, it wouldn't. He massaged a thumb and forefinger into his eyes to dash away the tears. He'd had enough of that. Maybe he could call Tina, his stepmom.

He thought about it as he passed dark buildings, their shop signs turned off and curtains closed. The bar had been down the little town's main street. How many more blocks was it? The cold air stung his fingertips, and after turning up the collar on his jacket, he jammed them deep in two pockets.

Tina, his stepmom, had always been kind. It was because of her that his dad had flirted with religion. She had that church she was a part of—the same church that man he'd met at Crossroads Truck Stop had run. Now, wasn't that a funny coincidence? Meeting a pastor on the day his mom passed? His stepmom's pastor. Kevin almost giggled at the thought. Had the big man in the sky brought him to Crossroads for just that reason?

"God doesn't exist, Kevin. You know that. Even if He did, there's no way He's good."

He sighed with relief as the brightly lit motel sign came into view. His feet were cold. Gusts whipped by, a reminder of the Canadian prairies' winter bite. It might be spring, but winter was still holding to the fringe. The wind burned his nose and the tops of his ears.

He thought about the pastor again then shrugged off the image. "Forget about God and go to bed."

Kevin promised himself he would forget as he stepped off the sidewalk and into the motel parking lot.

Check the truck.

The voice in his head sent pinpricks up his arms.

This late at night? No way.

Check the truck.

Kevin groaned to himself as he realized it was probably the best thing after drinking so much. He might sleep in, and with that camper there, it was best to make sure everything was in order and tightly locked up.

As he walked towards his semi, a soft glow caught his eye. The camper. Someone had a light on, but it was low and did nothing to illuminate the darkness. He also didn't see any shadow moving around inside. Good. He let out a breath he'd been holding and moved towards his truck's door, fumbling with his keys.

Did he even really need to check inside if it was locked?

Come on, Kevin. They'd have to have broken a window or something to get in. Everything's fine. Just go to bed.

He shook his head again in self annoyance and turned. As he did, his eyes wandered back towards the camper. Condensation on the windows told him someone had a heater going.

Good. If they have any girls in there, they won't freeze.

Then his eyes froze on the leftmost window. In the corner, he could just see outlines in the fog, beading water drops stretching each letter's shape. They showed up as blackness against the shine of the soft light within.

Help

The keys in Kevin's hands jingled as his hands trembled.

Oh, no. No, no, no.

Something in Kevin's chest constricted, and he coughed. Then fear of alerting whoever might be in that camper gripped him. He forgot about the room and turned back to his truck, unlocked it and climbed in, easing the door shut behind him, making sure it latched, then locked it.

His heart hammered.

Do something.

Why would someone write those words? He closed his eyes for a second to breathe, letting his liquored thoughts sort themselves out.

The pastor he'd met at Crossroads Truck Stop had been looking for his daughter. What if ...

No, it couldn't be her in that camper. He was too far past the city. But it didn't matter if it was her or not. He had to call it in.

It took him a minute to pull up Crime Stopper's number on his phone's browser. Then he spotted the flyer Austin had given him at Crossroads, the girl's face printed in black and white. She looked so young, her curls bunching around her cheeks. Amy Grill, the poster named her.

He picked up the paper with shaking fingers. It crackled slightly at his touch.

"Hello, this is Crime Stoppers. Do you have an anonymous tip to leave?" a woman's voice crackled over the connection.

"Yes!"

Waiting

ROSE

ROSE SAT AT THE back of the sanctuary, claiming the first pew before the double doors that opened to the foyer. Rachel had dropped her off on her way to work an hour before. A few volunteers walked around the church, but Rose was alone in the sanctuary. It was still early, and she didn't expect anyone to come pray with her until noon. Cushioned in silence, she no longer knew what to pray.

She felt utterly useless.

The torture of waiting was agony. But she refused to sit at home alone where the solitude would eat away at her heart. The solid pew under her was a familiar comfort. She needed that familiarity in the middle of chaos. She needed ...

Come home, Arthur.

She had sent him a text last night asking him to return. Now she wondered if it had been the right thing. Yesterday morning she'd felt confident that he needed to go find Amy, even if she wanted him at home. She'd felt it in her soul. But now? His messages and phone calls had been short, his tone often morose. Coming home was the right thing. It had to be. He'd gone nearly to Winnipeg and found no sign of her. Whatever it was God had meant him to do out there, he had to have done it, even if it wasn't bringing Amy home.

But ... how could it not be bringing her home?

God, you are taking care of Amy, aren't you? You will bring her home, won't you?

The more useless she felt, the more angry she became with herself. Perhaps sitting here was a bad idea. It gave too many chances for self reflection, and her self reflection had ceased to be helpful in the last few weeks. Perhaps she should move to the fellowship hall.

In the quiet, nothing distracted from the discomfort of living in her own skin. Pins and needles danced through her fingers and toes. A few times the feeling had vanished from her leg again, only to come back as a deep, incessant ache. She hadn't told anyone. Not yet. She wouldn't until it all became unbearable. But hiding it was exhausting.

The doors behind her squeaked as someone slipped into the room, and the arm of Abigail's wheelchair appeared in her peripheral vision. The woman didn't say anything. Rose also didn't look over at her but stared forward towards the pulpit at the front of the sanctuary. Rose smiled as her friend touched her arm but still held the silence.

They sat together for several minutes before Abigail spoke. When she did, her words pierced Rose's heart despite their soft, loving tone. "You're needed."

Rose closed her eyes and couldn't help pulling her arm gently away from Abigail's touch. It was like the woman had read her thoughts. Shame trailed on the edges of a creeping sore throat.

"You'll never not be needed. No matter what state of decline your body slips into, you will always be needed."

Rose wiped the tips of tingling fingers over her eyes, and Abigail handed her a tissue from a pouch hanging off the arm of her chair.

"Thank you," Rose said. The sore throat pulled any confidence from her words, but she was grateful she didn't croak as she spoke. "How did you know what I was thinking?"

Abigail rubbed her hands over her wheelchair's armrests. "I've had seasons of grief for my lack of mobility. I know what it looks like. That grief isn't wrong, Rose. It's necessary."

Rose nodded and dabbed at her nose with the now crumpled tissue. "It's true."

"Then why does it feel so wrong?" Rose finally looked over at her friend, letting out a shuddering breath.

"Because you've always been the one doing things, fixing things, helping people."

"I thought I'd learned to let go already."

"Grief is not linear, Rose."

"I suppose that's true." But she wasn't sure if the knowing helped at all. "Still being needed while I can't help is painful, Abigail."

Her friend looked at her with a worried question glinting in her eye. She took a few moments to think before she asked, "What makes you think you can't help?"

"Well, I haven't been. I'm stuck here with this." Rose poked a finger towards her walker, folded and slid in between the pews beside her. "I'm stuck sitting here while others search for my daughter ... Listen to me, I'm selfishly whining while Amy is in danger."

"You might be stuck here, but that doesn't answer my question. What makes you think you can't help or that you haven't been already? What lie are you listening to, Rose?"

Lie? Was there one?

"I haven't been doing anything."

"You've been praying."

Rose shifted her numbing rear against the pew seat. "It's not enough."

"Says who?"

She blinked at her friend, unnerved by her direct questions. "It's not helping."

"Rose," Abigail leaned forward in her chair and stared down at her motionless feet supported by metal footrests. "How do you know it's not helping?"

Rose opened her mouth but then closed it again, uncertain how to answer the question.

"I won't pretend to understand exactly how prayer works. I know it's not magic, not something we do that promises God will always fix things on our behalf. But I know it works. Even when His answer is no, or wait, or something else we weren't hoping for."

"And what if you have no words left to pray, Abigail?"

Her friend's eyebrows pulled together, and she laced her fingers across her middle. "Then maybe it's time to just listen." She swivelled her wheelchair back towards the doors. "Listening is an act of trust and expectation, Rose. Maybe it's time for prayers that go beyond words."

Rose knew her friend meant her advice as a comfort, but it was far from it. As she sat in silence again, her thoughts bounced back and forth, forming a headache behind her eyes.

After a few minutes, Abigail came back to ask if she was hungry and if she would like to move to the fellowship hall. Rose followed, feet shuffling across the carpet as she pushed her walker in slow, methodical movements.

The hall was bright, and though only Abigail and one other person puttered around the kitchen area, Rose felt less isolated. Her tension eased a bit when offered a warm cup of tea that relaxed her tongue from the roof of her mouth.

She endured more waiting.

It wouldn't be much longer, and Arthur would join her. She clutched her cell phone with one hand through the fabric of her cardigan as it rested in a pocket and lifted her cup to her lips with the other. A wave of tingling passed through her fingers, pain lingering at the edge of each prickly sensation. Her grip on the cup's handle tightened, and she closed her eyes, willing it all to pass.

As she set down the cup and shook out her fingers, the sound of shuffling entered the hall. Was it noon already?

Several people filed in and called greetings across the open space from the door to the kitchen. A woman with auburn hair and a long decorative scarf waved at Rose. Hillary. Her pale wrinkles attested to her age even as her hair colour tried to hide it. Rose smiled as the woman visited the crock pot of soup at the kitchen window before carrying two bowls over to Rose's table.

"Eat. Abigail's orders," Hillary said. Her matter-of-fact tone left no room to argue, and as Hillary sat, they both tucked in, though Hillary's enthusiasm for the food dwarfed Rose's.

More people entered, several Rose didn't know and many that she did. It warmed her heart. They were all here for Amy. If … if only Amy could see this. If only she could know how much they all cared for her.

Memories of her daughter's hateful words about the people of Hope Is Here Church sent a sharp pain through Rose's heart. In many ways, it was a justified emotion for her daughter to have had, but the growing crowd told Rose these people held more than rejection for her. They still loved her..

She doesn't know their care, does she, God? Is that my fault?

A handful of church board members entered the room, and behind them came Pastor Edwin from Barton Community Church. Pastor Edwin chatted with the men ahead of him as he pulled a soft hat from his head. People cared more than Amy would ever realize. Why did it seem so hard to show that care except after tragedy?

Rose shrugged the thoughts away as she noticed a girl and boy, whom she didn't know, enter the room. The girl's light Asian skin contrasted with the boy's darker yet still Asian hue as she confidently pulled him towards a table. The girl served him from the crock pot as he sat rigid in a metal chair.

Who were they? They must be kids from the high school. Rose wished Rachel was beside her. She would know.

Rose's last spoonful of soup was cold against her tongue, a silent signal it was time to return to the sanctuary.

Moisture collected at the edges of Rose's eyes as she looked around the sanctuary. So many people had come. The high schoolers caught her eye as the girl pushed the boy into a back pew before pulling out a string of beads. Rosary beads? A twinge in Rose's chest felt like a tug as she looked at the pair. Should she go over and introduce herself? Should she thank them for coming? Or would the attention just embarrass them? The boy looked exceedingly uncomfortable as he stared at his hands, only lifting his eyes for a second to look around and then abruptly staring down again.

Her old role as a pastor's wife pulled her towards them. The girl saw her coming and smiled brightly.

Rose kept her voice low as she greeted them. "Thank you for coming."

The girl returned her greeting with a firm handshake and a confident grin. "It's the least we can do for Amy," she said as Rose settled into a nearby pew. "I'm Peggy. I showed Amy around the high school on her first day."

"Its nice to meet you, Peggy." Rose nodded at the boy. "And who is this?"

"Oh! Rohan! Turn around and say hello."

Rohan turned and bobbed a nod at Rose.

"And how do you know my daughter?" Rose asked.

Rohan opened his mouth but closed it again, a shadow drifting over his eyes as she looked at her.

"Mrs. Grill?" Peggy asked.

"Yes?"

Peggy looked between her companion and Rose, her eyebrows drawing together as she settled her gaze on Rose again. "Mrs Grill, Rohan was with Amy at the party on Sunday night."

The boy seemed to physically shrink at Peggy's words.

"I'm so sorry," he whispered.

Was that fear? Was he afraid of her? The idea of someone being afraid of her was distressing, and she reached out a frail hand to him but placed it on the pew's back to rest in front of her instead of touching him. He'd shrunk back as her hand moved.

"Whatever it is you're sorry for, Rohan, I forgive you," Rose said. Each word echoed in her chest, and Rose knew she meant every one of them.

Rohan's eyes grew large.

"We lost Amy in the crowd," he said. "The house was so packed. Josh … Josh tried to find her, but it was too late."

"They've arrested Brad, haven't they?" Peggy asked.

Rose didn't know that name. She realized she'd been neglecting Amy and her new life. She should have known these kids. She should have made it her business to know. Pins and needles followed by a deep ache washed through her hands. The sensation crept up her arms as well. She swallowed, blinking away tears.

Rohan nodded at Peggy. "I don't know why, though. Don't know the charges."

"Well, thank you for being here," Rose said again.

"I told Rohan he needed to come for himself as much as Amy," Peggy said. "I just wish Josh could come as well."

"He wouldn't—" A ruckus from the foyer interrupted their hushed discussion, and everyone in the sanctuary turned toward the noise.

Rose's heart skipped a beat as Arthur pushed into the room.

"Rose!" he yelled into the silence. "Did you get the call? They found her!"

"See! I told you us coming would help!" Peggy exclaimed into the cheer as people all around the sanctuary stood.

Arthur rushed to Rose and pulled her up into his arms. "Did you get the call too?" he asked as he crushed her to his chest.

A hand still rested on the phone in her pocket. She'd been clutching it for hours, waiting for the buzzing sensation of a text from Arthur or Rachel. Now she pulled it out as Arthur half released her to stare at the screen. Notifications blinked across the lock screen, and she opened her phone to a missed call and messages from Rachel.

"I must have been so busy chatting that I didn't hear the phone," she said, ashamed for her lapse of attention. Her hand trembled. She hadn't felt the phone vibrate even once.

People gathered around them as Arthur held fast to Rose's shoulder and guided her walker into her hands.

"Where did they find her?"

"Is she okay?"

"When will they bring her home?"

"Can we visit her?"

"Arthur, what happened?"

All these questions were thrown at her husband as he led her from the sanctuary, but his focus was on the church doors.

"We don't know much," Gary answered from the edge of the crowd. "I'll do my best to keep you all informed as Arthur and Rose receive information. But, please, right now they need space."

Arthur nodded in thanks towards Gary as someone pushed the doors open and the smell of fresh air and a warm noonday sun welcomed them into the outside world.

"Where are we going, Arthur?" Rose asked, shaking slightly with a strange mix of weariness and adrenaline.

"She's been admitted to a hospital in Winnipeg," he answered. "Officer Thomas has asked us to meet her there. He's sending over the address in a few minutes. He doesn't have jurisdiction across the provincial border, but the local detective has been in close contact with him since they brought her in."

Rose sensed her husband's excitement behind the strain that pulled his voice in a strange way.

"Is she okay?" Rose whispered, unsure if she wanted a full answer.

"No. No, she's not."

Our Girl

ROSE

RACHEL DECIDED SHE'D REMAIN in Barton to look after the apartment when Rose called her. Arthur sped their small car down the street. A sharp turn into Echo Apartments sent Rose's heart into her throat. She gasped and grabbed his arm as her bottom shifted across her seat.

"You guys okay, Mom?" Rachel asked over the call.

"Yes! We just arrived at the apartment."

"We'll need to grab some overnight things for your mother." Arthur leaned closer to the phone as he spoke. "I'm sorry, Rachel."

"It's okay, Dad. Go take care of Amy."

After Rachel hung up, Arthur leaned close to his wife, and Rose breathed in his familiar musk while he planted a kiss on her lips. She lifted a numb hand to his face and almost whimpered when she couldn't feel the stubble of his unshaven face against her skin. She cupped her second hand to his cheek as well and felt warmth seep into her fingers there. Before he pulled away, he leaned his forehead against hers for a second.

"I'll need extra underwear and socks. Make sure you grab more for yourself as well. My winter coat, just in case, and ..." She faltered, her brain swimming with all the things they may need.

"We can buy anything we forget," he reassured her. "Wait here. I won't be long. Oh, do you need to use the bathroom?"

She shook her head no, and he left her in the car to jog towards their apartment, his duffle bag in hand. Rose wondered if he would take the time to place his dirty clothes in the hamper or if Rachel would have the honour of finding his soiled things cast aside on the living room couch. She hoped he would at least keep it contained in their bedroom.

She pressed her hand to her mouth as tears built in her eyes.

Thank you, God. Thank you.

But fear about what they would find once they reached the city crawled behind her prayer.

The drive was uneventful, and the miles slipped past them in a blur of tense silence and even more intense bursts of conversation. What would they find when they arrived in the city? Where would they stay? Did they have a plan for the short term or long term? Arthur did his best to smooth Rose's worries, saying they would take it all in stride and that being present was the most important thing.

Rose did her best not to force Arthur to stop for what she considered unimportant things like bathroom breaks and to stretch aching limbs. Her legs screamed silent hate at her for it, but speed was more important.

After the hours Arthur spent that morning driving home and a full afternoon and evening back in the car, his exhaustion was apparent as they pulled into a bustling truck stop. He wiped a hand over his face before unfolding her walker for her, setting it in front of the open car door and grasping her arms with gentle strength as she attempted to pull her aching body up onto her feet.

"Are you alright?" he asked, blinking sleep from his reddened eyes.

Could they make it into the city safely with him so tired?

"Just tired, Arthur," she assured him. She hoped the pinched smile she gave him was enough to cover her discomfort. Everything hurt.

"Gary and I stopped here yesterday before deciding to call it a night." He looked around, and she could tell he was reliving that first visit. "They have coffee."

"Coffee sounds wonderful."

His strong hands pulled her the last few inches to her feet. She flexed each muscle slowly before nodding for him to let go. He walked alongside her as she shuffled up the sidewalk and into the truck stop entrance.

The place smelled of oil and sugar. Rose wrinkled her nose at the strange mix. The convenience shop buzzed with truckers and travellers of all kinds who were stopping for the night or gassing up for the last stretch into the city. Arthur guided her past aisles of snacks that gave way to displays of small truck parts, oils, and accessories. He saw her safely to the door of the women's bathroom then left her to take care of his own needs.

When she emerged, she took a slow walk to the right, thinking to stretch her still shaking legs while Arthur purchased coffee and any snacks he desired. A large window that took up much of the far wall just past an open gathering area called to her. It looked out on a dark makeshift building with the words "Truckers' Chapel" painted on the door. A light at the side of the building illuminated the words, but the dark windows made Rose uneasy.

An empty chapel. How lonely.

She supposed it was no different from when any church was closed for the evening, doors locked and lights extinguished. Still, the noise of the convenience store and gas station at her back made her wonder how long those windows had been dark. Truck stops were busiest in the evenings, weren't they?

Arthur found her looking out the windows. A gentle touch of his elbow to her arm made her shift and smile at the two large to-go cups he held in his hands.

"These are hot," he said.

"Sensitive fingers?" she teased.

He grinned as he sipped from one of them, blowing through the opened slot in the lid before slurping loudly and blowing again. "Come on. Is there anything else you need before we get going?"

They hadn't stopped for a proper meal, but she didn't feel hungry.

Still, she thought of him. "We should grab you food."

He shook his head. "I still have snacks in the car. That's enough for me if you're not up for dinner."

He led her back towards the main doors and turned to lean his back into the handle, pushing it open for her. But a call from the check-out counter made Rose carefully turn, straining to see the man waving at her husband.

He was elderly and fanned a paper in the air as Arthur lifted his to-go cup in salute. "I'm going to write 'found' on every one of them, Arthur! Praise God!"

Arthur's tired grin crinkled the corners of his eyes, and Rose wondered at the age she saw there. She knew the same age lined her own face these days. Her hands shook on her walker handles, and she paused just outside the glass doors.

Forty-three feels more like I imagined eighty would. "Who was that?" she asked.

"Austin. Nice guy. I think he owns the place. He hung up posters of Amy and said he would hand them out to people for me."

"You didn't have any with you when you left, did you?"

"No, but Glen emailed the file to Gary, and Austin printed them out right back there in the office."

Arthur shook his head, though the smile was still twinkling in his eyes. He set the coffee on their car's roof before opening the passenger side door for her.

"He sounds like a sweet man."

They made it. Bleary-eyed though she was, Rose pressed her nose to the cold glass of her window as they passed the lit-up hospital. It rose above the street with closed in pedestrian walkways connecting buildings overhead.

It was far too late to stop tonight. They would have to trust their daughter in the hands of unknown doctors and nurses. Arthur searched for the closest hotel, his head whipping back and forth between the car mirrors and the signs that blinked at them from the darkness. City traffic was terrible at any time of the day, and around the hospital, it didn't seem to have lessened with nightfall.

Rose's gut flopped as Arthur took a sudden turn into a parking structure and the ground immediately slanted down. He left her in the car while he secured a room, and she blared praise music from the radio to hold back the parking complex's gloom. She sent texts to Rachel and Sarah. She phoned the hospital and chatted with the nurse, who informed her Amy was stable and sleeping. Her gut turned over when she learned they had to dose her with something to calm her. The strain in the nurse's voice said more than the words she used. Fear gripped Rose's heart as she ended the call.

God, I know you are with my girl, but help her know it too.

She felt like an emotional mess when Arthur came to get her and carry in their luggage, his expression pinched. She didn't want to ask how much the room had cost and for how long they had it. They had no way of knowing how long they'd need to be in town. But Rose hoped only a few days, and then they'd be taking Amy home.

"Not much farther." Arthur patted Rose's shoulder as he pushed her forward.

That proved to be untrue, even though they entered the hospital soon after. They lost their way despite asking for directions twice and signing in at reception. The hallways were wide, with white, blue, purple, and green lines painted on the ground that led the way to different clinics and departments. As time passed, Rose's heart throbbed for her daughter. Did she know her parents were coming? Was she wondering where they were? Did she know how many people had looked for her and prayed for her?

"Soon, Rose." Arthur squeezed her shoulder again.

God, where is my baby?

Arthur scanned the halls for a third person to ask for directions.

"Excuse me?" The woman he stopped was dressed in street clothes but wore an identification tag on her pocket.

She pulled black rimmed glasses from her face as she stopped and smiled at Arthur. He asked for directions to the inpatient ward where the nurses had told them Amy was located.

"You can follow me, sir. I'm headed in the same direction." The woman shook Arthur's hand as he thanked her, and Rose felt a weight lift from her shoulders.

Finally, someone who knows where to go.

"Don't be embarrassed," the woman said. "Getting lost in this place is normal. Most people who work here only know their own departments. My name is Dr. Miriam. What's your daughter's name? I visit patients in the wards regularly, though I'm a psychotherapist and am based out of the mental health unit."

When Arthur gave Dr. Miriam Amy's name, her face grew grave. "You're Amy Grill's parents?"

The woman slowed her steps a bit as she looked between Rose in her wheelchair and Arthur. "I'm so glad it was me you asked for help. Come, they've placed your daughter in a private room."

"You know Amy?"

"I wasn't on duty when she first arrived, but my colleagues have briefed me on her case. I'm headed there right now."

Dr. Miriam's pace quickened, hurrying them down the hall and through several nondescript doors.

How did anyone find their way around this place? Perhaps the doctor was taking them through staff-only halls?

When they entered the ward, everything was brightly lit and bustling despite the early hour. Dr. Miriam led them to a corner room where the door was closed. Still, Rose could hear shouting through the heavy wood. It seeped under the door and past its hinges like smoke that foretold a hidden fire.

Miriam placed one hand on Arthur's arm and nodded to Rose as she placed her second hand on the door handle.

"This will not be easy," she said. Rose could tell she was fortifying her own resolve by the wrinkling and subsequent smoothing of lines across the woman's forehead. "Remember, above all, right now, your daughter needs love, respect, and patience."

Rose nodded as she gripped the armrests of her chair.

Lord, help us all.

As the door swung open, the shouting turned to a scream that sent a dagger into Rose's heart.

Amid Her Screams

ARTHUR

WAS THE GIRL KNEELING on the bed really Amy? For a second, Arthur wasn't sure. Her face twisted in pure agony, and the sound coming from her mouth felt like knives in his ears. It stopped Arthur and Dr. Miriam both in their tracks.

Miriam recovered first and stepped back to close the door, sealing them all in with Amy's agony. Arthur could only watch as she then stepped around him and approached the nurses who stood to both sides of his daughter. Shock glued his feet to the floor. Both nurses looked ready to grab for Amy if she decided to bolt from the bed. The one on the right was a small woman, her blond hair pulled up into a tight bun, her shoulders rigid, her face holding genuine concern. On the left stood a male nurse. His dark blue scrubs hung loosely on his wiry frame, his hair cut so short, he was practically bald. The male nurse kept his distance, watching his counterpart and now Dr. Miriam for any sign to step in.

"Amy!" Rose yelled over the terrible noise, her arms stretching out towards her.

It took Amy a moment to hear her mother's call, but when she did, her scream stopped, replaced with physical shaking and whimpers that sent shivers down Arthur's spine.

"Mom?" Amy hugged the hospital gown to her chest. "Dad?"

"Arthur!" The urgency in Rose's voice as she pounded a fist on her wheelchair's arm jolted him back to reality.

He pushed his wife forward until her knees hit the side of the bed. The obstacle didn't stop Rose. She reached for her daughter with more energy than Arthur had seen her exert in weeks, pulling herself up to her feet and crawling like a child onto the hospital bed until she engulfed Amy in a hug. Arthur saw her body tremble and lifted his hands, ready to catch his wife if needed and pull her backwards. He swallowed, unsure how to feel but thankful the terrible noise had ended.

"Mom!" Amy choked on the word.

Arthur looked over at the female nurse who was clearly in charge, her expression flip-flopping between relief and concern for the pair on the bed.

"How is she?" he asked.

The woman reached for Rose's elbow as she pulled away from Amy to let both of them breathe. "Not in here. Dr. Miriam, Dr. Hillard will want to speak to you in the hall shortly. She stepped out but promised to be back."

Miriam nodded as she observed the scene.

"Arthur," Rose said, turning her head slightly backwards. "I need to lie down."

Arthur's heart jumped. He saw stability slipping away from his wife's frame and did his best to ease her down to the mattress, thankful for the nurse helping to support her shoulder as Rose's head touched the pillow. Amy curled into her mother without a single look at her father. They'd never been close, but after the anxious hours of searching, to not even receive a glance from her hurt. Hot shame washed in and up his esophagus.

"Now that she's calm, why don't you take Dad to talk to Dr. Hillard," the female nurse said as she looked between her male colleague and Arthur. "Don't worry about your wife and daughter," she continued as the male nurse set a gentle hand on Arthur's arm. "I'll take care of her. I think this is exactly what Amy needs."

"Rose has MS. Her medications are in her bag." Arthur stepped back, a guilt-laced relief expanding the airways in his chest as he swallowed the burning sensation lingering in his throat.

The female nurse only nodded.

Rose pulled Amy to her chest as if she was an infant. Her hands stroked her frizzy mass of curls. All her attention was on Amy, and Arthur was sure she didn't even hear the others murmuring around them.

Arthur let the male nurse lead him from the room, a bubble of tension popping in his ear as the door closed again. It seemed he couldn't do anything in there, but maybe out here was different.

"I know it might feel like you're being shut out right now," the male nurse beside him said as he watched Arthur's eyes cast about. "But from my experience, it's a man's job just to be ready, waiting, and willing to do the small things in situations like these. It will take your daughter time after what she's been through to reach for her father. That's normal. But she still needs you, and she will let you know when she's ready."

Arthur nodded at the man and stretched out his hand. "I'm sorry, I'm Arthur Grill. Thank you for taking care of Amy."

"It's my pleasure, Arthur. It really is." The nurse's face warmed, and a bright, toothy grin stretched across his thin face. His grip was firm, and Arthur welcomed the touch with two firm shakes.

"I'm John, and I'm here most nights."

"Nights?" Arthur wondered aloud.

John chuckled. "I'm on overtime right now. This place is never dull!"

"Especially in this ward, unfortunately," Dr. Miriam said.

Arthur had forgotten about the woman as she stood off to the side, waiting for John to give what comfort and advice he could.

"John. Could you grab a pitcher of water and some cups before you head out? And, yes, you should head out. Now that her parents are here, I'm hoping the situation will improve."

"Are you sure?" he asked. Arthur noted the worry in the nurse's voice.

Dr. Miriam nodded. "Go get some sleep. Dr. Hillard shouldn't be much longer." She said this while glancing at her watch and pressing a button on its side.

When John returned with a blue plastic jug and a stack of disposable cups, Dr. Miriam cracked the door back open and made her silent way inside for a second before returning to Arthur in the hall.

The infuriating feeling of helplessness was returning, but all Arthur could do was resign himself to lean up against the wide plastic handrail mounted on the wall behind him.

"Hallways are horrible for conferences. I wonder if we should wait in the family room, down a few doors?" Dr. Miriam asked. "Let me just check if it's free."

Her footsteps clipped on the smooth flooring, and Arthur folded arms over his chest as he settled back to wait.

Dr. Hillard was a large, round-faced woman whose small, high voice baffled Arthur when she first greeted him. When she leaned forward, the chair under her groaned.

"Amy told us she's on an antidepressant but couldn't remember the name. We also need her counsellor's full name and contact information, your family doctor, and the names and contact numbers for any other medical professional she's had regular contact with over the last two years." The woman paused to peer down at a clipboard she held then scratched out a few notes. "She told me it's been about that long since she's been getting therapy."

"I don't know the name of her medication. But Rose will," Arthur assured her. Even if his wife wasn't able to recall it, they'd grabbed the bottle when they hurriedly packed a bag for Amy.

Arthur wasn't sure he'd be able to retain all the information being poured out onto his lap and heaved a sigh of relief when Dr. Hillard handed him a list of what she needed. Communication between medical systems across provincial lines was limited, making it Arthur's top priority to gather everything Amy's team needed to treat her and to do it fast.

"Mr. Grill ... anger and aggression are normal reactions to trauma. Your daughter is exhibiting a high level of both. I am relieved to see her mother's presence soothe her. But it's early. From what Amy has been able to communicate to me about her past, she's suffered from a fragile mental state for some time, and it has often manifested in similar ways.

This may mean it'll take longer for her to be ready to leave the safety of the hospital." The woman shifted even farther forward, her dull grey eyes searching Arthur's face. "There is no telling how long of a road to healing your daughter has or how complete this healing can be. Abuse of the kind Amy has endured ... cuts deep. What your daughter has experienced will leave invisible scars for the rest of her life. She will require support for the foreseeable future, maybe indefinitely."

Arthur coughed. The paper in his hands crinkled as anger and grief warred in his heart.

"The amount of drugs in her system on admittance to the hospital has me very concerned." Dr Hillard's voice lowered, and Arthur wondered if she would fall off the chair as it groaned under her weight again. "Their levels are dropping steadily, but we might not be able to see the damage they've done until after she is completely sober. This means we'll need to wait to let her continue her regular medications for at least a few days. This next week will be very difficult."

They told Arthur about the forced injections Amy had been subjected to. He swallowed down bile as he listened to the report of her injuries. Still, they said it didn't look like the most recent physical abuse had gone as far as it could have. The full extent of it couldn't be known until Amy was ready to tell her story, and she was far from ready.

Would she even be able to remember it? Maybe it was better they never found out. Arthur longed for Rose as he sat alone in the family room with Dr. Hillard and Dr. Miriam watching him.

"Do you have any idea how long she will need to be in the hospital?" he asked.

"There is no way to know for sure," Miriam answered. "We hope only a few weeks, but it could stretch much longer than that. I understand you are from a small town. Do you know what kind of mental health facilities are available locally to you?"

Arthur shook his head when he admitted, "Very few. Most people have to travel out of town or use online services, even for basic counselling. Amy was blessed when she started sessions. Her counsellor was new to the area and her school."

"Are—if you or your family would like spiritual support during this time, we have a wonderful Chaplin on staff, Mr. Grill," Dr. Miriam offered. Worry creased the woman's face when he looked up at her.

"I'm a pastor myself," he admitted.

"Surely, even pastors need support. Especially in times like these." After a moment of silence, Dr. Hillard said, "Well, I believe this is all the information I need." She handed him one last paper with more notes scrawled over the page.

He squinted at the handwriting and wondered how long he'd need to wait before Rose could help him decipher the notes between the black printed text.

As Dr. Hillard stood, her chair gave a sigh of relief.

"We are here for Amy and your family for as long as we are needed," she assured him before leaving. "You will not be hurried out of the hospital. Cross province care and communication can be tricky, but we won't let her leave until there are plans and support in place."

Arthur knew the statement should be a comfort, but he still had so many questions. How long would they need to stay here? Would his job wait for him? Would they be able to afford the apartment if he didn't head back to town, back to work? How could he be a proper support to his family with all this uncertainty hanging over their heads? He might be a pastor, but was he capable of helping his daughter heal?

Both doctors left the room as Arthur had sunk into thought.

God, he prayed into the silence, *what now?*

Found

AMY HATED THE SHAKING and how she wasn't able to stop. Why couldn't she control it? Even in the arms of her mother, her body shook. It was exhausting. Someone covered them in a heated blanket as Rose ran her fingers over Amy's frizzing curls.

Just a few days ago, she had thought herself strong. How had she been so wrong?

As she trembled, it felt like tiny pieces of herself were flaking away. No matter how tightly she hugged them, she couldn't hold it all in place.

She'd done her best to answer all the officer's questions. She'd held it together when the door of the ambulance had slammed closed, leaving her with the pitying eyes of the paramedics. She'd started shaking when they wheeled her into the local hospital and again when they'd transferred her to the big city. How long had it been? She'd slept for a while. Had it continued during her sleep? Her muscles ached, but she didn't squirm in her mother's arms. No, she just held onto herself and let her mother be a second layer of protection.

"I'm here, Amy. I'm here," Rose whispered into her hair.

She shouldn't let her mother care for her like this. Rose was sick. She should tell her she was okay and let her sit in her wheelchair again. She could still hold her hand. That would be enough … wouldn't it?

"I'm here. Mom's here. Your dad is here too, and we aren't leaving. I've got you. I won't let go."

Amy heard shuffling around the room. Someone added a blanket to the bed and tucked them in.

"Mrs. Grill, you let me know if you need anything, and I'll get it for you. If you need to get up, call." That was the female nurse. She'd done most of the talking since Amy had been brought to this room.

She hated this room.

It grew silent except for her mother's gentle whispers as the nurse stopped her puttering and sat somewhere, watching them. Amy could feel the woman's eyes. She didn't want to hate her, but she did. The woman had helped the doctor examine her. Somehow, that examination had felt worse than being touched by any man. She'd started screaming halfway through it.

"I'm so sorry, Amy," the doctor had said. "We need to check for tears and internal damage."

She'd told them that only one man had touched her that way and it had been days ago. She was fine.

They still needed to examine her. At first, she'd been able to calm herself, she'd tried to hold still, she tried to be brave. But she just couldn't. Her body wouldn't stop shaking; it revolted against her will. They drew back as she screamed, and then she'd started to fight. She couldn't help it. She couldn't bear it.

Her mother's whispers had changed to words she couldn't quite catch as her hand slid from Amy's hair to her shoulder and arm, moving in gentle strokes as she lightly rubbed her presence into her daughter's awareness again. The tightness in Amy's chest slowly released. The shaking didn't stop, but she didn't fight it as much as warmth sank into her body. She slipped into sleep to the sound of prayers, and warmth enveloped her.

The quiet of the parking lot was oppressive as the night slipped away. The blowing air from the heater was both a comfort and an irritant.

Sleep came in short bursts, but the nip of cold that the heater couldn't completely drive from the camper woke her time and time again as it nibbled at her toes, fingers, and nose. She pulled the itchy blanket up to cover her face and curled tighter into a ball. Sleep pulled her back into the murky waters.

A banging from the camper door woke her with a start. Someone was fisting the door and calling in a loud voice. Her mind moved as if coated in molasses. Had they given her something again? The shouting moved inside the camper. The man across the room was up and calling through the door, curses spilling from his mouth like venom.

The door opened. A light flashed. Someone asked questions in rapid succession. An eerie few seconds of silence passed, and then the whole camper shook.

Amy screamed.

A large body shoved its way in as the man with greasy hair balled his fist and took a swing. Then the light flashed across his bed, searching.

Yelling and scuffling reached her ears from the outside as the man was pulled from the camper and the light came closer. A soft call slid under the noise, reaching for her.

"Hello? Is someone there?"

The blanket cocooning her was pulled, and a stranger's voice called to the outside before turning back to her and asking, "My name is Officer Miller. What's yours?"

Her tongue stuck to the roof of her mouth. Her answer came out on a rasping moan.

"Sweet heaven, are you Amy Grill?"

Amy didn't know if she had said yes or nodded. Had she reached for him? Instead of yelling again, the officer grabbed the radio from his shoulder and spoke with fast words. Then he knelt on the bed and asked if he could touch her before laying a tentative hand on her knee.

"Thank you, Jesus," he said.

Amy couldn't tell if he was swearing or praying. A light shone brightly, illuminating her corner, but hiding the officer in shadows behind its intensity. Something in her mind whispered that she should be afraid. What if he was going to hurt her like the other man? She needed to be ready to fight. But her body felt like jelly.

The camper rocked again as another person entered.

"Are you sure?" a gruff voice said.

The sound of rustling paper whispered as the second officer held up a white sheet of it.

"I have no doubt," the first officer said.

"My God. I don't believe it."

Then the paramedics pushed their way in, and the lack of space forced both officers to leave. Someone offered her a drink. With it, her voice returned.

"Can I go home now?" she asked.

"Yes, Amy. First the hospital, okay? But after that, we are going to get you home as soon as we can. Come on."

She shrank from the hands that offered help. But gentle words in soft tones coaxed her from the bed, and blankets were wrapped around her aching frame.

Her heart raced with fear as they held onto her, helping her step down from the camper to the pavement. Her legs gave way, and she was lifted onto a stretcher and strapped in. A part of her asked why she was letting them strap her behind velcro restraints. But her body refused to fight, and the tension she felt from being held down drifted in and out of her consciousness.

Officer Miller was at her side, asking her questions, his voice low and gentle.

"Did you get them?" she asked.

"Them?"

Amy whimpered when he turned and yelled, "She says there was more than one!"

He halted the paramedics for a moment and asked her more questions. His words tripped over themselves in her brain as she tried to understand.

"The man in the hotel room. Made me take a shower."

"What room number, Amy?"

But she couldn't remember. Officer Miller turned from her then and let the paramedics wheel her away.

She assumed they'd started looking then. Before lifting her backwards into an ambulance, she'd glimpsed a man standing by a semi truck and an officer clapping him on the shoulder as they both watched her.

As the doors closed her into another small space and as sad, kind eyes assessed her condition, she wondered, *What time is it?*

So warm, too warm. She couldn't breathe. The blankets were suffocating. The arms around her restricting. She pushed at them, struggling to get out.

Help! her mind yelled, and then it wasn't just her mind, it was her voice.

"Amy? Amy, what's wrong?"

She heard her mother. But she pushed, panic rising in her lungs as she gulped for air.

"Let me help you, Mrs. Grill," someone else said, and the arms around her fell away. "Give her space. It's okay. Give her a minute to remember where she is."

Amy ripped the blankets away and pushed them from the bed. Waves of red covered her vision, so dark they were almost black. She gasped for air. She swiped her hand over her face, trying to push the red away.

"Get OUT!" she screamed.

Her body wasn't cold anymore. No nip from the elements bit like it had in the camper. The faces that looked at her were filled with love and tears. She screamed even louder.She was strong again. No one would control her. The impulse of fear in her turned from flight to fight, and she stared at the woman in scrubs with blond hair pulled tightly back.

"Get OUT!"

Bittersweet

ARTHUR

ARTHUR IMPULSIVELY JUMPED OUT of his seat at the sound of rushing nurses. He'd ignored the call that sounded over the hospital intercom system while he'd been thinking. The cushioned back of the chair had welcomed his weight as he stretched. There was so much to take in, so much he would need to tell Rose. But as soon as more audible calls sounded and two nurses dressed in dark scrubs rushed past the doorway and down the hall leading to Amy's room, Arthur had a sinking feeling in his gut.

What if it was Amy? What if ... What if it was Rose?

He moved down the hall and spotted a light on the ceiling right before his daughter's room. It was blinking. The door stood ajar, but the noise from within warned Arthur not to enter. He stood in the hall, unsure of what to do as colour drained from his face while he listened to the language spilling from the room.

A nurse Arthur hadn't seen before pushed Rose in her wheelchair out the door. His wife was pale, and as Arthur stepped forward, the nurse nodded to him and let him take over. She returned to the room and shut the noise within.

"What's going on?" Arthur asked Rose as he pulled her chair to the side and crouched down beside it.

"Amy." Rose's hand trembled as she held her cardigan closed over her chest. When Arthur took her other hand in his, she squeezed his fingers tightly. "She woke up and just lost it." Rose steadied herself with a deep breath and released her cardigan to wrap a second hand around Arthur's. "Do you remember when she used to 'go red' on us? It's been a long time since she's completely lost it."

He remembered. Before they had sought a councellor a year and a half ago, Amy's tantrums and verbal abuse had been a regular occurrence in the home. She'd described the red waves that flowed over her vision, and they had dubbed her loss of control as "going red" because of it. Slowly, she had learned control, and her outbursts had decreased. Any fights in the last few months had been nothing compared to what they used to be, and they no longer used the term very often.

"It's like then, but ... but it's worse, Arthur. She–she lashed out at me."

"Are you hurt?" he asked, looking Rose over more carefully. Her blouse was slightly askew and her cardigan pulled crookedly over her sharp shoulder bones.

"Not badly, Arthur. I might bruise." She rubbed her chest. "She didn't mean to. I know she didn't. Her control is tentative. I can't imagine what she's been through." Rose let out a sob, and tears spilled down her face.

The grief in her eyes burned Arthur's soul.

"Any progress she made is gone, Arthur. It's gone. It's like our baby girl is gone."

"No! No, she's not gone, Rose. She's still in there."

He wanted to pull her from the wheelchair and cradle her in his arms, but the door opened and closed behind them. Nurses left the room only for more to enter soon after. The noise from behind the door seemed to have settled to a loud hum of voices, and Amy's screams had mercifully ceased.

"She's still in there," he said again as he looked at the door, a barrier between him and the daughter he had never understood but loved no less.

"What do we do, Arthur?" Rose asked.

"Wait," was the only reply he could give.

"More waiting? God, when will it end?" The despair in Rose's voice shocked him, and he looked back at his wife.

"I should take you back to the hotel."

"No! I'm not leaving." Rose's voice shook with emotion. "I promised her, Arthur. I'm not leaving. We are not leaving."

It felt like an eternity until the door opened again and a line of people exited the room. The last one was Dr. Hillard. She looked around the hall before stepping up to them and speaking in a lowered voice. "Mr. and Mrs. Grill, she needs to be moved to the psychiatric ward. I was hoping to keep her here for the next day or so. Another move may make the outbursts worse. But ... we don't have the staff to support her properly here."

"Psychiatric ward?" Rose looked confused. "I thought this was the psychiatric ward."

The doctor shook her head. "It's true we have many patients needing mental health support here, but not on this level. She needs more security. She needs staff trained in specific safety protocols." The woman's face saddened, and she picked at the edge of the clipboard still held in her hands. "I can help her body heal, but I don't have the tools to help her mind. We need the information I asked you for immediately, Mr. Grill."

Arthur nodded and relayed to Rose some of the questions he'd been asked as well as showing her the paper he would need her help to fill out.

"Of course," Rose said as she took the paper. "Pen's in my purse, dear."

The gift of a task, a way to help, visibly steadied Rose, and Arthur breathed in relief to see her take the job from his hands.

"Drop it off at the nurses' station as soon as you're finished." The woman shook her head as she left, her eyes dropping to her clipboard, back up to the hall, then back down again in a nervous manner.

What had those monsters done to his daughter to break her like this? A sour taste rose in Arthur's throat.

"Is there a room we can sit in to fill this out, Arthur? Then I think I need a coffee." Rose looked up at him with expectant eyes as she again rubbed her chest.

"I thought things would be better, at least ... after they found her," Arthur admitted. "I never expected ... But I guess I should have."

He felt empty as he looked over at his daughter's door. Rose must have seen it on his face, for she tapped her chair's armrest as if impatient.

"Let's get out of the hall, Arthur. And I still need that pen."

So Close

RACHEL

RACHEL WAS WORRIED ABOUT her sister. She was worried about her mother. She even worried about her father. The look on his face when he'd left in search of Amy had wrung her heart. The elation in his voice when he'd announced they'd found her still rang in Rachel's memory. But she worried about the crash that inevitably followed such a high.

The apartment was too quiet in the evenings, and exhaustion clung to her body, weighing her thoughts down along with it. Since her parents had left, she'd realized being alone while in this mental state wasn't a good idea. She longed to have her mother with her but knew she was selfish for it. As always, Amy needed her more, and Rachel would have to do without. But it was hard as a few days turned into a week of her parents being gone.

She was thankful for Glen and his family as she walked the cement path around the apartment building to their tiny backyard. Abigail had invited her over every evening for dinner. She'd even told her she could spend the nights if she wanted.

"Glen can sleep on the couch, and we can air out his room for you."

"No! No. Thank you, though," she'd assured them. "That's unnecessary. The meals are more than enough."

Rachel had also never been so tired in her life, and that first evening of getting home from work to an empty apartment and having to think about feeding herself had pushed her into tears.

Telling herself it was the stupidest thing to cry about hadn't helped. She'd cried again when Abigail had texted her and told her she was cooking extra and expected her at 6:30 sharp, no arguing allowed.

"Glen will walk you back home," Abigail had insisted that first night as well. "And make sure you lock your doors and keep a light by the sliding one on all night."

If the cement walkway hadn't been there, Rachel would have worn a path after the last week.

She knocked on the glass of the Edwards' sliding door, waiting for the seated figure of Abigail, planted before the stove, to wave her in. The main room's lights were shining brightly, and Rachel could see her friend was stirring a large pot. As the glass door slid aside, a wave of warmth and savoury scents welcomed her.

"What is that? It smells divine!" Rachel said.

Her words spread a smile over Abigail's face.

"Just good old chicken and noodle soup, dear. Come on in." Abigail pointed to a base cupboard to her left. "Grab the bowls, will you? The men will be late today."

Most of the dishes were stored low in the Edwards' kitchen. The cupboards had drawers that made it much easier for Abigail to find and grab what she needed. As Rachel found bowls and spoons, she thought she would prefer a kitchen much like this someday. Having the dishes lower seemed more practical. If you dropped something, it didn't have as far to fall. Decorative or rarely used dishes lined the top cupboards. Abigail even had wooden slats in her drawers to slide the plates into so they rested straight up on their edges instead of lying in stacks.

"How are you feeling today? How was work?" her friend asked.

"Tired. Boring."

"Bad boring or good boring?"

Rachel paused, a hand hovering over the table, a spoon poised to be placed by a bowl. "Good boring. Most people remembered to clean the lint trays after drying their clothes, and no one yelled at me. It was slow for a Thursday." Abigail nodded as Rachel continued. "Any day no one yells at you is a good day in customer service, even if it's slow."

"Now that's the truth!" the older woman said and lifted a ladle high above the soup pot in salute. When she dropped the spoon back into the soup, she rolled backwards slightly to turn and roll out of the galley-style kitchen towards the dining table. "Any word from your parents?"

Rachel shook her head. "Not much change. But now that Amy's system is clean, they can start introducing new medications to help ease her anxiety." Rose had tried to explain it all to her over the phone, but Rachel knew she was only grasping fragments about what the rest of them were going through. "The police have made a few arrests. I've been trying not to think about it, though."

"Any legal stuff is going to take a long time to move through the courts. It always does." Abigail's chair lightly bumped the table, and she shifted on her cushions. "And Jay?"

Abigail's question was soft, and Rachel finished laying out silverware on the table before she answered. "I don't know. But ... I haven't checked either."

Rachel brushed thoughts of her ex aside. "I'll get the soup from the stove. Do you want the whole pot brought over, or is there a smaller container I should use?"

"The whole pot is fine."

Rachel liked how Abigail and her family weren't fancy. Rose would have dragged out the soup tureen. But serving straight from the pot meant fewer dishes, and Rachel had learned how much Abigail hated dishes. She loved the countertop dishwasher the Edwards had, but it was small. Rachel wondered how many times a day Abigail had to run it.

The handles on either side of the soup pot were hot, sending Rachel in search of oven gloves before bringing it over to the table. After placing the large vessel on a trivet, she slid into the seat beside Abigail.

The woman placed her hand over Rachel's, but when she didn't speak, Rachel looked up from the warm hand to her face. "I'm okay."

Worry lines creased Abigail's forehead. "The breaking of any relationship is hard, Rachel, and you've been through so much upheaval in the last few months. Your dad ... mom ... and now Jay. I worry."

"I don't feel safe even thinking about him." Rachel's voice was small, and her fingers trembled despite the warmth of Abigail's hand.

"For what it's worth," Abigail said, gently squeezing Rachel's chilled fingers, "you did the right thing. At least for now. Jay has a lot of decisions to make, and I'm afraid he's going to be making them behind bars for a while."

Abigail lifted the lid from the pot and served them each a bowl of steaming chicken noodle soup. As the vapours filled the air in front of her, Rachel's stomach grumbled, and both women laughed, breaking the tension between them.

She is such a good friend.

Rachel realized how long it had been since she was able to truly call someone a friend. Abigail might be twenty-plus years her senior, but it didn't matter. Over the last week they'd laughed and cried together.

Abigail had never hidden her grief over Rachel's life choices but had also never shunned her for them. Rachel wondered at the fact she no longer had friends her own age said about herself. She'd never had many, but those special few had all been lost slowly as she clung more and more to Jay and her new way of life. She'd never taken the time at Barton Public High to build new relationships ... As the two women began to eat, she pushed the question aside.

"We still don't know if everyone involved in Amy's abduction has been caught. I don't know what kind of mess Jay is still involved in, and I'm afraid about how this mess might follow me." She stopped and wiped a drop of broth from her bottom lip. "Us. Amy and I both. I don't understand what she's going through. I'm not sure if I want to ... When I think of what Jay did. What he risked. What ..."

A shell had formed around her feelings for Jay over the last few days, and now when she stopped to knock on it with thoughts of what, if, and why, it sounded hollow. Her heart rang with the same emptiness when she shook her head at herself. "I'm sorry, Abigail. I'm tired tonight."

"Don't be sorry. I'm glad the boys are late so we can talk."

Abigail stirred the soup in front of her, squinting down at the floating vegetables. "You have to do, or not do in this case, what you feel is right, Rachel. It's all any of us *can* do in situations like this. But have you prayed about it?"

Rachel had. She'd been praying more the last week than she had in years. It felt strange to talk to someone she wasn't sure she believed in anymore. She knew she didn't believe in church, not the kind she'd been a part of as a child. Still, she prayed, and in the dark, lonely hours, it had brought her moments of peace. She felt her decision was right. But she didn't want to admit that the religious part of her was waking up again.

"I know you have questions, Rachel. I know you are searching. But can you promise me something?" Abigail set her spoon down, still staring into her bowl.

"Maybe. What is it?" Rachel asked when the woman paused.

"Can you promise me that you take God with you as you search for answers?"

"How do you do that when you don't know if you believe in Him anymore?"

Abigail's shoulders rose with a slow breath, and a smile spread across her face. Her red hair bounced around her cheeks as she looked up, eyes twinkling.

"God doesn't need you to believe to hear your prayers, Rachel. If He is real, if His love is real, He'll still be listening. Ask Him to come with you."

"Alright." Rachel swallowed the lump that had formed in her throat and pushed away her bowl. "I promise I'll at least try."

Abigail turned her smile back to her soup and cleaned her bowl.

"More?" Rachel asked her.

"Oh, yes!"

They both enjoyed a second bowl before Glen and Ben walked through the door together. Both men shook water drops from their jackets, and Ben ran a hand over his balding head, dislodging drops that stalled on his skin. Glen threw his work cap to the side of the door to hit an air vent, but Rachel wasn't sure any warmth would be blowing from it tonight. She wrinkled her nose at the distinct smell of fried foods that clung to Glen's work uniform.

"Ugh, I'm soaked through to the underwear, Mom!" he said, undeterred by Rachel's presence. She rolled her eyes as he shook his hair and showered the carpet with water drops.

"You're not a dog, Glen," Abigail said as she laughed at him.

"What's for dinner?" Ben asked, stepping away from the onslaught of water.

"Soup."

Ben groaned at his wife's answer and muttered, "Feeding a half-drowned man more water?"

"Ignore him. He's just tired," Abigail said to Rachel as her men passed the table to find their rooms. "Don't leave a wet spot on the bed when you change, Ben," she called after him.

When had it started raining?

Soon Glen joined them, now dressed in a white shirt and a plush pair of pyjama pants. The cartoon character design made Rachel smile, and Glen grinned at her.

"Best Christmas present ever, these."

He was so different from Jay. So open. Even though they were close in age, he seemed so young at times. But he had his stepmom's wisdom. Moments after he rescued her, she wondered what it would be like to be with Glen instead of Jay. But she had to reject that idea. He was a good friend, but she had a hard time taking him seriously. She couldn't date someone like that. She respected parts of his personality, but other parts, she just couldn't.

"You're not afraid I'll tell everyone you're a huge nerd under that skater facade?" she asked him.

"Ha! They already know." He grinned.

As Ben joined them at the table, the room grew quiet. The boys dug in, and Rachel offered to clear away her and Abigail's dishes.

"Take the umbrella home, Rachel," Ben said when she headed for the door.

"That's okay. I have classes tonight, Ben. I'll be driving, not walking."

"Take it. I haven't seen such large raindrops all spring. You'll be soaked before reaching your apartment. You can bring it back tomorrow." Ben was usually as silly as his son at mealtimes, but this evening his voice was low and tired. "It's dark too. Make sure you call when you get home after class. I want to know that the sliding door of yours is locked, or I'll come check it myself."

She grabbed the umbrella the family kept propped up against the sliding door's frame. She waved it at him.

Ben nodded and returned to his food, a satisfied look on his face. "Don't forget that call."

"Yes sir, Mr. Edwards," she called as she opened the door and the umbrella at the same time.

The rain bounced off the nylon fabric and misted her face for a moment before she pushed out into the evening, jumping over a puddle right in front of the door.

The family waved as she slid the glass closed.

Take God with you.

She wondered what her father would think of Abigail's words.

Will you come with me, God, even if I don't believe in you anymore?

But was it true that she didn't believe? Maybe Abigail had sensed she still had some kind of faith, and that's why she believed God would go with her.

The sound of rain filled her senses as she trudged home. She needed to grab her bag before heading to school. As she unlocked her parents' apartment to grab it, she shivered.

The rain continued as she drove to the high school. She was thankful her mother had left her car behind. Trudging through this downpour would have been miserable, and after the last few weeks, she hated walking alone at night. She never felt safe anymore as she imagined strangers standing in the shadows watching her. No one had been able to tell them if the men who'd tried to abduct her had been arrested.

Officer Thomas had told her himself that Roger, the man she met in the apartment stairwell weeks ago, was a gang leader. They didn't think he was the top honcho, but he was up there. He was also the one who had harassed Amy down on Main Street. She shook her head at the thought. Undoubtedly, this mess was tangled like a plate of spaghetti. Would she ever understand what had really happened?

Roger had conveniently disappeared from town shortly after Amy's abduction, and no one was talking. But would he be back? There was no way to know. Rachel's mind itched as she pushed the door open at the school's side entrance.

When class ended, the dark night welcomed her back as she made for the car. The rain had turned to mist that the umbrella did little to guard against. When she closed the door, the dullness of silence seemed to swallow her.

Class had been filled with chatter, and though Rachel hadn't joined in, preferring to sit back and listen, now its absence left an ache in her heart.

God, when did I become so alone?

The drive home was filled with silent tears.

Rachel pushed into the dark room with the weight of weariness on her shoulders. As she rubbed her eyes she felt for the side table and lamp between her bed, and that of her sisters. She groaned when her arm hit the stack of books she left there, knocking them onto the bed. She fumbled for the switch on the lamp then sucked in a breath and squeezed her eyes shut as the sudden light stabbed her tired eyes. She felt for the books and their edges with eyes still closed before settling down.

The sound of crumpling paper as she sat on her bed made Rachel jump back up, the heavy bodies of several books clutched to her chest. She tottered on her toes for a second of dizziness as the blood in her veins caught up with the suddenness of her movement. Once the sensation settled, she stamped her foot in frustration and turned around to survey the bed.

A crumpled and now flattened brown object stood out from the pale blue blankets like an offending stain. The light from the bedside table didn't immediately help her identify the object, and Rachel poked it gingerly with a finger.

The bag from the clinic.

The realization that it was indeed a now very crumpled brown paper bag that the receptionist had run out to her and not a smear of chocolate or something worse brought fresh tears to Rachel's eyes. The stress and fear of being alone for so long, paired with the lesson from her night class echoing in her head, made her feel fragile. All she wanted to do was fall into bed. But ...

If I dump it on the floor now, it will only get kicked into a corner or have to be dealt with in the morning.

"Don't put off until tomorrow what you can do today." That was how the saying went, wasn't it? She sighed, set the books still in her arms back on to the table and picked up the bag.

She tipped it over and let its contents scatter across the comforter.

The stack of pamphlets inside had all seen better days. She sifted through them while rubbing weariness from her eyes again. Titles written in bold scripts across front pages glared up at her; What to Expect When You are Expecting, The Five Stages of Grief, Are You or Someone You Love on Drugs, How Loneliness Kills. Rachel blinked at each with a sinking heart. There was nothing for her ...

A small pink scrap of paper that looked like it had been torn from a larger piece slipped from in between the glossy pages of an information sheet on infant immunizations. The handwriting squeezed onto the scrap caught her eye.

To the girl looking through the window.

Rachel flipped the paper over.

I don't know what you might be going through, and just wanted you to know, I see you.
"God is our refuge and strength,
a very present help in trouble."
Psalms 46:1

Rachel froze, fingers pinching the paper's pink edge. She read the message again and then a third time before turning it over to read the small print on the opposite again as well.

To the girl looking through the window.

The receptionist had stepped out of line. Handing out Bible verses and personal messages to patients without permission would be frowned on, seen as pushing religion on someone vulnerable, but she couldn't be upset about it.

I see you.

She read the paper a fourth time and then a fifth before laying it aside and shuffling the pamphlets into a pile and walking them out of the room.

When she returned, she laid the paper by the lamp on the bedside table and resigned herself to another night alone. But maybe, just maybe she wasn't as alone as she thought she was.

Decisions

RACHEL

RACHEL HAD THE OPENING shift at the laundromat the next morning. The rain had stopped, but the sky remained a heavy grey. She could smell the moisture in the air, and puddles sat in the gutters, gathering in every low spot on the sidewalk. She unlocked the laundromat's front door and stomped her feet on the entryway mat, shaking water from the rubber soles of her shoes.

Her breakfast of cereal sat heavy in her stomach as she re-locked the door and made her way to the back of the long room and the light switch panel. The back storage room door was wide open, and Rachel paused in surprise.

"Tracy, you better have just forgotten to close that last night," she muttered.

The overly chatty woman had come in to take over from Rachel around four o'clock the day before. Tracy had been in charge of cleaning and closing up for the night, and she'd been alone.

When Rachel peered into the back room, her heart sank.

The contents of the top shelves were now scattered all over the floor. Laundry detergent leaked from broken bottles, and dryer sheets lay about like spent confetti.

"Oh, God, no!" Rachel groaned as the smell of mixed soaps reached her.

She pulled her phone from a pocket and dialed her boss' number. Her heart hammered as she waited nearly five rings before he picked up.

"Hello?" His response was sluggish, and Rachel cringed.

"Hey, Donald, it's Rachel. We have a problem."

She ran shaking fingers through her hair as she relayed the sight to him. "Tracy was the one to close last night, right? For sure?"

"Yes!" the man barked, and Rachel heard something fall and shatter on his end of the line before she pulled the device away from her ear, shrinking from the noise.

"Do you want me to report it as vandalism? Or?" Rachel wasn't sure if Tracy had gotten involved with the man or not. She always talked about him disgustedly, but Rachel also knew the woman had been desperate. The mess looked very much like revenge to her.

"Yeah ..." His bark had turned to a grumble. "I'll be right over, Rachel. Do your best to get the place open for business, will ya? It's Friday!"

All Rachel could do was shake her head as the call ended, cutting off her boss' cursing. She walked back to the front desk to look up the police station's number.

It was pushing ten a.m. by the time Donald walked in the front entrance. Rachel had left the back room as it was but grabbed a few untouched supplies from a nearby shelf. She made note of what she grabbed in case the police asked her about it, even snapping a few pictures of the shelves as proof of where she'd taken it from.

"Where are they?" Donald yelled as he paced the aisle between washers and dryers.

"Do you think anything's missing?" she asked him, hoping it would send the man looking and stop the pacing.

"No ... don't know ... Everything is fine behind the counter, right?"

She nodded to him. "I don't see anything out of place. The paperwork looks fine. Cash looks fine. But you know I didn't close last night. So ..."

"Right. I'll have a look at those numbers, please."

She pushed her chair out of the way for him as he pulled another up behind the counter and the computer monitor.

Rachel knew how to count the cash she regularly emptied from the machines and had been making notes of the numbers since her first day of work. But other than that, she'd never paid attention to the business' finances. It wasn't her place.

Donald kept the cash overflow in the safe stashed in the back of the storage room. Her coworker Tim had a key to deposit the money himself when he worked, but every other day, Donald came in to take care of the money himself. They all took careful note of how much was left after closing out the register. Still, Rachel wondered. Some would have to have been left as there were customers using the machines when she'd clocked out the day before.

Donald shook his head and groaned but didn't tell her the damages or if anything was missing.

The bell above the door chimed, and a uniformed officer walked in. The freckles that peppered his face added youth to his profile. Rachel didn't recognize him from her visit to the police station. Donald checked his watch and cast the man a disgruntled look before pointing to the back and motioning that he would lead him to the mess.

"What happened?" the officer asked as Donald rounded the counter.

Did they know each other? The officer didn't introduce himself, but his eyes lingered on Rachel.

A shiver ran up her spine.

The chime rang again, and Rachel relaxed as Officer Thomas strolled in. He waved a hand at her and smiled, though his eyes looked sad, or maybe he was tired. It was hard to tell as he looked away and followed his colleague down the aisle of washers.

"The back room's been vandalized. Supplies smashed. No way to tell if something is missing back there yet, though." Donald's voice echoed towards her.

"And you opened for business anyway?"

Rachel couldn't tell which officer had asked. Donald grunted before the men's voices lowered and only muffled words reached her.

Rachel flip-flopped between relief at seeing Officer Thomas and unease at the whole situation as she waited alone at the front desk. When would life settle down again? Why did these things keep happening around her? She worried about Tracy and thought about calling her for a moment before deciding against it. If the woman was the vandal, she wouldn't answer Rachel's call anyway. She rolled her shoulders to ease some of her tension.

"Doing okay, Miss Grill?" Officer Thomas asked as he walked back towards her and pulled a notepad and pen from his uniform jacket pocket.

"Yes. Just tired and annoyed."

"I guess you're the one who'll be cleaning up that mess. I would be annoyed too."

That was a truth she had not allowed herself to think about until then.

"You got a mask to wear when you do it? Those fumes have gotten pretty strong." He looked down at the paper in his hand and scribbled out some words.

She hadn't thought of that and wondered if Donald could be persuaded to grab her some before he left.

"Now, Miss Grill. I need to take your statement. Can you walk me through coming in and finding the mess this morning?"

Rachel recounted how she'd found the back room in detail, doing her best to mark times and tell him what she had removed from the room to ready the laundromat for customers. He nodded as she spoke then asked about the day before and when she'd left Tracy to the late shift.

"She seemed fine to me," Rachel said. "She's always a bit on edge and likes to run her mouth when she doesn't get the hours she wants or needs."

She shrugged as Officer Thomas lifted an eyebrow.

"Do you remember how many people were in the building when you left? Any regulars we could contact?"

Rachel shook her head as the door chime sounded for a third time that morning.

"Thomas?" It was a third officer. His square frame reminded Rachel of a well chiselled boulder.

Officer Thomas held up a finger of pause to Rachel and turned to his colleague, who motioned his need for a private word.

Rachel pushed her back firmly against her chair, wishing she had decided to skip work that morning. But knowing that would have been out of character for her and put her under suspicion, she chided herself for the thought. The new officer's expression pinched as he spoke to Thomas. In turn, Thomas stood still as a stone. His back was turned to her, but he didn't even shift on his feet before his head slowly turned to look back down the aisle of washers.

The two men started walking together but split apart when they reached the aisle. Officer Thomas took the middle, and the new man split to the right.

What was going on?

Rachel stood for a second to watch both men move with determination when a fourth officer walked into the building and motioned for her to stay put. He placed himself in front of the counter. Was he guarding her? Apprehension tingled up her legs, and she felt her stomach flip.

Someone shouted a name she didn't know, and the first officer to arrive appeared in the door of the back room. Donald stood by his elbow but backed off as soon as he saw the two other officers converging on the room's doorway.

Rachel watched wide-eyed as the square officer reached the storage room first. She didn't hear what he said, but the first officer's face screwed up into something ugly. He looked past Thomas and directly at her. Her heart skittered in her chest as he lunged, pushing a shoulder past Officer Thomas. The third officer's large hand was on the first's in a flash as he caught up to Thomas. He grabbed his arm as if he was afraid the younger man would go for the gun holstered at his hip.

Officer Thomas shouted words into the first man's face that made Rachel cringe.

"What's going on?" she asked her guardian.

"Don't worry. Just stay where you are." It wasn't an answer to the question, but she sat down and pushed her chair backwards until it touched the wall, hoping it would shrink her presence in the room. It didn't, and she felt the first officer's eyes on her as he was led towards the front exit.

Then they all left. The sudden reduction of people in the building left the air chilled. Or maybe it was the drafts that had slipped in the door as Officer Thomas led his colleague away. Rachel blinked, her heart still fluttering in her chest.

"Rachel?" Donald asked. He was at her elbow. She hadn't heard him come behind the counter. "Do you know him?"

"I don't think so," she answered, unsure. "Why would they arrest one of their own? I didn't finish answering Officer Thomas' questions."

Donald's eyes were dark, and he seemed on edge as he opened his mouth once then closed it again. Finally, he decided to speak. "They said something about Jay."

"What?"

"Why don't you go home? I'll clean up here."

"What?" she repeated, frozen to the chair.

"I think … I think they found Jay. He must have told them something about that officer."

"Donald, do you know him?" She didn't know why she asked.

He turned when he nodded. But he didn't elaborate. "Look, Rachel. I know a lot of people in this town. Not all of them are good. They found Jay. I think you should go home and lock your doors." His eyes narrowed as he spoke to her.

None of this made sense, but the look on Donald's face frightened her. She wasn't safe here? Not even in the middle of the morning? She rose, trembling as he made to open the door for her.

If she wasn't safe at work, would she even be safe at home? Was she safe right now, walking down the street? The sun was bright, working hard to dry the puddles that lingered in the gutters. She was so tired. It felt like her very skin sagged on her bones as she walked past building after building. Was she being watched? How could she go on like this? When would life feel normal again? Could it ever?

God, why me? Why us?

She almost tripped on an uneven crack on the sidewalk and slowed her steps to look around. The floor-to-ceiling windows of the clinic glimmered in the sunshine as she walked past.

The panes were peppered with papers and posters advertising various groups and programs the Health Unit had available to Barton's citizens. She looked past them. A familiar face behind the reception desk looked back—the woman who had handed her the brown paper bag, her eyes soft and curious. She looked to the left and right as if watching for people before beckoning Rachel through the window to come inside.

Home

ARTHUR

ANGER BURNED IN ARTHUR'S chest. Its vehemence shocked him, but he refused to shake it off. He sat in front of Rose in her wheelchair, his backside pressing a deep depression into the hotel bed.

"She can't leave now," he said. His body trembled as he strove for control of his temper. This wasn't Rose's fault. He wouldn't snap at her, he promised himself. "We've only just come back together as a family. She can't leave."

"Arthur—"

"She can't leave, Rose."

"You can't stop her."

Arthur bit his tongue.

"You can't stop Rachel from going where she wants to, where she needs to, Arthur. We can't ... We can't control her life no matter how much we want to. It's wrong. It's part of the reason she left in the first place."

"We had rules. Rules, Rose. She broke them. That's why she left."

His wife let out a deep sigh. "Alright, there were many reasons she left. I won't argue about that, Arthur. But it doesn't change the fact that we can't stop her. And ... I'm not sure we should try to even change her mind."

Arthur looked away and swallowed. She was right, and he hated it. Rachel was eighteen. As a February baby, she spent her first few months as a legal adult finishing up high school. But with the year almost over, nothing could keep her in Barton Township for much longer, not even them.

"I need to go home," he said, looking at his hands.

"You can't stop her, Arthur."

"I know." His chest filled with an aching resignation. "Train up a child in the way he should go; even when he is old he will not depart from it." He quoted the Bible verse from Proverbs 22:6 under his breath.

Rose's eyes shimmered with moisture as she sat back in her wheelchair. "Rachel is strong, Arthur. She is smart, and driven, and far from old. She has time."

Yes, there was time. But what would they have to watch her go through, do, struggle with before she came back to them? Would they ever see her come back to the woman of God they'd raised her to be?

"I just ... I just want us all to be together, Rose."

Rose looked around the hotel room, avoiding Arthur's gaze. It was late evening. Rachel's call had come in just before they'd started preparing for an early night. His eldest daughter had told her mother about the arrest the police had made that day right in front of her. They'd gotten an update from Officer Thomas himself earlier, but the details had been sparse. Rachel filled in the few gaps that she could and then had told Rose her plans.

His daughter had visited the local clinic and talked to an on-staff nurse. He ground his teeth as he ran the advice Rachel had been given through his mind. She'd been told that if she didn't feel safe in Barton, she should leave. Or at least that was the gist of it.

Rachel had taken the advice to heart and, on returning to the apartment, set about job hunting in a city to the east, the opposite direction from where they were now. She'd told them she didn't want to mess with moving across the provincial border. Staying in Ontario was easier. The few cities in the northwest of the province were still much cheaper than Winnipeg, and she couldn't afford to go all the way east to Toronto. It was too expensive to live in the provincial capital anyway.

No, she'd move in the opposite direction from them. Arthur didn't know what he would have said or done if she'd told them she was moving to Toronto, a full two and a half day's drive away. They would never have seen her again. This way, she promised she'd come home for the holidays. Arthur wondered if she really would.

"I need to go home," he repeated. "I'll lose the job at Ham's if I don't." Rose sighed again.

God, what is your plan?

What do I do with a family so torn?

How do I hold us all together?

Is it even possible?

Too many questions bounced around his mind, and though he needed rest before the long drive the next morning, he sat there waiting, wishing he could hear the voice of God, wondering why he was so silent.

"Arthur?"

"Hm?"

"I love you."

Rose's simple statement sent a wave of warmth through Arthur's heart. He looked at her, her thin frame cradled in her chair, her pale skin, her frizzing hair. It was all so beautiful. He didn't deserve her, he knew that, but she was the one thing he could be sure of. As long as they were both on Earth, they would be one.

Saying goodbye to Rose the next morning was more difficult than Arthur had anticipated. He wheeled her to the hospital and up to the family waiting room. Since Amy had been admitted to the psychiatric ward, their visits had become more restricted, but Rose insisted on being available at all times.

"Are you sure you're going to be alright, and you don't want to come back with me? Not even for a few days?"

"No, Arthur. I've talked to the hospital chaplain, and he'll take me back to the hotel. I'll be fine."

The chaplain was an interesting man with a dark complexion and bright eyes that never stayed still when he spoke. He seemed well connected in the community and had assured Rose he would help her find a more affordable place to stay, enabling her to remain close to her daughter. Still, Arthur worried. But unease about a much depleted bank account was growing, and now he had Rachel to worry about. He kissed Rose's forehead again before squeezing her hand and walking away.

Strangers passed him without a glance on the wide city sidewalks back to the hotel. The morning was fresh, the air crisp, but the sun shone brightly, promising a warm spring day once it had risen above the tall buildings.

After collecting the car from the hotel parking complex, Arthur was glad to be leaving the city. How long would it be until he needed to return? A few days? Would Rose and Amy make it a week without him? It might be a Saturday morning, but Fred was eager to have Arthur back at the grocery store working. Sunday would see him carting stock through Ham's back rooms. The regular delivery of goods wouldn't happen until Monday and Tuesday, but weekends were still busy. His coworkers would be organizing for the impending influx of boxes and crates, shifting goods forwards and making room to place new goods at the back of shelves and fridges.

He never imagined he would miss Ham's Grocers, but a part of him did. As he sped out of the city proper, Arthur's mood brightened. Life would again be different at home, but they could only get better from here ... right? He didn't let himself think of Rachel yet. While on the road, he could do nothing about it. But when he was home, maybe he could change her mind.

Arthur paused at the now familiar Crossroads Truck Stop and looked for Austin at the counter. He felt a knot of disappointment when it was a younger employee manning the checkout. He smiled sadly at the picture of Amy taped up on the front display window. Austin had written *found* in bold black under her name.

We found her, God. But it's going to take time to put those broken pieces back together.

Arthur had wondered over the last few weeks if his daughter's soul was still missing. A darkness lived in her eyes, overshadowing the spark of defiance that had once been every present there. It sent shivers up his spine when he spent time with her. Their conversations had been few even while he sat beside her bed for several hours, giving her mother a break.

He had almost wept when Amy reached out to him for the last twenty minutes of that sit in and held his hand. It was the only time all week she'd touched him or allowed him to touch her. They had never been close, but he had thought his girls knew they were safe in his presence. He swallowed past the lump the memory formed in his throat.

"She has to reacclimate to what safe is," her doctor has said, voicing the tough truth of a terrible situation. "We all need to be patient. You need to love her in this mess, Mr. Grill, in order for her to move through it. You and your wife can be the lifeline that she follows to find her way out."

What does love in these kinds of circumstances look like, God? I can't fix her. I can't do anything for her, really. Sitting on my rear and waiting doesn't feel like love.

He'd been a man of action for years. It was part of why Hope Is Here Church had hired him as a young man. He and Rose had made the perfect "get things done" team. So, what did a "do it" kind of man *do* when there wasn't anything to do? He could work. He would do his best to make sure Rose could stay with Amy as long as she needed to. He could strive to get Rose what she needed to be comfortable. He could take care of Rachel if only she would let him. He would at least try. He had to.

As he walked back to his car, disposable coffee cup in hand, he glanced over at the mostly dark Truckers' Chapel. The main building partly hid it, but one of the windows was lit up, something Arthur hadn't seen before. He smiled, wondering to himself if they had found someone to open it. Austin would be thrilled if they had. Was that why he wasn't at the checkout today?

Thoughts of what lay behind him faded as he neared Barton, and the familiar houses on the outskirts of town came into view. Arthur's stomach rumbled. He should pick up some dinner for Rachel. Entering the apartment with food as an offering would be the perfect icebreaker before tackling hard subjects with his eldest daughter, wouldn't it? Everyone's temperament improved in the presence of food.

After stopping at the first local burger joint on the main drag, Arthur's stomach had to suffer the torturous and delicious smell seeping through the brown paper to-go bag resting on the passenger's seat. He should have stopped for lunch, but after Crossroads Truck Stop, he had let the push to get home drive him. He couldn't stop his fingers from searching the bag for stray fries as he carried it to the apartment sliding door.

The sun shone on the glass, obscuring his view inside, but he didn't think twice about sliding the glass sideways and calling into the dimness.

"Rose?" He caught himself as Rachel appeared in the kitchen doorway.

"Dad?"

"Sorry," he said, shaking his head. "I must be tired. Up for an early dinner?"

The paper bag crackled in his hand as he held it out to her. Rachel rewarded him with a soft smile, and he blew out a soft breath. "I got us both the same thing. I hope you don't mind."

Arthur crinkled his nose as he set the brown bag on the kitchen table. The room smelled of cleaning products.

"Seems like you've been busy today," he said.

Rachel pulled down a set of plates from the cupboard. "Sorry about the smell. I spilled some full strength floor cleaner this morning." She mimicked her father's expression, and the lines that formed over the bridge of her nose reminded Arthur of her mother. Rose was sensitive to smell and unafraid to let him know her distaste of unexpected scents, or him when he irritated her delicate constitution.

"The smell's not that bad."

"It was this morning. I had all the windows open for a few hours."

Rachel pulled the food bag to herself and drew out a burger and fries for each plate she'd set on the table. Arthur looked her over as she shook crumbs from the bottom of the bag before pushing a plate towards him.

"What?" she asked.

Was that apprehension he saw flickering in her eyes?

The look made Arthur pause before speaking and choosing his words carefully. "Nothing, Rachel, I'm just glad to be home and that the apartment isn't empty." Arthur shifted focus from his daughter to the food while he sat. "I hope you don't mind the onions and pickles. I couldn't remember how you liked your burger. But they're sliced big, so if you need to take them off, I can eat them. Can you pass the ketchup?"

Rachel eased a few ketchup packages towards him while subjecting him to her own slow visual appraisal. "You can have my onions."

He chuckled at the grimace she made while removing the white rings from in between layers of bun, meat, and lettuce.

"But thanks for the food. If you don't mind, I think I'll eat in my room. I have some studying to get done before Monday."

"Oh ... Sure." Disappointment pooled in Arthur's gut as Rachel stood from her place at the table, plate in hand. He'd hoped they could sit and talk. Had he said something wrong? She clearly already had her guard up. Why? Couldn't he be home for five minutes without her needing to distance herself from him? Hadn't they resolved their issues before he'd had to leave?

After Rachel left, the silence around him felt suffocating.

He grabbed his own plate from the table before heading into the living room and turning on the TV.

The Call

ARTHUR

RACHEL CONTINUED TO AVOID Arthur for the rest of the evening. After a phone call with Rose, he resigned himself to leaving her alone, only interrupting her studying to let her know he was headed to bed and that he'd cleared away the dirty dishes. She'd smiled, nodded, and then buried her nose back into a textbook.

He paused before closing the door. The ends of her hair hung in frizzy strands around her face, having slipped from the tie that held it in a ponytail at the nape of her neck. With her long legs curled up on the bed, hidden from view, she looked so much like Rose.

"Rachel."

"Hm?" The sound she made was both question and dismissal.

He closed the door.

She's not ready to talk. Give her until the morning.

When the morning came, Rachel was out of the house before Arthur. He shook his head at the sound of the sliding door closing as he dressed.

"Where is she going on a Sunday morning?"

Even he wouldn't be attending church. He wondered if Pastor Edwin and the small congregation at Barton Community Church were missing them as he packed a lunch and headed out the door for work. Did it matter if they were or weren't? They hadn't had time to get involved with people there, and everything going on in his life left little time to worry about it.

He and Rose had received numerous calls of celebration when Amy was found and a few notes of encouragement since then. But Arthur didn't expect much more. The small congregation of Barton Community Church couldn't do anything beyond pray for them.

Isn't that enough, Arthur?

When he stepped into the back room at Ham's Grocers, he was greeted with "Hello," and "Glad you're back, Arthur," from all across the room. A smile spread over his face as gratitude for the warm greeting bloomed in his chest.

At lunch, he sent a text to Rose. She replied, assuring him she was fine. Amy was tired that day and irritable, so she spent most of the morning in the hospital family room waiting. She would be accompanying her to a counselling session in the afternoon.

Arthur hoped that meant breakthroughs were happening.

Is it too soon to hope for that, God?

It probably was.

Arthur relished the return to work. Preparing for the next day's impending deliveries kept the whole store busy, organizing shelves and shifting boxes and pallets around the storage rooms.

Fred greeted him during second break, making sure Arthur knew how happy he was they'd found Amy and how good it was to see such a hard worker back home.

"You won't have to take any more time off for a while, right?" his boss asked, concern washing over his face for a moment before he smoothed it out and returned to a placid smile.

He's trying to stay polite, but he's put out by extended absences, Arthur realized.

"The plan is to work as long and consistently as I can, Fred. But Rose is still in the city with our daughter. We don't know how long recovery will take."

Fred nodded and patted Arthur's arm before walking away.

Penelope found him right before his shift ended as he hung the keys to the forklift in the small blue box mounted to the wall beside the hard hats and vests. He stood frozen for a moment as she enveloped him in a hug. The woman's all-business attitude was shockingly absent as she cried.

"I never once stopped praying for you, Arthur. I just knew you'd find her." Despite a handful of his coworkers looking on with raised eyebrows, he returned the small woman's embrace.

"Thank you," was all he could say as emotion strained his voice.

Penelope held the embrace longer than Arthur thought normal, but he didn't pull away.

"The prayers won't stop, Arthur. No, they won't," she declared when she finally released him. "And don't you worry, we will rework your shift schedule into whatever you need it to be. I will make sure of that."

Gratitude filled his chest to bursting as he left for home.

A text from Rachel informed him that they'd both been invited to the Edwards' for dinner that evening, but she wouldn't be there until six-thirty. Abigail wanted her to let him know he could head over whenever he wanted.

He decided he wasn't ready for people yet when he slid the glass door into the apartment open. The plastic mat right inside the entrance had been recently cleaned, and Arthur made a mental note to thank Rachel again. He let his jacket fall to the mat and slipped out of his boots, revelling in the feeling of the carpet as he walked over it with stocking feet. A full day of walking cement floors had left even his toes aching.

He almost called for Rose again but caught himself and sighed. It was good to be home, but the apartment felt achingly empty. Had it really ever been packed with people and warmth?

He found himself at his small computer desk, sifting through junk emails with a fresh cup of coffee in hand. Then he scanned through half typed correspondences he'd planned to send out to church boards and fellowships across the country. As block after block of text rolled over the computer screen, a question stuck in his mind. Was this what his family needed? Was it even what he wanted? Was it what he was supposed to do?

He let a finger tap the side of his mug. What did he want? What did his family need? He wasn't sure. What if a church in the city reached out to him? Would he be in the right space of mind to accept a call back to ministry? He and Rose hadn't even been talking about the possibility yet. She had so many other things on her mind. Moving to the city would be a huge change from small town life, and what about Amy? Was he moving too fast?

A notification sounded from his phone, and a second later, a green bar slid out from the right hand of his computer screen, showing that he'd gotten a new email. He clicked on it absentmindedly, a drip of coffee beading on his lip. He wiped it away with the back of a hand and set the cup down as he leaned closer to the screen. Was he reading it right?

Pastor Grill, we are writing to inform you of an opening at Crossroads Truck Stop Chapel. This position has been waiting to be filled for quite some time, but until now, the collaborating congregations supporting the ministry haven't had the funds to offer a full-time chaplain. Recently, their circumstances have changed, making filling this position financially possible. You are one of many ministers in our contact list. If you hear the call, please respond.

Arthur's fingers hovered above the keys. He couldn't believe it.

Pins and needles washed over him, lingering in his fingertips as he pressed the speed dial on his cell phone.

"Rose? Can you talk?"

"The truck stop? The one where we picked up coffee on the way into the city?" Rose asked. She sounded confused and tired. Arthur slowed his speech, giving her extra time to process his words.

"Yes, it's called Crossroads Truck Stop. You saw the small chapel there, right? I remember you staring at it through the building's side windows. Anyway, I just got an email listing them as a potential call to ministry."

"The chapel? At the truck stop? Really?"

"Yes, really."

"Well, what did the message say?"

"Not much. It just said all the local churches have decided to band together to make filling the long empty position financially possible, and they've sent out the call for a chaplain."

"Well, are you going to answer it?"

"I don't know."

Rose took a deep breath that sounded like a vacuum over the phone. "Well, why not?"

Surprise leapt within Arthur's heart at the sound of excitement in his wife's voice.

"A chaplaincy is more than a step down from Senior Pastor, Rose."

"Do we care about that?" she asked.

Did he care?

"Well, do you think we could live on a chaplain's salary?"

"Did they say how much they're offering?"

"No."

"Then why don't you ask them? Pursuing more information is never a bad thing, right?"

"I guess—well, okay then. I will."

Sweat beaded on his cheek where the cell phone pressed against his skin. He shifted the device to his other hand and ear, wiping the moisture away with a sleeve. Why was he sweating? It was just an email, just a possibility, nothing more. Maybe not even a good possibility. He wouldn't be able to judge more until he had the information.

"Arthur?" Rose asked softly. "Are you still there? Are you okay?"

"Yes. I'm still here." Why was his heart racing?

"Did you need something else?"

"No. I—I love you. I'll call you before bed."

Their call ended with her sending him her love as well. His heart felt like it was bouncing inside his rib cage.

God? What is this?

Arthur wiped more perspiration from his forehead before writing a short reply to the original message. He asked for more information and then tried to forget about it until a reply came in.

Arthur and Rachel arrived at the Edwards' sliding door at almost the same time. He nodded to his daughter as she paused on the walkway before turning into the small backyard space allotted to the apartment.

"How was your day?" he asked, one hand in a pocket, the other poised to open the door.

"Oh. Fine. Thanks for asking, Dad."

"Why are you avoiding me, Rachel?"

"I'm not avoiding you."

"Rachel..."

"Dad!" Rachel pointed at the door and Glen's face smiling at them both through the glass.

Arthur raised his eyebrows as his daughter laughed at Glen's playful expression and waved. The boy pulled the door open, his smile stretching from ear to ear.

"Pastor Arthur! It's good to have you home. Rachel! I've got something I want to show you."

Glen was dressed in the most ridiculous pyjama pants Arthur had ever seen, and Arthur's brows stayed raised as he let Rachel step into the Edwards' small living room space.

"Leave the glass open, Glen," Abigail called from the kitchen behind the combined living room and dining room. "Just pull the screen closed."

Walking into the Edwards' home felt like a warm hug. Maybe a warm hug that lasted a bit too long. Arthur was soon thankful for the open door as a cool breeze found its way inside. The kitchen was a mess of pots, pans, and utensils as Abigail and Ben worked together to finish dinner. Arthur smiled as Rachel immediately jumped up to the sink and started rinsing the worst of the prep dishes, clearing much needed space for the couple.

"Take a seat, Arthur," Ben said, motioning him towards the dinner table. "It'll be five more minutes."

Compassion's Way

ROSE

RELIEF ALMOST TRIPPED ROSE as she reached Amy's room. She'd laboriously shuffled her way behind her walker through the hospital halls as Reverend Daryl, the hospital's chaplain, guided her. He'd picked her up from the hotel and helped her most of the way, but on reaching the psychiatric wards, they'd split up, and Rose was left to herself and her stubbornly stiff feet.

"Mom!" Amy's smile of greeting was a balm to Rose's soul. When was the last time Rose had seen her smile so brightly? She couldn't recall even from the time before Arthur's dismissal from Hope Is Here Church. It had to be a sign.

Amy's new room was small but set up for longer stays with an armchair in the corner next to a table and a simpler dining room style chair to accompany it. The stationary bed and side table could have belonged to any modest bedroom, as well as the small wardrobe and dresser set against the left side wall. Amy sat on the bed, her legs crisscrossed in front of her. Scattered pieces of a puzzle they'd both worked on yesterday lay on the table.

"How was your breakfast?" Rose asked as she slowly moved into the room, leaving the door open to the hall.

Amy rolled her eyes and rested a chin on the palm of a hand as an elbow pressed into her knee. "It was oatmeal." Amy mock gagged on the word.

Rose laughed. "No fruit?"

Amy pointed to an unopened cup of fruit cocktail on the bedside table. Rose chuckled as Amy wrinkled her nose but held back a fully disgusted explanation of why she didn't eat the fruit along with her cereal. The sass her daughter exuded almost brought tears to Rose's eyes.

God, she is starting to sound and act like the Amy I know and love. Difficult as it may be, she is still here.

It looked like their day would start out better than yesterday's tears and agitation. Was the new medication working already? Or was Amy just getting used to her new surroundings? Rose prayed the peace and smiles would last as she sank into the armchair.

"Do we get to do something today? Or are we going to just sit in this room again?" Amy asked.

"We should take a walk in the garden. You like it there."

"We did that yesterday."

"Well, we'll do it again and then see how you feel. Wasn't the fresh air wonderful?"

Rose held her breath as Amy pinched her lips together, then she released it as her daughter shrugged and the moment of tension passed.

"Alright," Amy relented.

Waiting was difficult for Amy, but Dr. Miriam had told them stability and low stress would be key to stabilizing her anxiety enough that she could leave. That meant slow days and regular counselling sessions.

"Do you mind?" Rose asked as she stretched from her seat to reach the fruit cup on the nightstand. She paused as Amy eyed her, a strange expression on her face.

"Go ahead," Amy said after a second. Rose watched her daughter blink several times then looked away as she grabbed the small cup.

"If it bothers you, I can leave it there."

"No. I'm not going to eat it, so you should."

"Are you remembering something?" Rose asked softly as she held the cup but didn't open it.

"No." Amy's reply came too fast. "I wish I could pick my own food like I always did at home." Amy unfolded her legs and let them slide over the edge of the bed, placing both hands on either side of her knees. Her shoulders shrugged, and the cock of her head as she pulled it backwards reminded Rose of a turtle ducking into its shell for safety.

"We can ask Dr. Miriam if you're allowed food from outside the hospital in your room. If she says yes, you can write me a list."

Amy nodded and wriggled her toes then thumped her heels against the enclosed wooden platform the mattress rested on. It offered no space to store things or to hide in.

"Come, let's finish this and then visit the garden before your morning chat with the counsellor." Rose tapped the tabletop beside her displaying the jumble of puzzle pieces.

The morning moved along peacefully as Amy perched on the dining chair opposite Rose and started shifting puzzle pieces around. Still, Rose watched her carefully as the picture took shape.

With only a few pieces left to fit in place, Amy sighed, looked up, and shifted away from the small table. Rose watched as her daughter yanked on a blond curl, pulling the strand nearly straight before letting it go just to grab it again and pull harder.

"What is it?" Rose asked.

"Nothing."

"Amy ..."

Her daughter snorted at an unshared thought and rose from her seat to pace the small space from bed to doorway. She poked her head into the hall, looked both ways, then turned back to Rose. "Mom?"

"Yes?"

"Why did God make me broken?"

Rose faltered. "Make you—"

"You heard me." Amy's tone was sharp, and her expression held mixed emotions Rose couldn't interpret.

"God didn't make you broken, Amy."

"Yes, He did. He built me this way, and then ... He let me shatter."

Rose's mouth felt open, her stomach lodged firmly in her throat as she grasped at words of reply.

In the silence, tears flowed from Amy, but not the hot, angry tears Rose was used to seeing her shed. No, this time they ran slow as her daughter's eyes stared into space.

"Amy, we are all broken. That is what sin does."

"I'm ... more broken than normal."

Rose sighed, "Maybe, but maybe you just feel the wrongness of it deeper than most."

Amy blinked at her. The change in her daughter's expression stilled a measure of Rose's fear. She couldn't tell how Amy would react when emotion like this surfaced. Would Rose soon find herself calling for help from a ward nurse? Would Amy's anger rise above her emptiness and flood the room with shouting and curses?

Rose swallowed before continuing, "Sin ... it cuts deep, Amy, for all of us. Some people don't notice the damage or fool themselves into thinking it's normal. But you are not alone in feeling its bite. We are all broken. That's why Christ came."

Amy returned to the chair opposite her mother, her face frozen as she fought for control, for words. "So, this happened to me because of my sin?"

"Oh, Amy. No." Rose wiped her own eyes dry with the back of her hand. "No, Amy. This happened because of other people's sin."

"Why did He let it happen?"

Why, God? Why did you?

Rose shook her head as she answered in a whisper, "I don't know, baby. I'm sorry."

Amy looked down at the near finished puzzle again and pushed a connection flat where the cardboard edges had started to shift up.

Rose breathed a breath of relief as they finished the puzzle in silence, Amy lost in thought but blessedly calm.

The garden was down several levels, and Rose notified the nurses where they'd be going and for roughly how long as they left the ward. It was a blessing Amy had come far enough to have this freedom. Even though her daughter stayed silent through the elevator ride and averted her eyes from every stranger they passed, she lit up when they stepped out the glass doors into the sunshine.

The garden sat in the centre of the hospital buildings, enclosed on all sides by glass windows or white-washed bricks. The space was open to the sky, but the high walls kept the corners in shadows. Sun lamps hung in those places and benches were set just off the trail so patients could soak up natural vitamin D or use the lamps when it was absent.

A cement path wandered through planters. Dark fresh earth was piled in spots, freshly turned and waiting for spring planting. Soon the garden would be filled with colour, and Rose wondered if they'd still be there to see everything in bloom. The trees that grew from the centres of the larger plots were dressed in fresh green leaves, and new growth could be seen at branch tips. They found a bench for Rose, and she sat watching Amy walk the winding path over and over until a beeper sounded, telling them it was almost time for Amy's counselling session.

After accompanying her daughter back to her ward, Rose retreated to the family waiting room. She would join Amy again for lunch, but until then, her daughter needed privacy. That suited Rose fine. She was exhausted as well as frustrated at her exhaustion.

God, how can I be of any help in this condition?

It was a blessing to be able to walk the halls with just her walker and not require the wheelchair like their first week. Still, she grieved for her independence and health. Arthur had only allowed her to stay because she'd be spending most of her time in the hospital. If anything happened, she would have ample help. Rose's fingers trembled as she sat watching the local news play on the family room's television.

How long can we continue like this, God?

So many factors made their situation unsustainable.

I miss life as it used to be. Struggles and all. Oh, God ... I would have done things so differently if only I had known.

She knew that thinking that way wouldn't help, but the solitude created white space for her inner voice and its questions.

"Rose?" A soft knock sounded, and she looked up to see Reverend Daryl tapping the door frame with dark knuckles. "Oh, good, I thought you might have been sleeping," he said when she shifted in her chair to face his direction. "I have great news!" he continued. "I've found you a new place to stay."

Rose sat up, a spark of warmth lighting in her chest.

"Over the last week, I've contacted several organizations that provide accommodations for families in a health crisis. Most of them are at capacity with long wait lists. I didn't have much hope of finding you a room with one of them, so I turned to local churches to see if any families had a room to let for a decent price. Well ..." Reverend Daryl paused, the grin on his face stretching from ear to ear. "Compassion's Way, a home that's usually only open to terminally ill patients and their families, has an opening. They've acquired a second house. The extra rooms have filled fast, but, Rose, they have one left. It's on the main floor of the older home they use. It's not as up to date décor-wise as the new suites, and they've moved some of the long term tenets over to the new space for the duration of renovations on the older house. But this room is still livable and open for you. What do you think?"

At first, Rose didn't know what to say. Reverend Daryl's way of dumping out information at a rapid pace left her brain tired, but after a moment of thought, she asked, "How far is it from the hospital?"

"Just a few blocks farther west. I can still pick you up every day I come in for work. They also have shuttles that run from the homes to the hospital. You can sign up ahead of time for an additional cost."

"And what is the cost per night, Reverend?"

Rose almost fell off the chair when he told her the daily dollar amount. It wasn't even a quarter of the price they were paying for the hotel room.

"There are house rules and a house kitchen and rec room that all families share. Both will undergo renovations, but the room is yours for up to six months, Rose. What do you think?"

"I think it's an answer to prayer," Rose told him. She could hardly believe something like this would be open to them. "But Amy isn't terminally ill. How did you get a yes from them?"

"I told them about your health issues as well." The reverend lost his smile for a moment. "I hope that was alright, but having a caregiver in your situation and given Amy's history, I felt the need was just as great as anyone else."

It was true. Rose didn't mind him relaying their situation to others. After the missing person's report that went out for Amy and then the search afterwards, thousands of people would know at least pieces of their story. Maybe even the whole country. Considering the price of the room, she couldn't say no.

"You don't have to make the final decision right now, Rose. I can take you this evening to view the room and make sure the living situation is adequate."

She nodded. "And what about Amy? She won't be released anytime soon, but we are hoping day visits out of the hospital will be allowed soon."

"I'm not sure, Rose, but the home's caretaker will be on hand when we visit. I'm sure she can answer any questions you have."

The house was huge. Rose hadn't been sure what to expect when Reverend Daryl picked her up that evening, but a house that looked like an old-fashioned villa wasn't it. She could see why renovations were needed, and the beginnings of scaffolding ran along one exterior wall.

They must be starting work on the roof, Rose thought as she pushed herself up the first entryway step. The neighbouring house was more modern, but Rose could see the bones of a classic high class home under the vinyl siding and upgraded windows. She wondered if the two would mirror each other when the work was finished.

A smiling woman in a smart pantsuit greeted them at the door. Splashes of freckles brought character and youth to her face while she carried herself like someone closer to her forties or even fifties. Rose liked her instantly.

"Mrs. Grill, you are welcome here. Let me show you the room first, and then I'll take you downstairs to the rec room. How is your daughter?" The woman introduced herself as Trisha, and the room she led them to was just down the hall. "I noticed you came up the front steps. Did you see the side ramp? It's much easier for someone supported by a walker. Here is the room. I'm so pleased the first one down the hall was available for you. It will mean much less walking. What do you think?" As she spoke, Trisha pushed the room's door wide.

"Will it be enough, Rose?" the reverend asked. It looked like the man was bursting with excitement, and his energy made Rose smile.

The room was painted and carpeted in grey tones, but the yellow art hung on the walls gave the room some life. Two double beds and two side tables stood straight on, making it easy for Rose to walk up in between them. A closet snuggled beside an entertainment centre on one wall, and a small dining area sat across from it. Wear lines on the carpet showed high-traffic areas, but the room smelled fresh.

"Renovations are starting on the top floors first, beginning with the roof. We don't plan on making it down to this first floor for some time. There will be noise during the day, but since you'll be spending time with your daughter at the hospital, I hope it won't be too much for you. The kitchen might not always be open as we have moved most of the staff to the second house during renovations."

"Is there a fridge?" Rose asked.

"Yes. A small one is tucked away in the closet and a microwave as well."

"Then it will be enough," Rose said and turned to shake hands with Trisha.

"We can move you in as soon as tomorrow evening, Rose," Daryl offered as he spun in place, visibly pleased with himself and the situation.

"Yes." Rose said, returning his grin. "Thank you both."

She couldn't wait to tell Arthur. She hoped it would lift a portion of the weight that life pressed on her husband's shoulders. And two beds? Rose didn't know what God or the hospital staff had in store for Amy, but if needed, there was room here for her as well.

Thank you, God. Oh, thank you.

Crossroads Truckers' Chapel

ARTHUR

ARTHUR TRAVELLED BACK TO the city to spend the weekend with Rose. It was a huge relief to find her settling into the room at Compassion's Way. The drop in price from the hotel was a blessing to their bank account, but Arthur had been more worried about Rose's security. The key card locks on all the doors and the buzzer system used to let visitors in eased his mind. Most of all, it was good to see his wife content, even happy.

Amy was calm when he visited her at the hospital. Rose had filled a small soft sided cooler with snacks and juice boxes she now kept in the cubby of her bedside table. Arthur noted the stack of unopened fruit cups beside her lamp as well. Rose just shook her head at him when he turned to ask why Amy needed snacks if she wasn't eating the hospital meals.

He enjoyed the evening with Rose after they left Amy for the night. It felt like an eternity since they had been able to enjoy each other's company, and Rose seemed more at peace as she didn't wring her hands in pain or shift in her chair as they watched the news together. He reached over and took her hand. She squeezed his fingers and smiled at him without saying a word.

This is enough, God. It's enough. Thank you.

Prayer seemed to slip out of his mind and heart much easier than it had in earlier weeks. What had changed? Their life was still fraught with troubles, and looming unknowns plagued them, but the words didn't stick in his throat or mind anymore.

In the morning he concluded the change must be happening in him. Something once sideways had been righted and settled. He still wasn't sure what, but he was grateful. As he kissed Rose goodbye, it felt good to know he would miss her but would also not dread coming back to her in a week or two. Their situation was okay, not perfect, but okay. The knowledge that this level of separation was only for a time and in the future Rose could bring Amy home helped in the moments of loneliness that still ebbed and flowed by. His heart held a strange anticipation as he climbed into the car and headed down the highway towards Crossroads Truckers' Chapel.

Was stopping there on the way home really the right thing to do?

He still wasn't sure when he pulled into the parking lot. It was just after noon, and he hoped to be home before it got too late. But could he hope for that with all the questions and apprehension swimming through his brain?

He'd sent Austin a message telling the man his expected time of arrival, and sure enough, he was waiting just outside the convenience store's doors. The wrinkles around his eyes deepened when Arthur stepped up on the curb and accepted his handshake.

"I never imagined I would be showing you around the chapel. But God works in strange ways, Arthur. Let's see if He's used this mess of a world to bring you to us. Hm?" The elderly man motioned to the side of the building and the shipping container turned chapel. "I've got a friend waiting in there for you."

Blinds shaded the inside of the building from view, but Arthur could tell by light reflecting from the plastic's edges that lights were on inside. The blinds also moved in the slight breeze. Arthur wondered why the windows were open if the blinds were down as Austin opened the door and ushered him inside.

The smell of freshly painted walls lingered in the corners of the first room. The back wall was only a few large steps away, but the space opened to the right and left. Chairs were stacked against the left wall beside a small podium. On the right, a counter with a gleaming wooden top separated what looked like a reception area from the small sanctuary space. Past the counter was a hall, but how far back it led, Arthur couldn't tell. It looked longer than he'd first thought. The windows across from the entrance were open, shades up, and a breeze let in cleansing air.

"Sorry about the smell," a man said from the hall. "I had to close the windows after painting last night, so the room didn't get properly aired out. I'm Bryan. Welcome."

Arthur accepted the newcomer's hand and recognized the name that had graced the bottom of each correspondence he'd received about the chaplaincy. The man seemed friendly enough as he shook Arthur's hand with a firm grip, but something familiar about him made Arthur uneasy.

"First, I'll give you a tour," Bryan said. "Not that there is that much to see, but." He winked as he motioned behind himself and down the hall.

The building was compact but laid out in a surprisingly convenient manner. The first door down the hall revealed a small bathroom, the second, a meeting room with just enough space for a small table and a set of four chairs. Cupboards lined one wall, providing a small kitchen space.

So a meeting and lunch room. Convenient, I guess.

At the end, a third room lined with a couch and several bookshelves greeted them. Large windows looked to either side of the building, giving views of the parking lot as well as a neighbouring field.

"The books were donated by several churches some years ago," Bryan commented. "I've no idea how old they are."

Austin nodded and added, "It's been a great thing for many of the men who stop here. They're often lonely and bored from travelling the roads alone. The books give them a healthy escape. It's now up to the chaplain to decide what books to keep on the shelves and what to discard or ban. We used to get regular donations of faith-based fiction and not so faith-based titles as well."

Arthur had never imagined the small chapel would house a library, but he could see how it could be useful. It was better to have a good book to read at evening stops while long haul truck driving than to look for entertainment in less savoury ways.

"The chapel has been closed for two years," Austin said sadly as he backed out of the room. "It will be good to see the books being read again, and hopefully soon."

"The middle room has been used for counselling sessions in the past," Bryan said as they passed by the door on their way back to the main room.

"What kind of counselling?" Arthur asked. It had never been a large part of his ministry at Hope Is Here Church. "Conflict resolution and being a listening ear is, of course, a large part of my pastoral experience, but I never formally counselled anyone. I've not been trained in it."

Bryan nodded as if it was what he'd expected. "We hope our chaplain will be willing to take an entry level counselling course. The churches would pay for it, and any heavy cases need to be referred to licensed professionals, but most of the men who stop in are looking for someone to talk to. Our last chaplain found the training quite practical."

"Does Hope Is Here Church employ a licensed counsellor, then, Arthur?" Austin asked. "I thought most pastors offered at least marriage counselling to their congregations."

"I offered a premarital course, but that was it. The material was basic, practical, and helpful." He shuffled his feet as they reentered the small main sanctuary area. "When deeper counselling was needed, I had a list of contacts I could send people to. Pastor Edwin from Barton Community Church was one of them. He has a bachelor's degree in counselling alongside his seminary credentials."

Austin accepted the information with a smile.

"Now, here behind the reception counter is the office area. As the chaplain is often alone in the building, we found it more practical to have things out in the open. No hiding behind doors here," Bryan told him and made a point of pulling open the file cabinets stored under the counter. The desk area was cleverly built into the wall directly under one of the back windows. "Unfortunately, there is no computer. It was stolen. We're hoping a new or used one will be donated to the ministry before we open again."

The tour done, the men stood in the open space before the counter as they asked Arthur if he had any particular questions. He had many.

Did they have a list that went into the details of all tasks and expectations of the position? Was there to be any other staff? Who would the chaplain be answerable to? What risks did the job involve? What was the salary offered?

Working with people inside a church could be rough, and Arthur imagined working with people right off the street could be even worse at times.

Bryan did his best to answer questions, and Austin made notes of things they might need to iron out more thoroughly.

"What about living accommodations?" Arthur asked. "Hope Is Here Church owned a parsonage. I assume there is no such thing attached to a position like this, but we don't know the area. Are there apartments available to rent? Everything seems very spread out. Where did the previous chaplain live?"

"Ah. The last chaplain was a retired pastor from one of the supporting congregations. He owned his own home not far from here. But, Austin, don't you have a rental on your property?" Bryan asked the older man.

"Yes, I do. Needs some work on it, though. Been empty for a few months, and the last tenant did a number on the place. What about the Goffers? They have rentals as well."

Bryan continued to nod as Austin threw out names and more possibilities. "All in all, Arthur, we might be a small community, but there is affordable housing available. Does your wife work?"

"No ..." Arthur rubbed the back of his neck. He'd hoped any personal questions wouldn't delve too deeply at this interview. He didn't feel ready to speak about their situation with virtual strangers. "Health issues have kept her home for the last year, and she won't be able to work again."

Bryan leaned up against the counter and nodded. "I'm sorry to hear that. I am sure something affordable could be found. Any more questions?"

"Bryan, I should be getting back to the storefront," Austin said as he looked at his watch.

"Of course. I can take Arthur through the last few things, like the trial schedule and the fundraising requirements."

Austin left with a wave of his hand, and as the door shut behind him, Bryan dove right into what the chapel committee was asking of any applicants, including speaking engagements at each of the supporting churches. By the time they were finished, Arthur's head was spinning. He felt unsure as he climbed back into the car, a fresh coffee in hand. They wanted him to jump through more hoops before hiring him than he'd expected, more than he'd had to for the full time Senior Pastor's position at Hope Is Here. He wasn't sure if this was right. The roller coaster of it all sounded exhausting. He sent a text to Rose and then one to Rachel before pulling out of the lot.

God, I need wisdom and direction.

Bryan had not asked him why he'd been let go from Hope Is Here, and that bothered Arthur. He'd expected it to be one of the committee's first questions. Was it worth going through any more hassle in pursuit of the position before he knew what they would think of his family situation? He was grateful to not have had to speak of it, but ...

He just didn't know.

At present, the committee had no one else interested in the job. That was in his favour as well as the fact that they hadn't been able to find anyone willing to take it on two years ago when the last man stepped down. Maybe Arthur could ask the former chaplain some pointed questions if the committee would allow it.

Acceptance

ARTHUR

The man on the other end of the call had paused, and Arthur picked at a loose thread on the hem of his t-shirt as he waited. It had been several weeks since his meeting with Austin and Bryan. Still, Arthur hadn't felt the confirmation in his spirit he was looking for before accepting the chaplaincy. They were waiting for Arthur to give them the go-ahead to start the process of scheduling Sundays for him to speak at each church that subsidized the mission.

Instead, he'd asked for more time and permission to contact the former chaplain. He'd received the man's number the night before and had been told that early morning was the best time to contact him. Arthur never imagined he'd be pouring his apprehension out to a stranger, but he'd felt a distinct urge to lay it all out

"I stepped down because of my age, Pastor Arthur," the voice began. "I was already a senior when I took the mission on. You have many spry years ahead of you, I think. No mission is easy work. Don't let fear hold you back." They were wise words from a seasoned soul, but was it really fear Arthur was dealing with?

"I keep waiting for that feeling of peace I got when starting as the pastor at Hope Is Here or a burst of energetic excitement," he admitted.

"But all I feel is apprehension. It would mean another change for my family ... I have to be sure, Mr. Simon."

"Feelings don't always tell us the truth, Arthur. What does your wife think of all of this? Depending on what kind of woman she is, I have often found when we can't find the answers ourselves, God has given them to our life partners, and He uses them to point the way. Or at least nudge us in a general direction. If you and your wife are in agreement, that might be your sign."

Arthur had talked to Rose repeatedly. She liked the idea of being closer to the city and the access to medical facilities it would bring. But she worried about country life and moving out of province. Would they be able to find a doctor to take on her own case? What about Rachel? It would mean moving farther away from her. Was that right?

"Are you content where you work right now, Arthur?" Mr. Simon asked.

"I've gotten used to it. Working the stockroom of a grocery store is a far cry from a senior pastor at the largest church in town."

"So is taking on a chaplaincy. There is no acclaim for this job. You'll find the congregations supporting the ministry will soon forget you exist. Once a year, there will be conversations about if you are worth the money spent on the mission. There is also personal risk. I've seen criminals of all kinds walk through Crossroads Truck Stop. It's a hub. But it's also the perfect place to make a difference and plant seeds of hope in people's lives. Seeds you will rarely get to see sprout and flourish. It takes faith."

Arthur pulled the string on his shirt, and the hemmed edge gave way. Why couldn't he stop fidgeting? He felt like he was twelve years old again and speaking to his father about a misdeed.

"Being let go from a church you'd served for so long must have been a huge blow to your self-confidence. Maybe even to your trust in God."

"Yes. I can admit that. I questioned why He let it happen every hour for the first few weeks."

"Arthur, a minister is a minister no matter where he works or what circles he moves in. You can do the work of God stocking shelves just as vigorously as standing behind a pulpit on Sunday mornings." The older man coughed and muffled the phone for a few moments while he recovered. "I can't–I can't tell you what you should do. Keep praying, and ask your family to help guide you. Remember, what our society sees as success or failure is not how God measures it."

Failure. The word stuck like a burr in his mind. Is that what he was afraid of? After the last few months they'd gone through, it made sense.

"Thank you for your time, Mr. Simon. I'll think about what you've said."

A hole formed in Arthur's thoughts when the older man ended the call.

At work, Arthur went through the motions, but his mind was a cascade of questions.

What are you afraid of?

What will you do now?

What if you pick the wrong thing?

He had at least a full week before he'd be able to travel back to Rose. In the meantime, Bryan and the Search Committee for Crossroads Chapel were waiting. Even if he said yes, it wasn't a sure thing he'd be offered the job. The churches all had to agree he was the right man. Maybe it was better to get things started. He could always back out if he felt the need to, right?

Lucas threw a set of forklift keys Arthur's way as they passed in the hall. "Hang these up for me, will you? I forgot."

Arthur nodded at the supervisor. It was strange that he'd forgotten something like that. He was always reminding people to stick to the small rules that made important processes slide by smoothly.

When he reached the bottom of the stairs, Arthur hung the keys in place, matching the colour label on the chain with the label over its hook. He'd just come off break, and the ring of conversation happening around the lunchroom tables still echoed in his ears. He pulled a lobe to ease the sensation then grabbed a hard hat from the wall and headed off to look for his work crew.

Arthur was quiet for the rest of his shift, only communicating with Ben and Hammond in short sentences when necessary. Both men respected Arthur's mood, and things moved fast. It wasn't long before he walked back up the steps to the second floor to grab his lunch kit and head for home.

I should grab groceries before I leave, he thought. Rachel would appreciate not having to remind him or, worse, having to come herself.

As he left the lunchroom, bag in hand, the office door opened, and Fred stuck his head out. "Good, you're still here," he said and motioned Arthur over.

It surprised Arthur to find Lucas leaning back against the desk in the tight space as well as Penelope seated in an office chair behind him. She had one leg crossed over the other, and her foot bounced in the air as she pursed her lips.

"What did I do?" Arthur joked. But the three sets of eyes staring at him made him question if he had unwittingly made a mistake. Why else would all three of them be waiting to talk to him?

"Arthur," Fred began, but then shut his mouth and looked over at Penelope. "You ask him."

The woman raised an eyebrow. "Alright." Her foot stilled its bouncing, and she leaned back in the office chair before looking Arthur straight in the eyes. "Fred would like to know if you are still seriously looking for a full-time position elsewhere."

"Yes. I mean, of course I am. I have a family and—"

Penelope held up her hand, stopping him mid sentence.

Fred sighed.

Lucas shuffled his feet.

"Okay, you are scaring me." Arthur looked from one person to another, and the hair on the back of his neck lifted. "Am I being fired?"

"No!" Penelope said.

Lucas groaned softly and ran a hand through his hair. "Fred, just tell him."

"Well—"

"Fred, just spit it out."

Penelope's command made Arthur jump and Fred grimace.

"My nephew's moving back to town and ... needs a job. I've offered him a full-time position in back." Fred looked down at Lucas's boots, suddenly fascinated by the flecks of dirt they'd left on the smooth office flooring. "That means there won't be another full-time position available in back for some time."

Arthur's shoulders drooped, and his lunch bag suddenly felt uncomfortably heavy.

"I'm sorry. I know I promised that in time we would work you up to full-time."

"And generally we keep our promises." Penelope added.

Arthur noted the anger in the woman's voice. "When will he be starting?"

"Not for some weeks."

Arthur nodded but didn't know what to say.

Penelope stood. Her eyes flashed with a moment's anger then softened as she looked from Fred to Arthur. "We all know you need full-time, Arthur. If you have any other prospects ..."

With a swallow and a numbness akin to the day after being let go from Hope Is Here Church, Arthur listened to himself verbally give his two weeks notice.

"Alright, Arthur." Fred nodded. "I'll get the paperwork drawn up."

Lucas squeezed Arthur's shoulder as he ducked from the room, clearly unhappy but also unwilling to say anything against his boss' decision.

The office door closed as Penelope moved into the hall, and Arthur was left staring at the woman in shock.

She spoke softly as if to a child in distress. "Do not forget what God has already done for you, Arthur Grill. He can and will do it again."

Arthur stood at the kitchen counter, can opener in hand, sauce pot ready before him..

"I don't understand it, Rose. What have I done?" His free hand shook as he held the phone to his ear.

"You did what was necessary. And I am proud of you."

"It was like I had no control of the words coming out of my mouth. I mean, I could have waited. They said the man doesn't come for weeks, Rose, weeks."

Rose was silent for an agonizing moment. "I think God just made the decision for you, Arthur."

"Oh, Rose, come on."

"No, no, I don't mean He moved your mouth for you and forced you to quit. I mean he gave you an ultimatum, and your brain did the rest, just like He knew it would."

Could that be right? Was this new loss God's way of pointing ahead?

"But the money—"

"It will be fine, Arthur."

"Rose." Emotion burned Arthur's throat, and he held back tears of anger and doubt. "Why is this happening again?"

The can opener fell to the counter with a clatter.

"I don't know, not really, but ... Oh, Arthur, God has been so good to us."

His wife's sincerity flowed though the phone speaker, and he caught his breath as mixed emotion swirled in his chest.

"We've had financial stability up until this last year. Our daughters are almost grown. It's been hard, but Arthur, we have had such good years, haven't we?"

He opened his mouth to speak, but all that came out was a sound of strain.

"And even now, through this mess, we lost one job, and He handed us another. We lost our house, and He found us a new home. We lost our daughters, He has brought them back to us."

Arthur swallowed as his throat burned with bile.

"He's been so good, Arthur, even as we have doubted Him."

"Alright." He couldn't help the strain in his voice, the anger in his heart. She was right, but what did it change?

"Arthur, if you were still pastoring at Hope Is Here and someone like Paul or Jeff came to you with this exact story, what would you have told them?"

"I'm ... not sure."

Rose waited, and as her silence stretched, Arthur felt the swirling in his chest ease.

"I just feel so lost, Rose."

"I know. I do too. But He has been so good to us, Arthur, and He doesn't change. He's always had a plan. We need to trust it."

He nodded to himself in the silence. "If it was someone else, I would tell them to keep holding on because He never lets go of us."

"I love you, Arthur. Call Bryan."

When the call dropped, Arthur grabbed the can of condensed soup on the counter. He remembered the advice of Mr. Simon that morning. Rose agreed with the change. Still, his blood ran cold as he set the can back down to swipe through his contact list and find Bryan's number.

Lord, please let this not be a mistake.

Bringing Amy Home

AMY

THE END OF SUMMER poured a hot sun down on the city. Still, Amy shivered. She'd been in the hospital so long that stepping out onto the street scared her. She pulled the zipper on her sweater up the last remaining metal teeth then pulled her hands into the sleeves and crumpled the openings tightly closed with fists. Her mother stood beside her, one hand on her elbow, the other braced on a walker. Rose's skin glistened white beneath the sun.

She's too pale.

Amy knew it was her fault. Their trips to the hospital garden had never been long. Maybe she could help her mother enjoy the last few days of warmth ... if she was brave.

At that moment, she didn't feel brave.

Her father pulled the car up to the hospital's entrance. It had been months since her last long car ride. Would she make it? She'd done okay the last few outings. She'd gone shopping for new clothes and once to visit a restaurant. But after both, she'd sat shivering in her room for hours. The eyes of others, the ones she knew weren't really looking at her, crawled all over her skin.

She stumbled.

"Deep breath. In through your nose, out through your mouth," Rose whispered as she gently pushed Amy forward towards the open car door. Arthur held it for her. A nurse stood on Amy's other side, letting her mother take charge of coaxing her into the vehicle. The woman handed Amy's bag over to her father before leaning down in the doorway.

"Amy, remember your breathing. Remember, it's okay to ask your dad to pull over for a break. Try to do it before you're past your limit so he has time to find a safe place." The woman handed her a brown paper bag stuffed with others of the same size. "Just in case you get carsick."

"Are you sure I'm ready?" Amy whispered the question, and the woman smiled at her and nodded.

"You can do it. Even if it takes longer to get home than you hoped. You'll make it, and you'll feel better when you're in your own room."

Amy wasn't sure the woman was right, but she hoped she was.

It didn't help that the room would be one she'd never seen before. The one at the parsonage was long gone, and according to what she'd heard through emails from her old church friends, a new pastor was living in the house. The room she'd ended up sharing with Rachel at Echo Apartments was also gone. Her parents had moved out last week.

They told her about the new trailer house. Amy could hardly believe it. How could her father be okay with that kind of regression? The parsonage had been one of the nicest houses on the block.

Her mother had said she'd done her best to arrange her bedroom to match what Amy had at Echo Apartments. That way, it would feel more familiar. If she didn't like it, she could have the fun of changing things herself. It would be like being there when they'd moved in.

She knew Rose meant well. She knew she should be grateful, and a large part of her was. But a small dark spot in her heart ached and begged to scream her fury.

They shouldn't have touched her things. They shouldn't have moved before she'd come home. Weren't they thinking of her at all? They'd never thought of her, not through any of the changes that had come over the last six months. Not until ...

The door to the car closed, and Amy pursed her lips as the nurse helped her mother walk around to the front passenger's door.

You're being selfish, Amy.

But after everything she'd been through, didn't she deserve to be selfish? Half of her said yes, the other, no.

She got sick during the drive. Her mother told her once wasn't bad at all, but Amy hated how weak she felt and cried for a whole hour afterwards. Flat countryside flew by as their little car sped down the highway. Cornfields, wheat fields, and hay fields were all there with barns and farmhouses dotted through the landscape.

"Almost there," her dad told her as he peered through the rearview mirror.

Amy turned her eyes away. "Good to know."

Moving without me meant a much shorter car ride. I can close myself in my room soon.

She tried to grasp on to that positivity as it squirmed away.

Would it even feel like *her* room when she stepped into it? How would she react? Would the red waves wash over her vision again? Would she feel empty and cold, just like she'd been cold in that camper …

They passed through a small, spread out town before turning down a side road. "Crossroads" the population sign read. But the number underneath the name was three times bigger than Barton. How could so many people live in that dinky place? Manitoba was a prairie province. Was it the extra flat space that made the difference?

Amy couldn't tell if the new road was paved or just packed rock and dirt baked to hardness in the summer sun. It had a shine to it. A few more houses sat down this road. She sucked slow breaths, taking note of every white washed fence, blue trimmed window, or double car garage. They'd passed one large well-to-do home just for a small lacklustre cottage to appear next. She guessed the neighbourhoods weren't as organized by income out here as they were in town.

A second turn had them driving slower, and then her father pulled down a lane lined with trees. Amy noticed that people had tree lines planted around their homes almost like fence lines. Some fields were ringed with them as well. She wondered why. Her palms grew slick with moisture as her father slowed the car's speed. Then a break in the trees opened, and they pulled into a small plot.

She gaped at the tiny trailer house raised off the ground on cement blocks and dressed in a garish yellow with white trimmed windows.

"Welcome home, Amy," her father told her.
"Oh, my God," she said as her parents opened their doors.

She hated her new room.
    She hated the house.
    She hated the country.
    She hated her parents.
    She hated herself.
After two weeks of settling in, the trip back to the city came as a relief. Still, she refused to show it as she sat in the back seat, smouldering. Her skin itched, and her heart crackled with emotions.

God? Why didn't you fix things? Why did you leave me with this pain? People say they care, but that's a lie. I can see their irritation. I'm trying, but they hate me. They wish I hadn't made it back.

When they reached the mental health clinic, she almost slammed the car door on her father's hand and laughed as he held back an angry yell. She threw daggers with her eyes at him and her mother, daring them to scold her.

It was petty, and she knew it.

As soon as she turned away and headed for the clinic's entrance, shame crawled up her throat like a bad heartburn. She was better than this. But her reflex was to self preserve, to lash out. They deserved better than a daughter like her.

Her shame transferred to her shoulders and became a weight as she was ushered into the clinic's waiting room. Her mother would register her. So she sat and waited, staring at the cold linoleum flooring.

When her name was called, her mother walked with her behind the receptionist's desk and down a side hall until they reached a door labelled with Dr. Miriam's name on a gold plaque. Worry lined Rose's face as she placed a hand on Amy's back. The touch pressed clothes against Amy's irritated skin, and she moved forward to escape the contact.

The door opened to Dr. Miriam and her gentle smile. "Amy! I'm so happy to see you again. How are you?"

Amy grasped for the closeness she'd formed with the doctor over her hospital stay, but the new setting made everything feel different. Rose sat beside her for the first fifteen minutes of the session, and Amy met Dr. Miriam's questions with one-word answers and pursed lips. She listened while her mother described their new living arrangements and how Amy would be starting online schooling for the first half of the year.

Dr. Miriam made copious notes, and when they'd finished, she asked Rose to wait with her husband while she spoke with Amy alone. Amy gripped the fabric of her jeans and scrunched it tightly as her mother shuffled out of the room.

Amy watched her leave, the weight on her shoulders threatening to flatten her on the chair. When Miriam looked at her, the sound of her own heartbeat made it hard to concentrate on what the woman said.

"Now, Amy, tell me about your new home," the doctor urged.

"My mother just told you all about it."

"I know, but I want to hear about it from you. Different people experience things differently. Do you like your new room?"

Amy sighed and slowly released her grip from her jeans to lace her fingers together and rest them in her lap. She tried to keep them still, but it was hard. She needed to grip something solid. "I like the window in my room. I didn't have a window at Echo Apartments."

"That's great! What about the window do you like the most?"

"I guess ..." She paused, her tongue travelling over her teeth as her mind fought for words. "It opens. Lets the air in."

"Living in a windowless room could make you feel trapped."

Amy nodded. "It's good to be able to see outside." She shrugged and looked away from the woman to the door where her mother had disappeared.

"I like the hospital better."

"Really?" Dr. Miriam sat up and placed the end of her pen against her bottom lip. "Even though the hospital had so many rules? The window in your room didn't open. You couldn't go everywhere you wanted to." The woman cocked her head to the side, and Amy squirmed under her gaze. "You know, Amy, struggling with change is normal, and after going through the things you've had to endure, it makes it even harder."

"Yeah." It wasn't fair that she'd had to go through all that pain, that darkness. She refused to think about it and pushed images trying to work their way to the forefront of her mind further back.

"How are you feeling, Amy? Really feeling? You can tell me."

Amy couldn't bring herself to look at the woman and instead pulled the fabric of her jeans into her fists again

The doctor got up and stepped over to a wall of shelves that lined the room. Amy heard paper rustling and couldn't help glancing over as Miriam retrieved a jar filled with pencil crayons from beside a stack of crisp white sheets of paper. She laid one of these sheets and the jar of brightly coloured pencils on the chair Amy's mother had used.

"Why don't you use the writing techniques we used in the hospital, Amy? Show me how you feel as I ask questions. You don't even have to look at me while I talk. Take your time."

Amy looked at the jar and the bright pencils sharpened to points that looked to the ceiling. She chose a deep red one.

"Can I have a hard book to use as a desk?" she asked before she began to write, listen, and draw her feelings for Miriam to see.

Amy went to a second appointment with Dr. Hillard where they went over Amy's anxiety symptoms and the recommended medication change Dr. Miriam had scribbled down before they left her office.

Dr. Hillard nodded as she read the list and then checked over Amy's rash with gentle fingers. "I think it's a mild reaction to one of your prescriptions. We'll get you a cream to soothe it and change up some of these medications, Amy. Don't worry, we'll get this cleared up."

Amy kept her silence as her mother and the doctor went over the changes and any other concerns they might have.

"Now, Amy, do you have anything to ask me?" Doctor Hillard asked.

Amy shook her head and looked away, wishing she could curl up and melt into the metal chair.

"This week has been hard," Rose answered for her.

"And that's normal at this stage." Dr. Hillard assured them.

As they left the second clinic, Amy felt the weight on her shoulders start to slowly drip off. The sensation was strange, and she hugged herself and rubbed her hands up and down her arms as she sat in the car's back seat. The paper she'd used to draw and write her feelings lay beside her, a mass of red shapes with words she'd printed in black. There were spirals, dots, and stars. She hadn't been sure how to help Dr. Miriam understand what they meant, but somehow, the woman seemed to understand, at least in part. She liked not having to talk the whole session. It helped her relax and think.

She picked up the paper and studied it herself. Amy was no artist. Her lines were uneven and misshapen. But it was perfect—a jumbled, perfect mess, just like her. She didn't know why it made her smile, but it did. As she'd scribbled out the shapes, the tangle inside her mind had slowly started to shift. It had allowed her to give Dr. Miriam a tired smile as she left her office. Her silence with Dr. Hillard had been more from exhaustion than angst.

As the light shining into the car changed from bright daylight to a more subdued evening tone, Amy realized she would be happy to get home.

"Just one more visit with Dr. Hillard next month, and these trips will start to lessen," Rose told Arthur in the front of the car. "Monthly visits with Dr. Miriam will continue as we work on lining up counselling at a closer location."

Amy closed her eyes and tuned out her parents. The *whoosh* of wind outside the car window sang to her. Maybe if her heart settled into this new home, she would start moving in a more positive direction.

She thought of Josh and Rohan, of Peggy, and finally her old friends at Hope Is Here School. She missed her friends but dreaded seeing any of them after what she'd gone through.

Online classes would make forming new relationships hard. But maybe once she was well enough to step back into a high school building, that would change as well. Maybe ... maybe she could learn to trust again.

She decided she would hold on to that small spark and add a yellow star to her emotions page when she got home.

Visitors

AMY

Amy loved to let the crisp air of fall in through her bedroom window. As the weeks wore on and her online schooling started, she found herself curled up on her desk chair, staring out at the changing season. It eased the strain looking at a computer screen had on her eyes.

When September tipped into October, the window often remained open despite the promise of winter that crept into the evening hours. She only inched the glass closed as the sun went down and the evening grew too cold. As soon as the sun rose in the morning, she would open it again and breathe in the fresh yet slightly raw scent of fall.

Canadian Thanksgiving was just around the corner, and with it would bring the first visitors her parents would host in their new home. They all wondered how she'd handle it. Was she ready to see old friends? Would they bring back uncomfortable memories? If they did, would she be able to hold her composure, or would the red waves and her anger win?

Rachel would be visiting.

Amy didn't know what to think of her sister anymore. Her abduction had been Jay's fault, and Jay had belonged to Rachel. She struggled knowing it should have been her sister in that camper, not her, but she could never wish such an experience on anyone, not even someone she hated.

Did she hate Rachel? She asked herself that question as she sat next to her window, feet pulled up on the chair, knees pointing straight to the ceiling like slender mountain peaks. No, she realized, she didn't hate her. But she felt a sharp pain when she thought of her. Rachel had always been so good, and Amy, the opposite. Yet it was Rachel's choice that sent them down this terrible cascade of destruction. What would their lives be like if her sister hadn't moved in with Jay?

The closer they came to Thanksgiving Day, the more she thought about it. She spoke about it with Dr. Miriam. She wrote about it in the journal the psychiatrist had encouraged her to start. She made emotion pictures while holding the image of her sister's face in her mind.

Sadness and hurt were the topmost feelings that showed up in her words and drawings. Dr. Miriam said that was good. Grief often wore a mask and masqueraded as anger. She was grieving for so many things as she existed in a quiet, isolated world. Soon, it would be time to confront it. Soon, she would see her sister again.

When Thanksgiving morning dawned, golden light shone through her window.

The trees surrounding the property were a mix of evergreen and deciduous varieties. Deep green needled branches contrasted beautifully with their tall golden brothers. Amy didn't know the names of the golden ones, but the slow shift from green to a surprising shade of yellow had made her smile.

Guests wouldn't arrive until afternoon, and Amy spent her morning helping Rose carefully sort out the kitchen. The meal would be simple. All they were providing was the turkey and a few pies. Their guests would bring the rest.

Her mother moved slowly as she directed Amy to wash the few dishes left in the sink from the night before. No dishwasher existed in the small house trailer. How she missed the one they had at the parsonage. The feeling of nasty, soggy crumbs and other bits floating in the warm water were revolting. Rose had a hard time standing at the sink these days, so the job mostly fell to Amy.

She usually bemoaned the chore, but that morning her mother looked extra pale.

"I'm fine, Arthur," Rose had said when asked if she was alright. "Just tired. But I have good help. So don't worry."

Arthur had the day off but insisted on driving to Crossroads Chapel to check the building had made it safely through the night. After a break-in soon after he had started work there, he'd made sure he or Austin checked the small building over every morning and evening. Amy thought her father seemed happier than he'd been in a long time despite that stress. He was healing and moving forward. But her mother was a different story.

Rose looked tired all the time. Amy knew it was her fault. She was a strain on her mother's fragile health. It should be Amy caring for her mother, not the other way around. But ...

She promised herself she'd do a better job of taking Rose outside to sit at their small donated dining set. She told herself she'd even make her mother tea to ward off the fall chill. Fresh air was important. Amy knew that now after experiencing so long hidden away behind hospital walls. She could be her mother's doorway, just like Rose had been for her.

"What time are people coming, Mom?" she asked while rinsing a fork and placing it in the dish rack to dry.

"Around one-thirty if the drive goes okay. Rachel has farther to go, so she might be late."

Her sister had chosen to move in the opposite direction. Amy often wondered why since Winnipeg would have been a larger city with more schools to choose from.

Was it because she wanted to be as far away from me as she could? She's never liked me much.

But maybe there was more to it than that. Did Rachel feel responsible for what had happened to her little sister? Did she know it was all her fault?

"Amy dear, can you sweep before we have to start thinking of lunch?" her mother asked. "The bathroom also needs to be cleaned before guests arrive."

"I've never cleaned a bathroom before!"

"You're sixteen. How did that happen?"

Amy groaned in revulsion.

Rose smiled. "Come on. I can sit in the hall and give you step-by-step instructions."

"Fine." Amy shook water drops from her fingers before wiping them on a nearby towel.

I guess I'm more than a door for my mother. I'm her hands and feet as well.

After lunch, Amy helped her mother walk down the ramp that graced the outside of the house. It slanted gently, wrapping back on itself and ending exactly where the steps were planted into the loose dirt of the driveway. Rose sat at the outdoor dining set amid withering flower beds with a fresh layer of fallen leaves hiding broken, dried stems. Amy wrapped a blanket around her and set a mug in her hands.

Amy didn't like to sit still herself unless it was in her own room gazing out the window, so she walked down the lane picking up leaves of different shades before returning to set them on the table and sort in a colour line.

She was laying a half green and yellow leaf beside a full yellow one when a horn sounded behind her and a car pulled into the drive. Rose raised a hand in greeting while Amy found herself like a deer caught in headlights, unable to move. She watched the smiling familiar faces of Gary and Sarah as they opened doors and waved back.

It's just the Davids. They're nothing to be nervous about. They never judged you. They are good friends.

Her heart skipped a beat as a head of blond curls, shorter than her own but almost as springy, popped up from the back seat. Glen Edwards shouted her name and waved a bag of buns in the air. Had she known he was coming for dinner as well? Would he approach her? What should she do if he tried to touch her, hug her? Would she be okay if he tried to shake her hand? She tensed as he walked up to Rose.

"Mom's sorry she couldn't make it, Mrs. Grill," he said to her mother after meeting her at the table and bending down for a brief hug of greeting. "Dad got called into work, and she didn't feel it was right to come without him."

"I am sorry to hear that. But at least we still have buns," Rose chuckled.

Everyone but Amy laughed, and Sarah helped her mother stand and start making her way into the house. Glen flashed her a bright grin as he followed the older women.

Amy stayed rooted beside the table lined with leaves, letting out a held breath as Glen disappeared indoors. She watched Gary carry a large shallow basket that looked like it contained a casserole into the house. He looked back as he reached their front entrance, as if expecting her to follow, but she chose to stay where she was and watched as he closed the door. She would join them when she was ready and not before.

How long could she wait?

As long as I want to.

She shuffled the leaves back and forth, ruining the carefully laid out order.

After a time, her father looked out the door to check on her. But he didn't call her in. Not yet. He would soon, she knew. When she heard the sound of a second car's wheels on gravel, Amy refused to look down the lane. It could only be one person.

Her fidgeting hands froze as the sound of a door opening and closing echoed down the driveway. She shifted her gaze away from the table and over to the treeline when the empty chair her mother had used scraped the ground and groaned under the weight of a body. But she didn't run away, even though her feet itched. Her hands twitched. Red crept into the corners of her vision, but she blinked it away, rubbing her fingers together before letting her nails drag over her skin. They left light pink marks.

"Amy?" Rachel's voice asked.

She didn't say anything, only nodded.

"How are you doing?"

Finally, she dared a glance at her sister's hands, folded carefully in her lap. Two bags of pre-washed salad lay on the table between them, Rachel's contribution to the Thanksgiving meal.

"That will wilt in the sun," Amy told her sister. Water drops had already started to form on the inside of the plastic bags.

"They'll be okay for a few minutes."

Amy's throat hurt. Why didn't Rachel just go inside? Why did she have to sit down? Didn't she want to see Mom?

"Mom and Dad are inside. So are Gary, Sarah, and Glen. I didn't know Glen was coming."

"Glen?" Rachel shifted in the chair.

Amy still didn't look up, but Rachel's hands no longer sat in her lap but clasped the metal of the chair's arms.

"I didn't know he was coming either. Are Abigail and Ben here too?"

Amy shook her head and listened to her sister's disappointed sigh.

The wind blew and rustled the golden leaves on the nearby trees. A few let go, and Amy watched them flit their way to the ground.

"Amy?"

"What?"

"I'm sorry, and I love you."

Amy's hands froze halfway through shredding a leaf. Had Rachel ever told her she loved her before? Maybe when they were kids, but she couldn't remember. It definitely had never crossed her lips since they'd both become teenagers. Amy couldn't remember ever saying it to her older sister, either.

She nodded, her lips glued together by an invisible paste.

Rachel pushed the chair back. It dug little tracks in the dirt as she rose and grabbed the salad bags. "See you inside, then."

Amy listened to the sound of the front door opening and closing before she looked after her sister. She could see her shadow moving across the glass of the entryway window as someone else welcomed her.

Amy might not have been able to look at her, but she'd blinked the red away. It hadn't tried to come back as Rachel had spoken. That was good.

I can do this.

She breathed in through her nose and out through rounded lips.

She got up and walked inside.

"AMY!" Glen called across the open room from where he sat in front of the picture window. "What's hanging?"

What's hanging? Since when did people talk like that? She grinned at the bright-faced boy then turned the grin on Rachel, who sat beside him.

A Message

ARTHUR

ARTHUR PULLED AT THE collar of his shirt and the tie that wrapped around it as winter's chill crept into the car. He sat in the parking lot of Hope Is Here Church with the engine off. The cold tickled his nose and nipped at toes that were stuffed into his best dress shoes—the shoes he used to wear most Sunday mornings as he gave his sermons from the pulpit of that very church.

He groaned before pulling the tie completely off and smoothed its long satin length before draping it over his neck again and attempting a retie. He wished Rose was with him. He used to tie the garment around his own neck every weekend only for her to redo it when it inevitably went crooked. But she wasn't with him that morning. She was with Amy, spending a quiet Sunday watching the live streamed service of one of the churches local to Crossroads.

She'd told him she enjoyed quiet Sundays. Weekends used to be the busiest time of the week for them, after all. It was nice to sit back and be able to breathe, to not have people judging their every facial expression and word. He had enjoyed not having to worry about the constant criticism as well. But here he was again.

Hope Is Here Church looked the same from the outside. He had to admit, he was nervous to see if it had changed on the inside. Would walking through those doors again be a good thing? It could very easily be a terrible idea as well. Would his former congregation welcome him or listen with stony faces and closed hearts?

You won't know until you step through the doors.

Give it to God.

It's His job to soften hearts, not yours.

A thin layer of ice crystals and snow crunched under his feet as he walked—briefcase in hand, shoulders shrugged against the chill—into the front foyer. The cold amplified the sound as it bounced off frozen surfaces.

As the warmth of indoors hit him, he shivered, a release of the tension his body had held in an attempt to hoard its heat.

"Arthur!" a woman's voice trilled across the large entryway. "How was the trip last evening?"

"The highways are clear and dry," he answered while shaking hands with the church's secretary. "How are you, Gail?"

"Doing well. Nothing new," she replied.

Gail had been there the night of that fateful church board meeting, the night they'd dismissed him. She'd refused to look at him then, holding neutrality on her face. He wondered at the bright smile and ringing joy in her voice this morning. They'd been friends for years, but neither he nor Rose had heard from her since that night. She hadn't helped with the move or come to the prayer meetings when Amy went missing.

"Well, I'm glad to see you again," she said as she stepped back. It was a dismissal, and she kept the smile plastered to her face as she walked away.

Arthur didn't know what to do as Gail left him standing alone in the foyer. Where was everyone? It was thirty minutes before services were scheduled to start. Where was the greeter that usually stood by the door to shake hands with each soul that entered? Where were the board members that would oversee the offering collection for the day? Where were the ushers and Sunday School teachers?

Just as Arthur heaved a shuddering sigh, the door to the church office wing was thrown open, and a string of people filed out. Chatter filled the room, and bright smiles were flashed his way.

Gary rushed over and clapped him on the arm. "Sorry, Arthur, prayer time ran a bit late. Come on back, and we'll have a quick prayer with Pastor Jacobs."

"Prayer time? With the whole staff?" Arthur asked, surprised at the number of people that continued to push through the office wing's door and into the foyer.

Prayer before service had been an important step while he was serving at Hope Is Here Church, but they hadn't called in that large a group. The worship team and Sunday school teachers had met separately. The ushers and supporting board members of the day had been the only ones to join him in his office an hour before service, and their prayer time had never lasted more than a few minutes.

"Oh, yes. We all pray together now," Gary informed him with a smile as he clasped an arm around Arthur's shoulder and started to pull him towards the door now being held open by a smiling youth Arthur didn't recognize.

A lump formed in Arthur's throat as he was ushered towards his former office. Things had changed.

Of course they have.

Did you expect the new guy to do things your way?

It was all harder to wrap his mind around than he wanted to admit.

He thought for sure people like Bennett and Henry would push back against change. They'd always stalled him on the smallest of things with questions and counter opinions. They had caused outright dissension at times. What had happened to ease things? What was this Pastor Jacobs like?

Arthur didn't have to wait long to get his answer.

It wasn't the pastor's office Arthur was led to but the board room. Many chairs were still filled. Everyone was waiting for him. Arthur swallowed and coughed into an elbow as a fresh lump of fear stifled his airway. It all looked too much like that night ...

A short man with cropped and styled red hair smiled broadly at him from the far end of the table. He waved with hands that seemed too large to match his height. He threw a loud voice across the room. "Pastor Arthur! So good to have you this morning. We're all excited to hear your report from Crossroads Truckers' Chapel. Come in, come in! Gary, get the man a drink, will you?"

A bottled water rolled across the table, and Gary grabbed it up and made an offering of it.

"Now, gentlemen," Pastor Jacobs continued, "let us pray."

Once the prayer was done and the board members were let out into the hall, Pastor Jacobs wove his way past chairs to grasp Arthur's hand. The man's fingers engulfed his in a vice grip, and Arthur's grin almost became a grimace at the heavy shake. "Come, Pastor Arthur, I'll brief you on the layout of the service. I've changed the order of things a bit."

Arthur couldn't help but notice Bennett Yule hadn't been present for the prayer. The man had been the greatest burr in Arthur's coat while leading Hope Is Here Church. But even though he'd been difficult, it felt wrong to not see him among the other men. After looking over the bulletin with the boisterous Pastor Jacobs, who insisted Arthur call him by his first name, Jordan, he asked Gary where Bennett was.

"He stepped down from the board. You should see him in the congregation."

Arthur almost fell over at the news. "You can't be serious! Was he voted out? I can't imagine that man letting go before his term was up for anything and then not getting voted back in. He's always voted back in."

"I think he reconsidered after you left, Arthur. He's also aging quite a bit. But it's not right for me to tell his story. I'll help you look for him after the service if you want."

Arthur nodded as they walked into the sanctuary and found seats at the front.

The thumping in Arthur's chest stuttered as pressure built up behind his rib cage when he looked out over the congregation he knew so well but was no longer his. He felt more self-conscious than he had in years of public speaking. It felt like a continuous stumble as he progressed through his presentation of the work done at Crossroads Truckers'

Chapel. A large projector screen showed pictures of the mission and the few people Arthur had met during his first few weeks there. He smiled at the photo of Austin waving as he pulled open the front door in greeting and another one of the man posing in front of a shelf in the back room holding his favourite book up for the camera.

When Arthur finally finished and stepped down from the stage, the congregation applauded and smiled. The pressure in his chest finally eased, but the pain of regret remained a prick as he moved towards a nearby pew. A few people nodded his way as he looked out over their heads one last time. A little boy from the back waved. Was that Jeff and Mary Cooper's youngest, James? Arthur waved back before taking his seat.

He soon found out Pastor Jordan Jacobs was long winded.

Very long winded.

Still, Arthur enjoyed the man's animated speaking style that used waving gestures and voice inflections that nearly shook the room. He blinked when Pastor Jacobs even jumped while on stage to make a point then broke out into a full laugh with the rest of the congregation.

How on earth did this man get voted in as senior pastor here? He was so ... improper.

It was a wonder, and Arthur thanked God for the shrinking of fear, and, yes, even jealousy that he'd felt at the beginning of the morning. The pinprick of painful regret lingered but dulled as he listened. He couldn't compare himself to the short, loud man. He was just too different from Arthur to even try. Maybe God had known Pastor Jacobs was what Hope Is Here Church needed to be shaken up a bit—not as punishment but as the gardener tills the earth, making it ready for new seeds and fertilizer. It occurred to Arthur that maybe he'd sown all the seeds God had given him for these people, and it was time for someone else to plant a new kind of crop. He felt his darker emotions slip completely off his shoulders and pool at his feet.

After the closing hymn was sung, Pastor Jacobs clapped him on the back and led him down the aisle before the rest of the congregation filed out of the pews in an orderly fashion. Arthur stood with his replacement, taking turns shaking people's hands as they left and headed for the coffee room.

"One thing I've loved right from the beginning of pastoring this church, Arthur, is the coffee room and how often it's open. What a wonderful fellowship we enjoy each week! Just wonderful."

Everyone wished Arthur well as they moved past. Many gave a heartfelt "Hello" and a few tears. The smiles outshone the sadness. When the sanctuary was empty, he made his way to the coffee line and the familiar sound of chatter, laughter, and the happy sequels of children. It was all too surreal as he took a seat at a table beside Gary.

He was a bit speechless as conversation swept across the table filled with familiar faces.

"Arthur! It's so good to see you again. How are Rose and the girls?"

"We miss you, for sure. But hasn't God brought us an amazing new pastor? He keeps me spellbound with his antics."

"I'm so glad you came for the visit. I love your new calling and am happy to support you there."

Arthur did his best to answer the questions, but some of the comments stuck like splinters after rubbing a hand over rough wood. He found himself tripping over his own words, stuttering or merely shrugging.

Gary noticed his discomfort and shifted the conversation from Arthur to the church itself, knowing the surrounding men would jump at the chance to talk about the new programs and Pastor Jacobs' vision for them all.

"They are just excited, Arthur. It's still the honeymoon stage of having someone new on board."

"I know," he assured Gary and dipped his head in assurance. Still, that pinprick of pain jabbed. He rubbed at his chest, sliding fingers under his tie that hung slightly crooked.

He almost drained his coffee and ran when a new face slowly eased onto the chair at his left. Carefully combed white hair and a face that had aged in the months since he had seen him, looked Arthur up and down.

Gary coughed, but Bennett waved him off. "I'm glad you're here this morning, Arthur. You're looking well."

"Bennett, thank you." What else could he say? As Arthur watched, the man's age-lined face smoothed a bit. His old friend, rival, stumbling block—Arthur wasn't sure how to think of Bennett anymore—pulled a plain white envelope from his suit jacket.

"I've had a few good months to think, Arthur," the man said. "I don't regret the decision we made as a board. But perhaps—" Bennett's words stumbled to a stop, and he shook his head. "Here, this is for you. I will be praying for you and your family." The old man grunted as he stood again and walked away.

"Bennett!" Gary called after him and got up to follow, stopping the man at the coffee room doors.

Arthur watched as a few words were exchanged and Bennett placed a hand on Gary's elbow for a second before patting it and then pressing on.

Gary returned, shaking his head. "I'm sorry, Arthur."

"Don't be." The envelope was warm from being kept close to Bennett's chest, and Arthur slipped it into his own dress jacket. "I'll read it when I get home."

After the coffee was drained, Arthur made ready to leave and followed Gary and Sarah to a nearby restaurant.

"Our treat," Sarah had assured him. "You have a long drive, and I won't let you head out until you've had a good lunch. If we had more time, I would invite you over."

But he wanted to get home before dark, and winter meant shorter days.

He placed a hand on the door, ready to push his way out into the cold winter, but stopped short. Would this be his last visit to Hope Is Here Church? He felt a pinprick of pain again, and he rubbed his chest. He stepped away from the door and looked around one last time. He could just see the burgundy cushions that lined the sanctuary pews and the runner that carefully draped over the table before the pulpit. How many times had he and the elders of the church served communion there? Tears gathered.

"I loved you all. I still do," he whispered before turning to the door and pushing out into the cold.

Bennett's Letter

ARTHUR

He had loved them, and he'd done his best to shepherd Hope Is Here Church as its senior pastor. He knew God would honour that, despite all his failings and mistakes. Still, it was painful to say goodbye as he drove out of the parking lot, following Gary to his friend's favourite Asian restaurant on Main Street. The pinprick in his chest had eased during the service, but the chill that refused to be driven from his car amplified the pain. As he parked behind Gary and crossed the street, he was rubbing his dress shirt over his chest again.

He pulled his tie off when they sat down and rolled it before stuffing it into a pocket.

"Are you okay, Arthur?" Sarah asked.

"Just hungry and tired," he assured her.

They didn't linger on the meal like they would have in the past, and soon he was stuffing a to-go carton with leftovers and hugging his friends goodbye.

Sarah cried but smiled. Gary looked confident.

"God's got a plan, Arthur, and I'm just a phone call away," he promised.

The reconciliation of their relationship was a sweet blessing. Arthur promised himself he wouldn't neglect it.

The couple stood on the sidewalk by his car, winter coats zipped tightly closed, shoulders shrugged against the wind, waving, as Arthur pulled away and headed for home. He set the heater to blow on high as the winter landscape rushed by.

Arthur rubbed at his chest for most of the drive.

Home. Home. Home.

Rose was there, and that was where he wanted—needed—to be.

When he realized his foot was pressing heavily on the gas peddle, he forced himself to ease off. Gentle flurries began to fall, but the highways remained clear and dry as the wind swept it. Getting home safely was still more important than getting home fast, he told himself, flipping on the radio.

Again, the pain in his chest pricked. A flash of fear had him wondering if he was having a heart attack. He slowed the car even more.

No, God, not another problem, please. Not now.

All the scenic roadside stops were closed during winter, or he would have pulled in at the next blue sign bearing a white picnic bench in its centre. As he pressed a hand to his chest again, the envelope from Bennett crinkled. He should stop. He should read it.

It can wait.

He sped past high jagged cut rocks left over from road construction that had blasted and dug through the Northern Ontario hillsides until the landscape shifted to the flat, wide open spaces of the Manitoba prairie.

The pain became a rattle that sounded with each of his breaths.

Arthur pulled the car over on the highway's shoulder and pressed the hazard lights button on the dash. He sat back, focusing on breathing past the pain.

"God, not here. Rose needs me."

His hands trembled. Tears fell as fear, pain, and that aching question of "why" flooded in. He pinched his fingers into his eyes to flick the water away.

"Okay, God, I'm listening. What is it you need me to hear?"

Gentle music played over the radio, but Arthur ignored it then killed the sound altogether by turning the car key and extinguishing the engine. He needed quiet to hold himself together. He needed to listen.

When the purr of the car stopped, silence reigned. The rustle of Arthur's winter coat was loud in his ears, so he tried not to move a muscle.

He relished the silence.

The pinprick of pain in his chest jabbed again but gently this time. Steady breathing calmed him, and the hammering of his heart in his ears quieted.

No still small voice spoke in the silence. But he longed for it.

"Clear words, God. Clear direction. Clear healing. It's what I and my family need. Why won't you just speak to us?"

Would God understand?

Intellectually, Arthur knew He would, but resignation swept in as the pain in his chest eased even more. He turned the car back on, making sure the hazard lights blinked again.

He rubbed his chest one more time, and the envelope hidden there crinkled. He pulled it out. Its exterior was blank.

Arthur broke the seal and retrieved a folded sheet of paper from inside. Only someone Bennett's age would still use stationery with his name and address printed at the top. Arthur had to smile at the small detail.

Dear Arthur,

I was apprehensive when I heard you would be visiting Hope Is Here this week, but I felt compelled to write this letter. We have often butted heads, but I want you to know that I have always respected you, regardless of when we disagreed.

I regret how your dismissal happened. There should have been a congregational vote. You should have been allowed to say goodbye properly to the people you served for so long. There should have been explanations and transparency. For my part in taking that away from you and others, I am deeply sorry.

I still feel your leaving was right. Reading this will—I am sure—be uncomfortable. But please hold with me.

Many of us have watched you, Rose, and your girls struggle over the last few years. It pained us when our attempts to help, however inadequate they might have been, were brushed off. Arthur, your family has needed you for a long time. I do not regret that now they have you.

I have never felt such grief when I heard about Amy's abduction. Know your daughter will forever be in my prayers. Thank God she was found.

Thank you for your service to our church and your sacrifice.

Bennett Yule

Arthur let the paper fall and buried his face in his hands. As he sat with no one but God, he felt a tension snap in his chest. Slowly, warmth flowed in. Something unwound inside of him like a cord released from a tie and fell away. He didn't understand it, but the pain in his chest eased and then flickered out. He could breathe. With the opening of his airways came a flood of tears like he had never shed before.

The words he and Gary had exchanged while on the road together came back to him in a flood.

"We were all watching you breaking. I just ... You needed a respite."

Then Rose's gentle reminders of God's goodness and plan came drifting in. She'd often hinted she believed their dismissal was a good thing. Was she right?

Arthur reached over and fumbled in the glove compartment for the stash of tissues Rose always kept there.

Of course she's right.

Mr. Simon had been wise to remind him of the direction God gave to His children though their spouses. There had been multiple times during the first few years of their marriage when Arthur had been the one to remind Rose of God's blessings, His grace, and His plans for their lives. Looking back, he could see now how their roles had flipped as the years in full-time ministry had worn on him.

He hadn't meant to stop listening to her or to God. But siting in the stillness, he realized for the first time in years that he had. Had the shock of what he perceived as betrayal from Hope Is Here Church, sealed his ears to the truth for months?

I was so sure of the direction you had for me, I forgot to keep listening. Didn't I ...

He released a deep sigh as he wiped his eyes then his nose, tears now spent.

An ache settled in his chest, small yet unmistakable. Was it grief? Yes, he recognized it now.

It will always be there. Won't it, God? I need your help to keep listening now that my ears are open again. I'm sorry. I didn't realize I'd stopped.

The grief for yesterdays would dull with time, and soon the reality of God's love and how He had cared for them all through the turmoil of the last few months would become clearer and clearer. He would be able to look back and give an account of each moment God had pressed His hand to their heartaches.

Arthur hoped that time wasn't too far off as he laid Bennett's letter on the passenger's seat, turned off the hazard lights, and pulled back out onto the highway.

He was going home.

Tired and happy, he pulled into his driveway. He never thought a trailer house could look so beautiful. When had he come to accept it as a gift instead of a demotion? It didn't matter.

Warmth greeted him as he entered the small house. The smell of buttered and salted popcorn made him smile.

It was nearing dinnertime, and Amy sat in the small living room space on the couch, a huge silver bowl between her crisscrossed legs.

"Hey, Dad," she said, not looking away from the program she was watching. "Want some?"

"Where's your mother?" he asked, looking around before he set down his briefcase and shrugged off his outdoor clothing.

"Changing."

As Arthur hung his coat on the row of hooks beside the door, Rose shuffled into the room. She was wrapped in a blue house robe, ready for an evening of comfort.

"Good, you're home! I was getting worried." She smiled brightly as he stooped to kiss her cheek.

She turned and let his lips brush hers, placing a frail arm around his waist.

She smelled like popcorn laced with something sweet.

Amy groaned and rolled her eyes as she watched them, and Arthur reluctantly pulled away.

"We decided popcorn, cheese, apples, and ice cream were good enough for supper tonight. I hope you don't mind," Rose said as they both moved to the couch.

Amy patted the cushion beside her before holding up the bowl.

"I don't see apples or cheese," Arthur pointed out.

"I was just going to get them—"

"No," Amy interrupted as she handed the bowl off to him. "I'll do it."

Rose sat beside Arthur on the small couch, and soon Amy was back with a plate piled with roughly cut fruit and cheese. She squeezed into the small space beside him and immediately turned back to her show.

Arthur had no idea what she was watching and didn't really care as he dug one hand into the popcorn and curled the other around Rose's fingers.

"I love you," he said to them both.

"We love you too," Rose said back as she selected a few popped kernels for herself.

Arthur didn't expect to hear anything from Amy. It was a bit of a miracle that she'd invited him to sit so close. Usually, the middle of the couch was reserved for Rose, but a deep smile spread across his face as his youngest daughter turned to him and said, "I love you too, Dad."

Her voice shook as she said it, and she twisted away as her face contorted in an emotion he couldn't read. But Arthur believed her. For the first time in a long time, he truly believed her, and it touched a place deep inside that he'd thought would be cold forever.

Rose squeezed his hand and laid her head on his shoulder.

It was so good to be home.

The End

Sponsors

THIS WORK OF FICTION would not have been published without the generous financial support of ...

J. D. Ans

May God return your blessing to you in an even greater amount.

About the Author

Mary Grace van der Kroef is a poet, writer, and artist from Ontario, Canada. She enjoys the simple things in life, like a good cup of coffee and heart-to-heart talks with friends. She uses her writing to highlight those simple things while encouraging others and exploring her own inner world. She is a follower of Jesus Christ and writes from a Christian worldview. She believes every person, regardless of circumstance, is a creative being whose stories are important. She cherishes people's differences and believes diverse stories are imperative to understanding what it is to be human.

Call to Review

HONEST REVIEWS ARE ONE of the most important things for an indie author's success, and Mary is grateful for each person who takes the time to write a review or rate her books. If you enjoyed this book, please consider taking the time to review or rate it at your favourite retailer or review platform.

www.ingramcontent.com/pod-product-compliance
Lightning Source LLC
Chambersburg PA
CBHW020640120726
47906CB00001B/63